A SECRET GIFT

AMANDA JAMES

One More Chapter
a division of HarperCollins*Publishers* Ltd
1 London Bridge Street
London SE1 9GF
www.harpercollins.co.uk
HarperCollins*Publishers*
1st Floor, Watermarque Building, Ringsend Road
Dublin 4, Ireland

This paperback edition 2022

2

First published in Great Britain in ebook format
by HarperCollins*Publishers* 2021

A catalogue record of this book is available from the British Library

ISBN: 978-0-00-850499-1

Printed and bound in the UK using 100% Renewable Electricity
by CPI Group (UK) Ltd

Amanda James has written since she was a child and even asked her parents for a typewriter for Christmas. She never imagined her words would ever be published. In 2010 the dream of becoming a writer came true when she had her first short story published.

Originally from Sheffield, Amanda now lives in Cornwall and is inspired every day by the wild and beautiful coastline. She can usually be found playing on the beach with her family, or walking the cliff paths planning her next book.

 twitter.com/amandajames61

 facebook.com/MandyJamesAuthorPage

To Tanya with much love. Thanks for the Christmas crystals.

Chapter One

The calendar on the kitchen wall tells me three things. It's February, it's Friday and you've been gone three years. The last one's a lie. Has to be. Because you're here with me always. In my heart, my thoughts, your essence alive in every room. Late at night, if I half close my eyes, I can see you sitting in your chair by the fire. I can hear your footfall on the stair, your laughter on the wind as I open the bedroom window. I stare at the scene on the calendar. There's a bent and battered tree on a hill by the ocean. Its stark branches are silhouetted against a winter sunset, fighting with the wind to remain anchored. The tree and I have a lot in common. Melancholy waits in my depths. It's seeking a chance to break free – swim to my surface, claim my day. I mustn't let it. I've a job to do.

St Margaret's Residential Home sits at the top of a rain-soaked Newquay hill. Its windows gaze out over the town to the far Atlantic horizon, which today is a charcoal line, joining together sky and water. I wonder how Hope Trebarwith is today as I hurry up the steps. The old lady hasn't been well at all over the past two weeks. I've grown so fond of her with her daft sense of humour and wise words. I hate to think of a time when she'll be no longer with us, but then losing lovely older people unfortunately goes with the job of being a carer.

I hang my dripping coat up and look at the roster. Hope's still with us, thankfully, but Doctor Kelly is popping in to see her later. I make a cup of tea and take it to her room, tap softly on the door.

'Come in … I'm awake.' Hope's tremulous voice is barely audible through the wood.

I step in and set the tea down on the nightstand, flick on the little lamp. Though today her room is as dark as the horizon, it's large, and has the benefit of a big bay window through which in summer, sunlight pours like molten gold. Hope's propped up in bed, her head's fallen forward as if her neck's too weak to support it. Too many pillows. 'Morning, Hope. You don't look too comfy there.'

'I'm not.' Hope's voice is muffled as her chin's on her chest. 'That young 'un got me washed. She's too quick. Comes in like a bloody whirlwind, shoves me up like this and buggers off. Can't wait to be elsewhere, I expect. Mind you, I don't blame her.'

A quick plump of the pillows – and removal of two – allows Hope to relax and make eye contact. For a woman of ninety-four she's still got remarkably animated eyes. The colour of moss in sunlit rock pools, and always ready to smile. 'That's better, Hope. Now, I've brought you a cuppa and a couple of biscuits.'

I sit by the bed and hand her the mug. 'Thanks, Tawny One.' I smile at her pet name for me. She says my hair's the colour and texture of a lion's mane. 'It seems ages since I saw you, Joy.' She takes a sip of tea, cocks her head bird-like, scrutinises my face as if trying to remember our last meeting. Her memory, like her health, is rapidly failing.

'It was my day off yesterday, but I saw you the day before.' The puzzle in her face makes my heart sad. She clearly can't remember that at all.

Hope takes a bite of her biscuit and points the rest at me. 'Your name doesn't suit you today. Joy isn't joyful. Why's that?'

I consider skirting round the truth, but what's the point? 'It's three years since Sean died today. Still can't believe it.'

Hope's bushy grey eyebrows furrow and she purses her lips. Then her eyes widen. 'I remember now! He was your husband – a fireman, died in a blaze.' She jabs the remainder of her biscuit at me in triumph. Then she lowers her hand, sighs. 'Sorry, Joy. Is there anything I can do?'

'Not really, Hope. But it's nice to chat to you. How are you feeling today?'

'Not so bad for an old 'un. My ticker keeps playing up – and I've got this cough at night. It won't be long for me now.' Hope's matter-of-fact tone makes me smile. She always tells it like it is.

'I think that's a way off yet. Doctor Kelly's coming to see you later and—'

'Smelly Kelly, I call him.' Hope's eyes crinkle and she gives a wheezy gasp that passes for laughter. 'He's got more of that perfume on him than a pox doctor's clerk. It's to cover up the stink of cigarettes. He's fooling no one.' She taps the side of her nose. 'Least of all me.'

I laugh and brush a few biscuit crumbs from the duvet into my hand, tip them in the waste-paper basket. 'Well, I'd better get on. I've got quite a few people to see this morning and—'

Hope grabs my hand. 'Come and see me tomorrow, Joy.' The strength of her grip and the urgency in her voice surprises me.

'Of course I will, don't worry.'

Hope's eyes hold mine with such intensity and she juts her chin out. 'I mean it, Tawny One. No matter how busy you are, I need to speak with you. It's important.'

I take one of her long bony hands, light as a bird's wing, caress the prominent blue veins under paper-thin skin with my thumb. 'I promise I will. And I'll look in again later before I go home.'

'No need for that. Just come tomorrow.'

As I'm about to leave, Hope starts to cough, and it's some time before she can get her breath. I give her water and tissues. Making sure she needs nothing else, I go about my business. But all the time I'm working, chatting to the other residents, completing my duties, I can't get Hope out of my mind. I wonder what she's so desperate to see me about tomorrow?

My shift over, I make my way down the long creaky corridor to Hope's room and meet Doctor Kelly coming the other way. He's a big round man in his forties with a moon face and a nervous smile. 'Hi, Doctor Kelly,' I say, standing to the side to let him pass and trying not to smile as a strong waft of aftershave follows me. *Smelly Kelly*. 'How's Mrs Trebarwith doing?'

His button-brown eyes look down at me. 'Not too good, I'm afraid. She's developed a chest infection, should really be in hospital, but she's not having any of it. Her daughter can't convince her either.'

'Oh dear. Is she on antibiotics?'

'Yes, three times a day. If there's no change she'll have to have them by IV.' Doctor Kelly's mouth twitches at the corners. 'Bye now.'

I tap lightly on Hope's door, but this time there's no answer. I push it open and pop my head round. Hope's propped up on more pillows than when I left her, but she's sleeping peacefully. I creep in and tuck her duvet carefully in around her feet; she hates it when they get cold in the night. I whisper, 'Night, my friend. See you tomorrow.'

She mumbles something that sounds like, 'Happiness is within your grasp.'

I draw the curtains against the darkening sky over the ocean and think about that. Maybe it is, it just doesn't feel like it today. But I promise myself that tomorrow will be different.

Chapter Two

The owners of cats are deluded. They are in fact owned by the cat. Every morning it's Sebastian who's attended to first. Never mind how half asleep I still am, or how much I'm longing for that first reviving cup of tea, I have to give him a cuddle, wash out his food bowl, refill it and replenish his water bowl, before I even think of myself. Otherwise I'm plagued with yowls and ankle threading, often accompanied by countertop parading, until I submit. Because he's beautiful, adorable and cuddly, I never complain. He's such great company, though he doesn't have much to say. Unlike yesterday, the absence of gloom promises sunshine later, and patches of blue sky are already doing jazz hands through the light cloud.

Sebastian decides it's time for another cuddle, even though I'm sitting at the kitchen table eating toast. He leaps onto the table and walks right up to me, his enormous green eyes silently demanding my attention. I stroke his long black and brown coat and gently push him away to prevent him putting one of his huge paws in my toast and jam. He eventually gets the message and jumps down, runs over to Sean's chair and snuggles into the cushion. I expect he misses him too.

My eyes find my husband's photo on the mantelshelf above the fire. I took it when we were walking on Mawgan Porth Beach just down the road. He's smiling at me, his blond unruly hair blowing in the wind, kind blue eyes crinkling at the corners. Sean always looked after others before himself. That's why he was so good at his job. I wish he'd been terrible at his job. Wish he'd saved himself instead of his colleague. Selfish, maybe, but I could live with that if he was sitting opposite me now, chatting away, taking big gulps of tea from his blue and white stripy mug. I take a sip from it now. It comforts me to imagine that the imprint of his lips somehow remains, his lips on mine, not in the way I'd like, but at least it's something.

Because it's so nice outside, I decide I've enough time for a quick run down to the beach before work. Crisp winter days have a way of boosting my get up and go, while days like yesterday put me in Eeyore mode. Then I cut myself some slack – yesterday was the anniversary of Sean's death, after all. I get changed into my running gear and pull the door of Atlantic Cottage closed behind me. I take a breath and gird my loins. Running down the hill to Mawgan Porth will be a breeze, but running back uphill to the little hamlet of Trevarrian will be another matter. In fact, I'll have to walk most of it. I look at my watch and have second thoughts, then Hope's words from yesterday whisper in my ear – *happiness is within your grasp* – and I set off at a good pace.

By the time I reach the beach, the sun's out and a yellow crescent of sand cradles a subdued ultramarine ocean. I jog down the uneven sand-and-rock slope to the beach and set off along it towards the far cliffs, the windows of the white houses perched upon them, winking in the sunlight. In the distance, a slight figure in a red tracksuit runs toward me. I realise it's my friend Fiona, her distinctive white-blonde hair's lifting on the breeze and, as she gets closer, she raises a hand in greeting.

'Hi, Joy!' She puts her hands on her knees, gets her breath. 'I was only thinking about you yesterday … you know, with it being a bad day for you.' I put my hand on her shoulder, touched she'd remembered. 'I was going to pop round, but this guy I'm seeing dropped over unexpectedly with flowers and a take-away … I couldn't really turn him away.'

'Another new one?' I laugh. 'You've had more men than I've had—'

Fiona holds her hand up. 'Don't say it. But this one's a keeper. Mark's the only one that's made me laugh, made me feel like me again, since Bastard Face dumped me.'

Bastard Face being her ex-husband who did a runner with her cousin two years ago. I nod and hide a smile at her choice words. 'Well, I'm pleased for you. You'll have to introduce me.'

'I'll introduce you to his fit mate, too. It's about time you had another man in your life. You're only bloody twenty-nine – must feel lonely.'

'I don't think so, Fi. Thanks all the same.'

'Why?'

9

'It's too soon. Besides, I have Sebastian.'

'He's a damned cat, not a man. And look at you!' She sweeps a hand the length of me. 'You're gorgeous; turquoise-blue eyes, a fantastic figure, and all that messy hair! You've got a real surfer-girl vibe going on. Any man would be lucky to have you.'

I laugh at her eager expression and 100-watt smile. 'But I don't want any man. The only man I want, I can't have.'

'Aw, bless you.' Fiona pulls me into a hug and I feel awkward, patronised. I know she means well, but there's too many people going around blessing people all over the place. I don't want to be blessed. I don't want a man. I want to be left alone to get over the death of the love of my life in my own way, thank you very much.

I break away. 'Well, I must be off. Got to be at work by nine thirty.'

'I've got my car if you want a lift. I'm not due in the surgery until after lunch today. I'm giving the new girl the benefit of my medical secretary experience – so I thought I'd pop to Aldi to get a few bits this morning.'

A lift would be nice, but I can't face making pleasant conversation. The buoyant mood I had upon waking has drifted away on the tide. I tell her thanks, but I need the exercise and we part company, promising to meet up in the near future.

The walk up to St Margaret's is much more attractive today. The view from the top of the hill over Newquay looks like a painting. The town's peaceful under the hard winter sunshine and, beyond it, the azure ocean sends its playful white-crested waves racing each other to shore. Seagulls hang in a formation of six above the scene, broadcasting their raucous cries across the wind. I close my eyes and take a breath of salt air before going inside.

Before I do anything else, I must go and see how Hope is. The way she beseeched me yesterday to visit her today has been preying on my mind. It's more than a whim, a trick of her failing mental state. I don't know what it is, but I know it's something really important. To her, if to no one else.

Hope's face brightens as I walk in. She's sitting up in bed, a new yellow fluffy blanket draped over her knees. She gives me a little wave. 'Morning, Joy! Great to see you.'

I wave back and place her mug of tea on the nightstand as usual. 'You look much better this morning. The antibiotics must be working.'

'Not sure about that. I've just been coughing my guts up, but I'm all the better for seeing you.'

I sit down and pat the yellow blanket. 'Where's this from?'

'My daughter Jenny and granddaughter Emma came yesterday evening. Emma said she saw it and thought of me.' Hope gives a wheezy chuckle. 'Do I look like I'm yellow and fluffy? Not sure how to take it, to be honest.'

I laugh. 'It's lovely. Warm and cuddly.'

'It *is* nice.' Hope's smile then turns itself into a thin line. 'Our Jenny wants me to go into hospital, but no fear. I told her this is my final resting place. It was bad enough when I had to leave my family home after sixty-odd years, so I'm buggered if I'm upping sticks again.'

'Let's have no talk about final rests. Those tablets will work soon and—'

'Pass me that box on the dresser, will you, love. I asked our Jenny to bring it in.'

The small cardboard box is a bit battered and surprisingly heavy. 'Blimey, Hope. Have you got a few house bricks in here?' I place it on the bed beside her.

'Not house bricks, but pebbles.' Her face contorts and she gives a few hacking coughs. I hand her some tissues and water. 'Open it and get them out, would you, love? I haven't the strength.'

Running my hand under the flap, I open the top and take out a squat jar of pebbles. 'What are these for?'

'For you. You'll have to get your own from down the beach eventually, but these will start you off. I've been waiting for the right person to pass them on to for a good few years now. And I was beginning to think you'd never come along.'

I look at the jar of unremarkable pebbles and think there must be more to it if they are so important to Hope. Or maybe it's her mental state. 'Er, thank you, Hope. I can put them on the ornament shelf in my cottage and—'

'Ha!' she barks. 'You think I'm just gaga, don't you?' Hope chuckles and pats the top of the jar. 'These pebbles are for storing emotional energy – feelings, in other words.'

Shit. Now what do I say?

'I can see by your face you think I'm having a confused episode. And I don't blame you, love. I would in your shoes.' Hope smiles. 'But what I'm about to tell you will take a lot of swallowing. I've written you a letter too, because this blessed chest won't let me talk for long…' As if on cue, she has a coughing fit. When she's recovered, she hands me a letter that was under the yellow blanket. 'Read this later when you're home.'

'Okay. I will. But you need to rest now, Hope.' I tuck the letter into the pocket of my uniform.

'Plenty of time to rest very soon. I'm buggering off to a higher plane or whatever it is. Had a glimpse the other day, and I did like it. It looked warm and cosy, and I won't have to worry about putting the heating on. When I lived on my own, our Jenny always told me off about not putting it on, but it cost a fortune.'

I'm about to say she'll be with us a while yet, but change my mind. Instead I smile and take a surreptitious glance at my watch. I need to get on. 'Right, Hope, I…'

'I know you've got things to do, so I'll be quick and you've got the letter for later.' She fixes me with those rockpool eyes. 'Many years ago, I was given a death-bed mission by Patience, my mum's friend. I'd known her as long as I could remember and helped nurse her in her last days. She said she'd always known I'd be the one to pass on her mission to, because of my name. Hope. Apparently it's very common for "collectors" like us to have names like Hope, Patience, Joy, Grace and so on. Though not always.'

'What do you mean by "collectors"?'

'We collect the excess energy – or feelings. Feelings of joy, confidence, and courage for example. We collect them from those who have too much, store it in the pebbles and then bequeath it to the ones who are in need. Some don't use pebbles to store it. They keep it within themselves. I tried to keep an excess of joy once, but it made me too giddy! Felt like I was drunk!' Hope laughs but then coughs into her tissue. 'You might be strong enough to store it, but I'd say use the pebbles until you're used to the job. We collectors bring hope where there's despair, courage when there's fear, joy where there's sorrow.'

My goodness, Hope has a powerful imagination. Maybe it's the combination of drugs she's on? I think it's easier to indulge her. She needs her rest and I need to get on. 'R-ight. Why pebbles, and how do you store this energy?'

'The pebbles have the energy of the moon-tide and ocean in them. They're already open to receive more. When you hold one, they get hot and make your hands warm – heat vibration. You feel its energy. Like when you hold a crystal.' She puts her head on one side quizzically. 'You've held a crystal, I expect?'

'No. I'm not into that stuff.'

'Well you are now, love.' Hope's eyes crinkle at the edges. 'So you collect the excess feelings from one person, then transfer it from yourself to a pebble.' She flaps a hand at my pocket. 'The letter goes into all that. And the best bit is the person who's received it is compelled to help someone else with a random act of kindness. Isn't that wonderful?' Hope gives a wide smile. 'And I tell you, this world of ours could do with more kindness.' She sinks back, rests her head on her pillow. All that talking's taken it out of her.

'I can't argue with that, Hope.' I tuck her blanket round

her feet. 'Now, you rest and I'll pop back in later before I go home, okay?'

Hope doesn't open her eyes. Her skin looks clammy and she's developed a grey pallor. Today she looks every one and more of her ninety-four years. 'No need, Joy, thanks. I've got Jenny and Emma coming again.' As I stand, she opens her eyes. 'Don't forget your pebbles. They won't have any power left in 'em after all these years. I think it's only stored for a few months or so. But it will save you having to go to the beach to look for some.'

'Okay, don't worry.' I put the jar in the box and tuck it under my arm.

Hope reaches out a hand. I take it and she pulls me down to her level, plants a kiss on my cheek and whispers in my ear, 'Thank you, Tawny One. You have been so, so kind. And I can tell that if you choose to accept your mission, you will bring so much happiness to so many people.'

I'm about to answer, but already she's dropped into an exhausted sleep. Dear Hope. They broke the mould when they made her.

I'm so busy all day, I don't have time to think about Hope's strange imaginings until I'm ready for home. She's got me at it now, because I can still feel the imprint of her kiss on my cheek. Must be because my emotions are high. Unfortunately, in this job, I've seen people at the end of their lives before, and I don't think she can be far away from hers. On the way out, I hurry along the corridor to her room just to see how she is, but as I'm halfway along, the sound of weeping women stops me in my tracks. Oh no. I cover the last few metres quietly, but don't go through the open door. Hope's lying peacefully while by her bedside a middle-aged woman and a younger woman hold each other, sobbing their hearts out. My gut twists and I cover my mouth. Seems she's found her way home sooner than I thought. *Goodbye, Hope, my dear friend.*

I step back and quickly retreat the way I came. A knot of emotion rises in my throat and tears prickle my eyes. I tell myself I should be used to this. It's part of the job, part of life, and I need to hold it together. I concentrate on my feet thumping along the threadbare carpet, and at last I'm outside in the cold evening air. I take a gulp of it and swallow down an ache in my throat. But once inside the privacy of my car, I'm helpless to do anything other than allow my grief free rein.

Chapter Three

The next morning I'm sorting the laundry. I have the whole weekend off and I plan to walk on the beach, go food shopping, and then eat food that's bad for me while binge-watching anything that looks like it's likely to numb my brain for the afternoon. Too much thinking is bad for me, I've decided. I spent nearly all evening mulling over Hope's passing, the problems of the other residents, the meaning of life, fate, and what lies ahead. My mood shifted from steadfast and resolute, to a melancholy as deep and thick as an Alabama swamp. Does Alabama have swamps? I reckon so. I imagine it has those mangrove trees that grow round the edges, their branch-like roots spearing through the thick slime and gloop, reaching through the dark depths, to where unmentionable creatures slither in wait for unsuspecting prey.

I shudder. Light and vacuous is what I need today, no thinking. Thinking is banned.

I shove my uniform into the washing machine and

realise the letter from Hope is still in the pocket. I almost read it last night, but wondered if it might make me swampier. I'll read it in a minute with a cuppa and a digestive before I go down to the beach.

A few minutes later, feet up on the recliner, I crunch into my biscuit and unfold the letter. There're three sheets of paper. Blimey. Must have taken her ages in her state. Okay, here we go.

Dear Joy,

By the time you read this I think I'll be elsewhere. Once again, thank you for everything you've done for me. You're one in a million, though I must admit – it's time you got back in the classroom. You'll feel more fulfilled as a TA than a friendly ear and wiper of old people's bottoms. Of course, someone has to do it, but something tells me your destiny lies in pastures new. Talking of which…

Hopefully you'll accept your vocation as a collector. It's so rewarding. As I probably said to you (don't forget I wrote this letter before chatting with you), you'll bring happiness where there is sadness, hope where there is despair. Sometimes it could be a matter of life or death… And in doing all this, you'll be happy too. It is within your grasp. You might not think so now, given the last few dark years. But it is, and will be.

Now, down to practical things. You'll start seeing energy surrounding people – auras, for want of better word. It's their dominant energy or feeling at that time. Energy manifests from this – becomes physical somehow. The person has too much of it. Don't ask me how the bloody thing works. I was often puzzled by it all. Old Patience that passed it on to me said she used to ask questions in her head. Sometimes she'd get guidance and answers about what to do next. I never did... Patience said all collectors work slightly different.

Anyhow, these feelings are available to the collector like a virus, but a good one in this case. Through touch, breath, or even laughter – vibration through the air. The imprint of a kiss. The imprint of a hand on table, or glass. You get the idea. Once you've got it, transfer it to a pebble, and then pass the pebble to someone who needs it. You might wonder how? It's simple. Pebbles are small, easy to drop into a bag or a pocket. And another thing, I read once, when we die, all of our energy goes back into the universe. I understood it to be like the universe is like one massive pebble that absorbs it and then gives it back in some way. It's all to do with consciousness and, if I'm honest, I can't grasp it. But hopefully by now, I've been collected by the big pebble in the sky!

Right. Back to you and collecting. Thing is, you don't have to accept the mission. You already have the power to collect, from that kiss on the cheek I gave you. I'm hoping I did, or you'll wonder what I'm on about! Ha ha. I doubt you'll reject it, because you're a decent girl. It will become like second nature as time goes on. But you have to keep it all to yourself – others won't understand. And if you tell people, your collecting power will stop. It's lonely keeping it secret, but there you go. Try not to see it as a burden. Patience said it's been passed on from ancient times and the Druids. They knew about all about the earth, nature, the universe and magical things, apparently.

That's about it. I can't think of anything else you need to know. You could try asking questions if you get stuck. It worked for Patience. I had fifty rewarding years doing my collecting and saw some wonderful results…

And get back to school, maid. I just know that's what you should be doing. Goodbye, and good luck!

Your very dear friend,

Hope Trebarwith X

I realise my cheeks are wet and wipe them on the back of my jumper sleeve. Bless her heart. I will miss the old girl so much. And my word, that is one hell of a story. I put the letter down and drink my tea. Ponder on it. The whole thing feels so real… I brush my cheek where she kissed me but no longer feel the imprint. Then I tell myself off. Why would I? This is all just a fantasy Hope had. Ramblings fuelled by drugs and a failing brain. Mind you, I think she might be right about trying to get a job as a TA. I did four wonderful years in my local primary school, until Sean's death left me incapable of doing anything at all for a very long time. When it was time to return to work, there were no vacancies in nearby schools, so I took the first job going, which happened to be at St Margaret's. I do miss the children.

Sebastian looks at me from Sean's chair, stretches out his back legs. 'Right, mister. I'm off for my walk, then off to Newquay to do the food shop.' He says nothing. Yawns. 'Yes, I know it's boring, but it has to be done. I might bring you a treat if you're lucky.' At this, he gives a little meow and rolls on his back. Oh, to be a cat. Life would be so much easier.

Shopping completed, I walk out of Sainsbury's pushing a trolley piled so high, it will feed a small country for a week. I always get too much, but at least I won't have to do this trip for a while. I've got freezer stuff and I...

Oh my God. I stop dead.

There's a man ... a homeless man crouched near the wall; he's got a little box to collect money.

But he's wrapped in ... my heart beats like a hammer ... in misery. I can see it. I can actually see his – what did Hope say? My mind struggles for the word and my hands grip tighter on the handles of the trolley – his ... aura. It's black and red and it's writhing around him like a monstrous snake.

'Oh my God,' I say out loud and the man glances over at me, furrows his brow. He looks to be in his late teens, but his eyes are borrowed from a much older man. His dark hair's long and matted and his baggy combat trousers are stained and torn. The poor love. I want to make him better, take away his pain. *Maybe you can, Joy.* The whisper of an inner voice pulls me over towards him. But I stop after a few paces. This is crazy. I'm hallucinating. I tell myself I can't see this aura at all. It's a combination of losing Hope, her fairy story and the fact I've been feeling down about Sean and my life in general. My feet hurry me past, then I stop, dig my purse out of my bag and put ten pounds into his box.

'Thanks very much!' he says, with a grateful smile.

My eyes fill, so I just nod and rush to my car.

I put the shopping away on autopilot. My head is full of the homeless guy and the way I just chucked money at him and ran. What kind of person does that? And what the hell is happening to my mind? Focus. I need focus. There are toast crumbs on the countertop. I grab the dishcloth, run water through it. I must concentrate on the mundane to keep away the image of the writhing red and black light engulfing the poor guy in Sainsbury's carpark. As I wipe the side down, next to the kettle I notice Hope's jar of pebbles. Mine, now, actually. I need to put them away. Or, better still, take the pebbles to the beach and recycle the jar. For now, I'll just shove them in the cupboard. Out of sight, out of mind. I grab the jar, but instead of putting it in the cupboard, I twist off the top and pull out a flat, oval, eggshell-coloured pebble. The weight of it in my palm feels right, comforting. Hang on. Right and comforting, what's that supposed to mean? *It's a sodding pebble.*

I put the pebble on the kitchen table and notice it's almost the same colour as the wooden table top. My stomach growls, reminding me I'm supposed to be eating lunch in front of the TV, but I can't take my eyes from the pebble. What if Hope's story wasn't rambling? What if I can replace the homeless guy's misery with joy? Didn't she say that it could mean the difference between life or death? My sensible side tells me to stop, get lunch. Immerse myself in mind-numbing telly. My reckless side says go back to see the man. Take a pebble. What can it hurt? Nobody but me need know if it's some weird meltdown I'm having.

Grabbing the pebble, I shove it in my pocket. My stomach roars, so I take a huge bite from a hot-cross bun on my way to the door. Then I stop. One small flaw in this cunning crazy plan. I have to find an excess of joy or happiness to transfer to the pebble. And where the hell am I supposed to find that?

I use the carpark not far from St Margaret's and walk down the steep hill into Newquay town centre. Sainsbury's isn't far, but I didn't want to park there, as I have some joy to find. More scope in town – more people. Dear oh dear. My thoughts are becoming increasingly bizarre. I see a few unidentifiable auras cloaking people like a second skin as I walk by. I stare in wonder. Why are they unidentifiable? And why do some people have auras and others don't? Or am I only able to see some?

Thoughts like this chase around my head as I walk past the cinema, Holland and Barrett, The Cornish Bakery – the waft of pasties torments more angry rumbles from my stomach, and then on a bench to my left there's a young couple.

They are glowing.

Shining.

They have a curly-haired baby girl of about eight months balanced between them. She's dressed in denim dungarees and a pink shirt and has a little foot on each of their thighs, her hands held by each parent to support her wobbly attempt to stand upright. A vibrant aura surrounds them all. It's yellow and white and it smells of summer meadows. Smell? Hope never mentioned smells. I can hardly process what's happening. Joy is coming at me in waves, every bit as strong as the ones on the ocean beating against the rocks, out of sight beyond the shops. I put my hand on the back of another bench to steady myself. I find I'm grinning, almost breaking into laughter, as deep, rich feelings of joy and happiness rise inside me like a fat Harvest Moon.

The smiling man notices me, then looks away as he catches my eye. I must look crazy, holding onto the back of a bench gawping at them with a big daft grin on my face. He loses the smile, whispers something to the woman, and as her head switches in my direction, her smile dies too. Shit. I need to do something before their joy disappears because of my weirdness. Instinct drives me forward. 'Hi, excuse me for staring. It's just that you all look so happy, joyful. It's so wonderful to see!'

The woman smiles, more assuredly, but she still looks uncertain. And who can blame her? 'That's okay. Our little one is a delight, even though I do say so myself.'

'She certainly is,' I coo, and extend my hand to the little girl's cheek. Her big brown eyes shine with delight and she laughs and bounces up and down on her parents' legs. As I withdraw, I 'accidently' brush the woman's hand and the power of her joy seeps into my fingers. Immediately I'm intoxicated, just like Hope described. My heart's racing and my breath's coming in short huffs. I need to move on before I make a fool of myself and burst out laughing, fall over, or both. Saying goodbye, I hurry as fast as my unsteady legs will go to another bench and slump down on it. My fingers curl around the smooth pebble in my pocket, and as if I'm being guided by something, I will the exhilarating energy to leave me. Thankfully it goes as quickly as it came. I can breathe normally again, my head's clear and a peaceful calm fills the crater in the centre of my chest vacated by the Harvest moon.

I take a moment to let the whole thing sink in. Old Hope's story is true, then. Either that, or I'm having the same hallucinations. But it's so 'out there'. So incredibly impossible, mystical and magical. I've been brought up to think logically, scientifically. What's just happened is neither, and, I must admit, I'm not sure if I like it. Yes, I want to help people, but… Oh, I don't know. I can't seem to get my thoughts in order. Do I want such a mission? I've only done one and it's bloody exhausting. In point of fact, I've only done half a mission. There's a homeless guy who needs a pebble.

I hurry back through the town, checking every so often to see if the pebble's still safe. Why wouldn't it be? It's warm and cosy in my zipped coat pocket. I suppose the whole thing's so weird, I wouldn't be surprised if it vanished. Or turned into a frog. That's what happens in fairy tales … or do they turn into princes? I couldn't run with the weight of a prince in my pocket. Besides, my pocket's not big enough. Now, *those* thoughts are way too weird, even for me. I run up the steps to Sainsbury's carpark, thread through the cars to the spot against the wall where the homeless guy was. Except now he isn't. I quickly run around the corner of the building, but no. He's not there either. He's not inside, he's not in the other carpark. He's not anywhere. The prince has gone. Vanished.

Chapter Four

Two hours later, I can't feel my hands. The weather's turned and icy rain has spent the last while hurtling sideways at my face, its little needlepoints freezing my skin and making my nose run. I've covered most of Newquay town centre twice in that time, some of the side roads too, and scoured the central beaches from high vantage points. The idea that a homeless man is unlikely to be on a beach isn't lost on me, but I'm running out of places to look. There's an uncomfortable feeling taking hold in my gut. It's putting down roots. Sending shoots of disquiet into my heart. What if this mission actually *is* a matter of life or death? What if the guy has gone into some derelict building or back alley and taken his own life with an overdose of paracetamol? What if he used the money I gave him to buy them? What if I'm too late and it's all my fault?

Another half an hour's gone by and I'm at a loss. Maybe I'll try to find a homeless shelter and see if they can help. I fish my phone out of my pocket and Google homeless shelters in Newquay, but the signal's dodgy, perhaps because of the weather, and it buffers annoyingly as if mocking my desperation. I shove it in my pocket and remember Hope talking about asking for help. Why not? Might as well go the whole hog. Feeling a bit stupid, I wipe the rain from my face and whisper inside my hood, *Please, show me where to go.*

Nothing dramatic happens, but when I start walking again, my feet pull me towards the opposite end of town. I have a gut feeling I'm onto something at last.

Ten minutes after, I'm avoiding puddles on the narrow uneven pavement leading to where the iconic Atlantic Hotel sits atop a hill. Its huge white presence has gazed out over the town since Victorian times. As I'm passing The Red Lion, from the corner of my eye, I see a dejected figure drenched through, walking with an unsteady gait down the hill to the harbour. My heart jumps. It's the guy. Or I think it is. He's so soaked I can't make out the colours of his clothing. I think he had on combat trousers, but a black hoodie? This guy is definitely wearing a black hoodie. But where's the aura of misery? I set off after him, and as I get closer, I can make out the aura. It's the red and black snake again, but much weaker. It's writhing only intermittently, as if it's weak … dying. I continue with caution, keeping my back to the wall.

As he passes the Harbour Fish and Grill restaurant, he stumbles and swears out loud. Then he takes a moment – his forehead pressed against the menu in a glass case on the wall. I'm upwind, and the stench of booze and vomit cuts through the chill air, turning my stomach. He sets off again and I think I catch a sob on the air. Another aura's forming. It's eggshell tan, like the pebble in my pocket. It's solid, unmoving ... it's, I don't know. It's ... the word is shaping in my head. Desolation. *Oh God, no*. The man's hurrying towards the wall overlooking the harbour. He's struggling to the top. I close the gap between us, my hood flying off, my hair streaming out, wet strands tangling together across my eyes.

'Hey!' I call up to him.

He's astride the wall now, looks down at me through glazed amber eyes. 'What?'

'You need to come down. You'll injure yourself.' My voice sounds frantic. Aren't you supposed to be calm in these situations? And what a stupid thing to say. He knows he'll injure himself. That's his intention.

'Go away.' He lifts his other leg over the wall so he's facing away from me, looking out to sea.

'Please, listen. I can help you!' I begin climbing, but the wall's slippery with rain. God knows how he got up there so fast in his state.

'Nobody can. Too late,' he tosses to the wind. Doesn't look round.

Eventually astride the wall, I take a breath and put my hand gently on his shoulder. 'Please listen. I saw you in Sainsbury's earlier and gave you some money. Then I went home and thought about you. You're so young, and I could see you were totally miserable. I came back to see if I could help.'

This gets his attention. He peers at me as if he's looking through fog. Then he gives a crooked smile and his eyes fill. 'You gave me a tenner. Very much appreciated, kind lady.'

He's got a lovely smile, middle-class accent, local though, I think. 'That's right. I did. And now I'm going to help you down from here and we're going to a café to drink coffee. You need sobering up, and then we can talk.'

A dark cloud crosses his face. 'No. I've done with this shit. I'm going somewhere I don't have to think. Don't have people passing by, looking at me like I'm scum.' He shuffles closer to the edge, looks down into the harbour so very far below us.

'No.' I grab the arm of his soaking hoodie. 'No. Please. Please let me help you. I swear things will look better in a while.' I close my hand over the pebble in my pocket and try to find his. But he's wriggling away from my grasp.

'How the fuck are you going to help? You know nothing about me!' His unusual amber eyes darken in anger.

'Tell me your name,' I say, in what I hope is my commanding voice. I used to use it in the classroom.

It works. 'Jack.'

'Jack, please, I'm begging you. Let me take you for a coffee, some food as well if you feel hungry, and we'll talk this through. I promise I will make you feel better.' *If I could only get this damned pebble to you.* If I just hand it to him, he'll probably chuck it straight into the harbour, the mood he's in. 'My name's Joy, by the way.'

Jack wipes a mixture of rain and tears from his face and sighs. He says nothing for the longest time and I fear he's going to jump. I can hardly cope with the tension and then he says, 'I can't see how you can make things better. But I can see you'll not give up in a hurry.'

———————————

We sit opposite each other in the café on the high street. The rotund woman behind the counter eyes us with disdain from time to time. Not surprising really. Both soaked to the skin, dripping all over her floor, Jack wearing a faint aroma of vomit and alcohol. Despite him saying he wasn't that hungry, he's tucking into his pasty and chips as if he's worried it's going to be snatched away. I sip my coffee and consider how I'm going to slip the pebble to him. I'm guessing he's got to hold it in his hand for a while so he can absorb the joy. If he finds it in his pocket, he might hold it – wonder how it got there, but maybe not keep it in his hand long enough, the mood he's in.

He pushes his plate to the side and takes a gulp of coffee. I say, 'That will give you some energy for a bit. Drink up and I'll get you another.'

'Thanks. But I'm not that drunk, to be honest. What nearly happened just now sobered me up.'

'Why did it happen?'

'Want my life story?'

'Yes.'

One side of his generous mouth turns up and he shoves a hand through his long hair. Or tries to. The tangles prevent it – he's left with a bird's-nest effect on the left side. Under that grime he has a handsome face bordering on the striking. 'Okay. In a nutshell I come from a comfortable

31

background. My dad is an Oxford-educated Maths professor, Mum is a successful artist, my brother is a doctor. My parents' great hope for me to "make something" of myself was dashed into little pieces when I dropped out of uni. I was studying to be a vet, but my heart wasn't in it. I've always struggled academically, and it nearly killed me getting the grades I needed to get on the course.' Jack takes more coffee, stares out of the window at the rain-soaked passers-by.

No more seems forthcoming, so I venture, 'I'm guessing they didn't respond well to you dropping out.'

Jack gives a humourless bark. 'You could say that. Mum's not so bad, but Dad…' He shakes his head. 'He was incandescent. Talked about all the money he'd shelled out over the years on extra tuition and God knows what else. I had an ultimatum of going back to uni right then and begging for my place back, or he'd wash his hands of me. There'd be no more money from him. I told him to stick it up his arse.' He gives a surprised laugh at the memory, showing even white teeth. 'God knows where I got the courage. Dad said I was an ungrateful little bastard and needed to learn some hard life lessons. Then he grabbed a bag, packed some of my clothes and chucked me out.'

My mouth drops open. How could a parent do that? Okay, I don't see eye-to-eye with my dad, but he'd never have done something like that. 'How old were you when that happened?'

'It was a year ago, so eighteen. I turned nineteen last week.'

Only ten years between us, but I feel so much older – protective of him. 'And what did your mum do?'

'She begged him to reconsider, but what Dad says goes. She's always been scared of him, I think.'

'And your brother?'

'Andrew. He's six years older. Doesn't live at home. He's probably living with his girlfriend now. She's a junior doctor like him, but they've more training to do.'

'Right. And you've been living on the street for a year?' He nods. Poor Jack. I couldn't even stand it for a couple of days.

'Well, I was living on a mate's floor for a bit, and in another's shed in the summer. But his parents got wind and said I needed to go home. It's not so bad on the street in the summer. There's lots of tourists who chuck you a few quid when they've been on the beer. But the winter months are hard.' He sighs and says to the table, 'Last week some yobs gave me a beating and nicked my sleeping bag and money. They spat and pissed on me. Don't think I've ever felt so worthless.'

Instinctively I reach out and squeeze his hand. I swallow down emotion and say, 'Couldn't you go to a homeless shelter?'

'Yeah, I have been now and then. But they get pretty full and…' He shrugs. 'Oh, I don't know. Sounds weird, but I don't feel I belong there.' Under his breath he mutters, 'I don't belong anywhere.'

Better in the shelter than being out on the street in danger and freezing. I keep that thought to myself and say, 'What about Andrew. Didn't you get on?'

'Yeah. But he was the golden boy. I was jealous to death of him, even though he never gave me cause. He came to find me on the streets at the beginning and once a few months ago too. Begged me to come back to his. I said I was fine as I was. He gave me his address and said I was welcome any time, day or night. But I never took him up on it.'

I consider everything he's told me while we drink our tea. It's obvious to me that Andrew seems the logical next step for Jack. I can tell he'll fight against it, but into the silence I say, 'Jack, I know it feels like the end of the world now – but you have so much to offer. You'll feel differently in the future, I'm sure of it. You're a bright, lovely young man and you can be happy again. Practically speaking, I think staying with your brother is the way forward for you—'

'No.'

'Why not?'

'Because as I said, he's the golden boy. The one who never puts a foot wrong. It would be admitting defeat if I go begging to him for a roof.' A flash of irritation passes across his eyes and he shoves his hand through the other side of his hair. Matching bird's nests.

'You wouldn't be begging. He's offered and clearly cares about you.'

Jack snorts. 'Can you imagine, when it got back to Dad? I'd never hear the end of it. "That waste of space sponging off Andrew. Preying on his good nature," blah, blah.'

This irritates me. *Pride comes before a fall. Or a jump into the harbour.* My words are out before I can stop them. 'So, you'd rather kill yourself than feel humiliated, eh? That's ridiculous.'

Jack's head snaps from the window to my face, eyes flashing, mouth turned down at the corners. His face flushes. It's obvious I've shamed him. 'Thanks for the food, but it's time I went,' he growls. He scrapes his chair back and stands up.

Shit! Me and my big gob. 'Please, Jack. Don't go. Not yet.' I dig in my pocket for the pebble. He's ignoring me. Pulling his jacket on. 'Jack. Here, I have something for you.'

Without looking at me he says, 'I don't want your money.'

'It's not money, it's…' A flash of inspiration. 'It's my lucky pebble. Don't laugh. I know it will make you feel better.'

Jack looks far away from laughter. He glances at the pebble in my open hand. I hope he takes it soon, because joy is seeping through my skin like a honey dripper. He shakes his head, makes as if to leave again. 'Please, Jack!' The woman behind the counter bangs a cup down and tuts in annoyance.

'Jeez! Okay, if it means that much to you.' He snatches the pebble and goes to put it in his pocket but the jacket's still wet and the opening's stuck together. And then a few moments later, he stops looking for his pocket. An expression of wonder floods his face and a huge smile lights in his eyes like the sun rising on a dismal day. 'This pebble's awesome.' He opens his hand, stares at the pebble. 'My whole hand is warm and…' He glances at me and away. 'And I feel … happy?' Jack says in bewilderment, staring at me intently. He furrows his thick black brows and blinks away moisture. 'For some reason, Joy, I feel really *fucking* happy!'

'Right! That's enough. Be on yer way.' The woman bustles from behind the counter, arms folded across her ample chest, her expression reminiscent of a bulldog chewing a wasp. 'Not having the likes of you stinking out my café and swearing like a trooper. Out!' She jabs her finger towards the exit, her short-sleeved top revealing an underarm wobbling like pink blancmange.

Jack finds the woman hilarious and guffaws in her face. Her expression contorts in fury and she draws her wobbly arm back as if she's about to wallop him. I tell her we're going, grab a handful of jacket and drag him out into the street where, luckily, it's stopped raining.

I pull him to the side to let others past and he gives me a big hug. I hold my breath; God knows when he last had a wash. He steps back. 'Joy. You are fucking amazing. You're right about all this too.' Jack flings his arms out, almost knocking an old man's hat off. 'Life is precious and I nearly gave it all up.' He points a grubby finger at me. 'You know what? Some people would kill to be me. People with cancer, old people, people who are really disabled and shit. And *I* was about to end it all.' He shakes his head, incredulous. 'I need to learn a few hard life lessons, as my charming papa would say!' He laughs and leans against a shop window. 'I feel a bit dizzy to be honest, Joy. Maybe it's the realisation that I have a second chance at life.'

His speech is starting to falter. If I'd been holding the pebble this long, I'd be comatose, but I imagine it would take a bit longer for his desolation to turn into joy. He needs to put the pebble away now. It's done its job. 'Put the pebble in your pocket, Jack, before you lose it.' He immediately does as I ask. 'Now, what do you want to do next?'

Jack scratches his bird's nest. 'I reckon go to Andrew's. You were right about that too. He'll help me get back on my feet, then I'll see where we are. One step at a time, my dear.' He wags a finger. 'Let's not get ahead of ourselves.' Another guffaw startles a dog as it passes. It starts barking at us and its owner has to pick it up. Jack lunges at it, hand outstretched. 'Hey, puppy, don't get angry!'

'Jack, leave it. He might bite.' I grab his hand and lead him down the street.

'I wanted to stroke him, lovely little fella. His bark is much worse than his bite, I bet.' Jack chortles and catches sight of his appearance in Argos's window. 'Bloody hell, look at the state of me!'

I lead him up to the carpark and he follows, amazed at everything he sees. The colour of a child's hair, a daisy growing through the cracks in a wall, the pattern of a rubber tyre-mark on the road. The world is wonderful, apparently, and he's been too blind to see it. Long may it continue. At my car I say, 'Can I have your brother's address?'

'Why? Are you coming to stay too?' He creases up at his own joke.

'No. I'm taking you there.'

Jack flaps his hand dismissively. 'No worries. It's only at Whipsiderry, I can walk.'

There's no way I'm letting him out of my sight until he's

safely delivered to his brother. Despite his protests, I bundle him into the car and set off. Ten minutes later, I park up outside a plush apartment block overlooking Whipsiderry beach. Nodding at the long windows and generous balconies, I say, 'Nice place.'

'Yeah. Dad will be forking out for it. Doubt Andrew will be earning much yet.'

We both sit in silence looking through the windscreen at the apartment. Neither of us seem to want to make the first move. Then my stomach flips. It's only just gone half-four. There might be nobody in. A light comes on in one of the windows and I take the bull by the horns. 'Come on. Let's see if he's in. If not, then we'll go to mine for a bit – it's only ten minutes away.' I get out of the car.

'You'd do that for me? Take in a manky stranger?' Jack's eyes are bright as he comes round the car to join me.

'You're not a stranger now, are you? You're my friend. And remember, Jack. If you get down again tomorrow or anytime soon, give the pebble a squeeze and think about all the good things you have in life, okay?' Before he can fling his arms round me again, I hurry up the pavement and down the side path to the apartments.

Jack rings the bell and I stand behind him a few paces. Just as we think there's nobody in, light shines through the semi-circle window in the top of the door and it's opened. Andrew stands there looking at us, his mouth open. I know it's Andrew because he's just an older version of Jack. A cleaner one too, of course, and shorter-haired. But the handsome features and pale-amber eyes state that the two men are unmistakably related.

'Jack! Thank God you're okay. I've been so worried about you lately, man. Come in, come in.' He opens the door wide and ushers Jack through. Jack steps in and launches himself at his brother.

'Andrew, you're such a good person. I've treated you with contempt, but all that stops now. I'm a changed man.'

Andrew looks at me over his sobbing brother's shoulder and pats his back. 'There, now. It's okay, Jack.' He says to me, 'Won't you come in ... er?'

'Joy.' I smile and shake my head. 'No thanks. I'll be off, now I know he's safe.'

Jack turns to me. 'You must come in, Joy! You can't just leave.'

I dig in my bag for a bit of paper and a pen, and write my contact details on it. 'There you go, now you can keep in touch.' I give a beaming smile and he kisses me on the cheek. Andrew thanks me profusely, and then I head off back to my car.

A salt breeze heavy with rain comes at me straight off the Atlantic and I spread my arms wide in welcome, inhale great gulps of it. The knots in my chest begin to loosen and a light sensation settles in my heart. I've completed my first mission as a collector and it feels wonderful. Inside the car I turn the key in the ignition and notice my hand's trembling. I'm still euphoric – I saved a life today, after all, but my God, it's taken its toll. Exhaustion takes over from euphoria on the drive home along the coast road. To keep me going, I focus on my warm cosy cottage, a shit-load of junk food, rubbish TV, maybe a glass of wine and, of course, a cuddle with Sebastian Cat.

Chapter Five

S unday lunch at Mum and Dad's. Can I face it? I consider this as I drag eyeliner across my lid in an attempt to appear like I'm in the land of the living. If I don't go to my parents', there'll be endless telephone calls from Mum asking if I'm okay, yada yada. Best to just go and get it over with. I'll have to put on a show – be the great actress, tell fibs about how absolutely fine everything is, despite feeling like I have a walk-on part in my own surreal life at the moment.

I've tried to zone out any thoughts about collecting over the last few days since I helped Jack. The euphoria I felt having returned him to a safe haven with his brother soon faded. I've been going to work, coming home, refusing to think about more missions. If I allow it head room, it makes me short of breath, pushes me to the edge of panic. Why? Because it's not bloody normal, is it? It's beyond anything I've ever experienced and it makes me wonder if I've imagined the whole thing, because I'm still grieving for the love of my life. Having said that, I have seen auras – glimmers of colour draped around some people at work like old cardigans, but nothing I can identify, and nothing that 'speaks' to me. It could be that unless people have an excess of a positive or negative energy, the aura remains unidentified, or weak. The more I mull that over, the more likely it seems.

Looking back at the mirror, I do some more mulling. How washed-out I look. My light-blue eyes are grey today, and my skin matches them. No wonder, with the sleepless nights I've been having lately. I apply some foundation and blusher, add a few stokes of mascara and a slick of pink lip gloss. That's better. At least I look more alive now. My mess of a tawny mane needs a cut though. I'll be looking like Jack soon. I slip on some black jeans and a red jumper. This makes me look bright and cheerful. I'm ready for Act One of Lunch with Parents, in which the leading lady convinces the supporting cast she is happy and settled in her life. Normal. But as I get out of the car outside Mum and Dad's, my stomach churns and something tells me an Oscar will not be mine this year.

Mum pulls me inside and gives me a big hug. 'It seems ages since we saw you, sweetheart,' she says into my hair. I mumble into her shoulder that it's only been two weeks, but she ignores that, holds me at arm's length, peers into my eyes intently. 'Are you okay? You look a bit tired?'

Great. 'I'm fine, Mum. Just not slept as well as I might have recently.' I shrug my coat off, hang it on the coat rack by the front door.

'Oh? Why's that?' She folds her arms over her blue and white stripy apron, gives me the Spanish Inquisition stare.

'No reason. Sometimes I get like this in winter. Can't wait for spring.' I give her a big smile and inhale. 'Mmm, roast beef and Yorkshire pudding?'

Mum twists a few strands of escaped auburn hair back into a tortoiseshell clip, puffs her fringe out of her miss-nothing jade-green eyes and leads the way to the kitchen. 'Yes, it is,' she says over her shoulder. 'But don't think you can just change the subject, young lady. You're not yourself. Not yourself at all.' Apart from this recent collecting phenomenon, I've not been myself since Sean died. But I'm not going to divulge that to Mum, am I? She'd start going on about how I'm still young, that I can start again, like she often does. I do wonder sometimes if she knows me at all.

Dad's in the living room in his recliner, feet up by the fire, reading the paper, a beer by his elbow on the rickety little table we've had as long as I can remember. I decide to duck in to see him to avoid more interrogation. Mum's already asking me something else from the kitchen, but I ignore her and sit on the sofa across from Dad.

'Hello, love. How's tricks?' Dad puts the paper down and gives me a smile. I'm struck by how much older he looks lately. He's only fifty-eight, but his dark hair's almost white now, and his eyes, so like mine, rest on a flock of crow's feet. Mum's the same age but looks so much younger. Perhaps it's the being out in all weathers catching up on him. The building trade isn't kind to young men, never mind older ones.

'I'm good, Dad, thanks. I—'

'No, she isn't, Derek,' says Mum from the doorway. 'She's not been sleeping and anyone can see she looks knackered.'

I sigh and think about the Oscar. 'Mum, how many more times? I'm fine,' I say to the fire.

She comes in and perches on the arm of Dad's chair and they both regard me as if I'm some unfathomable curio in a museum. 'You sure, love?' Dad's trying on Mum's concerned face, and unfortunately it fits.

'Yes!' I do a forced laugh. 'Now, can we talk about what you've both been up to?'

'Oh, the usual. Been in the shop three days and then helping at the nursery. Same old,' Mum says with a sigh. She always makes out that being an assistant in her sister's bakery is a chore and working with her best friend at the local nursery too, but she loves both. I've watched her in the shop, laughing and joking with all the customers. She's the life and soul.

'Yeah, same here. Working. It's bloody freezing at the mo,' Dad says, stretching his sock-clad feet closer to the open fire.

'Still on those new apartments as you come into Newquay?' I ask.

'Yep.'

The fire crackling's the only sound as we all look at each other, enveloped in an awkward silence. Mum says, 'Right, do you want a glass of wine, Joy?'

I'd like a barrel. 'Yes, please. And I'll come and help you with the roast,' I say, half rising from my chair.

Dad flaps me back down. 'No. Your mum can manage, let's have a catch-up.' Mum rolls her eyes and leaves us.

I look at the fire again. A catch-up? Dad and I have never been good at talking about anything meaningful. I picture his face as I run a scenario in my head of me telling him all about my new-found mission. I hide a smile. He sighs and I look back over to him. He's pressed his lips together and appears to be thinking. I'm about to ask about his hobby – gardening – just for something to talk about really, when he says, 'Are you happy working at the old people's home? I mean really?' He frowns and knits his brows together.

Not this again. He's mentioned it a few times over the last few years. 'You know why I took the job, Dad. It was the only thing going when I needed to go back to work after Sean.'

'Yes. Though you could have been looking for something else all this time, couldn't you?'

'I could. But to answer your question, I am happy there … mostly. Some of the residents are really lovely and I have made some good friends.'

'That's nice, but you're a clever girl. I think you could have made more of your chances early on. If you'd gone to university and—'

Mum comes in with the wine and her death stare cuts his sentence short. 'Now, Derek. Joy hasn't come here for a lecture.' She hands me a glass of red, which I inhale half of before she's drawn another breath. 'Lunch will only be ten minutes.' She glares at Dad as she walks past. 'Play nice.'

'Deb, for goodness sake. I'm just looking out for our daughter,' he says to her disappearing back.

A tumult of emotion is swirling in my chest and I clench and unclench my jaw to try and calm myself. Looking out for me? I'm twenty-nine. And it's not true. All he does is criticise. I've never felt good enough for him. A disappointment. As far back as I can remember, whatever I've done has always been the wrong thing for him. The only good memories I have were of us swimming and sometimes surfing. He's always loved the sea.

'You know I want the best for you, Joy. I was just saying, if you'd have gone to uni, you could be doing anything now. Your choice would be so much wider and—'

'You know why I didn't go to university, Dad,' I say through gritted teeth. 'I met Sean and fell in love. You never approved of that though, did you? Me, chucking in my university place to set up home with the man I loved?'

Dad shifts in his seat, crosses his legs, sets his chin. 'I didn't see why you couldn't have waited until later. You could have got your degree and then been in a better position to—'

'No!' Anger ejects the word, taking me by surprise. I can't stop others following on either, in hot, staccato sentences. 'I didn't want to wait. And I'm glad I didn't now. My husband is dead, in case you hadn't noticed. Every second I spent with him was precious. Every. Single. One.'

Dad's mouth falls open and he spreads his hands. 'Don't get upset, love. I know you loved him; I just want the best for you in life. That's all.'

Mum sticks her head round the door. 'What's the shouting about?'

I shake my head and gulp some more wine.

'I said the wrong thing as usual, Deb.' Dad sighs and folds his arms.

Mum puffs her fringe at him and wipes her hands on her apron. 'Marvellous. Look, lunch is more or less ready, why don't you come through and sit at the table?' She leaves the room and Dad and I stare at each other.

Words are lining up on my tongue again. But they aren't angry, just coated with sadness, bewilderment and needing release. 'I've always felt that you're disappointed in me, Dad. I always seem to come up short, no matter what I do. I suppose I could do better at life, but I've stopped trying, to be honest. I certainly will never win your approval.' My voice is shaky, carrying with it the threat of tears.

To my surprise, Dad's eyes glisten and he shakes his head, unable to look at me. 'I had no idea you felt like that. I just wanted better for you than I had for myself. You were such a clever clogs right from being a little girl ... you had dreams of being a teacher even back then.' He clears his throat and says to the fire, 'I remember you lining your teddies up and pretending to teach them their times table. Then when you got the TA's job, I was over the moon for you.'

This is a first. 'You were? Then why didn't you tell me?'

'Tell you what?'

'That you were over the moon – proud, even. You have never once told me you're proud of me ... do you know that? Not once.' The shake in my voice has more of a wobble building now, so I gulp down the rest of my wine to wash it away.

'Oh…' he says in a voice so quiet, I can hardly hear it above the crackle and pop of a shifting log in the grate.

I can't look at him. Might as well just go in to lunch and forget about all this raking over the bloody past. What good will it do? I stand up. 'Mum will be back in a minute to tell us to get a move on. We'd better go in,' I say, nodding at the door.

'I'm sorry, Joy. I didn't realise. I'm no good with words … I *felt* proud of you, but never said it out loud. I was brought up in a household that didn't really go in for emotions.'

He tries a laugh that sounds more like a cough and I glance over my shoulder at him. Then I have to catch hold of the door frame to steady myself, because his head's encircled by a dull yellow light, the kind you'd get from a dirty low-wattage bulb in a dark cellar. There's a smell of mould too. The light spreads down the outside of his arms, his legs, defining his entire body. A feeble margin of … what? I concentrate and then it comes to me. Worthlessness. He feels inadequate, devoid of confidence. So all of his bluster and bravado is just for show. Maybe it always has been.

His face seems to have elongated, as if a weight of misery is pulling it earthward. God, I've had it up to here. What with the shock of being thrust into the 'collecting' world and the trauma of saving Jack – I can't cope with this. With his hopelessness. And I'm worried sick about my mental health. What if all this is imagined? What if there's no such thing as collecting, and I'm having a long-overdue breakdown? 'Look, Dad. It's okay, let's not dwell on it all. Lunch is ready.'

He stands but makes no attempt to make a move. He looks thoughtful, folds his arms, puts his head on one side. 'I suppose me "going on at you", as you'd say, is just my way of being ambitious for you. That's all it is. I've never made much of my own life, after all.'

A thought strikes me and morphs into words. 'If you're not happy with that, do something. It isn't too late, Dad. Be ambitious for yourself, not me.'

'Nah. I've never had the gumption.' He smiles, showing all of his teeth. Dad always does that when he's embarrassed or unsure. 'I'm not brainy like you.'

This is the most open and honest he's ever been with me. He looks like a little boy. I remember Grandpa Tregear, a big man with massive meaty fists, a ready scowl, a gruff voice … a man of few words, and suddenly it's all becoming clear. My heart lurches and I want to hug him. 'You *are* brainy. You just need a bit of confidence.' The sickly yellow glow surrounding him deepens. *A bit of confidence? That's an understatement.*

Dad shakes his head, turns his mouth down at the edges. 'Thing is, I had a chance of going into a new business with my old workmate, Barry, last week. He came from Penzance 'specially to seek me out on the site. Been looking all over Cornwall for me. We'd lost touch, see.' Pride flushes his face for a second or two. 'He's come into a bit of money and is starting his own small construction company. Wanted me to be manager … eventually be partner, maybe.'

'Then why on earth did you say no?'

Dad does an upside-down smile. 'Too chancy. What if it goes belly up? No. Besides, all that responsibility – sorting people. It's not for the likes of me.'

This is crazy. As manager, Dad would have more money, and probably not be doing such back-breaking outside work either. This old mate obviously believed in Dad, if he'd taken the trouble to come and find him too. I don't know what to say to him. Instinctively I step forward and give him a hug. 'You could always ring Barry and say you've changed your mind.'

Dad gives me a quick squeeze and we step back. The hug's over. He sighs. 'Technically I haven't said no, yet. Said I'd think about it.' We walk into the kitchen–diner together. 'But that's what you always say, isn't it? To be polite, like.'

That thought lifts me. It's not too late to change things. Mum's rushing around like a scalded cat, so I pitch in and put the roast potatoes in a serving dish. 'What do you think about Dad turning this job offer down?' I ask her.

She harrumphs and stirs the gravy. 'Less said about that the better. Suffice to say, I think he's a bloody fool.'

Dad does a sheepish laugh and carves the beef. 'Right, that's enough about me. Let's sit down and have a nice meal, eh?'

While we eat, the talk turns to the weather, me telling fibs to Mum that I'm absolutely fine, what's on TV, Sebastian, and the possibility of me returning to the classroom. I dropped it in as a goodwill gesture, partly to cheer Dad up, but I am considering it more seriously than I realised. Mostly during the whole time, however, I'm thinking that if this collecting is real and not my mind playing tricks because of my ongoing bereavement, I should allow myself to try. If I can help my dad, I should. Then I think about how to collect some confidence for Dad. And, more importantly – from where?

Chapter Six

The next evening I'm back in front of the mirror going through the same procedure as I did yesterday. Eyeliner, eyebrows, mascara, blusher, lipstick. In my head, an escape plan is growing at a greater rate than the thickness of my eyelashes. Why did I agree to meet Fiona for a drink? I'm tired, I've had a busy day at work, and by the time I've walked down to The Merrymoor Inn in this weather I'll look like Worzel Gummidge. As if illustrating that thought, a barrage of hailstones machine-gun scatters across my bedroom window. Right. I chuck down my hairbrush. I'm calling Fiona and saying I've got awful period pains.

I find my mobile on the kitchen table and just as I'm about to dial her number, another thought gallops in stage left. If I stay at home on my own, I'll start thinking about Dad and all the collecting stuff again. Then I'll worry that I'm losing my marbles on the one hand, and, on the other, if I'm actually sane and collecting is real, I should be doing more to help people find happiness, instead of sitting around endlessly worrying about everything. But if I keep my mind occupied by keeping my pub date with Fi, I can put off any big decisions until tomorrow. Hail attacks the window again. Okay. I'll go, but I'll only have one glass, so I can drive there.

As a stiff wind from the Atlantic blows me through the pub door, I see Fiona is already there. She's a vision in sparkly purple top and green jeans, waving like a windmill from a bar stool. Her white-blonde hair is in two long pigtails which makes her look like a cross between Pippi Longstocking and Gretel. On anyone else, the outfit would look odd – but Fiona rocks quirky and cool. 'Quick – bag that table over there and I'll bring the drinks!' she says, scrabbling in her bag for her purse. 'Glass of Merlot?'

I nod my thanks and grab a table for two at the back. Why she's so anxious about the seats, I have no idea. It's not as if the pub is anywhere near busy, it being a Monday night out of season. It's a big place and I'd guess there's about only ten of us here in total. It's a different story in summer. Then, the pub is heaving with tourists as it overlooks Mawgan Porth beach, and has a lovely decked area with outside seating, good food too. She hurries over, an expression on her face sour as a lemon, and nods at the table. 'Not that one. This one!' She hurries past to a larger one with four chairs near the window and plonks our drinks down.

'Why do you want a bigger table? There's just us two.' I follow, sit opposite and notice she avoids looking at me.

'I like to be able to spread out.' To illustrate, she puts her coat and bag on the chair next to her and expels a big puff of air as if she's run a marathon, not just walked over from the bar. She's acting weird. Shifty. I fold my arms, give her one of my mum's hard stares.

'You okay, Fi? You seem a bit … I don't know. Nervous?'

'Nervous?' She raises her eyebrows and does a high-pitched laugh. 'Why would I be nervous?' A tide of pink is creeping up her neck and her grey eyes flit to my face and away, like two unsettled butterflies.

There's an uncomfortable silence while Fiona checks her phone and taps the keyboard. A bit rude, to say the least. 'How's stuff with Mark?' I offer, to instigate conversation.

She shoves her phone in her bag. 'Oh, he's great. Great, thanks.' The butterflies cast about for a place to land and she tugs on one of her plaits. 'Yeah. Great,' she finishes lamely.

So we've established Mark's great. Now what? 'Work at the surgery going okay? No stroppy poorly people giving you grief at the reception desk?' I do a laugh that sounds like I've borrowed it from Scooby-Doo. She's got me acting weird now. Wish I'd stayed at home with my circular worries.

'Yeah. No problems at work.' Fiona's butterflies hover over her clasped hands and she sighs again. 'How's things with you?'

'Oh you know…' *I've been given a death-bed gift. I'm now a collector of excess positive energy so I can help those who need it.*

It can mean the difference between life and death. I saved a guy from suicide just the other day, as it happens. It's my mission to bring happiness wherever I can. 'Same old, same old.' She smiles and I take a sip of wine. This conversation is like pulling teeth.

'I need to go running more, but this weather is just awful. It never seems to stop raining lately.' Fiona flicks both plaits over her shoulder, and then pulls them back again.

I return her feeble smile and we both do synchronised sipping. Since when did we have nothing to say to each other? We usually chat non-stop, but a weather report and a few words about work is all we've got tonight. I tell her I need the loo, but, in reality, I just want to step out of this awkward atmosphere for a few minutes. While I'm in there, I decide to have those period pains after all, and cut the evening short. Because life is, isn't it? Too short to waste time struggling to make something out of nothing.

As I approach the table, I see Fiona talking on her phone. When I sit down, she flushes and ends the call. 'Just my mum.' She places the phone on the table and points at it, as though she needs to clarify who was on the other end of the line.

I take a sip of wine and gear myself up to tell the fib about my period, when in walk two guys. They are both tall, good-looking and a bit windswept. One has short dark hair and a neatly trimmed beard, dressed in jeans and a blue and yellow checked shirt, the other's clean-shaven, has blond curly hair, and reminds me of a surfer, except he's wearing a smart navy suit and shiny shoes. Well … shiny apart from a few mud spatters from the deluge outside. To my surprise the beardy one looks over and waves at Fiona. She waves back and says, 'Blimey, it's Mark and his friend Brad! I knew he was meeting him tonight, but I didn't know they were coming here.'

Any guilt I might have had about telling a fib to get away early disappears when I look at my friend's scarlet face and listen to her wobbly explanation. That is a dead-cert lying voice if ever I heard one. Mark and Brad are walking over, clutching pints, asking if they can join us. Now it all makes sense. The weird behaviour, the grabbing a bigger table, the looking at her phone. I've been set up. Set up with a surfer in a sharp suit.

Mark smiles at me and offers his hand. 'Nice to meet you at last. Fi's told me lots about you.'

I shake his hand, watch his soft brown eyes for any sign of shiftiness, but see none. Maybe it is really all coincidence... Yeah, and in a mo, maybe a pig will fly in and order a gin and tonic too. 'Nice to meet you too, Mark. I've heard similar.'

Mark inclines his head to Brad who's giving me the once-over, his navy eyes crinkling in a smile. His teeth are incredibly white, his nose perfectly straight, definitely handsome enough to be a model, and I'd put him at about thirty-three. 'This is my good buddy Brad, back home for a while. We grew up together round here, but he's made it huge in that big London.' He slaps Brad on the back, pride in his face.

Brad offers his hand across the table. I take it and he lifts mine slightly, says in a voice like melting honey, 'Hello, Joy.

How very lovely to meet you.' For a moment I think he's going to kiss the back of it so I quickly withdraw. A frown momentarily furrows his smooth brow, then he gives me a killer smile and a wink. 'Don't worry, darling, I don't bite. Unless you want me to, of course.'

Dear oh dear. What a complete tosser. Brad laughs as if it's the funniest thing he's ever heard, and Fiona gives me a half-smile and a meaningful look. Possibly an unspoken apology for setting me up. Possibly just wind. Right, Joy. Time for an exit. 'Sorry to be a party pooper, but I'm so tired. Think I need an early night.' I drain my glass and note the surprise on all three faces. They look like someone's given them an electric shock and I have to hide a smile.

Fiona says, 'Really? Can't you stay just a bit longer?'

Mark says, 'Go on, Joy. I'm sure we'll have fun. Brad will feel like a gooseberry if you leave, won't you, mate?'

Brad nods and does a pouty face. 'I will. And I'm sure you'd love to hear about the exclusive boutique I'm opening in Truro. I have six shops in London and this will be the first in Cornwall.' He gives me a dazzling smile. Then he leans forward, elbows on the table, giving me an intense gaze as he describes the boho-relaxed, yet stylish women's wear he deals in. When he says he could see me in all the latest creations, in fact he could see me as the perfect model to launch his new website, I turn away to get my coat. What a load of bull.

'Nice offer, but I have a job, thanks,' I say to the floor as I shrug my coat on and stand up. When I look back at him, I have to sit down again with a thump and stare at the shimmering magenta sunset of an aura Brad is wearing.

'You okay, love?' Fiona asks.

I nod slowly, my mind going into overdrive. What is the name of it? Pride? No. Not quite. Conceit? No. It's on the tip of my tongue … *confidence*. 'Yes, confidence!' Shit. Did I say that out loud? By the strange looks they're giving me, I'd say that would be a yes.

'What do you mean, Joy? What confidence?' Fiona asks.

Thinking on my feet, I blurt, 'I was just wondering how Brad became *so* successful and I realised it must be confidence. You have bags of it, I can tell.' I give him a warm smile, look directly into his eyes and lean forward across the table. This simpering act will kill me, but I need to do a spot of collecting.

Brad leans forward too until our faces are only a hand apart. 'I do, Joy. And that's not all.' The magenta shimmer is beginning to change around the borders … towards his lower half, it's going lilac. No! I have to get his confidence before it becomes lust, or whatever energy is trying to muscle in. I grab his hand, squeeze it hard and a huge surge of power races along my arm and chest, physically shooting me backwards into my seat.

'Whoa!' I say, and laugh out loud at their shocked expressions. 'Thanks for that, Brad.'

'Thanks for what?' he asks in a wary voice, moves closer to Mark.

'Just being you, dahlink!' I stand up, fling my arms out dramatically and bow to the table. Bloody hell, this confidence is crazy! I need to get out and home, transfer it to a pebble. Pronto.

Fiona stands up too, takes my hand and whispers, 'Are you on something, Joy?'

'On something?' I take her bewildered face between my hands. 'I am indeed! I am high on life.' I let go of her face and turn in a circle. 'High on possibilities, on lights hitherto hidden under bushels. From this day forth I will build a bridge across the terrifying abyss.' I do some more flinging of my arms. 'I shall stride across that bridge and forge a new path for others. Light a way through their darkness and bring laughter into their brave new world!' My smile's so wide, it feels like my lips are made of overstretched elastic. But the look of alarm on everyone's faces is enough to prompt, 'So farewell, dear friends. I shall see you anon!' With that, I grab my bag and stride out of the pub.

The rain's coming at me sideways, icy, straight from the Atlantic, but I don't care. My feet have wings and I wish I'd walked down here, instead of driven. I feel like a run. Never mind, I have achieved my aim, and the means to that arrived in the most unexpected of circumstances. Out of adversity comes great stuff, or whatever the saying is. I have an abundance of confidence to give to my dear old dad now and I have completed another mission. Well, almost. I have to get it to him, but that will be easy. How wonderful am I? How utterly marvellous? I can hardly believe how great I am at this job. I jump in the car and drive home up the windy hill, chastising myself for worrying about collecting and if it was real. Of course it is! I shall never doubt it, or myself ever again!

Chapter Seven

Tuesday morning dawns, after a fashion. Not much of a day to write home about. Through the kitchen window I watch a crow alight on my fence-post next to the apple tree, its branches stark against an ashen sky. The crow cocks its head to one side, tries a caw or two, then cocks it the other way, as if waiting for an answer. None comes, so it hops along the fence and flounces off over the barren winter field. I sigh. Must be nice to be able to just fly away. I'd fly somewhere sunny. When is spring going to make an appearance? It's March tomorrow, so hopefully a few green shoots will give us a sign or two in the next few weeks.

I pour some milk on my cornflakes and sit at the kitchen table, push them round my bowl for a bit. Wish I could shake this mood. I'm grumpy, not only because it's only a Tuesday morning and it's cold and grim out, but because I've called in sick and there's nothing wrong with me. Well, that's not strictly true. I'm shattered because of the collecting last night. Old Hope never told me how exhausting it would be. Yes, I was tired after rescuing Jack, but it was so hard letting go of the incredible high I had last night.

In future, I must always carry a little bag of pebbles in case of unexpected collections like I had from Brad. Because I had no pebble, by the time I got home from the pub, I had a huge struggle to let go of the surge of confidence washing through me. I felt invincible. Powerful. I remember picking a pebble out of the jar and then feeling like Bilbo from *The Lord of The Rings* when Gandalf asked him if he might see the ring of power. Bilbo thought he'd handed it over, but he'd put it back in his pocket instead. He couldn't bear to part with it. Same here. I managed it in the end, and then an avalanche of fatigue flattened me.

I shovel in a few mouthfuls of cornflakes and push the dish aside. I should have gone into work, but couldn't face it. The fact that I was loath to give up the confidence has been playing on my mind. Could it be that's what I'm lacking, like Dad? Maybe not as much as him, but enough to make me feel bereft after I transferred it to the pebble. Sebastian jumps up onto the table and sticks his head in the remainder of my cornflakes, lapping at the milk as if he's never been fed. I whisk it away and deposit the soggy mess in the bin. Washing my hands at the sink, I think of a long lonely soul-searching day stretching ahead, and tears prick my eyes. Time to get out, shake this off, go and find Dad at work before I become a soggy mess too.

By the time I pull into the little carpark overlooking Lusty Glaze beach, I'm feeling more myself. The thought of Fiona, Mark and Brad's faces looking like startled rabbits has kept me giggling at intervals during the ten-minute drive from Trevarrian. Patches of blue have torn strips across the ashen sky, giving it a ripped-jean effect, and the little pebble of confidence is in my pocket, waiting for its rightful owner. I'm wearing gloves as a precaution.

The site office is an island in a sea of muddy puddles and gravel. Graham, my dad's boss, gives me a wave through the window and opens the door.

'Hello, Joy. What brings you here? Nothing wrong?'

Graham looks like a thinner version of Homer Simpson, except he's not yellow. His hair is, though – testament to an over-use of cheap hair dye to hide the grey, Dad tells me. 'Hello, Graham. No, everything's fine. I just wanted to have a quick word with my dad, if that's okay?'

'Sure. I'll give him a buzz.' Graham quickly tells Dad I'm here and then we look at each other awkwardly. He's been Dad's boss for years, but we don't know each other that well really. Just the basics.

'How's Laura and the kids?' I say.

'Grand, thanks. Would you believe our Oliver is starting big school this year?'

'Really? It doesn't seem two minutes since he was born.'

'Tell me about it.' Graham shakes his head and picks a hard hat up from the desk, turns it round and round in his hands.

'Time flies, eh?'

'It does. Can't believe it. Oliver finishing primary school

and our Ella's only two more years to do.' Graham puts the hat down and looks at me, his eyebrows raised. 'Oh, just remembered something. Your dad was saying you might be looking to be a classroom assistant again.'

'Er … yeah, I had been think—'

'Cos there's a job going at their school. It was in the newsletter last week.'

'Which school is it?'

'Mowhay Academy, out towards Summercourt.'

Now my interest is piqued. Mowhay is a lovely little school with a wonderful reputation. It would be a dream to work there. I'm about to answer, when Dad crashes through the door, sweeping his hard hat off, his expression worry personified. The sickly glow still envelops him, but it's giving way to something else – it's purple and growing in strength. Worry. It's worry.

'You okay, love?'

'Yes, fine. I just needed to have a word.' I give him a reassuring smile. I should have realised my impromptu appearance at his place of work would have given him cause for concern.

Graham jams his hat on and opens the door. 'I'll leave you to it then. See ya, Joy.'

'Bye, Graham.'

As soon as the door clicks shut Dad says, 'What's wrong? You never come to my work. Is it your mum? Has she had an accident or something?' He shoves his hand through his hair and his Adam's apple bobs a few times.

'No, Dad. Honestly, there's nothing wrong. I just wanted to see how you were feeling after our talk the other day. I had hoped you might be still thinking about taking your friend's offer up. It's never too late to go for your dreams.' I lean against the desk in what I hope looks like a nonchalant manner while I unzip my coat pocket and run my fingers across the pebble of confidence. It's still there. Where else it would be? I have no idea, but nothing would surprise me these days. It has to be a quick transfer and I hope that my dad will fall for my plan, no questions asked.

'You've come here to work, to ask me that?' Dad frowns. 'Couldn't you have phoned? I nearly had a bloody heart attack when Graham said you were here.'

'I wanted to give you something too. Close your eyes and hold your hand out.'

His frown deepens. 'Eh?'

'Just do it.'

A deep sigh. 'Okay then.' He does as I ask.

Whipping out the pebble, I place it in his hand and close his fingers around it. 'It's a lucky pebble, Dad. When you have it close, you'll feel like you can do anything.'

Dad twists his mouth to the side and gives me a withering look. Little does he know that this is the absolute truth. Then his eyes widen and he blinks rapidly at the dark triangular pebble in the centre of his palm. 'Oh … well … thanks, Joy. I…' He looks away, draws a hand down his face and blows heavily through his mouth. 'I'll be going back to work now,' he says in a faraway bewildered voice. The sickly yellow aura is being subsumed by a magenta sunset, almost as dazzling as Brad's.

My heart soars. It's working! It's obvious that my poor father is struggling to comprehend the swell of confidence ballooning in his chest. And, being Dad, he won't want me to see how he's feeling. Time for me to go. 'Okay, Dad. But promise me you'll give the new career some serious thought. Call me soon.' Giving him a quick peck on the cheek, I leave the office, but rounding the corner, I give a quick backward glance. I can't be totally sure from this distance, but I think Dad is smiling.

Back at home, I open up my laptop, type in the local council's job page, open it up ... and then close it again almost immediately. Do I really want to put myself through the stress of applying for a post, waiting for a reply, and then if successful, more stress preparing for the interview? I get off the sofa and wander into the kitchen, flick the kettle on while still pondering. No. Life is much simpler as it is. Get up, go to work, do my job and come home. It's easy, apart from missing the lovely ones like Hope when their time is up. Why leave all that behind to go into an often-stressful TA role? Preparing for OFSTED, making sure I'm following the teacher's plans etc.? Meetings after school. Nope. I'm best leaving well alone...

Ten minutes later, I finish my coffee and find as if by magic, I've opened the page again and am scrolling through all the jobs. There it is – *Mowhay School requires an enthusiastic teaching assistant to join our dedicated team* ... blah, blah, *past experience is essential.* I download an application form and watch my fingers hover over the keys. What happened to leaving well alone? Hope's voice is whispering in my ear: *It's time you got back in the classroom …* and Dad's joins in too. My own inner voice says, *Get on with it!* I take a deep breath and fill out the form.

———

Before starting dinner, I'm contemplating doing a spot of spring cleaning to assuage my guilt about chucking a sickie. I can't remember the last time I cleaned behind the sofa, so the dust bunnies must have created a whole warren by now. I run some hot water into a bucket and grab a cloth and squirty cleaner and gird my loins to go back into the living room. Then my phone goes off. Oh good, saved literally by the bell.

'Hello, Dad.'

'Hello, Joy. I wanted you to be the first to know…'

The happiness in his voice is unmistakable and the pause, full of excitement. 'Know what? Don't keep me in suspense!'

'After you'd gone today, I rang Barry and we decided to meet at lunchtime. I agreed to work with him as manager with a view to becoming partner in the near future if all goes well!'

'Yay! That's fantastic, Dad!' I put the cloth down and do a dance round the room.

'It is. I was a bloody idiot for not doing it earlier. Feel a bit bad for Graham, me handing my notice in after all this time. But from next month I will be the manager at Barry Hale Construction.'

I stop dancing and catch sight of the big, daft grin on my

face in the mirror over the fire. I know the answer already, but I can't help but ask. 'What made you change your mind?'

'Er … well, you did with your nagging, mostly. The thing is … I know you'll think this is silly, even though you gave it me … but that lucky pebble really made a difference. It was as if it gave me confidence – the push I needed.' Dad gives an embarrassed laugh. 'Yeah, your old man's lost it.'

'You haven't. You've found it! Found the confidence to go for your dreams, and I'm so pleased.' I clear my throat and take a deep breath to stop my emotions getting the better of me.

'Well, it's really odd, but I feel like a new man. It's remarkable,' Dad says in hushed tones.

'That's brilliant. I bet Mum will be over the moon too. What have you done with the pebble?'

'It's in the glove compartment. I felt too giddy with it in my hand and even in my pocket! I'm not mentioning it to your mother, though. She'll think I'm nuts. Hell, *I* think I'm nuts!'

I laugh. 'Whether it's the pebble, my nagging, or just that you've eventually started to believe in yourself after all these years, just go with it and trust your instincts, Dad.'

'I will, Joy. And thank you. Righty-ho. I'm going to break the news to your mum. Speak soon.'

'Bye, Dad. Love you.'

I always end calls to my parents like that, but Dad usually just grunts 'Yup' or 'Okay'. But today he says, 'Love you too.'

A week later, I'm just walking through the door from a tough day when my phone pings in my pocket. Sounds like an email alert. Probably another bit of junk. What I need now is to pour a glass of wine and have a long soak in the bath. I might even infuse it with my new bergamot-scented bath bomb. The high life is not lost on me.

In the bath, my mind rehashes the day. Sadly, we lost another resident, Jim Grady. He was a charming old gentleman who always had a kind word for everyone. Never complained about anything, even though he wasn't in the best health and had more cause than some. He passed away in his sleep this afternoon at the age of eighty-nine. A good death, but I've seen too much of it over the past few years. I need a new start. Jim's passing has affirmed I've done the right thing applying for that job. I've probably got no chance though. Loads of people will be going for it.

Wrapped in my fluffy turquoise dressing gown, I make a salad while my quiche for one is in the oven. Why do they have to label things 'for one'? It just emphasises a person's Billy No Mates status. Rubs your face in it. Anyone can see by the size of it, how many people it's for. Taking my tray into the living room, I try to get comfy on the sofa and switch the TV on. Though I'll probably fall asleep, no matter what's on. Why can't I get comfy? There's something hard poking into my thigh … my phone. I shove a forkful of quiche into my mouth, check my emails and nearly choke. I've been invited to an interview next Tuesday. Oh my gosh. I'm suddenly wide awake!

Chapter Eight

From the outside, Mowhay School looks more like it belongs in New England than old Cornwall. The white clapboard structure, smart grey tiled roof and a beautiful stained-glass arched doorway at its entrance depicting children at play, give the combined impression of age and beauty that only buildings of the past can. Patches of land border the periphery, from which sprouts a variety of vegetables, roses, shrubs and wicker sculptures. I grab my bag and poly-wallet with a lesson plan and notes inside, and take a deep breath. I don't want to leave the safety and comfort of my car, but they won't do the damned interview out here, will they? Drive-thru interviews. Now there's a thought. Yes, and evidence of my nervous state.

Kelly Land, the receptionist, gives me a tour of the place. The school might look old fashioned, but, inside, it is very modern. The building comprises six state-of-the-art classrooms, complete with the best computers – one for each student – and a well-equipped kitchen and dining room. Lovely art and music studios are housed in another, similar structure built in the grounds, and in a third is a small science lab. I knew it was an excellent school, but not the full extent of it. There's a wobble in my belly, which threatens to topple the little confidence I've mustered this morning. Maybe I should have asked Dad for his pebble.

I look up at the ancient arched beams in the ceiling, kept from the original building, and the breath-taking simplicity of it all. I'm impressed with Kelly, too. Ostensibly, she's the receptionist and secretary. She isn't called a receptionist or secretary however, but Front of House. The headteacher said that as the first point of contact to visitors and parents, her task was to demonstrate that the school was a showcase of educational excellence and achievement. Blimey. I've just spent the last twenty minutes on my own, visiting classrooms and talking to staff and pupils. Such switched-on, polite kids. It would be a dream to work here. Now I'm scheduled to go back to the office.

'Joy, come on in,' Kelly says, stepping into her comfortable office, or 'welcome room', as it is known. The office is decorated with beautiful hand-made tapestries, woollen rugs made from alpaca wool (they have three of the animals in the grounds), and the floor is scattered with bean bags. Kelly has a bespoke desk and chair made by a local carpenter and her own kitchen and toilet in the adjoining room. The woman herself is around forty, tall, slim, and dressed in clothes similar in style to the tapestries. A long green linen tunic, and matching trousers, are embroidered with bright meadow flowers and beads. Kelly pushes back a tumble of titian hair from her eyes as she pulls out a seat for me.

'Thank you,' I say with a genuine smile. She's one of those people who put you at ease. Kelly's calm blue eyes and direct manner release the remaining few butterflies I have fluttering in my belly out into the early spring sunshine.

'So, are you ready for the interview in half an hour?' Kelly points at the coffee pot and I nod.

'I'm certainly getting there, thanks. The school is stunning and the people are friendly too.'

'They are.' Kelly nodded, pouring coffee into a yellow mug. 'All the staff are. We're like a little family here.' She takes a plate of biscuits from under the desk and offers it to me. 'There are some who say we Cornish are cliquey or stand-offish with those from up-country. But I haven't noticed. Must be a nasty rumour put about by those evildoers over the border in darkest Devon.' She winks at me and hands me the mug.

We talk about the structure of the day, and I get to ask lots of questions. All of it is familiar, but one or two things are new, like the gardening lessons and pupil-led projects every Friday. I try not to get my hopes up, but I so want this job. It would be a very much-needed breath of fresh air in a dark, stuffy room. Then Kelly runs her finger down a page in front of her. 'Oh, the head asked that you eat lunch with her in her office with the other candidates, just to help you get more of a feel for the school and allow you to ask more questions – that okay?'

'Of course. That would be great,' I say, all the while

worrying that I will spill my food down my new red dress bought especially for this occasion. We'll all be judged, of course, while we're supposedly socialising. I have to be on my guard at all times. Luckily my formal interview will be over by then, but I can't relax fully. 'Um, how many candidates are there?' I ask in what I hope sounds a casual manner.

'We had three Friday, three yesterday and three today. We'll make a decision tomorrow.'

My heart sticks in my throat and I wash it down with coffee. That's a lot. But what do I expect for such a sought-after school? 'Right. Where are the others?'

'They will all be here any moment. They have been shown around by various members of staff and, like you, they've had time to go in the classrooms. You're the first to get back.'

I hope I haven't been too quick. Maybe it looks bad that I'm first with my nose in the coffee and biscuits? But then, I was supposed to be back here by the time on the schedule. Telling myself to calm down, I glance up at the door as two women are shown in. They are both older than me, but that's not difficult. One looks to be around thirty-five. Tall, very thin, dark short hair and a nervous smile. The other, mid-forties, plump, rosy-cheeked, with blonde curly hair and a bubbly laugh. Kelly introduces us and we shake hands, pretending to be relaxed and jolly while furtively sizing each other up. Or maybe it's just me.

Tall and Thin is called Beth, and Plump and Rosy is Carla. We chat amongst ourselves, drink coffee and eat biscuits for a while. I discover that both have loads more experience than me. I'm the only one whose current job isn't in a school. So, by the time Kelly takes me down the hallway to the interview room, I have a tsunami of nerves surging through my veins and an ocean of nausea splashing around my stomach.

The interview went well. Really well, I thought. But then I remind myself not to get too confident. There's the lunch with the head, Helen Brearly, to get through now. She seemed nice enough during the interview and ten-minute lesson delivery, but I wasn't sure if she was genuine. Outside her office, I bunch my fist to knock, but the door opens before I make contact.

'Joy, come in, come in!' Helen says, stepping to one side and ushering me to a comfy chair next to a small table, upon which a nice selection of sandwiches and salads are arranged. Carla and Beth are already here. 'Take a plate and dig in.'

I take a plate and also a quick glance around the room. It's obviously trying to be bohemian like Kelly's welcome room, but it just lacks something. The prints perhaps are too colourful, the scatter cushions placed too carefully and the whole area, though attempting to come across as relaxed, is just too … I toss a few words in my head – neat. Yes, neat is the word.

As we help ourselves to food, I give Helen the

surreptitious once-over. I was too 'rabbit in the headlights' to notice much about her in the interview. She's very much like her room. And she's wearing similar attire to Kelly, cool-lemon linen trousers, an embroidered white and lemon long tunic with a cord belt. Yep, definitely has the boho vibe going on. But then the ebony sharp-edged bob, scarlet lips and carefully drawn brows over green glassy eyes wouldn't look out of place in a corporate boardroom.

Helen's fingers brush mine as she passes me a cup and I note how cold they are. Perhaps Helen isn't human at all, and actually a robot made by the kids in the science lab. They couldn't agree on the look, and therefore the robot's body was trying to be one thing, and her head another. I smile at my mad thought and then another, less frivolous one arrives – *Perhaps she's trying to be something she's not.*

'Please sit, tell me all about your view of this place so far,' Helen says, sitting behind her highly polished desk – again more suited to a boardroom than this office. The smile is encouraging, yet I have the impression that it's trying hard not to be fixed.

'Thanks, I have had a lovely morning. It's a wonderful and inspiring school,' I say, sitting on a rattan chair; a beanbag would be a mistake, given the fact that I have a plateful of food and a cup of tea in my hands. Carla and Beth nod and echo their agreement. This makes me feel better, and I place the mug on a little footstool and take a bite of an over-full tuna sandwich.

'Splendid! So you think you'd like to work here?' Helen raises her arched brows and crunches her perfect white teeth into a celery stick. At first, I think the celery is bleeding, but then realise it's Helen's red lipstick coating the ridges.

And who says 'splendid' anymore? Perhaps we've been sucked into a 1940s black and white film. 'Yes, very much so,' I say, my sandwich poised next to my mouth; then to my horror, a dollop of tuna, sweetcorn and mayonnaise plops onto my new red dress. My cheeks have a go at copying the colour of my dress, while Helen leaps to my aid with a napkin.

'Bugger, that was bad luck,' she says, shooting me a sympathetic glance while vigorously scrubbing at the stain.

I attempt a laugh that turns into a snort. 'Never mind. It will come out in the wash, hopefully.'

'Yes, should do. Perhaps put it in water as soon as you get in,' Carla says as if she's an expert, and smiles at Helen as if she's scored a point. Beth says nothing.

I mentally take charge of the situation before the atmosphere in the room becomes any more awkward and force myself to laugh more convincingly this time. 'Oh yes, I know. It'll be fine.' I give Helen what I hope is a winning smile and pray that there isn't a kernel of sweetcorn stuck on a canine. 'I was wondering if I could clarify something?'

'Of course, that's what this meeting's for, really.' Helen picks up her coffee cup and regards me over it with those keen green eyes.

As I'm about to ask her question, I note that somehow Helen's plate of food is half gone, even though I'd only actually seen her eat a celery stick. Perhaps she is a robot after all.

'Okay … at interview you asked me some of the things I would do if money was no object.'

Helen nods and drinks more coffee.

'If you remember, when looking at the history curriculum, I said it would be great to actually get the kids to construct a tipi. You know, to help them get a better understanding of what it might have been like to be a nomadic Native American and to have to live in one? Not that they could know properly of course, as it wouldn't be accurate … I mean, we couldn't go around killing buffalo and using their hides to construct one, and also these students have comfortable homes and modern technology to go home to at end of the day, but…' My words run out. Damn it, I'm just burbling on and poor Helen looks slightly bemused. Or is she trying not to laugh? The aroma of warm tuna wafts from my chest into the still air of the office.

'Yes, I remember. A great idea and not too expensive,' Helen says, the corners of her mouth twitching into a brief smile.

It is? Relief floats tentatively in my chest. I have to make this crystal clear though. 'Thanks. So there would be a possibility of perhaps building one … in the grounds?'

'Yes, of course. I'm sure you could substitute buffalo hide for manmade materials, just this once.' Helen turns one side of her mouth up. 'We could ask Bob, the caretaker and groundsman. He'll supply wood and such, and the children might bring in sheets or something.'

'That's a great idea,' I say, hoping I'm not being too sycophantic. Carla and Beth are looking at me as if they wish I'd disappear in a puff of smoke. But they have as much chance as I do to make an impression. It's not my fault if they aren't taking it. 'Brilliant that the children would bring things in too.'

'Yes. Our parents will be only too happy to supply ideas. Also, our children are used to thinking for themselves, taking initiative; they will love a tipi challenge. They know they have to achieve their very best, and they are prepared to do autonomous learning and unsupervised study. In fact, they could construct a number of tipis, not just one – in groups, of course.'

I can't help but feel that I'm winning at this 'not an interview' interview. Helen gives us all a friendly smile and offers cake. I take a slice and break it into three pieces. Only a complete idiot could manage to miss her mouth now. Even so, my eyes follow the cake's path to my mouth with the intent of a hawk on a field mouse. Success.

Carla asks a question about the history of the school, which, although interesting, is hardly the most relevant, and Beth says she has an idea for getting the children to become more involved in short-story writing. It seems a bit complicated and Helen mostly nods and looks out of the window. A few minutes later, Helen dabs a napkin at her mouth and sets her plate down. Blimey. Once again, she's consumed the whole slice as if by absorption. 'More tea? Coffee?' she asks, though I expect she's just being polite and probably has other things to do. Nobody does, so she calls an end to proceedings and says we'll be hearing whether or not we were successful by telephone tomorrow.

In the car I heave an enormous sigh of relief. Thank goodness that's over with. In a small corner of my head, on a sun-drenched beach, there's a little figure of hope relaxing on a comfy lounger, confident that the job's mine. In the rest of my head, there are storm clouds of doubt gathering out to sea. The little figure of hope is blissfully unaware they are moving swiftly towards it. My job is to think positive – make sure the clouds shed their load elsewhere. I start the engine and think happy thoughts.

Chapter Nine

I can't concentrate on anything the next day. After an early shift at St Margaret's, I'm home again doing the laundry while checking my phone for the trillionth time. No missed calls, no messages, nothing. Helen said I'd get a call, whether it be bad or good. The bad would include a little debrief, intended to help in future job hunting. Would there be future job hunting? The way I'm feeling right now, I wouldn't bet the farm on it. I've become unused to this type of stress. One thing about working at the care home, you couldn't call it stressful. The interview process was short and to the point, too. I was offered the job there and then. Why couldn't Helen have done that? It's not as if I'm applying for MI5, is it?

Watching a huddle of bruised clouds gathering directly above my garden and over the washing on the line, I'm reminded of the little figure of hope on the beach. I've a sneaking feeling it's going to get drenched, just like my washing. Then my phone goes off in my pocket, scaring the hell out of me. Unknown number. Oh God. It could be Helen. I stare at my phone while my heart's doing the rumba. Then my finger takes charge and swipes the screen.

'Hi, Joy. It's Helen Brearly.'

Does her voice sound a bit flat? Gosh, it does. She's about to deal a death blow to my career with an expertly placed robot hand… 'Hi, Helen, how are you?' Hopefully my high pipe and broad smile will compensate for her flat tone. She can't see my smile, but she will be able to hear it. She's made her decision, so what does it matter? She's talking again and I give myself a metaphorical clip round the ear'ole. *Concentrate.*

'… and the competition was tough, as I say, but we were blown away by your confident manner and easy way with the children. The tipi idea was particularly inventive, and something that we can achieve practically and fairly quickly.'

Hang on. She's saying nice stuff about me … very nice stuff. 'Oh, thank you. I'm glad you liked it.'

'So, I'd like to offer you the post, if you still want it?'

She would? And if I still want it? Is she mad? I stare at the washing and notice the sun's stabbed a few daggers of gold through the huddle of clouds, and a helpful breeze is shooing them away towards the ocean. 'Oh my goodness! Yes, of course I want it! I can't believe it. I thought when I heard your voice that it was going to be a no.'

'My voice?'

Shit, she sounds surprised. Why did I have to say that? I take a deep breath and say, 'It was probably just me, thinking the worst. There was nothing wrong with your voice.'

'I see.' Great. Now she sounds frosty. 'Okay, well I know it's a bit unorthodox, but we need you asap after Leslie, your predecessor, chose to leave her post so abruptly.' The derision is unmistakable. I remember the poor woman had a breakdown, according to Kelly, so she hardly 'chose' to leave, abruptly or otherwise. I decide to keep that thought to myself, however. 'How much notice do you have to give in your current post?'

'A fortnight. Is that okay?'

'Right. That will mean you start after Easter, so we'll have to limp along until then with supply.'

'Sorry, I don't think I could leave any earl—'

'Not your fault. Quite understand. And will you be around today at home, after school ends? I'll get Gilly Holmes, the teacher who you met yesterday, to drop some files over, so you can get up to speed. School policy and so forth. Gilly has a few bits for you too. She should have given you all this yesterday but forgot. She can be scatter-brained, sometimes.'

'Yes, I'll be here. Thank you.'

'Okay, see you after Easter. Any questions, email Gilly. Bye now!'

Helen's ended the call before I can draw breath. Wow. My head won't process what's just happened. Sebastian comes in and meows at me, starts winding himself about my ankles like a fluffy mohair thread. I laugh, pick him up, bury my face in his fur. 'Sebastian,' I whisper in his ear. 'I got the job ... I got the bloody job!' Sebastian looks far from excited and yawns in my face. Putting him down, I call Mum to share the news. She's so thrilled and says she will let Dad know when he gets home. She also says we must go out for a celebratory meal soon. Then I ring Fiona and she's over the moon too.

'That's amazing! How about we go out for a drink tonight to celebrate? I promise Brad won't be there.' She does a little sheepish laugh.

'You organised that "chance" meeting the other week, didn't you, Fi?'

'Eh? What makes you think that?' Her tone goes up a few octaves.

'Apart from the guilt in your voice? I think it was bloody obvious. I mean, you were acting all shifty just before they arrived at the pub, and you're a rubbish actor.'

She snorts down the phone. 'Okay, you got me. But I only wanted you to meet someone nice. I worry that you're lonely, and Brad is gorgeous, isn't he?'

'If you like a narcissist with a vacuous brain, yeah. Perfect.'

'Oh, he's not that bad…'

'He is.'

'Okay, he is. But he's pretty.'

'Pretty awful.'

'Right. I can see there's no convincing you. We'll go out very soon, yeah?'

'Yeah. Speak later. Bye, matey.' I end the call, but the phone rings immediately. Unknown caller.

'Joy, it's me, Jack.'

'Jack, how lovely to hear your voice!' I sit on the sofa

and Sebastian joins me, using my knee as a scratching post. 'Ow!' I tip him off onto a cushion.

'You okay?'

'Yes, just my cat getting a bit too boisterous. How's stuff?'

'Stuff is bloody fantastic, thanks to you. Can't really take in how fast things have moved. I have a job working at a homeless charity – just voluntary for now, but they are really pleased with me and say it could be paid work before long. I'm doing talks in shelters too, giving advice and encouragement to people who come in, and my mum has given me a lump sum to help me get a place of my own! She was so thrilled that I was turning my life around, that she told Dad she was helping me, and that was that! First time in her life she's stood up to him. Andrew and his girlfriend have been wonderful too. And I'm so happy that I can help people who are struggling, just like I was.'

That reminds me of what Hope said about people I help being compelled to bestow random acts of kindness. Jack's doing that in spades. 'Wow! I'm so thrilled for you, Jack!'

'I'm so thrilled for me too! And if you hadn't come along that day when I was about to … well, you know what … then I wouldn't be here at all.'

'It was my absolute pleasure, Jack,' I squeeze out through a lump in my throat the size of a golf ball. Then we talk about things in general, my new job, I even tell him a bit about my life and Sean.

Then Jack says, 'Anyway, must get on. Can we meet up again in person soon – have a proper chat?'

'Of course. Can't wait.'

'Okay, Joy. Speak soon, and thanks again from the bottom of my heart.'

'Bye, Jack. Take care!' My, my. What a wonderful day I'm having so far!

One not-so-wonderful thing has to be done next, and that's to ring St Margaret's and give Lucy, my manager, a fortnight's notice. I could do it tomorrow, but I want it done and off my mind. My heart gets a little heavy as I scroll through the contact list, remembering all the friends I've made and all the people like Hope I've looked after over the past few years. I will miss all of them, but it's time to move on. After I end the call, tears catch me unawares and I allow them to fall unchecked for a while. St Margaret's was a job that allowed me to get back on my feet after the darkest time in my life, and for that I'm grateful. Also, sometimes you just need to cry. And Lucy was so nice about it all, and wished me all the best. I promised I'd look in now and then in the future, and I'll keep my promise.

But now I need to do something positive. Before lunch, I'm going to jog down to the beach and back. I've neglected my fitness lately and despite the sun's best efforts earlier, it still looks a bit overcast, so should be ideal running conditions. After that, I'll have a nice lunch and maybe even have a glass of wine to celebrate the job!

As I trudge back up the lane, I realise that trip wasn't really one of my brightest ideas. Sweat trickles down my back, between my breasts, under my arms, and strands of damp hair stick to my face as the sun climbs higher in the cloudless sky. The weather forecast said we were in for some lovely spring weather. But this feels more like July. When at last I step into the cool of Atlantic Cottage, I give a huge sigh of relief. Now for a quick shower, then I'll make lunch. On my way upstairs I notice I left the milk out, and while enjoying the cool wave over my skin coming from the open fridge door, I hear a knock on the front one. *Shit! Who's this, now?* Much as I like Fiona, I so hope it isn't her, or even Mum come to surprise me. I just wanted to relax this afternoon. I hope it isn't anyone else either, as I hardly look my best and am wearing the delicate aroma of eau de Sweaty Betty.

The weirdness of that thought strikes me as I take a quick glance in the hall mirror and remove a smudge on my cheek with a wet finger. It *has* to be somebody, doesn't it, unless the shrubs along the path have somehow uprooted themselves and are tapping on the door with twiggy hands. When I open the door, I wish it were Fiona or my mum. In fact, anyone else but this guy in a grey suit, looking down at me from under dark lashes, a hand shading his sky-blue eyes from the angling sun.

'Hi. Sorry to bother you, but Gilly Holmes asked me if I'd drop off some files.' He lifts an armful of them to illustrate. 'It is Joy Pentire, isn't it?'

Though it has a slight Cornish lilt, the timbre of his voice reminds me of Aidan Turner's in *Poldark*. And apart from the eye colour, he could be the actor's understudy. I feel his gaze sweep my dishevelled appearance and I notice a few damp patches clearly visible through my thin shirt. Crossing my arms protectively over my chest and aware that my flushed face could probably cook a small chicken, I clear my throat, smile slightly and say in my best assertive voice, 'And you are?'

He pushes his dark wavy hair from his forehead and says, 'The deputy head from Mowhay School, Jowan Williams.' He juggles the files, offers his hand and takes a step forward, which forces me to take one back like we're performing some crazy Baroque formal dance. The deputy head? Some rapid-fire questions machine-gun my senses. Why is he here instead of Gilly? And why didn't I meet him yesterday? Should I ask him in? I can't be doing with entertaining right now. Not dressed like this, at least. It's all so unexpected.

I shake his hand quickly and then drop it, re-cross my arms and say, 'Hi, Jowan. Nice to meet you. Err … would you like to come in? Though I am on my way out again in a few moments, so…' A lie, but needs must.

Jowan glances at my appearance again and almost imperceptibly raises an eyebrow. To my horror, that tiny movement causes another embarrassing surge of blood to my face. It's obvious that he either doesn't believe me, or that he thinks I'm in the habit of going out looking like a sack of…

'No worries, I'll be in and out in no time,' he says. 'Just need to tell you what each file is, and it's a bit tricky balancing heavy files on the doorstep.'

'Of course, come through.' I usher him in, and follow with a sigh. Just wonderful. And to think that my day started so well.

He stands in my kitchen looking around. 'What a lovely home you have, Joy.' He nods at the table. 'Shall I put the files here?'

'Yes. And thanks, I do love my little cottage and this area.'

His generous mouth breaks into a smile which adds a warmth to his eyes as they crinkle at the corners. 'Yeah, it's great here. I live just down the road from here at Mawgan Porth. That's why Gilly asked me to drop these, as it's on my way. I'm off to a meeting in Newquay now, and then won't be going back to school afterwards.'

'Oh, I see. How come I didn't see you yesterday at the interview?'

'I was on a course. Senior management development and all that malarkey. Very boring, but has to be done.'

'Right.' I nod at the files. 'Bedtime reading for me.'

'Hardly.' He twists his mouth to the side and lifts a file. 'This is almost as boring as my course, I think. Helen does love a good set of policies.'

Hmm. Not very professional. 'Every school has them.'

Jowan stokes the stubble on his chin. 'Oh, of course. These ones are, let's say, very comprehensive.' He quickly explains what's in the files and then stands looking at me, arms folded.

I fold mine again, having forgotten about my damp patches temporarily. What's he gawping at me for? I wonder if he expects a cuppa? I ought to offer one really, but I feel such a mess. 'Um, I'd offer you a drink, but I'm just popping down to The Merrymoor to meet my friend.' His eyes sweep the length of me and he does the eyebrow thing again. Bloody hell!

'Right, okay.'

'When I've had a shower and got changed,' I say pointedly. 'I've just been out running.' Though why I feel the need to explain myself, I have no idea.

'I'd best be off anyway; don't want to be late for the meeting.' He smiles and walks past me to the front door, leaving behind him a subtle waft of delicious aftershave. As he opens the door, in stalks Sebastian, and immediately rubs himself around Jowan's legs. 'Wow! What a beauty,' he says, scooping him up. I expect my cat to protest and wriggle free as usual. He always takes a while to accept newcomers. But no. No, he settles into the crook of Jowan's arm as if he's known him forever, purring like a traction engine.

'Sebastian, you'll get hair on the poor man's suit,' I say, holding out my arms to take him.

'I don't care. I adore cats.' Jowan's eyes mist over. 'I recently lost mine. Old Bella had been with me since I left uni … can't get used to not having her around.'

'Oh, I'm sorry. Must be hard.'

'Yeah. She was fourteen though, so a good age. Had a good life too.' He tips Seb into my arms. 'Okay, I won't keep you any longer. See you after Easter.'

'Yes. Thanks so much for bringing the files over.'

'My pleasure. Nice to have met you, Joy.' He raises a hand in farewell as he walks away down the path.

As I watch him drive off, I feel a proper meanie, pretending I was going out. Jowan seems a nice guy. He likes cats, so he's got to be decent. And Sebastian warmed to him immediately, which is unheard of. Why didn't I offer him a cup of tea? Who cares if I'm a bit sweaty and look a mess?

In the shower, I puzzle over this question again and ask myself another. Would I have cared so much if it had been Gilly on my doorstep, and not a very attractive man? The answer is no. Which leads me to another question. Why? I shouldn't be attracted to him, should I? After Sean died, I knew I could never be with anyone else and have resigned myself to a life of singledom. Then my sensible head tells me to stop worrying. It's okay to find men attractive. I'm only human. Mostly, I'm annoyed with myself for acting the way I did just now. If the poor man ever comes by again, no matter how I look, I will be polite and offer him a cuppa.

Chapter Ten

W hy did I agree to start a new job? I was perfectly okay at St Margaret's. But no. No, I had to put myself under lots of stress and upheaval. Easter's over, and that's why I'm standing in front of the mirror at stupid o'clock, wondering if I have the bottle to get through my first day, *and* if I'm wearing the right outfit. Grey trousers, black comfy shoes and a yellow and blue checked shirt. Children like bright colours and I want to come across as cheerful and non-threatening. But will the staff see me as some kind of clown? I was in for inset day last week, so hopefully they know I'm not. And what about my hair? Or mane, as Hope would call it. Up or down? Up, probably, as I don't want to suffocate a child while I'm leaning over their shoulder to help them with work.

Taking some deep breaths, I remind myself that I've done this before as I tame my mane into a plait. I've done it before and very successfully for four years. Helen Brearly wouldn't have appointed me if I'd been no good. It had been a tough field, yet she'd chosen me. I'm just getting rattled for no real reason … although I've been a bit disconcerted regarding my 'collecting' life lately. It's been very quiet recently. In fact, non-existent. Maybe there'll be no more people to save and I've had the shortest career in collecting history. Hope said it was a lifelong thing, but it might not be in my case. And in the end, do I really want the responsibility of being a collector?

Then I think – not for the first time – it all still might have been a figment of my over-active imagination brought on by loneliness and missing my darling husband. Maybe it's gone now. Just an aberration. If it has, would I mind? I stretch my top lip into an arc and apply a slick of pink lip gloss. Yes, I think I would. Dad's so much happier these days, and if I hadn't become a collector – real or not – he'd still be muddling along in his old job, painting over his inadequacies with a pompous veneer and a condescending top coat. Jack's story has been a success too. But can it continue? So far, it's been a bit too easy. What if I get something wrong? Maybe I could do more harm than good. This brings me round to worrying about the whole responsibility thing again. Right now though, I need to shelve it and focus.

Okay, time to get gone. I give myself one last glance in the mirror and leave.

———————

It's lunchtime, and, once more in front of a mirror, in the Ladies, I wash my hands and smile at my reflection. The morning went *so* well. I adore the children in Gilly's class, even Callum Pengelley, who likes to pick his nose and wipe it on the nearest person's sleeve. I avoided being that person by a hair's breadth, and explained – supplying him with a tissue – that it isn't amusing, not in the least. I further stated that doing such things at the age of six is frowned upon. He screwed up his freckled face and appeared to be puzzling this, but then sneezed all over my hand. Nice.

Gilly is lovely to work with. I stick to the lesson plans, but she encourages me to use my initiative too. This afternoon can't come soon enough, because she asked me to explain my tipi-building idea to the class. We hope to source the materials, get Bob the caretaker/handyman to make a few designs and then build it over the next few weeks. Can't wait. I've not had much interaction with Helen, beyond the staff briefing this morning. She seems a little aloof. Jowan was there and asked how I was doing on his way out of the staffroom. I chatted to him a bit on inset day too – he's really warm, welcoming and friendly. Obviously trying his best to settle a new member of staff into the school routine, which is more than can be said for Helen.

The non-teaching staff are really friendly too. I've got attached to Daisy, one of the dinner ladies, already. She chatted to me for ages on inset day and she gave me a wave today at breaktime. Daisy is one of those round-faced, pink-cheeked, curly-haired, bubbly women who always seem full of the joys. She looks about thirty-eight, but is actually in her mid-forties and already has two grandchildren. I decide to join the lunch queue for some hot food. I'll have cottage pie and veg, maybe some apple pie and custard too – save me cooking tonight. Daisy comes out of the kitchen with a metal tray of cottage pie … and my wave stays frozen in mid-air before I drop my hand. Although she's smiling and chatting to staff and children in the queue, the outline of Daisy's body is shrouded by a dull-green light. It's as though she's walking through algae. Hmm. My collecting 'aberration' is not over, then.

'Daisy,' I say when I get to the end of the line. 'Are you okay?'

'Me?' She does her trademark guffaw, her bright blue eyes round. 'Of course. Why do you ask?'

I study the sickly aura around her and can't decide what the hell it is. Is it despair? Is it sadness? She's staring at me, the serving spoon hovering over the cottage pie, a question in her eyes. And something else. Something else is in her eyes … desperation … powerlessness? It's covered by her laugh and her bubbly nature, but I can see the edges peeling back. 'Um, I don't know. Just a feeling I have that you're not quite yourself.'

Daisy laughs again and waggles the spoon at me. 'Barking up the wrong tree there, Joy. Want some cottage pie?'

I can hear grumblings about having to wait from hungry kids behind me, so I say, 'Yes, please, Daisy. And some apple pie?'

Daisy obliges with a nod and a smile and I move away. I'll try and catch her before the end of school; this is neither the time nor the place to press her.

As I eat, I try to keep an eye on Daisy, but after a few minutes, she goes back to the kitchen and her colleague takes over. How can I begin to find out what's making her feel so hopeless? She's already putting up walls, and I don't know her well enough to rock up and demand to know. How *do* I know, anyway? I can't tell her the truth, can I? But if I insist that I know there's something wrong, she'll think I'm some kind of psychic ... it would be easier if I were.

As I'm pushing the last of the apple pie around the dish, Gilly comes into the dining hall. She's a popular teacher and closer to the children's age than the rest of us. I think she said she was twenty-five, but with her slight stature, elfin features and long dark hair in a ponytail, she looks even younger. I watch her high five some Year Six kids as she walks past their table, and then she spots me and hurries over.

'Can I join you?'

'Of course! I'm Billy No Mates at the mo.'

She grins and chucks her bag on the table. 'I was going to eat a sad cheese sandwich in the staffroom that I shoved together this morning, but couldn't resist the smells coming from the kitchen.' She grabs some money from her purse and tosses it down. 'Back in a mo.'

I move my tray away from her bag as the strap has fallen in some custard on the edge of it. Then I wipe it off with a tissue and hang it on the back of her chair. The wallet-purse has fallen open and I try not to nosy at the photos in the side compartment, but don't succeed. It's a handsome young man in an army uniform. He's smiling at the photographer with love in his eyes. I'm guessing the photographer was Gilly. They make a nice couple. I sip my drink and wait for her to come back.

'I decided on fish and chips! The cottage pie looked nice, but I fancied something with chips.' She nudges her purse out of the way with her tray and sets it down. Then she notices the photo, shoots me a puzzled glance then puts her change away, and rapidly zips away the soldier.

Gilly tucks into her food, but I think she seems a bit quiet. Did she think I'd opened her purse? 'Your purse fell open, and I couldn't help but notice the photo of a soldier. Hope you don't think I was being nosy!' My laugh sounds a bit pitchy, because that's exactly what I was being.

A frown creases her brow and she takes a sip of juice. 'No, course not.'

Okay then, not very forthcoming. But I'm not put off. 'Is he your boyfriend?'

Gilly's green-flecked hazel eyes avoid mine. She sighs and stuffs a chip in her mouth and mumbles through it, 'He was, but we aren't together anymore.'

'That's a shame. You made a nice couple.'

'Hmm. Known each other since Year Ten. Broke me when we split.'

Gilly attacks her pudding as if it's done something to annoy her, and I decide not to ask anything else. She obviously doesn't want to discuss it. He must have really hurt her when he ended it. 'Right … that's a shame.'

'Yeah. Had to be done though.'

Oh? This sounds as if she's the one who ended it. 'Your decision, then?' I ask, and then kick myself. So much for keeping quiet. 'Sorry. You might not want to talk about it.'

Dabbing her mouth with a napkin, she shakes her head. 'No, I don't mind. As I said, it broke me, but it's all in the past now. Me and Steve had dated since we were fifteen. We were inseparable, we liked all the same things, and were best friends as well as a couple. After uni, his plan was to be a solicitor, mine was always to teach. I never wanted to do anything else.' Gilly pauses and lets out a sigh. 'But then his elder brother Craig got killed in Iraq. It hit Steve so hard. Really hard. Anyway, he changed his plans, left uni and went into the army. Seemed he thought he could take the enemy on all by himself. Avenge Craig's death somehow.'

She finishes her pudding and I say, 'Death affects people in different ways.' Don't I know it. 'He must have been suffering so much.'

'Yes. I don't think he was thinking straight at the time, but despite me being against it, he joined up and that was that. He knows that I'm anti-war and can't abide the fact that our young men and women are sent to police areas, to protect the interests of big business. Oil is the key here. And so many poor people who live there die needlessly too. Our people lose their lives in roadside bombs, and for what? So some fat cat in London can buy another yacht?' Gilly's eyes flash in anger. 'It would be a different matter if we were fighting the Nazis in World War Two, but we aren't.'

Wow. I've opened up a can of worms here. 'Yes, I can see that…'

'I didn't finish with Steve straight away because I loved him too much. But after he was posted overseas, it was so hard to keep in touch. When he came home on leave one time … he…' Gilly blinks, takes a moment and takes a sip of juice. 'He proposed to me. Said he'd missed me so much and couldn't bear us to be apart. But I said no. There was no way I was going to be an army wife, living here, there and everywhere. Never putting down roots long enough to make a life. Hating his job. In the end, he said he'd leave the army, but I could tell he was only saying that to make me happy. I wouldn't make him choose, so I told him I'd met someone else. It was a lie, but that was the only thing I knew would make him leave me alone.'

'Oh, Gilly. I'm so sorry.'

'Me too. I broke his heart. But there we are. These things happen.' She looks at her watch and says brightly, 'Ready for afternoon school?'

Ignoring her question, I ask, 'How long ago was this?'

She looks out of the dining room window at the kids playing on the field. 'Nearly two years … and I miss him every day.'

I fiddle with my spoon, 'Do you still love him?'

'No. I don't know … yes, I suppose so.' She shrugs. 'Too late now anyway.' As she says this, an aura spreads over her head and down her arms, lengthening her outline like a shadow at sunset. It's orange and red and it's … longing? Regret?

'It might not be too late. If you really love him, then please tell him. You'll work something out.'

Gilly sighs and the aura fades. 'Thanks, Joy. Nice of you to care, but it's over and done.' She stands up and gives me a big smile. 'Okay, Mrs Pentire. Time for you to tell the class all about the exciting tipi task we have lined up over the next few weeks. Ready?'

I stand too, knowing I'm beaten … for now. 'Yes, Miss Holmes. Let's go!'

We had a great afternoon. The children were so enthusiastic about building a tipi in the grounds. Many of them are confident and outgoing, which can lead to potential clashes with each other as they try to assert dominance. Tristan, a farmer's son, asked if he could bring his pony in. He said his dad had a rifle too that might be useful. David, a sensible and down-to-earth boy who 'likes to learn new words', shook his head and said, 'Don't be preposterous! A rifle is not permitted in a school.'

I defused the situation, explaining why that wouldn't be possible. He seemed confused and disappointed when I told him that these people were not the baddies, like the old films would have us believe. 'Yeah, well, I'm going to get some feathers from our cockerel and paint my face when the tipi is done,' Tristan grumbled. I decided to leave that one for now.

In response to our request to bring in some old sheets or towels to use instead of buffalo skins, Ellie, an outspoken and lively girl, said she was going to grab the duvets off all the beds. Her mum has loads, apparently. Gilly said that wouldn't be a good idea and she should ask her mum's permission before bringing anything in. Ellie rolled her eyes, huffed, and said of course she'd ask first. Otherwise it would be stealing. Gilly and I caught each other's eye and tried not to laugh.

We deliver the children safely to their parents at 3:15 and then I remember Daisy. I'd hoped to catch her at the end of lunch, but totally forgot as I was engrossed in Gilly's story. I hurry to the kitchen, but find I've missed her by about ten minutes. Damn. I'll make sure I get in early tomorrow and try and catch her before she starts meal prep. Her colleague said they start about 8:15. Back in the classroom, I tidy everything away and check the lesson plans for tomorrow. I'm so happy to be back in a school. I've missed the chatter of six year olds and their enthusiasm for simple things. I'm as excited as they are about the tipi build. Some of it is because the idea was mine. It will be a fun task. On the way home I think of poor Daisy and Gilly. They aren't having much fun at all. Hopefully I'll be able to help them.

Chapter Eleven

Next day finds me in school just before eight, so I'm hoping Daisy's going to come through any moment. I hurry down to the kitchen–staff locker area and wait. This feels a bit weird. Me hanging about an empty locker room trying to look nonchalant. What am I going to say if anyone comes in? The teaching staff have their own area, so it will look odd. About to change my plans and go up to the main corridor to wait until Daisy comes in, I hear a muffled sob from the loo at the end of the room. I move towards it and stop a little way off, straining my ears. Another sob, this time unmuffled. Do I say something? Would I embarrass the person who's come in here for a quiet cry? While I'm debating, the door opens and out comes Daisy, dabbing her eyes.

She startles and then pretends to look for something in her handbag while surreptitiously wiping her eyes. 'Oh ... hello, Joy,' she mumbles, clearly mortified to see me here.

'Hi, Daisy. What's happened?'

'Nothing much. Sorry you had to see me like this.' She flaps the tissue at me and goes over to the sink, runs water into it. Then she gets a clean tissue, wets it and then dabs it against her pink cheeks and under her puffy eyes. She looks at her reflection and me behind, and her chin wobbles.

'Can I do anything to help, Daisy?'

A quick turn of her head. 'No. Nobody can.' Then her shoulders start to shake as silent sobs wrack her body. I hurry over and put my arms round her, which makes the sobbing worse, so I guide her over to a low bench and we sit down together. The dull-green algae is back, coating the outline of her frame. Its name forms in my head. Defeat. She's defeated … given up. I hand her a tissue and after a few moments she says, 'It's my husband. He lost his job six months ago and he's taking it out on me. Especially when he's had a drink. Gary's always been quick-tempered, has given me a slap from time to time over the years … but now…' She releases a long juddering sigh. 'Now he uses his fists.' She rolls her sleeve up and shows me the bloom of a huge, livid, black and yellow bruise on her forearm. 'There's more like that on my belly and back … he never marks my face.'

My heart's pounding as fury at this man I've never met surges round my body. How could anyone hurt someone like Daisy? Bloody coward! 'That's terrible, Daisy! Have you told anyone?'

She shakes her head, her bright-blue eyes clouded with despair. 'No. You're the first. I don't want to burden my friends. My three kids have left the nest now – getting on with their lives. I can't tell them, especially not my eldest,

John, because he'd go round and give his dad a good hiding. I couldn't cope with all that … with what it would do to our family.'

'But you can't just put up with it, Daisy. He might put you in hospital eventually. You have to get out of there.'

'I've no choice. I've nowhere to go. No money for my own place.' She shrugs. 'Besides, when he gets a job, he should be okay again. He says he loves me, and he's always sorry afterwards, so…' Daisy's words run out and she shrugs again.

'Men like him are always sorry, but it will happen again. I've heard about this kind of thing too many times.' Daisy sniffs but says nothing. 'Do you love him?'

She swallows and twists the wet tissue round her finger. 'I've asked myself that question every day for years … and if I'm totally honest with myself, the answer is no. I started falling out of love with him a long time ago when he had an affair, but I stayed with him because the children were small, and, as I said, there was nowhere we could have gone. My parents were the type who believed that if you made your bed, you had to lie in it.'

'But surely if they knew how serious the situation is now, you could stay with them temporarily?'

'No. Dad's gone now, and Mum's in a home. She has dementia.' Daisy pats my knee. 'Anyway, thanks for listening, Joy. I didn't mean to burden you, but it just came out. I had a rough time last night and am feeling sorrier for myself than usual. I'll be okay when I've got my face on.' She flashes a big smile, pulls out her make-up bag and goes over to the mirror.

Her make-up and jolly façade are part of her coping mechanism. A mask to hide the misery behind. Bloody hell, what an awful dilemma! Poor Daisy. I'm sure there are options for her, and help out there, but she's so defeated she won't be looking for them. I could try and help; she could stay with me for a bit. But I know instinctively the initial move has to come from her. She has to get the courage to say enough is enough. I go over and put my hand on her shoulder. 'You haven't burdened me. I am here for you whenever you need me. And if you want somewhere to escape to while you figure out your next move – you can come and stay with me.'

Daisy's eyes find mine in the mirror as she puts a trembling hand to her mouth. 'You'd do that for me? You've only known me five minutes.' Her eyes swim again and she puts her hand over mine. 'That's one of the kindest things anyone has ever said to me. You're such a lovely person, Joy.'

I smile. 'So, you'll come?'

Daisy shakes her head. 'No. But thanks for the incredible offer. I'm sure it will get easier soon.' The sickly green aura is fading, so perhaps she really believes that.

All through morning school, thoughts of Daisy are buzzing around at the back of my mind like a swarm of angry bees. What she needs is courage. Courage to do what she should have done years ago, and that's pack up and leave the brute of a man, who's not fit to be called a man. He's a snivelling coward. I need to collect some courage, but where from? It's not the kind of emotion that you find an excess of, willy-nilly around the place. Happiness or confidence is much easier to source. Who do I know who's courageous? I'm still puzzling on this when Molly Sanderson waves at me from the back of the class. I go over. She's adding information to a picture she's drawn of Native Americans setting up camp. 'Miss Pentire, do you think the Native Americans were better fighters than the cavalry? I do. It's just that they lost 'cos the cavalry had more better weapons and stuff.'

'I think you could be right, Molly. But there was a famous battle that the Native Americans won. The leader of the cavalry made some very big mistakes.' Molly fiddles with her shiny red ponytail, her brow furrowed in concentration, as I tell her all about the Battle of Little Bighorn.

'Colonel Custard was a bully and a show-off, I reckon,' she says, drawing an arrow sticking through a soldier's hat.

I hide a smile. 'His name was Custer, not Custard. And yes, I think you might be right again, Molly.'

'Their leader, Crazy Horse, was clever and brave.'

'Yes, very courageous.' As I say this, the name of someone I know who was also very courageous in battle, drops into my head.

———

Harold Robinson is sitting by his window poring over a book with a big magnifying glass. At ninety-six he's still alert and very much with us. His door's partly open and I stand for a few moments watching him. A uniform of smart trousers, shirt and tie, is always worn, even when he's relaxing in his room, like now. Harold's very particular about his appearance. Once a soldier, always a soldier, I suppose. Harold's posture is resolutely slouch free and he occasionally smooths his white hair which is still pretty thick and parted down the side, while his keen green eyes, larger than life through the glass, dart back and forth across the page. I imagine him as a young man in his war days and what he must have seen. I'm about to knock, when he looks up and sees me. A huge smile animates his expression and he says in surprise, 'Joy! How lovely to see you. Come on in.'

I go over and kiss his cheek, soft as velvet, and place a box of chocolates on his lap. 'Lovely to see you too. How are you, Harold?'

'Grand, my dear. And thanks so much for these.' He puts his book down and looks at the chocolates. 'Have you changed your mind and come back to work here? I do hope so.' He gives me a cheeky wink.

'No. Just visiting. I did wonder if I could pick your brains, though?'

'There's not much left of 'em. But you're welcome to try.' Harry chortles, opens the chocolates and pops one in his mouth. 'Want one?'

I take one and we chew together in mutual appreciation for a few moments. 'The children at school will soon be doing a project on the war, and I wondered if you'd mind telling me how it was for you. You were there at the D-Day landings, weren't you?'

'I was indeed. But I'm not sure my memories would be appropriate for little ones. It was pretty "hardcore", as my great-granddaughter says.'

'Oh, of course. I would only give them the gist.'

Harry puts the chocolates aside, clears his throat and sits ramrod straight. 'I couldn't talk about what I saw there for a long time. I had nightmares, you see. Terrible nightmares that went on for twenty-odd years. Still have them now and then, if I'm honest. My wife used to wake me up sometimes, said I'd been yelling. No counselling back then, of course.'

Thinking of all those young men living through hell and then just expected to get on with life, brings a lump to my throat. I swallow it down and say, 'How old were you, Harry?'

'Just twenty.'

'Dear Lord.'

'There wasn't much evidence of him around when we landed on Gold Beach, to be honest. The Yanks had it worst on Omaha, but we lost a lot of men that day.' Harry pauses and looks out of his window over the rooftops of Newquay towards the Atlantic, but I can tell he's seeing The Channel in his mind's eye many years ago. 'There were land mines and machine-gun fire. Once you see what those things can do to a body, you never forget. Nor the screams and cries of the men cut down. It was like a living hell.'

'How did you find the courage to keep pressing on up the beach?'

Harry looks at me and raises an eyebrow. 'No choice. We could hardly pile back in the landing craft and go home, could we, maid?'

I shake my head. 'No. But even so, I think you were all very brave.'

Harry's blue eyes narrow as he considers this. 'Yes. Yes, we were. We were terrified as well. Some of the boys – and they *were* boys, almost – were frozen with terror and we had to slap them out of it. I suppose I found my courage in the fact that we were defending our country from evil.' He gives me a hard stare. 'Because the Nazis were certainly that. All those civilians dead in the Blitz, the countless innocents bombed, cut down in their prime. And then there was the anger. I had a lot of anger at the injustice of it all – that's what drove me. Revenge for them. The dead, the dying. That's where my courage came from, I suppose.' Harry gives me a brief smile, his eyes shining with pride. As he's been talking, around his shoulders has settled a midnight-blue aura like a cloak. I don't have to wonder what the name of it is this time. Before it has chance to fade, I leap up and shake his hand.

'Thanks so much, Harry,' I say, as his courage slips quickly along my fingers and swells in my chest. Adrenaline's doing the rounds and my heart's thumping like a hammer. I feel like I can take on an entire Panzer division single-handed.

'My pleasure. You off so soon?'

'I am.' My voice sounds breathy, as if I've run upstairs. Must be fight mode kicking in. I take a breath and hold it for a count of four. Then I continue. 'Got to get home and feed my demanding cat.' Closing my hand around a pebble I keep in my pocket for emergencies, I allow Harry's courage to rush into it like an oncoming tide. Phew. My heartbeat slows immediately and my breathing returns to normal.

Harry puts his head on one side and frowns. 'Are you alright, Joy? You look a little flushed.'

'Yeah. Fine. I want to pop off now and write up what you said, while it's still fresh in my mind.'

'And feed the cat.'

'Yes. That too. I'll come and visit another time ... you've been more helpful than you'll ever know, Harry.' I squeeze his hand and he gives me a lovely smile.

Driving home, I wish I could have told Harry what just happened. He would be so pleased that his fighting spirit is being useful again. That something he has will hopefully be helpful to a woman who's being abused by a brute. But he probably wouldn't believe my story. What right-minded person would? Besides, as Hope told me, if I blab about it, the collecting won't work. A thought occurs. How did she know that? Has it ever been tested? I'll never know. But one thing's for sure, I won't be the one to do the testing.

Chapter Twelve

The next morning I'm hanging around the locker rooms again like a bad smell. I hope Daisy won't think I'm being too pushy and back off when she sees me. Hearing footsteps, I put my hand in my bag to take the pebble out of its little velvet pouch, but it's one of Daisy's colleagues. She's an older lady, stout and prone to grumbling. When she sees me she stops and huffs. 'Oh? You lost?'

'No.' I try a smile which slams into a force-field frown on the woman's large forehead. 'I have something for Daisy and thought I'd catch her early.'

The woman shakes her jowls. 'She's ill. Left us in the lurch today. I'm going to have to work like the clappers, 'cos there's only two of us left.'

'But she can't help it if she's poorly,' I say.

'Hmm. No help to me though, is it?'

I decline to answer and hurry out, worry about the cause of Daisy's illness speeding me on. What if her vile husband has really done some serious damage this time? I could go and see her at lunchtime if I knew where she lived. Would Kelly let me have Daisy's address, I wonder? Probably not. And what excuse would I come up with anyway? I can hardly say I want to go round to see if she's okay, Kelly would think it strange. I've only worked at the school five minutes – Daisy and I are hardly bosom buddies. Once again, all through the first few hours, my mind is with Daisy, not on the job. Gilly asks if I'm okay and I realise I've been staring into space. I must go and see Kelly at breaktime.

At first, predictably, Kelly is not happy about sharing another member of staff's personal details. Then I say I understand, but I'm worried about Daisy and can't really divulge why, because it would be a breach of confidence. Kelly reads my face for the longest time, as if the reason behind my concern for Daisy is written upon it. Then she says, 'It's more than my job's worth to give you the address.' Then she turns her back on me, looks out of the reception window and says, 'There's some nice brightly coloured cottages on Hurley Lane. The blue one is especially eye-catching.'

It takes a moment for the penny to drop, but when it does, I say quietly, 'Thanks. Maybe I'll take a look.' Then I hurry to the staffroom, Googling maps as I go.

Lunchtime finds me parked two doors down from the blue house and biting my nails to the quick. What if Daisy is just off sick, and it's nothing to do with her husband's violence? I'll feel a bit stupid. Having pondered on this for a few seconds, I dismiss it. So what if I feel stupid? At least I will have made sure she's okay. And if the brute is in his lair? I'll pretend I'm selling something. But what? I have no leaflets, no produce, nothing. Hmm. Okay, I have it. I'll pretend I'm from the church, volunteering to help people in the area with errands. I'm a doer of random acts of kindness, don't you know? A regular little ray of sunshine. I kind of am anyway. So it's the truth. Not the ray of sunshine, but the doer of kind acts. *Joy, for goodness' sake, stop procrastinating and go.*

At the door, I look around me. The house looks well cared for, neat front lawn, clean windows, tidy path. Those who pass would imagine the inhabitants lead a happy, ordered life. Normal. How wrong they'd be. The plan I thought of in the car feels flimsy, fragile and shallow. It's construction is at the mercy of a stiff breeze. This is all way out of my comfort zone, but I've brought courage in my pocket. If all else fails, I can hold the pebble for a few moments. Balling my fist, I raise it to knock, and then notice a doorbell. My doorbell doesn't work, but this one does, and the cheerful jingle-jangle heralds my arrival through the house. I swallow my nerves, rehearse my little ray of sunshine speech and wait. Nothing. I press the bell and add a gentle knock, just to make sure. Nothing. Then the upstairs window opens a crack and a pale white face, half obscured by a floral curtain, peeps down at me. 'Joy?' Daisy says in a half whisper. 'What are you doing here … and how do you know where I live?'

I ignore the last bit. 'Just popped round to see how you are. See if you needed anything.'

'It's just a stomach bug. I'll be fine tomorrow, thanks.'

Her furtive manner and trembling voice tell me otherwise. As does the livid bruise on her cheek as the curtain blows back on the breeze. Daisy grabs the curtain and covers her face again, but it's too late. I've seen. 'Daisy, let me in, please. I need to speak to you.'

Her words tumble out in a rush. 'No. I'm fine, thanks for coming, Joy. You'd best be off or you'll be late for afternoon school.'

I'm pretty sure she's alone, and that she's trying to get rid of me before the creature comes back. I open my mouth to say something else, but Daisy goes to close the window. I stop her by saying, 'I'm not going until I've seen you.'

'Please, Joy. Just go.' Her eyes dart up and down the street.

'No.'

The window slams and, a few moments later, a clatter of footsteps grows louder inside the house. The front door swings open and Daisy stands in front of me, but a little to the side, the left side of her face angled away from my gaze. 'Okay, you've seen me. I'm fine.' The door starts to close until I push past into the hallway and close it behind me.

'I saw your cheek when you were upstairs, Daisy. You aren't fine at all.'

All pretence is dropped as she glares at me, raises her arms in frustration. 'For God's sake, Joy. He's only gone to the bookies. He'll be back in about fifteen minutes. He can't find you here!'

Fear contorts her face and a single tear makes a slow journey over the raised black and red lump of her cheek. I palm the pebble of courage and take her hand in mine. 'No. He can't find *you* here. Pack a bag and I'll take you to mine until we can figure out what to do.'

Daisy shakes her head and tries to pull her hand away from mine, a puzzle in her eyes about why there's something hard and round in it. But I hold fast. 'No I can't … and what's that…?' She pauses as the courage seeps into the heel of her hand.

'It's a lucky pebble. It might sound mad, but I find they help at times like this.' My eyes hold hers, as she struggles to comprehend the surge of D-Day strength which must be firing the cylinders in her fight systems.

When I'm sure she's not going to drop the pebble, I unclasp her hand and say, 'Will you come with me?'

Daisy opens her palm and stares in bewilderment at the small dark-brown object cradled there. A lopsided smile puffs up her good cheek and her light-blue eyes twinkle with wonder and something else. Realisation that she can do it? That she can leave the brute of a man who calls himself a husband? I hold my breath. The smile fades and her eyes turn an arctic blue. 'Yes, I will. I bloody well will. This is the last time that bastard will ever lay a hand on me. And if he were here now, I'd give him something to think about!' Daisy grabs a walking stick from the hall stand and whacks it against the banister.

Not wanting to be a referee in that eventuality, I slip my arm through hers. 'Understandable. But not right now. Let's get you packed.' I lead her to the first step on the stairs, which she takes, then stops.

'No.' Daisy's eyes flash and her breathing quickens. 'Gary deserves to pay for what he's done to me all these years. Why didn't I see it before?' She slaps the walking stick on the banister again and whirls round to the front door, poised for Gary's entrance.

Damn. She's got an overload of D-Day courage now. I glance at my watch. We're running out of time. From my other pocket I pull the little velvet pouch I kept the pebble in and say, 'Daisy. Drop the pebble in here so it doesn't get lost. Put it in your pocket and let's go.'

'Why? I like holding it. I think it must be lucky, like you said.' Daisy stares at the pebble in her hand as if it's the Holy Grail.

Swiftly I scoop it up, tip it into the bag and shove it into her dressing gown pocket. 'Listen to me. We have to go. I need to drop you home, then dash back to school before I get the sack. And I quite like my job.' I finish with a brief smile and all but drag her upstairs.

Ten minutes later, we have three holdalls and a suitcase stuffed full of Daisy's life. I bundle her and them into my car, and screech away from the blue house like a formula-one driver. As we round a corner, Daisy thumps on the window and swears at a weaselly-looking man, smoking a cigarette outside the Spar shop. He's cracking the ring pull from a can of something, and never notices her.

'That's Gary, I presume?'

'Yeah. Scumbag!'

'Hmm. Never mind, you've done it now. You've finally

found the courage to leave the scumbag to choke on his scum.'

Daisy grins and hugs herself. 'I have. I really have…' she says in awe. 'And, Joy, I could never have done it without you.' She pats my shoulder. 'I honestly don't know how to thank you. Taking me into your home like this … I'm a relative stranger.'

'You did it all by yourself.' *Kind of, with old Soldier Harry's help.* 'I couldn't have forced you to leave if you didn't want to. And you're not a stranger. You're a friend. The kids at school all love you, and kids are never wrong.'

Daisy says nothing, just looks at the passing scenery near my home and sniffs. She fishes a tissue out of one pocket, and, from the other, pulls the velvet pouch. 'Thanks for this too. I don't think it's a mad idea at all. I think it's lovely … makes me feel stronger, and I'll keep it near me always.'

I nod and smile as I swing onto the drive of Atlantic Cottage. *Not too near though. We don't want you in jail any time soon, because a scumbag's been found beaten to a pulp with an old walking stick.*

Oh my goodness, this breakfast is delicious. I could get used to this. My waistline might not thank me, though. I wipe the last bit of toast through the remains of my fried egg and pop it into my mouth. Daisy's there straight away with the coffee pot and offers more bacon. 'More? I don't think so. I've consumed more calories last night and this morning than I normally do in a couple of days!'

Daisy does a mock sad face. 'Oh. You didn't like the chicken and leek pie and raspberry crumble and custard I made you last night?'

'I loved it! But if I keep this up, you'll have to roll me out of here.'

Daisy laughs. 'It won't hurt you. There's nothing of you, maid.'

I pat the little bump of my tummy and shake my head. Daisy collects my plate and takes it to the sink. Her cheek is still displaying a yellow and blue hue, but it's not as swollen as yesterday. Daisy's not going into work again today though, as no amount of make-up would disguise it. I move to the sink and put my hand on her shoulder. 'You know, I don't want you doing all the cooking and tidying while I'm at work. Have a rest and put your feet up.'

'I'm fine, Joy. I can't sit around doing nothing. Besides, it's the least I can do to thank you for rescuing me and letting me stay.'

'Nonsense. You rescued yourself.' Daisy gives me a little smile and runs water into the bowl. 'Has he tried to contact you again?'

'I blocked his number. But our John messaged last night. I told him I was okay, and I'd explain today. So he called this morning early to ask what was going on. Gary phoned him last night and told him I'd disappeared. I haven't told John why I left – just said I needed some time away from his dad to think.'

Worried that Gary might find her, I ask, 'You haven't told John where you are, have you?'

'No. Just that I'm staying with a friend.'

'Good.' I stretch and yawn as Sebastian flies through the cat-flap like a bullet. 'Hey there, boy. I wondered where you were. Want your breakfast?' Sebastian meows at me and jumps on Sean's chair, stretches a leg to the ceiling and starts to wash his bottom.

'I fed him earlier before you got up. Such an affectionate little chap.'

'Oh, I see.' I laugh. 'Didn't take long for you to abandon me, did it?' I tap his head and he gives me a green glare. How dare I disturb his ablutions?

'Would you like me to make you a sandwich for lunch, Joy?' Daisy says, her head in the fridge. She insisted we went to the local supermarket last night and bought enough food for an army.

'No. I'll skip lunch after that big brekkie, thanks.'

'That's no good. You need your energy, on the go all day with those kiddies. Now off and get ready. You'll be late.'

I laugh. 'Yes, Mum.'

Bob the reluctant handyman is ready on the playing field after lunch. I've decided he's the type of man who is happy in routine and the familiar, but any divergence from that is a broken spoke in his smooth-running wheel. Helen seemed to think he'd leap at the chance of a new project; she obviously doesn't know him very well. On the three occasions I've spoken to him, I've received a few withering looks down his long nose and at least two raises of his bushy grey eyebrows. Nevertheless, he has erected six wooden tipi frames with long poles, just as they would have been by the Native Americans – though Bob's poles probably came from B&Q, and most definitely not from the Great Plains of the United States.

When I talked to him at first about the tipis and showed him pictures, he scratched his head and said he could do it, but that the Cornish weather would probably drench the children's efforts and blow them over. I said we'd wait until the forecast was good and hope for the best. I also told him that in the event of bad weather, we could disassemble them and reassemble them another time. Bob sucked his teeth and said he was sure the Native Americans wouldn't have had to do that. I smiled, and said that in fact that's exactly what they did, because they were nomadic and followed the herds of buffalo across the plain. Bob raised an eyebrow and muttered something I couldn't hear. I got the feeling that he thought tipi erecting wasn't in his job description.

The frames look pretty good, and just the right height for the children. We decided full-size tipis were a bit ambitious. 'Excellent work, Bob!' I say with a big smile.

Bob sniffs and flicks his dark brown eyes to mine and away. 'I always do a job right, whether I reckon it'll work or not.'

'Right. Thanks, Bob.' I nod over to the playground where Gilly's lining up our class. 'I'll give you a shout if we need you.' Bob sniffs again and walks off. Maybe he'll come around when he sees what a great job the children make of the coverings.

———————————

By the end of the school day we have made fantastic progress. We managed to get the sheets fixed on all six structures and the children have decided on their roles for when we are 'living' the Plains Indians' experience. The entire class are fired up by the project and can't wait to start decorating the 'buffalo hide' with animals, hunting figures, stars and moons.

Gilly and I walk back to the classroom after the children have left and chat about the way it's gone. 'I'm as excited as the children about decorating the tipis tomorrow,' Gilly says with a chuckle. Through the window, she points to the clear-blue sky swept of cloud by a gentle breeze. 'Let's hope this weather keeps up.'

'It's set fair for the rest of the week, so all should be well.'

'I think I'm going to have a walk on the beach before dinner. It's ages since I've been.'

'Lovely. You live in Truro, don't you? So which beach do you go to?'

'I like to go to St Agnes and walk along the cliff path. Steve's folks live there. So does he when he's home, and we used to walk along there often...' Gilly's voice tails off and she looks at me as if she wished she'd just kept that to herself. 'No idea why I still like to go there. There's plenty of other beaches.'

'Perhaps it's because that's where you and he were happy. Maybe you feel closer to him when you walk there?'

She shrugs and picks up some exercise books. 'Maybe. All water under the bridge now.' A faded sunset sheen clings briefly to her outline, and then it's gone. 'Right, I'll take this lot home and mark it before I go for my walk. See you tomorrow, Joy.'

From the window, I watch her hurry towards the carpark, the sun sprinkling conker highlights through her shiny dark ponytail, and let my thoughts drift to Daisy. Since helping her I've had to admit to myself that collecting is actually real, as strange and crazy as it seems. No matter how much I've tried to argue it away, say to myself the reason the pebbles work is because I convince the recipient they are lucky or magical, that it's plain auto-suggestion and not magical at all … I know I've been kidding myself. As Gilly drives off, I wonder if she'll be the next on my collecting list. There must be something I can do to help her tell Steve how she really feels. The faded sunset she was wearing was longing, I think, edged with doubt. All she needs is to believe that their love isn't lost, that it's worth fighting for. To have faith. So … where am I going to find some of that?

Chapter Thirteen

I n the quiet of the classroom at the end of the day I put
the finishing touches to a display, tidy the crayons and
books, and allow myself a few minutes to take stock. My life
is hurtling along at the moment, seconds racing to become
minutes, minutes to become hours, all trying to scramble as
fast as possible to get past the finishing line of day's end.
There doesn't seem time for me to draw breath. On the one
hand it suits me, as I have little time to think about the past
and dwell on the emptiness in my heart, always present
since Sean left. But just sometimes, it can get a bit too
frantic.

Now, as I perch on the edge of the desk, I reflect that
despite the hectic rush, I'm beginning to remember what it
was like to be me before I lost Sean. I loved my job, and here
I am now; back in the classroom. It's as though a part of me
that has been missing for three years has clicked back into
place. I'm whole again. Is this new post the reality of me

finally taking the first step on the path of moving forward? A wave of emotion sweeps through me. I'm back in the classroom, but I'm not the same as I was before, am I? My life isn't the same. When I go home tonight, Sean won't be in his favourite chair, I won't hear his voice as he comes in the door shouting that he's home. Releasing a sigh, I tell myself to be positive. That these facts aside, my feet are on a tentative new path. A new path with familiar edges of my past lining the sides to strengthen it. Coming back to school was a good move. The best move.

Back home, I find Daisy in the kitchen, bags packed and beaming like a lighthouse. Where the hell is she going? The answer is obvious, but I hope I'm wrong. 'Daisy?' I nod at her belongings. 'You're leaving?' My heart's teetering over a precipice as I imagine weasel Gary persuading her to return to him.

'Yes. I'm going to John's. Just until I find myself a place.'

Phew! Thank goodness for that. 'He knows about you and his dad?' I fill the kettle and flick it on.

'Yes. He went round to ours this morning and found Gary paralytic. He'd vomited all over the sofa and was lying like a dog in his own filth. John helped clean him up and asked him why I'd left, and Gary eventually told him. Said he'd given me a good hiding and that I deserved it. John just managed to keep his temper and told him if he ever came near me again, he'd kill him. Then he phoned me and made me tell him everything. I didn't intend to, but it all came out. All the horrible things he's done over the years…' Daisy blinks away tears and grabs a tissue. 'Anyway, I agreed I'd go and stay with him and his wife for a while.' She sighs and gives me a big smile. 'It's such a relief though. I can't tell you how much it's helped to get it all off my chest.'

I hug her. 'I bet it is. Though you know you can stay here if you like. You don't have to rush off.' I toss a couple of teabags into mugs and pour on boiling water.

Daisy smiles and squeezes my shoulder. 'You are so kind. But John and Heather have offered, and it will be nice to spend a little time with the grandchildren too. He's coming to pick me up in half an hour.'

Sebastian looks up from Sean's chair and yawns at me. 'What will we do without Daisy to look after us, eh, Seb?'

Sebastian doesn't answer, but Daisy says, 'I promise I'll give you an extra portion of lunch at school every day!' She hugs me again, and, in a strange way, even though she's only been here a day, I realise I'm going to miss her. When Sean died, I didn't think I'd ever get used to living alone, but I did after a while. Though I can't say I like it. It was nice having another person in the house, however briefly.

Stepping back, I do a mock-horrified face. 'Don't you dare! I'll never fit into my new jeans.'

We sit at the table and sip our tea, chat about my day and her immediate plans. Then John arrives and off she goes. The house feels really quiet, as if it's lost something. A bit like the silence in place after the end of a party, when lots of people have been bustling about, laughing, joking, their energy crackling through the air. Daisy had a similar effect. She's such a big personality, happy, bubbling over with enthusiasm for life. On the surface, at least… Now I know it was just a façade. I've been allowed a glimpse into the darkness that was her reality. 'Was' being the key word. Because of Harry's courage, she's all set for a new life. One in which her happy façade is now the truth.

Sebastian meows at me and takes a flying leap onto my lap. I stroke a finger behind his ears. 'Okay, my boy. We've sorted Daisy, the next quest is to find some faith for Gilly. How hard can it be?' He purrs and closes his eyes. Looks like I'm on my own there, then.

The weight of ages is present in the narrow, cobbled streets and waterfront of Truro, and nowhere more so than in the lofty cathedral. I Googled before I left, and found there has been a place of worship on the site since the twelfth century, and the ancient church was incorporated into the main cathedral that was built in the 1800s. The Victorian stained-glass windows are apparently some of the best in England, some say Europe. I once visited when I was a child, and don't really remember much about it … because buildings aren't very exciting when you're eight or nine, are they? But as I leave the bright sunlit afternoon behind and step inside the cool, cavernous, stone-clad interior, the beauty and grandeur of the cathedral literally takes my breath away.

Surrounding me, set into extravagant carved stone, are so many beautiful arched and round windows made of shimmering blue, yellow and red glass. The sunlight sets them afire and in this animated light, the religious scenes depicted seem to move of their own volition. I walk towards the front, taking in the jaw-dropping architecture and scenes. The time and effort, not to say dedication and love that must have gone into the many years of its construction, are overwhelming. I'm not a religious person in the traditional sense, but I'm certainly a spiritual one. I can feel the presence of human endeavour and belief. Of faith.

There are only a few people here right now, and they seem to be just wandering, having a look round, like me. I take a glance at the information dotted here and there and find that the front is called the nave. At the nave, an elderly woman is constructing a stunning flower arrangement. She has long white curly hair, and is wearing a mid-calf rainbow kaftan over dark leggings. The yellows, oranges, reds and golds of the flowers reflect the huge stained-glass windows high above her, and there's something vaguely iconic about the way the light envelops her frame. Perhaps she's a depicted stained-glass figure that has escaped into the modern world.

I sit quietly on a pew, watch her work and contemplate my mission. I've been puzzling over it for a few days, and had originally decided to pop down to our local church and see if I could purloin some faith from our lady vicar. But something held me back. It seemed a bit dishonest. I know I did the same thing when I collected the courage from Harry, and felt fine about it, but for some reason the taking of faith from a vicar without her knowledge seemed sneakier. Then, after school today, I decided to come into Truro, shopping. This isn't unusual for me on a weekend, but it is when it's after school. Nevertheless, something made me come and walk past all the shops until I got to the door of this monolith of a building.

Faith is everywhere here. Steeped into each block of stone, pew and window. Perhaps all I have to do is reach out a hand and absorb it? As I place my palm on the wooden seat next to me, instinctively I know it won't work. I need to collect from a person, not an inanimate object. Looking up, I catch the eye of the flower arranger. She has twinkly deep-set blue eyes in a weathered face. I'm guessing she's around the eighty-year-old mark. Her radiant smile shrugs off at least ten years though, and she gives a little wave with a tiger lily. Then she turns and goes back to her task. Something tells me she wouldn't mind a chat, as long as I speak quietly. I get up and walk over.

'What a gorgeous arrangement,' I say with a smile.

'Thank you. I do love it.' She holds out a hand. 'My name's Gloria.'

I shake it. 'Nice to meet you. Mine's Joy.'

'Joy. How wonderful. Are you full of it?' Her eyes are full of mischief as she looks into mine.

'Full of what?'

She gives me a cheeky wink. 'Joy? You should be, standing in this amazing building.'

I gesture to the huge rose window. 'Yes. It's certainly an uplifting place.'

Gloria puts the tiger lily to her nose and inhales before placing it in the centre of her display. 'I adore it here. I've been doing the arrangements for forty years now, ever since I lost my family.' A cloud sails briefly across her sunny expression.

Her family? What, she lost them all at once? I don't voice that question, of course. 'Oh, I'm so sorry to hear that.'

'Thank you. It was a long time ago, but I miss them every day.'

Not sure what to say next, I offer, 'Does being in this place help?'

'Oh yes. Doing the flowers and being here was my saviour when they died.'

I watch her for a few seconds. Either I ask a difficult question or just move on – let the conversation end. But then Gloria might think I didn't care enough, and that's not true. 'Can I ask what happened?'

'Yes. My husband and ten-year-old twin boys were involved in a pile-up on the M5. They were killed outright.'

The impact of this slams into my consciousness, stealing any coherent response. I just put my hand on her shoulder and squeeze it. The loss of Sean nearly ended me, so God knows how she kept going when her entire family was snuffed out in one fell swoop. Then I say, 'I cannot imagine how you survived that.'

'At times, neither could I.' Gloria sighs and stands back to admire her work. 'But my faith got me through.'

I smile as if I understand, but I don't. If my entire family died just like that, I would question my faith, not embrace it. But then we're all different, thankfully. 'I wish I had your belief. It must be very comforting.'

'Belief is everything. Without faith, what are we?' She turns to face me, her expression serene. 'We all need direction, to be led along the one true path; without it we're lost.'

Gloria puts her hand on my arm, and as she does, her faith draws a glowing gold margin of light around her body, and a heady scent of incense fills my nostrils. I think of Gilly's need. This is my moment, and I'm sure Gloria wouldn't mind if she knew. 'There are so many lost people who need help, Gloria.' I slip my hand on top of her cool blue-veined one and give it a squeeze. A tickle of static creeps along my fingers and my senses immediately become calm and assured. It's as if the tide has washed over sun-baked rocks in midsummer, cooling, soothing, reviving. The feeling gathers momentum and I'm aware of Gloria's puzzled expression, as if at a distance, shimmering like heat-haze on tarmac. Before faith overwhelms me, I grasp the cool pebble waiting in my pocket, close my eyes and breathe out … it's done.

'Are you okay, Joy?'

Am I? Is it okay to take a bit of someone's faith, even though they have bags of it? I look her in the eye. 'Gloria. If you could share your faith with someone who really needed it, would you?'

'Of course.' Her kind eyes twinkle with knowing. 'But faith can't be given. It has to come from within. You have to believe.'

My guilty eyes slide away from hers. *It can be stolen, though.* I pick up my bag and slip it over my shoulder. 'Yes, thank you, Gloria. I must be off now, but it's been wonderful to meet you. Please keep up the good work, and I'll hopefully see you again one day.'

———

A few days later I'm relieved to see Daisy's back behind the serving counter at lunchtime. The suggestion of a bruise is still discolouring her cheekbone, but I'm guessing nobody else but Daisy and I can detect it under her make-up. Her larger-than-life persona is centre stage, and this time, it's a genuine performance. I could hear her belly laugh before I joined the lunch queue, and I watch her laughing and chatting with every child she serves. Her grumpy colleague – whose name I can't remember, so I just call her Grumpy Woman in my head – is sending 'hurry up' daggers at her. But Daisy's cheerful force-field is so strong that the daggers just clatter, ignored, onto the floor at her feet.

'Nice to see you back, Daisy,' I say. 'You seem more like your old self today.'

Her bright smile turns itself up another few watts and she squeezes my arm. 'Thanks to you, lovely Joy, I *am* my old self. The old self I haven't been acquainted with for many a year.'

She spoons a mountain of chicken casserole and roast potatoes onto my plate and Grumpy Woman's eyes nearly pop out in disapproval. 'That's enough, thanks, I won't be able to move from the table!' I lean in and whisper, 'How's living at John's going?'

She whispers back, 'Great. But I will be getting a place of my own once the old house is sold. I put it up for sale yesterday, and I'm looking into a divorce too. Gary's agreed. John's had a word or two...' She raises her eyebrows meaningfully. 'Seems like Gary's moving to Spain to stay with his brother. Good riddance, I say.'

'We'll never get to the end of the queue at this rate, Daisy!' Grumpy Woman snaps, huffing up to us, folding her arms under her bosom as if it's in need of propping up. Which, looking at her ample cleavage straining under her overall buttons, might not be far from the truth.

Daisy gives her a wink and hands me my plate. 'Okay, Melody, keep your hair on.'

She's got to be joking? I'd never have had GW down for a Melody! I put my plate on the tray. People with a name like that should be smiley, kind-eyed and always on the brink of bursting into song. 'Thanks, Daisy. I'll see you later, and keep me posted of any developments.'

The weather's been kind over the past few days and the tipis are almost done. This afternoon Gilly and I are working outside with the class. They're putting the finishing touches to the decorations on the sheets – the 'buffalo hide' coverings – and Jowan is coming along soon to take photos for the school newsletter, and chat to the children about the whole process. Callum Pengelley added some of the contents of his nostrils to his 'hunting scene' (actually just unrecognisable bold red, green and orange daubs of paint) on the side of his group tipi. He was stopped pretty smartish from doing the same to the other surfaces by David and Ellie. David was 'most displeased' by Callum's 'total disregard' for the wishes of the wider group, and was disgusted by Callum's 'unnatural preoccupation' with his own snot and bogeys. Tristan, who of course is Callum's best friend, had made good his threat to bring in cockerel feathers, but thankfully not his dad's rifle, and was only prevented from painting his face 'like a savage' by Gilly at the last moment. Gilly explained why it wasn't appropriate, and he was eventually mollified by being allowed to stick the feathers on the tipi instead, declaring the feathers were worth the extra work he'd had to do to 'collect' them. I expect there's a bald cockerel somewhere in north Cornwall who'd beg to differ.

Ellie is giving David a verbal rocket for adding a brown eye to the white horse she's painted before the thing is dry. He's struggling to remain composed, but fully accounting for his decision, while dramatically gesticulating each word with his paintbrush … just as Jowan comes along in a white shirt. Three chocolate splats land down the front of the shirt, and the fourth leaves a horizontal streak across the bridge of his nose. I cover a giggle with a gasp as I hurry over with a remnant of cloth. Seems like we have our Native American war-paint after all. Tristan nudges Callum and they crack out laughing at Jowan's ruined shirt while David stares aghast at his handiwork like a meerkat on guard.

Dabbing at the paint is ineffectual, and my efforts only

spread it into a huge coffee-looking stain over most of his front. The worst thing is the red tide of heat rising up my neck and cheeks as I become aware of his firm chest under the cloth in my hand. Not sure what to do next, I'm relieved when a diversion for my predicament is provided by Gilly. 'Tristan! Look what you've done now. You really need to be more careful.'

'It wasn't Tristan, it was David, and an accident, Miss Holmes,' Jowan says while putting his hand over mine, stopping it mid-scrub. 'Don't worry, Miss Pentire, I think it needs a washing machine.' He smiles at me and I'm sure he notices my cheeks. But then his gorgeous blue eyes hold mine in an intense stare and a shiver of excitement shoots through my stomach and other places. It's a long time since I've felt anything remotely like that. I'd actually forgotten I had other places. Then the spell is broken. It's the way he does a slight double take and furrows his brows. I turn away, take the cloth and my red face over to Ellie and her runny horse eye. I make a much better job of stemming the stream of brown through the white paint, than I did through the white shirt.

'David. You really need to be more careful. Have you apologised to Mr Williams?' Gilly asks.

David's meerkat stare morphs into woebegone. 'I didn't mean it, Sir. I was just waving my arms about.' He demonstrates then, still with the paintbrush in his hand. 'Oh…' Paint lands on the grass near Jowan's feet, just missing his shoes. 'I'm sorry again, Sir.'

'It's okay, David. Perhaps you could just keep your arms

still for a bit now?' Jowan raises an eyebrow at David, and smiles at Gilly and I.

Gilly is only just holding it together. Her shoulders are shaking and she's got her hand clasped over her mouth. Jowan takes over the situation, placing his hand on David's shoulder and shepherding him over to me and Ellie. 'Right. Can you tell me all about how you built this magnificent structure, while I take a few photos?'

I wander round the group, helping out where needed, while thinking about my reaction to Jowan. It's not just today, I realise; I often act out of character around him, or get flustered like I did just now. I've already admitted to myself that I find him attractive, but then anyone would. He's got a warm, friendly personality too. But sometimes my reaction to him is a bit over the top. Just now, with the blushing, for example. It's teenage behaviour. Anyone would think I'd never touched a man's chest before. This puts me in mind of Sean and guilt pokes me in my own chest. He was my everything, and here I am, drooling over Jowan.

'Can we have you in this one too, Miss Pentire?' Jowan's voice behind me jolts me out of my ponderings.

I turn to find him pointing a camera at me. 'Me? Nah, the kids did most of the work.'

Jowan tilts his head and gives me a slow smile, which makes me look away. 'You're too modest. And it was all your idea. Without you, this whole project would never have happened.' He waves his arm at the tipis and children putting the finishing touches to their hard work. 'Just look. It's really something.'

Six tipis stand tall and colourful in the sunlit playing field. A variety of horses, buffalo and Native Americans around campfires adorn all sides, lovingly painted by the children. Their immature depictions seem all the more beautiful because I know how much they've enjoyed the project. 'The kids do seem to be having fun, I must admit.'

Jowan leans in closer. 'They are loving it, Joy. Now, can you stand over there with Gilly? I'll gather the children together.'

I do as he asks, and he's just about to take some photos when Helen waves from the bottom of the field and starts towards us. She's wearing a too-tight green dress which ends just above the knee, restricting her movement, and by the look of her wobbly gait, her high heels are sinking into the grass. 'Hello everyone!' she says in a big, bright voice that sounds like she's borrowed it from a gameshow host. A gentle breeze lifts her shiny bob, which she quickly smooths, and she treats us to a wide smile, and a red lipstick mark on her front tooth.

'Hello, Miss Brearly,' the children chime, standing like little angels in the presence of the headteacher.

'Well, I'm very impressed,' Helen says, looking round at the tipis, hands on hips. 'Very impressed indeed.' She walks around them and then returns to us. 'And you're here to take our photo for the school newsletter, Mr Williams?'

Our photo? She's going to be in it, when she's done nothing? I glance at Gilly and she gives me a quick eye roll.

'Yes. Class Three, Miss Holmes and Miss Pentire. They have all done brilliant work,' Jowan says – I think a little pointedly – as he gathers us all together again.

'I'll slip in at the front too,' Helen says, patting her hair. 'Just to show everyone how pleased I am with all this wonderful work.' Her voice is again on the brink of gameshow as she beams at the children.

Jowan's normally sunny expression clouds over slightly, then he sighs and stands back a few paces. 'Okay, gang. When I say cheese, you say *pleeease*.' This causes a few giggles and Jowan begins snapping away.

At the end of the day, Gilly and I are tidying the classroom. I've been wondering how to give her the 'faith' pebble for a few days. The little velvet pouch in my bag is ready and waiting, but I can't just whip it out and slip it into her pocket. She'd think it weird and probably take it out and put it to one side, or chuck it in the garden or something. Collecting, I've discovered, throws up quite a few problems, but there's no handbook. It would be fantastic if I had someone to share things with. Someone who collected too. But the chances of that are pretty slim to none. How would I even find them if we aren't allowed to discuss it?

'She gets right on my nerves sometimes,' Gilly grumbles, stacking a jar of paintbrushes next to the crayons on the shelf.

'Who does?' I ask absently, still wondering how to complete my mission.

'Helen. Haven't you been listening?' Gilly frowns, and tightens the band on her swishy ponytail. I've noticed she does that when she's frustrated or grumpy. And just lately she seems to be both more often than she used to.

'Nope, miles away.'

'Helen annoyed me when she just rocked up and took centre stage for the newsletter photo. You could tell Jowan was pissed off.'

'Yes, I noticed that. It was a bit pushy to say the least, though I suppose she did give me the go-ahead. She seemed quite enthusiastic when I raised it at my interview.'

'Hmm. She's enthusiastic about anything as long as she doesn't have to do any of the work. I reckon she has a degree in delegating. Pain in the arse, holier than thou, "I know best" bloody Brearly. I hope the lipstick tooth shows up in the newsletter.'

This isn't like Gilly. Okay, she does moan a bit, but she's not normally quite so snippy. I wipe some glue off a table top and an idea surfaces. Maybe I can kill two birds with one stone. See what's bugging Gilly and slip her the faith pebble. 'Gilly, do you fancy coming over to mine for a meal tonight? Nothing fancy, just my renowned signature lasagne and perhaps a glass of wine?' I chuckle. 'You could even stay over, so we could have more than one?'

'Oh, I'd love to, but…' She grabs her planner and runs her finger down the page. 'I've still not organised my lesson for tomorrow afternoon, and it would be just my luck for Helen to swoop in unannounced, just as I'm winging it. And I was going to do a bit of research for the trip we were talking about…' Gilly looks at me and turns her mouth down at the edges. I'm about to suggest another time, when she slaps the planner on the desk. 'Oh, sod it! You only live once, and all work and no play makes Gill a dull girl!'

'Excellent! Talking of work, I think we've done enough for one day, don't you?' I say, offering her my arm and grabbing my coat.

'I do indeed. Let's get out of here before old lipstick tooth pops her head round the door.'

Arm in arm, we rush out to the carpark, giggling like a couple of schoolgirls.

Chapter Fourteen

I'm in the kitchen making the sauce for the lasagne when Gilly arrives. She's been home first to grab her overnight bag, and I'm guessing to plan a quick lesson for tomorrow. She's nothing if not dedicated. On the doorstep, I relieve her of a bottle of Merlot and a box of chocolates. 'You didn't have to bring anything, and we need to go careful with the booze. It *is* a school night, after all.' I laugh and show her in.

'Yeah, but tomorrow's Friday. We can scrape through, and then relax on Saturday.'

Hmm. I'm not sure I like the sound of that. I'm no party pooper, but having a hangover with a class of thirty lively six and seven year olds would be hell on wheels. 'I'll be the sensible one and stop us when we've had ample sufficiency, as my grandma used to say.'

Gilly laughs. 'She sounds as if she was brought up under Victoria.'

'Her name *was* Victoria, actually!'

Oh God. I might have to put a stop to the wine sooner than I predicted. Gilly's had two glasses already and we've not even sat down to eat yet. Sebastian is struggling to be free of her over-enthusiastic petting, so I explain he's not allowed at the table, though he is, and Gilly pouts in disappointment as I remove him to the safety of Sean's chair. 'Poor little lamb, not allowed to sit at the table with us, eh?' she asks with a giggle.

Gilly does seem in very high spirits, which is in part down to the wine. But I'm thinking that the great mood is just an act, a camouflage. There's a sadness and irritability waiting ... lurking underneath, like a shark a few feet below a sunlit ocean. Putting the lasagne, garlic bread and salad on the table, I ask, 'How about a glass of water? Pace ourselves?'

'Aw, spoilsport,' Gilly says and pulls a mock-angry face. I think the shark is showing the tip of its fin.

I place a glass of water in front of her and subtly move the wine out of her reach as I make room for the salad dish. 'This lasagne is superb, Joy,' she says, tucking in as if she's scared of someone snatching her plate away.

Passing her the garlic bread, I smile as she takes four pieces and lines them up around her plate as if she's a kid making a pattern of her food. 'I'm glad you're enjoying it.'

'It is absolutely delicious.' Gilly's green-flecked hazel eyes sparkle with pleasure and she wipes sauce from her chin with the back of her hand, crunches into the garlic bread. 'I rarely bother making stuff from scratch, little point with just me on my own.'

I can relate to that. 'When Sean was alive, I always made food from scratch. Nowadays, it's only a few times a week. Must get back into it.' Her owlish expression, complete with garlic butter lip gloss, makes me pause, a forkful halfway to my lips. 'What's up?'

'Is it still hard? You know, living without him?'

A bit blunt, but then she's had a few. I consider how much to share; it will bring the mood down, after all. Yet, she did ask. 'Yes. Sometimes it overwhelms me … the fact that he'll never walk through that door, or that I'll never hear his voice or laughter ever again.' A lump rises in my throat, so I take the forkful and wash it down with water. 'But it's getting better. Or it's happening less often, I suppose you'd say. Sometimes I imagine him sat over there in his favourite chair, or that I hear his laughter outside in the lane, some summer nights, when the window's open. But mostly I accept he's gone, and try to get on with things. They say time's a great healer. I think that's rubbish. But it has scabbed over the open wounds of my grief, I suppose.' I wipe my mouth and reach for the wine. 'At least we had seven wonderful years together. He was the love of my life. Not everyone has that, and so I feel blessed and grateful.'

Gilly tears up and thrusts her empty wine glass my way. As I fill it, I realise I've not talked about Sean as openly to anyone for ages without crying. This is both worrying and reassuring. Reassuring that I'm coping more, but I worry that I'm leaving him behind. Sean's still so real to me. I can't bear him to fade away. To become nothing more than a memory. My eyes copy Gilly's, so I dab at them with a bit of kitchen roll and laugh. 'This is turning out to be a really jolly meal, eh?'

She laughs too and takes a big gulp of wine. 'I did ask.' The last bit of food is chased round her plate with a half-moon of garlic bread and deposited into her mouth – a total eclipse. 'Thing is...' Gilly stops and strokes her chin. 'Thing is, what you said hit home to me. I know I was never married, and never lost anyone in that terrible, terrible way. But Steve was the love of my life and I let him go. The more I think about it, the more I realise it was the wrong thing to do. All that stuff about not agreeing with him going into the army, it's true, but mostly I think it was my way of making sure I didn't get hurt.' A big sigh. 'Sorry, you don't want to hear this.'

'Yes. Yes I do. I know you've not been yourself lately. Talking might help.'

'Haven't I?' Her eyebrows knot together over the bridge of her nose and her gaze telescopes out. 'No, I don't suppose I have. I guess the not wanting to get hurt thing was because Dad left us when I was ten, and we never saw him much after that. He would come back at Christmas, but he got married again and had more kids. I always felt like second best, you know?' I nod. 'Like last year's broken toy. Stuffed under the bed and forgotten about.' Her bottom lip wobbles so she takes more wine.

'That must have been hard. Do you see him now?'

'He calls sometimes and we meet up a few times a year. But it's always awkward, as though he's doing a duty rather than actually wanting to be there. He's like a poor understudy for my old dad – the old dad that I adored and who broke me totally when he went. Of course he is the same man, but he's lacking in ways I can't even put my finger on. The trust and love are gone, I think … on my part at least.'

Poor Gilly. She looks so young and vulnerable right now. 'So, ending it with Steve was you protecting yourself. You couldn't allow your heart to be broken again. Makes perfect sense to me.'

Thoroughly miserable now, she gives a brief nod and hides her face in her hands. Speaks through her fingers. 'The worst thing is, it's too late now to do anything about it.'

I smile, thinking about the pebble of faith in my bag on the sofa. 'It's never too late. All you have to do—'

'He's got someone else,' she wails, still through her fingers. 'I saw him last week in the supermarket. I guessed he must be home on leave and was just plucking up courage to speak to him, when a woman came over and popped some bananas in his trolley. She's all legs and boobs. They looked very cosy together. And it was at that exact moment that I realised I still loved him and had made a monumental mistake. Fucking typical.'

So that's what's been troubling her. Great. The idea of another woman on the scene hadn't been in my little plan. Now what? She removes her hands and waits for my response. *Something positive, Joy. Quick.* 'She might not be his girlfriend at all. She could be just a friend.'

I get an unhelpful eye roll and a snort. 'How likely is

that? She was about his age with long curly blonde hair and big blue eyes. She was all over him.'

'What, kissing him?'

'No. But she put her hand on his arm and laughed at something he was saying.'

Not great, but hardly conclusive evidence. 'Hmm. You have to be sure, Gilly, before you abandon all hope.'

'How can I do that?' She throws her arms to the side, nearly tipping over the remains of the wine bottle. 'Rock up at his mum's and ask if he's got a new girlfriend?'

I think for a moment. 'Not quite. But nearly. Rock up at his house and say you saw him from a distance in town the other day and thought you'd pop round for a catch-up. It might be devastating, if it's true he's got someone else. But you can't stand not knowing for sure.'

Gilly closes her eyes and rubs her temples with her forefingers. 'No. No, I can't.' Then a sigh. 'Okay, I'll do it.'

This is a surprise. I expected an argument … maybe it's the booze talking. 'You will?'

'Yeah. It's killing me not knowing who she is.' She drains her glass and reaches for the bottle which I snatch out of her grasp, before her fingers close around it. 'Hey! There's only a bit left.'

'The bit that broke the camel's back.'

'That's not the right metaphor.'

'I don't care. You'll thank me tomorrow.'

'Hmm.'

I leave her staring into space, probably imagining her meeting with Steve, while I clear the table and go over to my bag. With the faith pebble in hand, I go back and sit down opposite again. 'Now don't laugh, but I'd like you to take this with you when you see Steve.' I place the velvet bag on the table and push it towards her.

Frowning, she picks it up, feels the weight of it in her hand and then tips it. The striped white-and-black pebble sits in her palm, and she looks at me, puzzled. 'What's this?'

'A pebble.'

'Duh. I can see that, but why have you given it to me?'

'It's lucky ... magical. I have a lot of them for different occasions.' I stop, amazed at how easily this half-truth slips from my mouth. 'This one will help you have faith in your love for him, and say all the things you really need to say. Even if he is with this other woman, it will help you have the courage of your convictions. You need to tell him that you were wrong, and explain exactly how you feel about him. It's never too late.'

'Eh?' She shakes her head and closes her fist around the pebble. 'No way. If he's got someone else, that will be it... I...' Gilly's eyes grow round. 'I...' She blinks a few times and then slaps her other hand down flat on the table. 'Bugger it. You're right! I *will* tell him how I feel!' She's half-laughing, half choked with emotion. Opening her hand, she looks at the pebble and shakes her head. 'Shit, Joy. Either this thing is helping me believe in him, or I've had one too many!'

I laugh. 'A bit of both, I think.'

Closing her hand over it again, she stands up. 'I'm going there right now. No time like the present!'

Bloody hell, Gloria's unquestioning faith is taking over

here. 'No. Not now, he might think it's a bit strange, you randomly turning up at this time of an evening.'

'So what?' she tosses across at me, her eyes alight with devil-may-care.

'You've had too much to drink, and how would you get there?'

Gilly jumps up, grabs her coat and bag. 'I don't care. I'll get a taxi, or walk the ten miles if I have to! I know he still loves me. I can feel it!'

I jump up too and slip my arm through hers. 'Look, come and sit down and get comfy on the sofa. I'll make us a coffee and we'll talk through it all. There's cheesecake too, if you'd like some. After, you can have a nice shower before bed.'

'But that's wasting time, isn't it!' She looks at the pebble as if she's expecting an answer, and then her knuckles grow white as she tightens her grip around it again. 'No time like now.'

'How about you go first thing before school, hmm? You'll have a clearer head and Steve will be more likely to listen to you then, than if you turned up now with just short of a bottle of wine in you. Come on, sit down and we'll talk.'

She regards me through narrowed eyes, but says nothing. After I've managed to settle her, she cuddles a big scatter cushion to her chest and stares awestruck at the pebble. I suggest she puts it away in the bag for safe-keeping, as it might get lost in amongst the cushions. 'No. I want to keep it with me … even though I think I must be nuts for imagining it's lucky, or magic, or whatever you said.' Her bottom lip sticks out like a petulant child's.

This isn't a good idea, because I don't trust her to keep it with her overnight – not with her being three-sheets to the wind. For all I know, she'd take off to Steve's in the middle of the night, ready to do or die. 'You're not nuts. If you believe the pebble's magical, it will be. That's what I've found.' Not strictly true, but a little white lie won't hurt here. 'And you *can* keep it with you.' I sit next to her and quick as a flash, snatch the pebble and slip it into the bag. Silencing her protest with a raised forefinger and my best teacher's expression, I take the bag and put it into her coat pocket. 'But *not* in your hand. The pebble will be safe here until the morning. I promise.'

Gilly rolls her eyes and expels a whoosh of air which sounds like a punctured bike tyre. To complete the strop, she throws herself back against the cushions and folds her arms. I hide a smile. 'Seems like you've made the decision for me,' she says through gritted teeth. But at least she's not got Daisy's D-Day 'leaving the landing craft' look about her.

'That's because I'm taking care of you.' Another eye roll. 'So how about that cup of coffee?'

She considers this and sighs. 'Only if there's cheesecake.'

The cheery beep of the alarm clock at 6:30 a.m. the next morning has a backing track of torrential rain drumming against my bedroom window. Marvellous. It was a good job the tipis were completed yesterday, but I dread to think how they'll look after a thorough drenching. Maybe it's given animation to Callum's hunting scene. Unable to put off the inevitable any longer, I swing my legs out of bed and slip on my dressing gown. Sebastian is waiting by his dish in the kitchen. Always on time. I wouldn't be surprised to find he had a wristwatch under his fur.

'Hello, boy. What would you like for breakfast this morning?' I hold up two packets of cat food. One is tuna, the other is salmon. He yawns at the tuna and meows at the salmon. 'Salmon it is, then.' If anyone could hear me, they'd think I was losing it. Hope they can't. Checking over my shoulder to make sure Gilly's not in the vicinity, I notice her coat is gone from the back of the chair. Has she gone already? I tip the salmon into Seb's dish and set it down before hurrying to the hallway to see if Gilly's shoes are still there. Nope. And neither is her car on the driveway. God. I hope she didn't go over to Steve's in the middle of the night. I give her a call.

'Gilly, where are you?'

'Just pulled up outside Steve's. Feeling a bit worse for wear.'

'Not surprised. Isn't it a bit early to knock on his door?'

'I'm going to wait until seven. I can't leave it any longer or I'll not get to school in time.'

'Okay. Have you got the pebble?'

'It's in my pocket. It all seems a bit daft now, to be honest.'

'Trust me, it's not. Make sure you have it in your hand when you go up the path, okay?'

'If it makes you happy. Right now I'm going to eat a

banana and drink a bottle of water – both stolen from yours. Hope you don't mind.'

She sounds defeated rather than ready to take on the world. Hopefully the pebble will make all the difference. 'Of course I don't mind. Remember, tell him the truth and from your heart. You won't go far wrong.'

This sage advice plays on my mind while I eat two slices of Marmite on toast, drink a mug of tea and watch sheets of rain play hide and seek with my view through the kitchen window. Hope everything will work out for Gilly. She deserves some happiness. But then, don't we all?

Chapter Fifteen

G illy certainly deserves something other than happiness right now. My heart is doing the jive and a salty sweat-moustache keeps beading itself along my top lip, despite being wiped off every few seconds with the back of my hand. I've already had to fend off an awkward question from Helen as to Gilly's whereabouts in the staff briefing, mumbling something about taking a phone call from the bank, and now I'm all alone in the classroom. Alone, that is, apart from thirty children who are already restless and scenting blood. Like pack animals, it's uncanny the way they know things aren't quite as they should be. They can sense my weakness. I gulp and fire off the third, *Gilly. Where the hell are you?* message, and ask the children to take out their books and get ready to talk about the poems they wrote yesterday morning.

'Miss Pentire, you're not supposed to have your phone out in class,' Ellie admonishes in a high-pitched voice, which strips away my super-thin veneer of confidence like acetone.

'You're allowed to if you're an adult and it's important.'

She raises an eyebrow. 'And where's Miss Holmes today?'

Over my shoulder as I pass by her table, I reply, 'She's in an important meeting, shouldn't be long.' She'd bloody better not be. On the back row Callum Pengelly's inspecting something disgusting on his finger, so I hand him a tissue.

'But she's *never* in a meeting in lesson time,' David says, narrowing his eyes at me, as if he knows I'm lying my head off. Bloody hell, what is this? I feel like I'm a teenager being caught by my parents coming home at 3 a.m., drunk and incapable.

'Well, she *is* today, David, okay?'

David pulls his neck in and looks sidelong at Ellie. She does round eyes at him and shrugs. Yeah, well good. They need to know who's the damned boss around here… I just hope it's me.

I ask for volunteers to read out their poems, and of course, Ellie's and David's hands are first up. I'm relieved, because I know they both wrote reams, so that will give me a bit more breathing space while I decide on the next activity. My phone vibrates a message into my thigh and I slip it out of my pocket and hide it behind a propped-up book on my desk. It's from Gilly. Thank God!

So sorry, Joy! Steve and I got carried away catching up, and time got away from me – be there any minute. Please cover for me!! Xxx

A bit late to ask that. I've been covering for her since briefing, and it's now ten past nine! I'm miles away, annoyed, distracted and vaguely aware of David's droning voice, when the door opens and in walks Jowan. The droning stops and so does my heart, or it feels like it might. Why does he have to be so attractive? Also, why's he here, and how the hell do I explain where Gilly is? My heart wakes up and does a quick panicky gallop. Jowan runs his hand through his dark curls and gives the class and me a disarming smile. 'What a wonderful poem, David. Do carry on,' he says, resting a hip against my desk. David starts up again and Jowan leans down towards me, whispers, 'Where's Gilly? Helen's asked me to do an impromptu observation. She was coming, but got held up.'

Now what? Another lie? It's a good job it's not Helen instead, or Gilly would be up shit creek. 'Um… She's been unavoidably detained. Won't be long though.'

He loses the smile. 'Unavoidably detained?' Jowan's dark brows furrow over his bright-blue eyes. I nod. 'And how long will she be?'

Clearing my throat in the hope that a plausible answer will appear on my tongue, I look away. This is awful, I want to curl up into a ball and put my fingers in my ears. Luckily, David's just finished, so I lead a round of applause. 'Well done, David. That was fantastic!' Jowan claps too, but I note he's still not smiling. Then I say, 'Yes, Ellie you're next. Shh, everyone.'

We listen in silence to Ellie's reedy and dramatic intonation. She flings her arm to the side and nearly slaps David in the face. This elicits a half-cough half-snort from

Jowan and he walks over to look out of the window, just as the door flies open and Gilly barrels in looking like Worzel Gummidge's understudy. 'Sorry I'm late, everyone!' she says and then her smile freezes when she notices Jowan. She puts her things down and tries to smooth her wind-blown hair and straightens her back. 'Mr Williams, how nice.'

He inclines his head slightly. 'Miss Holmes.'

'We've been reading our poems out for Mr Williams,' I say in a voice which sounds like I borrowed it from Helen.

'While you've been unavoidably detained,' David says with a pointed look at his teacher. God, that kid's got the hearing of a bat.

'Miss Pentire said you've been in a very important meeting,' Ellie says, looking at me for confirmation.

'Never mind where I've been. I'm here now.' Gilly breezes round the class giving out information sheets, and explaining that we're going to be looking at theories about how the dinosaurs disappeared from the planet.

There's no time for me to say anything to Gilly, but, ten minutes in, Jowan takes her to one side by the store cupboard and they have a quick whispered conversation, which not even David's radar can pick up, by the look of frustrated concentration on his face as he leans in their direction. Jowan leaves shortly after, and Gilly gives me an eye roll. I'm guessing she's going for nonchalance regarding the whole situation, but the red blotchy tide inching up her neck gives her away.

At breaktime Gilly grabs my arm, nearly spilling my coffee, and drags me over to a quiet corner of the staffroom. 'Thanks so much for covering for me. And I'm so sorry I landed you in it.'

We'd not discussed it in full at the end of the lesson, as she'd slipped out before I had time to find out what she'd been up to. I'd only managed to tell her that Helen had been asking questions this morning. Still smarting at being landed in it, I keep my voice low and say, 'God knows what you'd have done if Helen had been observing instead of Jowan. What were you thinking?'

The blotches on her neck flare again and join the dots with the roses in her cheeks. 'I wasn't bloody thinking. I was in bed with Steve!'

'You were what?'

She giggles, her eyes glittering with devilment. 'You heard.'

'Oh, right. So while I was struggling to put Helen off the scent and lying to Jowan, you were shagging Steve's brains out? Nice.' I huff and fold my arms, a little angry, but I admit, secretly glad the mission worked.

'I really am sorry.' Gilly twists her mouth to the side and pats my arm. 'Truly I am. But emotions just overtook us. His parents were on holiday, so we had the house to ourselves and he was so thrilled to see me.' She hugs herself, a rainbow aura of happiness almost solid in the air around her. I'm surprised everyone can't see it, it's positively indecent.

'And the mystery woman?'

'She's someone he knows from the army. She's back

home on leave and he arranged to take her out, but now that's not happening.' Gilly beams and squeezes my hand. 'And guess what else? He's not on leave, he's left the army! He's training to be a PE teacher with help from a bursary scheme for ex-army people. Isn't that fantastic? So we'll be able to see each other all the time – have a proper relationship!'

Forgetting to be grumpy, I put my coffee down and give her a hug. Then the rainbow aura snakes under my skin with the intensity of a Class A drug. Not that I've ever had any, but I imagine the effect is similar. Wow! With a great effort, I swallow down laughter and the burning desire to dance with wild abandon round the staffroom, and get a grip of a spare pebble in my pocket. I keep these like other people keep tissues. Experience has taught me I could need an empty pebble at the drop of a hat. Happiness is sucked deep into it like an explorer in quicksand. Thank God. At last I can breathe again. Heaving a deep sigh, I say, 'I'm overjoyed for you, Gilly. Really I am.'

'Thanks.' Her eyes swim and she sniffs. 'Thanks to your encouragement and daft pebble, I told him exactly how I felt. Told him that I'd been a bloody fool and that I missed him every hour of every day since we'd parted. I also told him there was never anyone else, I'd just made it up to put him off. It was at that point that he kissed me and we kind of ended up in his bed.' A lovestruck, wistful expression settles over her features, and then over her left shoulder I see Helen making a bee-line for us from the other side of the room.

'Helen at six o'clock,' I hiss out of the corner of my mouth.

Gilly looks past me. 'I can't see her.'

'That's because you're looking at twelve o'clock, not six, you daft mare.' I grab her hand and turn to leave, but we're too late.

'Gilly, there you are. Can we have a word?' Helen heads us off, steps to the side and sweeps her arm to a vacant chair.

'Oh, we were just going back to the classroom a few minutes early to set up for next lesson,' Gilly says.

'I'm sure Joy can make a start – it shouldn't take long.' Helen's tone makes it clear this isn't open for negotiation.

I leave them to it, glad I had the foresight to tell Gilly I'd said to Helen there'd been a big problem with Gilly's bank this morning, and she'd been trying to sort it. Hopefully Gilly's good at thinking up big fibs on the spot like I've had to be recently. On the walk to the classroom I consider my collecting journey. So far it seems to have been successful, but it could have gone horribly wrong. Well, to be fair, it did go wrong for a bit, didn't it? Me trying to teach a class with no warning and no plan, with the deputy head watching. There is a time and place for bequeathing pebbles, and last night while Gilly was drunk was neither of those. Perhaps my enthusiasm gets the better of me sometimes.

Still, I've got a really powerful pebble of happiness to store for a later date. So all in all, it's been a hit. Thinking of Gilly's face full of love and contentment makes my heart swell. I feel like I'm really making a difference in people's lives. Old Hope was right. Happiness is within my grasp.

Quite literally at the moment, as it's in my pocket. I wonder who its recipient will be?

———

The wind gets up and spits a few raindrops at me as I walk to my car after school. The tipis were ruined by the earlier deluge, but they'd served their purpose. And we have the photos for posterity. Bob had dismantled them in record time. I've never seen him look so happy. After all the shenanigans of last night and today, I'm looking forward to a simple meal, a bath and an early night. Gilly said that Helen gave her a mild ticking-off for being late. Reading between the lines, Jowan hadn't let on that I'd been taking the class on my own, just that she'd got there five minutes after the start. We owe him.

As I open the car door, Jowan's voice comes through the next car's open window. 'You did a good job this morning, Joy.'

'Oh, thanks,' I say, bending down to his level. 'It was a one-off, obviously. Gilly is never late.'

'Yeah, that's why I kept it to myself.' He smiles and starts the engine.

I smile back. 'Not like you to be going home so early.'

'Yeah. My mum's not well … I'm popping a few things over to the hospital for her.'

I had no idea, but then Gilly did say he keeps his personal life fairly personal. All I know is he's divorced, but no kids. 'Really? Sorry to hear that.'

'Hmm. Unfortunately, I don't think she's got more than

a few weeks.' He gives his head a quick shake as if he's dismissing emotion. 'Anyway, see you on Monday.' He raises a hand and drives off before I have a chance to respond.

Poor Jowan. I hope he has someone he can confide in – someone to share the burden with. I get in my car, and slipping in beside me is the uncomfortable feeling that he's quite alone. Thoughts of Jowan sitting forlorn and miserable beside a hospital bed fill my head on the way home. Something tells me my thinking-cap needs a wash and spruce up, because I'll be needing it before long.

Chapter Sixteen

The swimming idea I had upon waking still holds water as I set off down the steep hill to Mawgan Porth beach on Sunday morning. Okay, there might be a bit of a nip in the bright clear April air, but a cobalt-blue sky has rolled itself out as far as my eye can see, and an egg-yolk sun is gathering strength as it climbs. Whether I'll actually go through with my swim after I set my big toe in the Atlantic, which has been in the chiller over winter, remains to be seen, but for now I'm doing it. Maybe Dad will come with me soon, he loves sea swimming. A radiator comes on in my heart, as I remember the great time I had with my parents yesterday over lunch. For a change, I'd suggested they came to mine, and the difference in them both since he's started out in the new partnership is nothing short of remarkable. Him, because he's doing something he's always wanted to do and he really believes in himself, and Mum is so much happier because she's living with someone who is fun to be around.

Happy people tend to transfer their happiness onto others, even without a pebble, and to me, this morning is full of hope and new possibilities in every little crocus head and wild garlic flower peeping through the burgeoning hedgerows. Bird conversation twitters through the still salt air, punctuated intermittently by the sigh of the ocean, and interrupting at a distance, the rumble of a tractor in a furrowed field. Uplifting. As is Dad's new idea. He's started a scheme for disaffected youngsters with few or no qualifications. Two local boys are working alongside him at the moment, learning about the necessary skills of the building trade. The business is paying them a fair wage while they learn, and he said the transformation in the way they conduct themselves and talk about the future is absolutely miraculous. I could have said the same about him.

An image of Hope's rockpool eyes, full of life and sparkle, comes to me and I smile. Random acts of kindness like Dad's and Jack's after receiving their pebbles are like tight little snowballs packed with love, sent rolling down a slope and gathering momentum as they go. Daisy and Gilly have yet to pass on theirs and I'm looking forward to finding out what they do. Thinking about them brings Jowan to mind and I wonder how his mum is. It must be so hard to lose a parent, and hopefully the day I lose mine is years away. Maybe Jowan will need a friendly ear on Monday, but how will I lend it without being too obvious?

Rounding the bend in the road, I see the wide expanse of Mawgan Porth beach is dotted with just a few dog walkers and families with young children. It will fill up a little more as the day grows warmer, it being a Sunday, but it won't get too busy out of season. This is how I like it. It feels like the beach outside the summer months is able to breathe, free of crowds, the stab of beach tents and windbreaks, populated only by a few seagulls, the odd jackdaw, and a scattering of locals.

As I set foot on the beach, a playful wind sneaks up behind me, snatches a handful of hair and wraps it around my eyes like a blindfold. Wresting it free, I twist my mane into a scrunchy and when I look up, in the near distance, there's a guy coming towards me who looks familiar. Hands in the pockets of a dark green hoodie, shoulders hunched, dark hair blowing in the wind. Jowan? It could be, but maybe it's because I was just thinking about him. As he draws nearer, I realise it's definitely him. Odd. Then I remember he told me he lived at Mawgan Porth that day when he came round unannounced. I shrug my swimming bag higher up my shoulder and move towards him, noting that, unusually for Jowan, his expression is closed, his mouth a grim line, eyes fixed on the swift movement of his feet over the damp sand.

When he's only a few steps away I say, 'Hi, Jowan, how's tricks?'

As if he's coming out of a trance, he stops, raises his gaze from his feet and stares through me. Then he blinks a few times and heaves a sigh. 'Joy. Nice to see you.'

He doesn't look particularly pleased to see me. He doesn't look anything, except completely out of it. His eyes are red-rimmed and I'm guessing sleep's been a stranger to him over the weekend. 'And you. Though I hope you don't mind me saying, you don't seem yourself.'

Jowan's bark of humourless laughter is like a slap. 'You could say that.' He looks at the huge white breakers bashing themselves against the cliff edge, and when he turns back, his eyes are full of unshed tears.

Great. Looks like I put my foot right in it.

'I'm not myself. My mum died in the early hours of Saturday morning.' He wipes his eyes with the back of his sleeve and clears his throat. A brownish-black aura is winding itself around his arms and torso like a jungle creeper. Grief.

My stomach constricts. 'Oh, Jowan,' I put my hand on his arm. 'I'm so sorry. I didn't realise it would be so soon.'

'Neither did I. Neither did the doctors and nursing staff. But there we are. Only sixty-one … doesn't seem fair.' He gives me a wobbly smile and looks at the sea again.

Poor man. Right now, he looks like a lost child in need of a hug, and someone to make the monsters disappear from the dark corners of his room. But I don't hug him. Why? Because he's the deputy head? Because it might be awkward? Something else? Something else, such as I might hug him with something more than friendly concern? Something like I'm drawn to him and don't know what to do about it? Annoying pulses of heat creep into my cheeks and I turn to look at the sea too. This isn't the time for self-analysis, for God's sake. 'Do you want to talk about it? We could go for a drink?' I nod over to the Merrymoor Inn.

'Um … not sure,' he says, his eyes still watching the rolling blue ocean's peaks and troughs dappled with shimmering sunlight. 'I've drunk far more than was good for me this weekend.' Scrubbing a fist over his stubbly chin he adds, 'Not sure I can face a pub full of people either. Wouldn't mind the chat though?'

I nod, and before I can talk myself out of it, I say, 'Of course. How about you come and have a bite to eat at mine? I can make us a full English?'

'That sounds good.' He smiles. 'I've substituted booze for food, and it's beginning to tell on me.'

'Okay. Let's get going.'

His hand on my arm stops me. 'You could come to mine instead? It's nearer.' He points at a white bungalow on the far cliff, its windows winking in the sun. 'Might be too knackered to walk all the way up that bloody hill to yours.' His smile's more sheepish than wobbly this time.

'Are you sure you're up to cooking?'

Jowan does a hippo yawn. 'Hmm. I'll have a go.'

'If you show me where everything is, I'll do it.'

'Really? That would be brilliant, thanks.'

We set off back up the beach. 'Got bacon?'

'Yep.'

'Eggs?'

'Yep.'

'Bread?'

'Yep.'

'Mushrooms?'

'Er … possibly.'

'Tomatoes?'

'Now you're pushing it.'

Jowan's house is amazing. Totally and utterly. Floor-to-ceiling picture windows open onto a patio-balcony and lush garden which provides a windswept view of golden sand, while the ocean draws a navy line across the horizon, dividing itself from the lighter blue of the sky. A few nervous clouds breeze onto the stage, but only have a walk-on part, thanks to the strengthening sunshine. This stunning vista, complete with salt air and gull cries, would be the perfect antidote to any worries or woes for me if I lived here. Ordinarily, I expect Jowan feels the same, but his woes right now are many and deep. He's standing next to me staring out of the window, while he listens to me waffle on about how wonderful the view and house are, but I can tell he's not really present. The aura's gone though.

I move towards the large, bright and well-equipped kitchen, find a big smile for him, and say, 'So let me crack on with this Sunday brunch, eh?'

Jowan turns and looks at me as if he's forgotten I'm here. 'Ah, yes. Thanks. I'll show you where everything is.'

While I cook, we talk about anything but his mum's recent passing. He's the only child, and he tells me this house was his parents', but his dad died not long after Jowan's marriage failed two years ago, so he came to stay with his mum for a time to lend some support, but never left. His dad apparently had had his own architect business and had designed and built his 'dream home'. 'I intended to move on, get my own place, but Mum always asked me to stay a bit longer. She was lost without Dad. And then she got the cancer diagnosis just over a year ago. It was as if her body had obeyed her wish to be with Dad. Anyway, I stayed.'

I glance over at him as he sits with his elbows on the kitchen table, propping his head up with both hands, as if it's too heavy for his neck to hold up by itself. Maybe it is. I've noticed his eyes closing once or twice when there's been a lull in the conversation. 'Your mum would have appreciated you staying with her, I'm sure. You must have been a huge comfort to her.'

'Yeah. I'm so pleased I could be here at the end… But I wish she'd managed to stay in her own bed watching the sea, listening to the gulls, as she'd planned, instead of in a sterile room that stank of disinfectant, fear and hospital dinners. Those smells get embedded into the walls somehow.' Jowan rubs his eyes and takes a swallow of coffee. 'The staff were all wonderful, of course. I've never met anyone in the NHS who didn't wear their caring loud and proud like a badge.'

The image of his mum dying peacefully in her bed watching the sea, but her inability to do so, has put a lump in my throat, so I busy myself putting eggs and bacon on a plate, and then I carry it over to him. 'I found a tomato after all.'

'That's a relief.' He smiles and takes a bite of toast. 'I couldn't possibly have eaten it without a grilled tomato.'

That brief smile transforms his face and he becomes the cheerful Jowan that I know. But then sadness floods back, sweeping any levity away on its riptide. My heart goes out to the poor guy and I don't know what to say to make it better. Something practical might help. 'Eat up and then have a nap. I won't say things will look better afterwards, but at least you'll have more strength to face the challenges.'

'Thanks, Joy.' He reaches out and gives my hand a squeeze. 'You have gone out of your way to be a friend.'

The look in his eye and the strength of feeling in his words make me embarrassed. 'Hey, it's only a fry-up.'

'It's more than that. You're here to lend an ear. To help me. It means a lot.'

We eat in silence for a few moments, then a thought occurs. 'Is there anyone you'd like me to call for you? You know, to tell them about your mum?'

A quick shake of the head. 'I did that yesterday, thanks. Well, all except Felicity – my ex. Not looking forward to that one, as our parting was not amicable … but she and Mum got on well. She'll be devastated.'

Dying to know what happened between them, I say in a casual manner, 'Sorry that it didn't work out.'

'I'm not.'

Not much there to go on. 'Oh, right.' There's an awkward silence broken by the scrape of my fork and knife as I scoop up the last bit of bacon.

Jowan puts his head on one side and dabs the corner of his mouth with a bit of kitchen roll. 'We hadn't been getting on for a while. She was badgering me to have kids after we'd agreed we'd wait until she was twenty-eight. I'm six years older than her and I thought she needed time to live a little. Also, I wanted to establish my career, so we'd be financially ready.'

'Hmm. So how old was she when she wanted to try?'

'Twenty-four. Just a few months after we got married.' He balls his fists and scrubs them over his dark curls. 'I managed to put her off for about eighteen months, and then we had an almighty row one evening when she'd come in drunk after seeing her friends. She slapped down an ultimatum. Either we start trying for a family in the next year, or she was leaving.'

'Wow. That must have been a shock.'

'Yes, it was. I felt like a walking sperm-bank. Is that all she wanted me for? She'd changed completely. Felicity had a great counselling job at the local youth centre which she used to adore, and we had a great circle of friends and a loving family, but everything suddenly came second to having a baby. I mean, I could understand it if she was in her thirties and the clock was ticking, but at barely twenty-six?'

'Tricky. What did you do?'

'Like an idiot I agreed to it, but said in six months' time, not immediately. She agreed to the compromise, but then went bitching to her friend about me. That was her biggest mistake ... it ended us.' Jowan drains his mug and thumps it down, making me flinch.

'Hey, maybe it's not the best time to be going over all this. I'm sorry for asking about it...'

'No. I don't mind really ... it's all water under the bridge.' He sits back, folds his arms, stares trancelike at a memory over my left shoulder. 'Maggie, her friend, had always had a thing for me. She'd once come on to me at a party not long before the wedding, and I'd told her to back off. But she clearly had an axe to grind – smarting over the knock-back, I expect – because once she'd seen the cracks appearing between Felicity and me, she told Felicity that I'd been the one doing the flirting and that I'd done it even after we were married.'

'Oh no. Did Felicity believe her?'

'Yes. She never even asked me about it, just decided to get "even" and slept with one of my "friends". So that was us over.'

I look at him, incredulous. 'My God, she must have been in a mess to have done something like that.'

Jowan shrugs, picks up his empty mug, looks in it and puts it down, gently this time. 'She must have. She said she was sorry, begged me to take her back after she realised Maggie was lying. But I couldn't trust her after that. It's a cliché, but she wasn't the woman I married anymore.'

His bottom lip wobbles and he picks up our empty plates, takes them over to the sink. 'I'm so, so sorry, Jowan. You've had a rough few years, to say the least, haven't you? Losing your dad, your marriage and now your mum.' I grab our mugs and start towards him, but stop as I see his shoulders start to shake as he runs water into the sink. The jungle creeper is back and putting fresh shoots out across his entire body. Oh God. Poor, poor guy. Setting the mugs back on the table, I go up behind him, put my hand on his back, and he turns into my embrace, sobbing on my shoulder.

I hold him tight, wishing his pain away, whispering *it's okay* into his ear. But it's not, is it? It's not okay and I don't know how to make it better. The happiness pebble I have at home is in my mind, but it wouldn't be right. Jowan needs to grieve. The loss of a loved one is a dagger-wound, deep and raw. But it's a pain that must be endured and worked through, studied and analysed. To be shaped with tears, anger, regret and acceptance, until it at last fits into the hole that loss has carved through your heart. Over time that hole will heal, though your heart will be for ever changed. Grief is a necessary part of healing. I should know.

After a few moments Jowan's sobs subside and he holds me at arm's length, his head tipped away from my gaze. 'I'm sorry, Joy. I've soaked your lovely top.' He gives an embarrassed chuckle and turns back to the sink, bracing his hands against the edge, and lets out a deep sigh.

'Never mind about my top. It's an old one I wear when I go swimming, as it's easy to shove on over a wet swimsuit. Now, I think—'

'Oh, you were going for a swim today? Great. I've really ruined your morning, haven't I?' He turns round, sniffs and wipes his eyes.

'You certainly have not. I'm glad to be here for you. Now, as I was about to say, I think you need to have a nap. Come on.' Surprising myself, I take his hand and lead him into the living room and sit him down on a comfy green leather sofa. 'Put your feet up.' He frowns and looks as if he's going to protest, so I plump some cushions and point at them, and he wordlessly lies down. Spying a red and yellow checked blanket tucked under a chair, I grab it, shake it out, and cover him with it. 'You need to sleep right now, okay?'

Jowan's eyes, glittering with tears, match the colour of the sunlit ocean through the window behind him. Once again, he looks like a lost child and I'm almost overtaken by a desire to kiss away his pain. What the hell? But then a cheeky grin saves me as he salutes and says, 'Yes, Boss. I'll go to sleep, I promise.'

The jungle creeper's fading, thank goodness. But flustered at what I almost did, I make a big production out of finding my bag and coat, then say brightly, 'Hope to see you in a few days or so, or will you be off longer?'

He furrows his brow. 'Off?'

I give him an incredulous look. 'Work.'

'Oh, I'm not having time off.' He does a hippo yawn and makes himself comfier against the cushions.

That's nuts. 'You must. You need time off to take stock. And there's lots of organisation to do when someone's died. Funeral stuff ... all sorts.' The tickle of tears behind my eyes catches me off guard. That's all he needs, me blubbing too.

'Sorry, Joy. This must have brought everything back ... about your husband, I mean.'

Sean's death has never been a secret, but I had never told Jowan about him. Must have been Helen, or maybe Gilly. I swallow. 'A little. But don't worry, lots of things bring it back.'

A sympathetic smile, 'Yes, I suppose they must.' Then he ponders for a while. 'I might take a few days, actually. Come back on Wednesday. Will you tell Helen for me?' Jowan closes his eyes. 'I can't face speaking to her today ... just so tired.'

This is *not* something I expected, and certainly not what I want to do at all. Though instead of telling him this, I say,

'Of course. Don't worry.' I move to the door and call over my shoulder, 'Have a good sleep and I'll see myself out.'

'Hmm. Thanks, Joy … really appreciate you coming round … and…'

Turning in the doorway, I realise why he's not finished his sentence. Jowan is fast asleep.

Chapter Seventeen

Clammy hands and a dry mouth. Not the best combination when I'm trying to be self-assured and confident. Locking the car, I hurry across the early-morning school carpark, pulling my jacket tighter against the fresh wind. Why am I getting in a pickle about telling Helen about Jowan's mum? Okay, it's not the pleasantest of tasks, but nothing to get worried about. Yes, I know she can be a difficult person to talk to, but this should be a straightforward imparting of information. Pop in the office, tell her, and pop out. That's it, all done. Perhaps it's because the fact that I nearly kissed Jowan yesterday has been playing on my mind ever since. Maybe I'm worrying that as soon as I mention his name to Helen, my face will light up like a red traffic light.. I'm ashamed of myself.

Inside the main corridor, I smooth my hair and check my appearance in the double doors, try to put yesterday from my mind. But it won't be silenced. What was I thinking? Not only would a kiss have been ridiculous, it would have been highly inappropriate. The man is grieving for his mother, for God's sake. For the life of me I don't know what possessed me. No matter how much my charitable side argues that it would have been a kiss of comfort and nothing more, the wicked side slaps this down for the lie it is. It chants, *Joy fancies Jowan, she likes him, she wants him*, over and over like a bully in the school playground, and no teachers are there to stop it.

Maybe the bully's right, but it isn't happening. Especially not at the moment … and especially because I still love my husband and miss him so much. An ocean of frustrated tears waits behind my eyes as I stand in front of Helen's door and bunch my fist to knock. Furious with myself, I blink them back and go for it. 'Enter,' comes Helen's voice through the wood.

'Hi, Helen. I came in early to catch you for a quick chat.' My smile feels nervous, awkward.

She looks up from her desk and closes a file with a sigh, obviously not thrilled to see me. 'I have a few moments. Anything wrong?'

Helen's hard scarlet slash of a mouth and those green glassy eyes have me tongue-tied. 'No. I mean, yes … well … kind of.' I sigh and gather my wits. Her frown deepens. 'It's Jowan's mum. She sadly died in the early hours of Saturday morning, and he asked if I'd let you know.' Her mouth stops being a slash and forms an O instead, so I press on. 'Also, he won't be in until Wednesday, with everything to organise and so forth.'

'Oh, my goodness.' She places her hand on her neck, traces a red manicured fingernail along her jawline. 'Poor

Jowan. That was quick, we thought she'd have a while longer yet.'

'Yes, Jowan said as much yesterday. He's devastated, poor guy.'

'So, how come you saw him yesterday ... and he asked you to tell me?' Her attempt at casual doesn't work, because the words have spiky-sharp edges, especially around the word *you*.

'I ran into him on the beach. We live close by one another.'

Helen stands up, folds her arms, her carefully applied thick dark eyebrows almost joining together over the bridge of her nose. 'On the beach? He just casually asked you to tell me news that was so devastating to him? That doesn't sound like Jowan at all.'

What's that supposed to mean? Does she think I'm making it up? Making my voice calm, I say, 'No. Not on the beach. I went to his house to make him brunch. He'd not slept or eaten properly since he found out. I could see he needed a chat and a good meal.' Why do I feel like I'm having to account for myself, as if I've done something wrong? Maybe because Helen's glaring at me as if I'm something nasty she's scraped off her shoe.

'I see. That was kind of you.' She scrabbles in her bag for her mobile phone and moves her finger down the screen, saying abruptly, 'I'll phone him now. Thank you for telling me.' Then she sits down, swivels her chair round to face the computer. I'm left looking at her back. There's no doubt I've been dismissed.

Mum's apple crumble is second to none. I scrape the last remnants of custard and apple around my dish and spoon it into my mouth. Then I sit back on the kitchen chair and expel a loud belch. 'That was incredible, Mum.'

'So was that burp. Where are your manners, young lady?'

'Pardon me for being so rude. It was not me, it was my food. It got so tired of being below, it just popped up to say hello,' I finish with a smile. I'm over at my parents' for Sunday lunch but Dad is out training his apprentice on some construction skill or other.

Mum's unimpressed with my little rhyme. 'Hmm. Anyway, I reckon she fancies this Jowan.'

I've just told her about Helen's odd behaviour on Monday morning. Her analysis is a bit out of the blue. 'How come?'

'Helen's obviously jealous of you. She hates the fact that you were there for Jowan and she wasn't.' Mum sniffs, sits back and folds her arms. 'It's not rocket science.'

'Nah … she's a control freak, that's all. Hates that she wasn't the first to know and had to be told by a lowly TA.'

'Mark my words…' She gives me a knowing look. 'Besides, it's obvious you like him, and I bet he likes you too.'

Bloody hell. How does she do this? Mothers must develop an inbuilt detector of their child's innermost feelings immediately after they've given birth. Mum has always been able to read me like a book. Even when the pages were illegible to me. Not sure about the him liking me bit, though. I treat her to a withering look. 'I do like him, but not in the way you mean, Mum.' Then I jump up and clear the table so she can't stare into my eyes or notice the red blotches rouging my cheeks.

'Then why have you gone redder than a pillar box?' she says to my back.

'I haven't.' I keep my back turned and rinse the plates, hoping she'll shut up.

'You have. Anyway, it's not a crime. Maybe you two can get together when he's had time to settle after all of his upset. You're young and it has been three years since—'

'For God's sake, Mum. There's nothing between us. He came in on Wednesday and barely spoke to me. Poor guy's really going through it. And as I keep saying, I don't want anyone else.' I take a deep breath and turn round. 'Anyway, what news from Debsville this week?'

Mum looks at me as if she has more to say on the subject of Jowan, but thinks better of it. 'I've not done much apart from the usual, to be honest. Though I have been a shoulder for my friend Maggie. She's really worried about her son… I'll tell you more when I've made a drink.' Mum flips the kettle on for coffee while I go through and make myself comfortable on the sofa. The patio doors frame a riot of colour in big terracotta pots. Daffodils, purple crocus and a rainbow of primroses turn their faces to the spring sunshine, and Marmaduke, our old ginger cat, sits on the fence watching the birds on the feeder with saucer eyes. When I was about twelve, I remember Dad bringing him home from a building site where three kittens had been found abandoned in a sack. So that must make him seventeen. Blimey.

'Can't believe Marmaduke is seventeen,' I say, taking a mug from Mum as she sits down opposite.

'He's not done bad for an abandoned little scrap, has he? And time marches on.' Mum's got a sad, wistful look in her eye. I often wonder if she's really happy at the bakery and helping out at the nursery. Maybe she needs something just for herself.

'True. So we must make the best of every day. Did you think about joining the choir I told you about?'

'Yes, I did. And I've joined the beach cleaning group.'

I raise my eyebrows. 'Beach cleaning? That's a new one on me.'

'Ah well, you see, you don't know everything about your old ma.' She gives me a cheeky wink and shoves an auburn tress out of her eyes. 'I'm a natural counsellor too, so Maggie says.'

'Maggie from the nursery?'

'And the beach cleaning group too. She joined when I did … she said she might pop over later.' Mum's eyes flit away from mine and she looks out at Marmaduke again.

'Oh. Well, I'll get off when I've finished this,' I say, taking a swallow of coffee.

'No, stay. She'd love to meet you.' Mum looks back and away. Is it me or does she seem a bit shifty?

'Really? Okay. But I won't stay long, as you said she was worried about her son and might need a chat.'

'I'm sure she will want to have a chat to you, though. But yeah, she's concerned about Liam. He's twenty-seven and just come back from London where he's been living for three years. Lost his job as a chef in a fancy restaurant and is living with Maggie and Greg until he finds somewhere. Maggie says he stays in his room the whole time, and has lost that sparkle he used to have.'

Mum changes the subject then and we chat for a few moments about Dad's new apprentices and how he loves what he's doing now. Then the doorbell rings. Mum says it will be Maggie, goes to answer it and comes back in followed by a tall thin woman, with close-cropped dark hair and large chocolate-brown eyes which scrutinise me carefully as Mum introduces us. Maggie's mouth tips up at one side as she shakes my hand and says, 'You are every bit as gorgeous as your mum said you were.'

'How nice of you, I—' My words are stopped by a guy popping his head round the door. He's dressed in a stylish red top, black trousers and expensive-looking leather brogues. He's tall, dark and has very similar eyes to Maggie, though his only give me a quick flick and away. Must have learned from Mum.

'This is Liam, my son. He was at a loose end, so I persuaded him to get out for once.' Maggie ruffles his expertly quaffed hair. 'Spends far too long in his room alone, don't you, boy?'

Liam slaps her hand away, a little too forcefully, I think. 'I'm not twelve, Mum.'

Maggie either doesn't notice, or ignores the flash of anger in his eyes as she pinches his cheek and says, 'Aw, diddums. You'll always be my baby.'

Liam's face turns pink and he draws his full mouth into

a pout and blows down his nostrils. Stepping forward into the awkward silence, I stick my hand out. 'Hi, Liam, great to meet you.'

He nods, shakes, and then folds his arms across his chest, jams his hands under his armpits, looking like he'd rather be anywhere else but here. 'Hello, Liam. Can I make you a nice coffee, or something stronger?' Mum asks, heading for the kitchen.

'Something stronger would be nice,' Liam says with a half-smile. 'A glass of red wine if you have it, thanks.'

'At this time in the afternoon?' Maggie asks, with a frown.

'Yes. Why not?'

She perches on the edge of a chair like a nervous bird. 'Well, you're driving, for one.'

Liam pulls some car keys from his pocket. 'God, I'm only having a glass. But be my guest.' He tosses them over to her.

'Charming.' The look Maggie gives her son would curdle milk. He doesn't respond, just flops down on the sofa, like a puppet cut from its strings, and closes his eyes. It's obvious he's totally deflated and at the end of his rope. But if Maggie's always like this, it's no wonder.

Deciding he needs a friend in his corner, I say, 'I'll have a glass of wine, Mum. We can't have poor Liam drinking alone.'

Maggie sighs and goes to join Mum in the kitchen. Liam opens his eyes, gives me a smile and says, 'Thanks.'

'I could tell you'd just about had enough there.' I sit on the chair opposite.

'You could say that.' Liam looks over his shoulder, leans forward and says out of the side of his mouth, 'I think our wonderful mothers are trying to set us up.'

For a moment I'm not sure what he means, then my mouth drops open. 'Romantically?' A nod and an eye roll are my answers. Mum's shifty manner starts to make sense. Maybe she's been taking lessons from Fiona. 'Bloody sneaky or what.'

'Yep. I was browbeaten and emotionally blackmailed into coming over. There I was on the computer, doing job applications, until Mum breezed in and blathered on about being worried about me and that I'd lost my spark. Said she wanted me to meet new people and get my face out in the community. She said Debs knew lots of people and she might put a good word in for me jobwise if I got to know her. Soon as I walked in and saw you, I knew what her real plan was.'

'Hmm. I suppose it could be true. Mum does know lots of people.'

'Nah. This is the third time in about six weeks.'

'Really?'

'Yeah,' he says and pretends to hang himself with an invisible noose. His laugh is a bold, deep rumble and his eyes sparkle like polished conkers. 'So, wanna set a date for the wedding?' His wide smile's infectious.

'Ha! Yeah, how about next week?'

We laugh and then he says, 'That's my parents' goal. To get me married off to some nice local maid.' The wide smile falters, turns to a grim line. His expression darkens and a faraway look clouds his eyes. An overwhelming aura

AMANDA JAMES

crayons a thick black line around his entire body. I don't have to wonder what it is, because this emotion is almost tangible. Sadness. Deep sadness. I feel like he's looking into an abyss. He's on the edge and thinking about stepping in.

'Why are you so sad, Liam?' I say quietly.

Running his hand over his hair, he sighs and says, 'It's a long and depressing story.'

'I'm here to listen, if you want to talk?'

Liam closes his eyes but a lone tear escapes and rolls down his cheek. 'Not sure it would help.'

My collecting sense kicks in, and I think of the happiness pebble in my bag. 'It might. But we can't do that here, obviously. Do you want to escape? Go for a walk on the beach?'

I get a grateful look, but then he says, 'I'm really not good company, you know.'

'That's because you need to get whatever it is off your chest. You'll feel better once we're walking. The sea air will give you a lift.' I stand up and shrug my coat on. 'Come on then.'

Standing up too, he glances to the kitchen where we can hear our mothers laughing about something. 'They won't be laughing in a minute, when they come in with the drinks and find us gone.' I'm pleased to see the black line around him is fading.

'We need to let them know we're going.' I laugh. 'We can't just cut and run. Besides, they'll be thrilled we've hit it off so quickly.' At this, a look of panic sweeps across his face, so I add, 'Hey, I'm only joking. I'm certainly not

188

looking for romance.' This is true, but I must admit I feel a bit put out by his reaction. Am I that unappealing?

'Me neither.' Liam puts a hand on my arm. 'But you *do* seem like a lovely person.' Just then, in come our mums. They see his hand on my arm and they beam at each other. Dear God, how obvious are they?

'Why have you got your coats on?' Maggie asks, handing a small glass of wine to us both.

Liam answers for us. 'We thought we'd go for a walk and a chat, if that's okay with you, Debs? Sorry I haven't had time to get to know you.' He downs the wine in one and sets the glass on the table. Our mothers stare at him, horrified.

'Thanks for lunch, Mum. Tell Dad hello and we'll speak soon.' I down my wine too, and we leave, laughing like hyenas.

The sun turns the peaks of the high dunes to shimmering gold as I pull the car into a space at Crantock beach. Though it's not the closest beach to Mum's, Liam asked if we might come here, as it's his favourite. He's been quiet on the fifteen-minute drive, but the dark margin has, thankfully, stayed away. Now he looks at his expensive shoes and pulls a face. 'Maybe not the ideal footwear for a beach walk. Didn't really think.'

'Take 'em off. Go barefoot, I always do,' I say, and get out of the car.

Liam gets out too and pulls his shoes and socks off and

rolls up his trousers to the knee. 'Oh, it's so good to feel the sand between your toes. It seems like an age since I've done it.' His eyes light up and a huge smile puffs his cheeks.

'No. London doesn't have many beaches, does it… I'd wither up like an old walnut if I couldn't be next to the ocean.' I roll my jeans up. 'It's in my blood.'

'Mine too. London suffocated me … I only stayed for one reason.' His smile's gone now and he's staring at the sand between his toes.

Unwilling to hear his sad story in the carpark, I slip my arm through his and drag him towards the steep path through the dunes and the entrance to the beach. At the apex, by the tufted marram-grass, we give our tired calf muscles a break, and our breath is taken by the climb, but mostly, the view.

'Wow … I have missed this. I didn't realise how much until right now.' Liam stands with his hands on his hips, taking deep breaths of air, marvelling at the vast expanse of golden sand edged by the dunes, the white horses galloping across a choppy cobalt ocean, and the River Gannel, steaming in from the right, as if relieved to be at the end of its journey.

'It's a wonderful beach,' I say, and point to the row of luxury houses on the hill opposite. 'My dream would be to live in that house there, the white square one, with all the huge windows. It has a swimming pool in the garden. I saw someone splashing in it one day.'

Liam says, 'Wow.'

'Imagine, living in that house, with this view, *and* a swimming pool in the garden? Heaven.'

'Wow,' he repeats. He nods and sighs.

I laugh. 'Are you going to say anything else, apart from wow, today?'

'Wow.' Liam chuckles, and sets off at a run down the other side of the dune, his arms windmilling in an effort to keep upright. I watch him while running my fingers over the smooth, cool pebble of happiness in my pocket. Maybe I don't need it after all. The ocean, sky, salt air and sand underfoot seem to be doing the job for me.

We walk along the beach with the wind in our faces until we get to the shoreline. 'Wanna paddle?' I ask.

'Try and stop me!'

Refreshing, might be the nicest way to describe the Atlantic's temperature, so our paddle is a quick one. The wind's woken up and is taking great delight in wrapping my hair around my eyes and making my nose run. We walk through the shallows for just a few moments then walk back up the beach to the protection of the dunes and flop down next to each other on the sand.

'Do you know what? I feel so much better already,' Liam says, shielding his eyes against the sun to watch a slightly built woman being dragged along by a couple of huskies.

'The beach and ocean will do that to you. Lifts the soul.'

'That's what I need. A bit of soul lifting.' Liam glances at me, gives me a smile.

'We can leave your sad story alone, if you like?'

Liam considers this. 'I'd rather get it off my chest, if you don't mind?'

'Of course. When you're ready.' Something strikes me. Ever since I started the collecting, people have been opening up to me right away. Okay, I have always been a good listener but, nowadays, strangers I've helped have been eager to share their stories with me. It's a good job, or my task would be much harder. Maybe it's all part of collecting.

He lets a huge sigh out into the wind and says, 'I'm gay. I know that shouldn't be a problem these days, but it is for my parents, particularly my dad. But I'm not just sad about that, mostly it's the break-up of my relationship. I was living with a man, Henry, in London. He was the owner of the restaurant I worked at and I adored him – thought we were for ever – but I found out he'd cheated on me numerous times, and to him, I was like a toy. Something to be played with, controlled. Henry dictated what I wore, what I did, everything. My appearance had to be perfect at all times, and I was never allowed to do what I really wanted. I once asked him to come down here to see how beautiful my local area was, but he said he'd rather die than come to such a backward arse-end of the universe.'

Liam pauses, looks away up the beach and I say, 'But that's terrible. I can see how much you love it here. How did you meet him?'

'I went to London to escape my parents, even though it killed me to leave this place. But I thought if I got a good job in the capital, I could save some money and then come back. Maybe start my own business here. Unfortunately, my boss turned out to be Henry and I fell for him.' Liam grabs a handful of sand and lets it trickle through his fingers into the breeze. 'Oh, he was wonderful in the early days, of course. Never put a foot wrong. Then once I was hooked on him, had moved into his place, he completely changed. By then it was too late. Never really saw what was happening, as he didn't become a monster all at once. He morphed little by little. He knew I'd have done anything for him.'

The black margin's coming back, thickening around his shoulders, arms. 'I'm so sorry, Liam.' I weigh the pebble in my pocket and add, 'How did you find out about his affairs?'

A humourless bark. 'Henry told me. Took great delight in it one night when I'd made his favourite meal. He swept it from the table onto the floor, told me to clean it up and then to pack my bags and leave. He'd got tired of me, I was too old for him – he wanted young blood. That was a joke, considering he's forty-two. My job at the restaurant was gone too. I...' Liam wipes away tears on the back of his sleeve. 'I had no choice. I had no savings, as most went on smart clothes and those stupid expensive shoes I had on today. Henry insisted I dressed well. I had to pay him rent, and contribute to bills too. When he kicked me out, I'd no real friends to turn to, as I never met any; a chef's job is pretty full-on and I worked late most nights. So, I had to come home ... cap in hand ... to my homophobic parents.' The margin extends, paints itself along his torso and wraps a coil around his chest.

We sit in silence for a while. Maybe I should give him the pebble now, but I know instinctively that if he has more to say, it needs to come out first. He needs to unburden himself totally before happiness can be let in. How I know this, I have no clue. The intuition of a collector, I suppose. Encouraging him to say more, I ask, 'Why did your mum try to pair you up with me then?'

'Because I never told my parents. How sad is that, Joy? Twenty-seven years old and still in the closet to the people that are supposed to love me the most.'

'Bloody hell, Liam.' I give him an incredulous look. 'How come?'

'As I said, they are homophobes. Years back, a friend of the family's son came out. My dad told us about it and called him all the vilest words. Said he was filth, and if he were his son, he'd disown him. Mum agreed, but said people are more accepting now. I almost blurted it all then, but the look in my dad's eye was enough to shut me up. I don't think I've ever seen hatred like it. It made me feel worthless. Subhuman. But then Dad always made me feel like shit. I've never been good enough.'

My throat constricts as his words take effect. It reminds me a bit of how my and Dad's relationship used to be. Not to the extreme he described, but I certainly never felt good enough. 'Liam, can I give you a hug?'

Wordlessly, he pulls me to him. 'Thanks for listening, Joy. You really helped.'

We break apart and I can see his dark aura is still there, yet it doesn't define him as completely as it did before. It looks more like the sky before a storm, than during. 'I'm glad I could help. Talking is often the best medicine.' I fiddle with the pebble in my pocket and pretend to sort through some grey ones on the sand to my right. 'But we need to do something practical to get you back on track. I'll ask around about a job.'

'Thanks, Joy. You're a star. And for what it's worth, if I

was straight, I'd certainly want our mums to matchmake.' He gives a little smile.

I laugh. 'Thanks. I think.' Then I take his hand and place the pebble onto his palm, close his fingers tight over it. 'Here's a lucky pebble. It will cheer you up.'

Almost immediately, the coil releases his chest and the sun breaks through the storm. 'Hey, it must be magic!' Liam looks at his palm in awe, then gives me a stretchy ear-to-ear smile. This is enough to send the rest of his sadness skittering away in the wind, like the tattered coat-tails of a nightmare. 'Wow! I feel fantastic.'

'Good. But put it away for now and keep it safe … only take it out when you really need it.'

Liam continues to stare at the pebble on his palm, so I whip it away and stick it in his pocket. 'Now, let's get walking. I'm getting chilly.'

Arm in arm we stride up the beach, and from time to time Liam looks across at me, with a wary expression. 'That pebble really felt like it had a powerful kick of something … must be cracking up more than I thought,' he says after a while.

'I have a jar of pebbles at home. If you believe they're lucky they will be.' The wary expression turns to disbelief, so I change the subject. 'And, Liam. If everything gets too much at home, you can stay with me for a while, okay?'

He stops and looks me in the eye. 'Seriously?'

'Yep.'

Liam's eyes fill and he covers his mouth, but words escape through his fingers. 'I can't believe how wonderful you are. Thank you from the bottom of my heart, Joy.'

'Don't mention it. And we should meet up soon. It won't do to stay in your room and dwell on things. You'll lose your spark!'

'God, don't turn into Mum!' He gives me a playful push and pretends to run off.

I catch up to him and he grabs my arms, dancing me round and round while people look on, bemused. 'Stop, you're making me dizzy!'

He throws back his head and laughs at the sky. 'You've made me dizzy. Dizzy with new possibilities, and I feel like I've known you for ever.' Then he grows serious. 'Thanks again so much, Joy.'

'You're welcome. Let's go back. My good deed for today is done.' We link arms and hurry towards the dunes. As we do, my heart swells, as if I have my own pebble inside it.

Chapter Eighteen

Gilly's acting weird around me. The last few days at work, every time I come into the staffroom and go over to her when she's talking to someone, she shuts the conversation down and gives me a big false grin. She reminds me of the Cheshire Cat. Then she whisks me away and babbles about the weather, or something equally inane to fill the awkward gap between us. I asked if she was herself the other day, and she did a high-pitched giggle and asked who else would she be?

Jowan, on the other hand, is quiet with me. True, I didn't really pal around with him much before, but I expected a bit more of a rapport between us since I was round at his the other weekend. Put him on the sofa and covered him with a blanket. *Nearly kissed him, don't forget that.* I shove that thought into a cupboard and block it. I want to ask him about his mum's funeral and how he's coping, but there's an invisible wall around him. At first, I assumed it was because he was struggling in general, but he's been almost his old self with others. Odd. But it's probably for the best. There's no room for my silly crush or whatever it is I've got for him. He's my boss, after all. Besides, I've decided to stay single; having a relationship with him would definitely complicate my work life.

Walking to the classroom after lunch, I see Daisy across the playground and she gives me a cheery wave. She's very much back to *her* old self, thank goodness. Better than her old self, actually. And I found out what her random act of kindness as a consequence of receiving the pebble is. Yesterday lunchtime she told me that she's staying behind to run an after-school club once a week. She's teaching the children to bake. Wonderful! I bounce into the classroom thinking about how great it is that Daisy's turning her life around, and Gilly's on the phone. As soon as she sees me, she flushes scarlet, ends the call, and starts rushing about putting paper and coloured pencils on each desk, ready for afternoon school. I'm about to ask her what's going on, when chattering children pile in like someone's shaken them out of a paper bag from a great height. It will have to wait.

———

Daisy's recipe for leek and potato soup and homemade rolls is so simple and delicious. Well, the soup is, the rolls are still in the oven. Liam's coming over for dinner and I'm so looking forward to seeing him again. We have texted each other most days and I really feel like I've known him forever. He's so easy to be around, and we have the same daft sense of humour. Hope he's open to my suggestion about his parents I've had flitting through my mind this week. But it could ruin things between us.

I'm pouring a glass of pinot when the doorbell goes, so I take it with me to answer the door.

'Oooh, how did you know that's exactly what I needed?' Liam asks, grabbing the glass from my hand and taking a big gulp.

'Oi! That was mine, and nice to see you too.'

'It's wonderful to see you. Joyful, in fact!' he kisses me on the cheek and sweeps past oohing and ahhing at pictures on the wall, my decor, and, lastly, Sebastian. 'You didn't tell me you had such a gorgeous creature living with you!' He kneels next to Sean's chair and fusses over Sebastian, who's lapping it up. First Jowan, now Liam ... must be because he misses Sean. This gives me a little kick of sadness, but the pain's not enough to bring me to my knees as it would have done a year ago, thankfully.

'He is gorgeous, and he knows it.' I tickle Seb under the chin as I pass by to the kitchen with Liam on my heels. I'm wondering if he's got the pebble on him, because he's certainly a different person from the one I met at Mum's. I can see a faint aura of happiness forming – his is not a rainbow like Gilly's was, but a flicker of orange flame, like the heart of a fire on a cold winter's evening. Hmm. This makes me wonder if the pebble will eventually lose its power if it's handled all the time. That was one of the many questions I would have liked to ask Hope. She did mention that they lose it if they're left in the jar for a while ... but did that apply to use too? Seeing as I can't ask Hope, maybe I'll just have to find out through experience over time.

'Hmm. Something smells delish,' he says, lifting the lid from the soup pot and sniffing. I take the lid, slap his hand away and point a finger at a chair next to the table.

'You're certainly much happier than you were, Liam. It's great to see.'

Liam turns to me, chocolate eyes lit with merriment. 'I am. I've had a few positive replies to my job enquiries, and my parents have left me alone, by and large. Mum thinks we are an item, so that has a lot to do with it!' He laughs and fiddles with something in his pocket before he sits at the table. I can guess what.

'And how did she get that idea, I wonder?' I put my head on one side and give him the laser stare.

He's the picture of innocence. 'Erm … no idea.'

'Hmm. So, we have soup and fresh rolls and butter, followed by a little rocket salad with baked salmon. Sound okay?'

'Sounds incredible. But I hope it's ready soon, I'm starving!'

We chat about his job news and he tells me he's waiting for a couple of phone calls. These jobs are not what he really wants, but hopefully they could lead to better things. While I plate up the salmon, I'm wondering how to broach my suggestion about his parents. Best just to go for it, I think. Taking a breath, I place the salmon in front of him and say in what I hope is a causal manner, 'Have you thought again of mentioning your sexuality to your parents? You'll feel better with it out in the open, I think.' I sit down opposite and refill his wine glass, the chug of the liquid loud in the stony silence.

Liam takes a mouthful of salmon and says out of the corner of his mouth, 'I already told you what would happen if I did, Joy. Besides, it's easier to let them think you and I are in a relationship.' He's not joking this time, and the atmosphere has gone from buoyant and upbeat, to sinking ship on a stormy day.

'Hmm. Sorry to bring you down. It's just that I hoped they might have mellowed a bit. And I always feel better if I get things that are important to me out in the open.'

'But then your parents are normal, not like a couple of throwbacks from Victorian times.'

'I wouldn't go so far as to say normal, but they aren't bad.' I smile and he sends one back. 'Just give it some thought, hey?'

Liam shrugs. 'If it makes you happy.'

About to reply, the doorbell stops my words and I frown. 'Who's this?'

He laughs and takes a sip of wine. 'How the heck should I know? It's your house.'

Fiona is the last person I expected to see. She's been a bit stand-offish since that night at The Merrymoor when I did my crazy person act after the nicked confidence from the charming Brad went straight to my head. I asked her over for a meal a few weeks ago but she had some flimsy excuse. 'I was just passing and realised I'd not seen you for ages. Can I come in for a cuppa?' Her smile is unsure, her eyes beseeching. She's not rocking the Pippi Longstocking hair tonight, it's been wound into a plait around her head and she looks more like a traditional little Dutch girl.

'You can … but I do have a guest for dinner.'

Her expression is a cross between curiosity and disappointment. 'Oh. A male guest or a female?'

'Male. Liam, I—'

'Right. I won't interrupt, then.' She sighs and pats my arm. 'I'm glad you're moving on at last.'

I'm about to tell her it's not like that, but I notice she's only just holding it together. Something's happened and she needs a friend. 'Look. Why don't you come in for a drink? The more the merrier, and it's ages since we had a natter.'

Fiona and Liam get on like a house on fire. I wonder how much of that is due to Liam's electric personality because of his constant handling of the pebble in his pocket. When he pops to the loo, Fiona grabs my arm and whispers, 'Where did you find him? He's gorgeous and totally lovely!'

'He's the son of my mum's friend. And we *are* just friends, actually.'

'Yeah right! I see how he looks at you, and you him.'

About to tell her she's way off the mark, I change my mind. Why not play Liam's trick? Why not let her think we're romantically involved? It would stop her arranging another Brad for me. Stop Mum too. It might actually be mutually beneficial for Liam and I. I tap the side of my nose with my forefinger. 'You can think what you like. Now, tell me what's upsetting you. I can tell there's something.'

Immediately, her eyes fill and she blinks away tears. 'Oh it's me and Mark. I might have done something stupid…'

'Might have?'

'Okay. I did. And Mark's found out. I really thought we could make a go of it, but I went and ruined it all.'

Liam comes in then and she says she'll tell me another time. Over coffee, Fiona asks him what he does for a living. 'I used to be a chef in London. I adored it, but I lost my job and can't seem to find another here.'

Fiona folds her arms and sits back in her seat. 'When you say chef, do you mean a proper fancy-type chef, or someone who worked in a fast-food place?'

He laughs. 'How very dare you! No, a proper fancy type.'

'Hmm.' She narrows her eyes, and gives us both a mysterious grin. 'In that case, I might be able to help. My cousin's the head chef at Rick Stein's over in Padstow, and he was saying the other day they're looking for a sous chef. I can put a word in, if you like?'

Liam's face lights up like a thousand stars. 'If I like?' He laughs. 'Really? Yeah, that would be fantastic!' He gets up and gives her a kiss on the cheek.

'Careful, you'll make Joy jealous,' Fiona says with a giggle.

I give Liam an exaggerated wink over the top of her head to stop him blowing my cover. 'Yeah. Go steady, Liam.'

Liam, obviously enjoying the game, comes over and takes me in his arms, whispers gobbledegook in my ears and gives me a lingering kiss on the cheek. 'I'll never give you cause to be jealous, darling,' he says with feeling. My God, he's a good actor. I give him a playful push and change the subject, my mind a jumble of conflicting thoughts. It was nice to be held, even though it was make-believe. Being held is one of the little things I used to take for granted when Sean was alive, and miss more and more as the years pass. Little things like a hug, a kiss, a reassuring touch of the hand, I've since realised are actually the huge things. They are forged by love. Protective amulets with which to adorn ourselves, giving us warmth and comfort as we move through our daily lives.

Apart from Liam just now, the last time I was in a man's arms was Jowan's. Even though there was no romance involved – I was only comforting him as he cried – I've thought about that moment too often lately. It buzzes into my conscience like an annoying bluebottle, and then buggers off before I can swat it. Then it waits, just out of sight, ready to buzz in again another day. Maybe I need to get some super-strength fly killer.

———————

A week later, I'm half-wishing I'd said yes to the party Mum wanted to throw. As usual, I said no fuss, just a quiet meal. But then it's a bit boring, having a birthday meal with just your parents, isn't it? You don't turn thirty every day, after all. It would be odd if you did, as you'd be ninety, three days after you were born. Can't see humanity surviving at that rate. My reflection smiles at that surreal thought and I dab some blusher on my cheekbones and fluff my hair. Will I do? Standing to the side, I smooth my turquoise silk dress over my hips and wonder if my stomach is sticking out too much. This is the first time I've worn this dress, and it *is* a bit clingy – I turn to the front again – and a bit low cut. I'm only going out for a meal with my parents, so maybe it's a bit over the top? *No. It's fine. Besides, you get precious few chances to wear a dress like this. Get going.*

About to turn away, my reflection frowns at me and I move closer to the bedroom mirror. I'm sure there are some new lines across my forehead. I fluff my hair again and pull a curl or two over my eyes to disguise them. It's no fun, this getting older lark. In my head comes a memory of Hope's creaky laughter and I imagine her quipping, 'You're nothing but a baby, Tawny One. Get out there and knock 'em dead.' Who I'll knock dead I have no clue, but at least I'll feel a bit special for a change.

As I hurry downstairs, I think about how I don't really mind being thirty. My collecting, and life in general seem to be going well. Collecting and delivering don't exhaust me like they did at the beginning. Must be getting used to it. My body must be able to absorb it as a normal activity. I've also got a wonderful new friend in Liam and, best of all, he has got the job at Rick Stein's, thanks to Fiona. He was like a dog with two tails when he came over to tell me. He reckoned it wouldn't be too long before he could afford to move out of his parents' and start to make a new life here in the place he loves. Life at home for the moment is better too for him, because his mum is over the moon that he's 'seeing' me. I can't help but feel it's all wrong. Best to come clean, but it's his life. And I must admit, the situation suits me at the moment.

Thinking of Fiona, I'm pleased I could help her with her little problem too. When we met for coffee the other day, I could hardly believe that she'd acted so rashly. She'd kissed Brad when she was drunk and Brad 'slipped up' and let it out to her boyfriend Mark. I realised that she's not as confident as she always makes out, and hides it behind a devil-may-care attitude and crazy dress-sense. Understandable after being dumped by her husband, but she needs to let Mark know exactly how she feels and how sorry she is. I have a confidence pebble ready if she needs it. I nicked some from Liam when he came round to tell me he'd got the job.

———

Mum answers the door, her face competing with the colour of her hair and her eyes sparkling with excitement. 'Happy birthday, darling!' she says, throwing her arms around me.

'Thanks, Mum. You ready?'

'Not quite. Come in for a bit.' She looks over her shoulder and back at me, gives me a stretchy smile. Hmm, weird. She's up to something.

'But you said we'd go straight off. Where's Dad?'

'In the living room, come and see him. You can open your presents too.'

'Okay … but you said we'd open them at the restaurant —' I'm left talking to the back of her head as she leads the way inside.

Instead of going into the living room, Mum goes to the dining room and over her shoulder, even though the light is off, I think I see a cold buffet on the table, which has been extended. What on earth?

Then, as I walk in, the light goes on and up goes a shout… 'SURPRISE!'

Chapter Nineteen

The shock has my stomach clenching, then it flips over. I can hardly believe my eyes! In front of me, laughing and clapping and blowing streamers, are Gilly, Fiona, Daisy, Liam and Jowan; Sonia, Charlie and Brenda, my three old friends from the care home; Polly and David, two other TAs from school ... and Helen, of all people! Mum and Dad too, of course. There's a silver banner on the wall saying *Happy 30th Joy!* And sparkly helium balloons with the number *30* on them cluster together in all four corners of the room like gossiping guests.

'Oh my goodness. Who on earth organised this?' I put a trembling hand to my mouth.

Mum points at Gilly. 'There's your culprit.'

'Gilly? How did you find my mum and dad?'

'Never mind all that now! It's time to party,' Fiona says, holding up a bottle of prosecco. Music starts and Mum propels me towards the table. Dad pulls a seat out, sits me down and hands me a glass of bubbles. Then everyone starts talking at once, filling plates and handing me gifts. I can hardly speak, I'm so overwhelmed, so I take a long pull on my drink, and as the crisp, cold liquid hits the spot, excitement takes the place of shock.

Gilly comes over with some food for me and I ask a hundred and one questions about how on earth it all happened. 'How did you find my parents?'

'I found your dad. He told your mum, and then she contacted Fiona and your old workmates. Fiona contacted Liam, and I organised people from school, obviously.' She lowers her voice. 'Helen overheard me ask Jowan, and she asked if she could tag along.'

I giggle. 'I did wonder. But how did you find Dad in the first place?'

'You told me the name of his new company.'

'I did?'

'Yep. And I noted it down in my "Joy's birthday organisation" file. It's been a real challenge, sorting it with you snooping round all the time.' Gilly's eyes roll dramatically.

'That's why you've been acting all weird and suspicious, then!'

'Moi?'

'Yes, you. Every time I walked into the staffroom or classroom, you clammed up and acted odd.'

Gilly laughs and goes off to get a refill and Fiona takes her place. 'Happy birthday, you old woman!'

'Eh? You're two years older than me.' I poke her on the arm.

'That's a vicious lie!' Fiona bats her eyelashes and flicks

both her plaits over her shoulders. She's in full-on Pippi Longstocking mode, and dressed in a red and gold sparkly pantsuit.

'How are you and Mark?'

'He's not interested. So there we are.'

'You can't have tried hard enough. I could tell he was crazy about you.'

'Look, this isn't the time for my woes. It's your birthday!'

Just then Mum comes over with a huge white box in her arms, decorated with red ribbon. Dad comes in behind and they stand there grinning like fools. 'Happy birthday from me and Dad.' Mum plonks the box on my lap and kisses me on the cheek, then Dad does the same.

'Thank you. And goodness knows how you kept the secret of this surprise party, Dad. You're hopeless, normally.'

'Why do you think I've been "busy at work" whenever you come over?' Dad laughs.

'Open it then,' Fiona says, leaning over my shoulder.

I look at the box, wondering what on earth it could be. This is one of the best bits of receiving presents, the anticipation. I undo the bows on the ribbons, and lift the lid. Inside there's a lovely wetsuit and on top, a white envelope. 'I needed a new wetsuit; how did you know?'

'You might have mentioned it from time to time,' Dad says with a smile. 'Now open the envelope.'

Mum's watching me, her eyes shining. I rip it open and inside is a voucher for a surf shop in Newquay. For … I look at the back. Four hundred pounds! 'Blimey!' I say, looking from one parent to the other in astonishment.

'Now you can get that surfboard you've been meaning to get the past five years or so but never did,' Mum says and hugs me. 'It's about time you did something just for you, instead of worrying about others all the time.'

My heart swells with love for them both. It's true. I have been meaning to get back into surfing for years. I was never out of the water as a kid, and through my teens I would regularly spend the day riding the waves down at Mawgan Porth with my friends. But surfboards are expensive and I had other calls on my finances, especially after Sean died. 'Thank you so much.' I hug them both and blink back tears. Then I prod Dad in his middle. 'And you can come with me sometimes.'

'Me, surfing?' He frowns and shakes his head. 'I don't think so.'

'Not surfing, swimming. You know you love it.'

'But I never have time nowadays.' He puffs out his chest and affects a posh accent. 'I'm a partner in my own construction business, don't you know.'

'I do. But even posh executive types get a day off now and then.' I hug him again and whisper that I love him into his ear. We're not a very demonstrative family, in terms of verbally spelling out how we feel – well, my parents aren't – so I was influenced by them as a kid. But Sean changed all that. He used to tell me exactly how he felt all the time, and me him. But I know Dad especially gets embarrassed, so *I love yous* are spoken few and far between. I often say I love them at the end of a phone call, because it's easier when there's distance, not face-to-face. Dad rarely returns it. Besides, until his recent transformation, when he found his confidence with a little help from me, feelings between us had been strained. Thankfully, nowadays, it seems as if we've started over. In that moment when I leapt up to hug him, my heart made the decision to underline that new start. Bugger his embarrassment. We need more declarations of love in this world, not less.

My mouth feels like it's been set in curlers at the edges. Constant smiling and laughing is wonderful, but a nice sit down with my feet up to relax for a bit would be good too. My head's still up in the clouds, while my body is struggling at ground level. What an evening it's been. Anxious that I will miss someone, I've been diligently trying to speak to each and every guest and endeavouring to spend an equal amount of time with them all. Jowan's the only one I've not managed to speak to yet … I think. Whenever I've caught his eye, he's looked away, or is that my imagination? Perhaps I want to avoid him, and I need to stop being so silly. I take a big gulp of prosecco and make a bee-line for him.

'Jowan, great to see you here,' I say, putting my hand on his shoulder.

He turns from Daisy, smiles, and his face goes a bit pink. 'Happy birthday, Joy.' As his lips brush my cheek and I inhale his spicy cologne, I'm irritated that his closeness has transferred his flush to my face.

'Thank you. And all this was such a surprise,' I burble unnecessarily, given that he was here when I was surprised by everyone.

'Yes, your face was a picture.' Jowan clears his throat and glances around. *His* face is a picture, actually. A picture of awkwardness. I'm about to ask how he's feeling now after the funeral and so forth, but he waves at someone, I'm not sure who, and says, 'Back in a mo.'

I watch him scuttle away and disappear into the kitchen. Hmm. If that wasn't avoiding me, I don't know what was. 'Happy birthday, Joy,' comes Helen's voice from behind me. Oops. She's another person I've not spoken to yet.

'Thanks, Helen,' I say, turning round to face her. Then my next sentence gets stuck in my throat, because over the top of her smart two-piece grey suit, she's wearing a vivid violet hue. But what is it? It has no smell, but it feels ... uncomfortable ... painful.

'You don't look thirty. Not that I know what the "age" thirty looks like. Is it tall, short – what? Odd thought, that.' She gives a high-pitched giggle. And I realise she's merry. Very. But the violet aura suggests she's far from happy. Bright eyes, a stretchy grin, a giggle on her lips, while underneath she's a wild animal caught in a snare.

I force a laugh. 'Yes. I think age is just a number really. It's how you feel that matt—'

'I'm thirty-seven, soon be forty. I wonder what *that* looks like?' Her eyes narrow and she's suddenly very interested in her fingernails. 'Look at this.' She thrusts an indigo nail at me so fast, I have to hoick my neck back. 'I had a manicure yesterday, that Shellac stuff, you know? And one's almost hanging off.' Helen swirls the dregs in her glass and mutters into it, 'Waste of bloody money,' as she downs it.

Oh dear. She's going to regret this tomorrow. Luckily, it's

the weekend. Grabbing a plate of sausage rolls, I hold them out to her. 'These are really nice, Helen. Try one.' *Soak up the booze before you fall over.*

Helen tucks her dark bob behind her ears and recoils. 'No thanks. I feel a bit …' she circles her hand in the air and belches, '… you know? In fact, I might need a breath of air.' She gazes around as if looking for a way out.

What a good idea. 'Come on, Helen. I'll show you the shortcut through the patio doors, just here.'

She mumbles something incoherent and allows me to propel her into my parents' large back garden. There's a nip in the air, as it's been a bright and sunny May day, free of cloud, so I guide her down the path and into the summerhouse. I flick the lamps on and draw the blinds. It's not that much warmer, but judging by her comedy drunk wobble along the path, I figure she could use some privacy and a sit down.

Helen flops down on a floral rattan sofa and sighs. 'This is nice. I've always wanted a summerhouse. I live in an apartment though, so that's unlikely!' She laughs like a hyena, as if she has not a care in the world. Her aura tells me she's lying.

'How are you feeling, Helen?' I ask, sitting in a matching chair across from her.

'It has a fabulous Atlantic view, so I can't complain.' She ignores my question and twirls a hand in the air as if she's a member of the Royal Family waving from a car. 'I have everything I want. A sumptuous apartment, more money than I need in the bank, a career that everyone respects, and…' She makes a triangle of her fingers and taps them against her lips. 'And…' Clearly adrift, she stares through me, lost in thought.

'How are you, Helen?' I try again. 'Shall I get you some water?'

A quick shake of the head. 'And … totally alone,' she finishes, bewildered, as if the realisation has only just hit her. Helen notices my frown and dismisses it with a flap of a hand. 'Oh, I have friends at school, but they aren't friends really. It's because I'm the head – their boss. My old friends I lost touch with, they are either all married or with partners and have kids. I was too busy building my career to do those things. And for what?' The *what* comes out as a bark as her voice threatens to give way to tears. 'It's all a lie, Joy. A lie … my whole life. I never wanted this.' She gives me an intense stare. 'And I am so … so miserable,' she whispers, her emerald eyes brimming with tears.

To say I'm stunned is an understatement. But it explains why at the interview and since, I've thought Helen was trying to be something she's not. She's not a teacher, not at heart. The poor woman's been living a lie. 'I had no idea, Helen.' I get up to comfort her, but she waves me away.

'Of course you didn't. Nobody does.'

Sitting back down I say, 'But why did you work so hard to achieve everything you have, if you didn't want it … or didn't you realise, until it was too late?'

Helen ponders this, staring through me again. 'A bit of both, I think. But mainly I did it because it was expected of me. My parents pushed me hard. Mum especially. She pushed me out at birth and kept right on pushing!' She does a shunting movement with her arm and gives the hyena laugh again. Brittle, humourless. 'I never liked teaching, and hate being a head even more. There's nothing I'd like better than to open a little shop by the sea and sell my paintings instead.' The tears spill over and chase each other down her cheeks. 'The main thing is that my parents are proud of me, though, isn't it? So proud.' Sarcasm clings to each and every syllable. 'Dad's a vicar, and tells anyone in his congregation who will listen about his clever daughter, the headteacher.'

Helen looks so vulnerable. The usual strident personality and dynamic business-like approach have disappeared. I am looking at the true Helen, and right now she is thoroughly miserable and trapped within a cage of her own making. Freedom. She needs to be set free. But where do I collect a surfeit of freedom? It's not a commonly found type of emotion like confidence, happiness, joy or courage, is it? Or maybe I could find out a little more. If she finds happiness, then that might set her free... If I can help her, I will. 'I'm so sorry, Helen. It's not too late to change direction. There's no reason why you can't get that little shop if you really want to. Is painting what you do in your spare time?'

'Yes. It's what keeps me sane.' She smiles and shoves her hands through her bob. 'If indeed I am anymore.'

'So why not leave your job and start afresh? Your parents will just have to cope with it. If you're not happy, then you must do something about it. Life is too short.'

'Yes. It's something I've considered, but it would come at a great cost.' Helen glances at me and away.

'But you said you had money in the bank and—'

'Not that kind of cost,' she snaps. 'It's a bit delicate … no idea why I told you any of this, really.'

Possibly because you're more than a little bit pissed. 'Because it helps to talk?'

Helen's eyes flash, 'Does it? Not sure you could help with this one. It's called unrequited love, in old-fashioned terms. I'm in love with someone at school, but he's not interested. But if I left, I'd never see him … and I couldn't bear that.'

Wow. That's a surprise. She blows her nose on a tissue while I wonder what to say next. 'So, have you told him how you feel?'

'Yes. That's how I know it's unrequited.' Helen enunciates this carefully, as if she's spelling something out to a child slow on the uptake.

Hmm, she's more like her old snippy self now. 'You told him you loved him?'

She snorts. 'Of course I didn't tell him I loved him. That would be too crass, even for me. It was a while ago now, I asked him out on a date. He said, thanks but no thanks. He wasn't looking for a relationship.'

Who is this guy? We only have a few male members of staff … and Bob the caretaker, of course. I can't see him and Helen together though, to be fair. 'Um …' I begin, then think better of asking her who it is. If she wants to tell me, she will.

'Exactly.' She points the broken nail at me and laughs more genuinely this time. 'Not much to say to that. I bet you're dying to ask who it is.' Her eyes dance, full of mischief. I shrug and smile. 'It's the delectable Jowan. Who else would it be really, in our school?'

My mouth drops open and my stomach churns. Jowan? My earlier thought of making her happy runs and hides in a corner. Did I want to try and get Jowan and her together? And my mother must be a witch. She said Helen fancied him the other week! Helen's studying my face, head on one side, eyes narrowed. *Say something, Joy.* From somewhere I find, 'Oh? Well, he *is* a lovely man.'

She twists her mouth to the side. 'Hmm. I did wonder if you had a thing for him. You seem a bit cosy. You know, meeting on the beach and then going to his house and all?'

'Eh? A thing for him? I went to his house because he was upset about his mum's death, and I was helping out,' I snap, indignant that she would imply it was more than that. And once again having to acknowledge that Mum was right about Helen being jealous of me.

Helen puts the palms of her hands up towards me. 'Okay, don't get on your high horse. Just making an observation.'

My cheeks and the tips of my ears are on fire, for two reasons, I realise. One, because Helen's observation is correct, and two, because I've only just admitted it to myself properly. I've been pushing feelings about Jowan away like a Victorian heroine, but now the lady is quite undone. The idea of Helen and Jowan together has planted a little seed of jealousy in my gut and it's growing like a magic beanstalk. In fact, if I'm honest, the idea of Jowan with anyone is most disconcerting. Most disconcerting? God. Even my thoughts sound Victorian. Pulling myself together, I blurt, 'Okay.

Well, you could try again. Maybe when you asked him, he was still getting over his divorce.'

Helen leans forward, hope in her eyes. 'Do you really think so?'

No. No I don't. And I have no bloody idea why I said it. 'It's worth a try.'

The violet aura is fading to lavender. 'I mean, what have I got to lose?'

Your pride and a more strained working relationship if he says no ... but what if he doesn't? 'Exactly.'

'Thanks, Joy. You've convinced me. I'll go and find him right now!' Helen leaps up, a radiant smile on her face.

'No!' I stand too and grab her arm as she hurries past. 'I think it might be wise to do it when you're sober.'

'I've had a few, but I'm not drunk,' she says, glaring down at me. Then her eyes soften. 'But I reckon you might be right. I'll wait until next week – plan it out.'

I'm about to answer when Mum opens the door. 'There you are, Joy! We've been looking everywhere for you. It's time for your cake.'

'Cake!' Helen trills, clapping her hands. 'That's just what I need right now.' She nudges me and hurries up the path back to the house.

'Is your headteacher a bit squiffy?' Mum asks in a low voice as we follow on.

'You could say that.'

A few minutes later, the lights are dimmed and Dad comes in with a huge white and pink cake in the shape of the number thirty. His face is lit by the same number of candles, and in the orange glow he looks like a happy pumpkin. Placing it on the table, he says, 'Wishing our girl the best birthday ever.' He puts his arm round Mum and pulls her to his side. 'We couldn't have chosen a better name for our wonderful daughter, because she brings joy to all who know her.'

'She certainly does,' Mum says and dabs at the corner of her eye with a tissue.

'Happy birthday, my love,' Dad says. 'You make us so proud.'

I make them proud? Wow. This is a first from Dad. Declaring such stuff in public and without embarrassment. My throat's too full of emotion to reply, so I make a little heart shape with my fingers. Then, his eyes bright in the candlelight, Dad says to everyone, 'Come on, you lot.' And starts them off with a wobbly 'Happy Birthday to you…'

Everyone claps and waits as I lean towards the candles amid shouts of 'Make a wish!' and 'Don't set that mane on fire!' Taking a deep breath, I make a wish and blow. Three puffs and some candles refuse to be snuffed. Helen leaps in from my right and does the job. I wonder if she made a wish. I also wonder if it was the same as mine? When everyone claps again and the lights go on, I notice Jowan's not there.

Liam sidles up to me a bit later as we're munching the cake. 'Okay, my darling?' he asks, giving me a big cakey kiss on the cheek.

'I am, thanks. It's been a lovely evening. Such a great surprise.'

'Good. I'm glad it went well. I've met some new friends too, which is nice.' He polishes off the last few crumbs and then adds, 'Oh, and that nice Jowan guy told me to pass on his apologies. He popped off home early as he had something to do.'

'Right. I did wonder where he went.'

'Yeah. I was telling him how much I adore you, and he suddenly said he had to go.'

Liam's eyes twinkle with mischief as I digest this bit of information along with the cake, which suddenly tastes too sweet. 'You told him you and I are together?'

'Of course I did. Because we are. Aren't we?' He winks and goes off to refill his glass.

My thoughts are in turmoil, crashing into each other like a dozen inebriated Helens in my mind. Did Jowan leave because he was upset I was with Liam? Or did he leave because he genuinely had something to do? And what the hell am I going to do about Helen? My collecting duty tells me what I should do, but don't I have a duty to myself? What about my own happiness?

Chapter Twenty

A week has passed and I'm still none the wiser. Luckily, work was very busy as we hurtled towards half-term. We had a few out-of-school trips, and a visiting local author came to do assembly. Gilly and I organised it, so it left precious little time for pondering on Jowan, Helen and myself. Apart from when I'm wide awake in the middle of the night, that is. Then, every crazy thought I can dream up crawls from the deepest recesses of my mind and does a devil dance. The thump of its feet pounding in my head and blocking the gateway to sleep. Jowan has continued to be distant, and I can count on the fingers of one hand the times he's actually spoken directly to me. Helen's been the same. Apart from last Monday, when she asked me in hushed tones to please keep what she told me to myself. The rest of the time she's been quiet, preoccupied, and has virtually ignored me. I can understand why. She's obviously embarrassed.

Today's Saturday, however, and I plan to forget all my

woes and get out in the Atlantic on my new surfboard. As I have my board, I drive down to the beach instead of walking, and soon I'm on the sand, a bounce in my step, the fresh wind tugging at my hair. The sky's the kind of blue a child would paint, with a yellow spiky sun in the corner of the page, peeping at me from behind a fluffy white cloud. As always, my spirit starts to rise when I'm next to the ocean and I take in a huge breath of salt air, then slowly exhale and stretch my hands to the heavens.

Five minutes later I'm still gazing out to sea. Okay, no more stalling. It might have been nearly eight years since I've been a surfer girl, but the waves are just right today, the wind's fairly calm, and it's time. The surfboard under my arm, I set off at a jog to warm up and get the blood flowing. Once my feet hit the water, I catch my breath, but keep going and paddle out to wait for my wave. Astride the board, I bob gently and look back at the land. The beach has a few dog walkers and families with children, but because it's only just past ten, it's fairly quiet. Beyond them, the beach climbs steeply to the dunes, and beyond those, the headland, dotted with houses, shelters the beach in the crook of its arm. One house draws my eye. Will Jowan be home? Will he be looking at the ocean from his living room, watching me, just a dot on the waves?

Shaking him from my thoughts, I see a wave and go for it, paddling for all I'm worth. I feel the swell behind me pick up the board, and in my head, I visualise myself springing up into a crouching position in one fluid movement, just as I used to in my youth. A surge of adrenaline. *One, two, three, up!* And miraculously I am. I am up and I'm riding the wave. The roar of the ocean in my ears, the wind whipping wet strands of loose hair across my face, the bounce of water under my feet, I'm alive. Alive and connected to the energy of the universe. The wave breaks all too quickly, but I did it. I did it without much of a problem or making a fool of myself. 'Whoop!' I yell to the gulls, and they yell back.

After an hour, I am well and truly pooped, but what a wonderful time I've had. I drag my weary feet and my board back to the carpark, picturing myself wrapped in a fluffy towel after a hot shower, drinking hot chocolate with squirty cream and reading my new novel. It's a suspense and set here in Cornwall. Can't wait.

'Sebastian, get your nose out of my hot chocolate!' I hurry to the kitchen table where I left my mug a few minutes ago to pop to the loo, but I'm too late. Sebastian is hoovering up the last of the squirty cream, completely ignoring my instruction to do otherwise. He looks up, his whiskers dripping white, when I clap my hands and make a shooing noise, but all he does is lick his chops with relish. Great. There's no way I'm drinking that now. I scoop him up and plonk him on the chair. 'That was *my* treat, Sebastian. I was really looking forward to it!' He gives me the slow blink and licks his chops again. Then the doorbell goes. Great. Who the hell is this now?

Pulling my dressing gown tight around me, I pad along the corridor and open the door. Liam's standing there with a split lip clotted with blood and a black eye. He has a suitcase and a big bag at his feet too. 'Oh my God, what happened?' I ask, ushering him through.

'Dad happened,' he says over his shoulder. 'I told him I was gay and he laughed. Said I was joking. I asked him if he saw me laughing, so…' Liam's voice breaks and he sets his bags down in the kitchen. Covers his face with his hands. Through his fingers he blurts, 'He said I disgusted him and I was no son of his. I said thank God for that, because who wants a bigoted piece of shit for a father? Then he hit me and I hit him back.'

'Oh, Liam.' I take him in my arms and he cries for a while. 'Come and sit down, I'll make you a hot chocolate with squirty cream. I'm having one.'

He gives me a watery smile and blows his nose, wincing as his lip starts to bleed again. 'Might have to drink it through a straw.'

'Luckily I think I have one somewhere.' I rifle through the cupboards. 'What made you tell him?'

'Partly because of you. You said I should tell them.'

I stop rifling. Did I? Shit. Yes I did, and now Liam's got a split lip. Damn it! Maybe I was letting the success of collecting go to my head. Imagining I knew the best for everyone. This is a timely reminder that it's not all plain sailing after all. 'Oh, I'm so sorry, Liam,' I begin, but he doesn't hear me.

'He was banging on about how you and me make a lovely couple and did I think we could make it work? Was it serious? Shit like that. I couldn't lie to him anymore… And you know what? Even though the worst happened, which I knew it would, I'm glad I'm out. It's as if a huge weight has been lifted.'

I put milk in a pan and chocolate powder in two cups. 'Well, that's the main thing. You have to be true to yourself. Let your feelings out. It's no good bottling everything up.' The irony of that little speech is not lost on me. Because that's exactly what I'm doing, isn't it? Bottling everything up. Not coming clean, not being true to myself.

Once the drinks are ready Liam gingerly sucks at the straw, but the action sets his lip bleeding again, so he settles for spooning the cream into his mouth instead. 'This is good. It's ages since I've had squirty cream.' Then he becomes serious. 'Nobody's mentioned the suitcase-elephant in the room. You know you once said I could stay, Joy?'

'I did and I meant it. *Mi casa es su casa.*'

Relief floods his face. 'Thanks, Joy. It won't be for long, just a couple of weeks while I find a nice place.'

'You can stay as long as you like.' Then the doorbell goes again. Great. The idea of an afternoon indulging in hot chocolate and reading quietly has melted away like the squirty cream.

'Fiona ... oh, and Mark,' I realise, as I open the door fully. 'Nice to see you together.' I smile, though it feels a bit overstretched across my teeth. Great that things have worked out, but I'm not really dressed for entertaining.

Fiona, on the other hand, is wearing sparkly silver tights and a green mini dress with yellow ribbons in her trademark plaits. A bit much, even for her. 'Why are you in your dressing gown?' is her opener. 'You got Liam in there?' she adds, with a lascivious wink.

'I have actually, but it's not what you think.'

'Never is,' Fiona says with a throaty laugh and pushes past, dragging Mark behind her. 'We've got some great news to share. Get the kettle on!'

Flustered that I just allowed her to barge in when Liam needed a bit of space, I hurry along behind, wondering how we'll explain Liam's condition. But I needn't have wondered, because Fiona is already giving him the Spanish Inquisition.

'A fight,' Liam says to her, shrugging and catching my eyes with his big brown ones. He looks like a deer in the headlights.

'Yes, Liam. I can see you've been in a fight, but who with? Or should that be, with whom?' Fiona sits at the table and pats the chair next to her for Mark.

'Um...' Liam says, turning scarlet and looks into his mug of hot chocolate.

I fold my arms and lean against the worktop. 'He might not want to share those details, Fiona,' I say, pointedly.

'Ooh!' Fiona glances at me and back to Liam, eyes twinkling with excitement. 'Did someone come on to Joy, and you walloped him?'

'No,' I say, and sweep a hand across my dressing gown. 'I'm just going to get changed, and please leave the twenty-questions out while I'm gone, okay?'

She salutes. 'Yes, ma'am.' As I leave the room, I hear Fiona say in a low voice, 'Is that your suitcase, Liam?'

Back in the kitchen a few minutes later, I see Liam's

making two more hot chocolates and Fiona's babbling on about how perfectly things have worked out for her and Mark. 'You came round to Fiona's way of thinking, then?' Liam asks Mark.

'She wouldn't take no for an answer.' He laughs. 'But I'm glad she didn't, I'd be lost without her.'

'That's why we're here. To tell you the big news!' Fiona says, drumming both forefingers on the kitchen table. 'We are getting married! And in the meantime, we're moving in together.'

My heart leaps and I run over and give her a big hug. 'That's the best news! So happy for you.'

'Thanks, Joy.' She flips her beribboned plaits over her shoulders and beams at me, an aura as pink as her cheeks blooming around her. The scent of fresh strawberries fills the room. More unadulterated happiness for me. I glance at the jar of pebbles next to the tea caddy. I need to do a spot of collecting while I have chance.

'This calls for a biscuit with our hot chocolate!' I declare, and go to the cupboard for the biscuit tin and a crafty pebble. After I've offered biscuits, I give Fiona another hug and a whoosh of happiness rockets into my core, almost lifting me off my feet. Quickly I thrust my hand into the back pocket of my jeans and grab the pebble. Phew.

'You okay?' Liam asks. 'You looked like you were going to fall over just then.'

'I'm fine. Just really happy for Fi and Mark.'

We sip our drinks for a few minutes while Fiona sprays us with a rapid machine-gun fire of information about rings, venues and bridesmaids. 'And guess what else? We got two cats from the rescue centre the other day and we think one's pregnant!' We ooh and ah, but I'm not sure a house full of kittens is the best idea with them both out at work all day. Then she suddenly changes tack and says, 'So who punched you, Liam?'

Liam looks at me, startled. She's put him on the back foot with that unexpected curve ball. 'As I said, Fiona, Liam doesn't want to go into all that,' I say.

'Can't Liam speak for himself?' she counters, the spark of mischief back in her cool grey eyes.

I do love her, but sometimes she goes way over the line. I'm about to say as much when Liam says, 'It's not a secret. I may as well just say what happened and get it all out in the open, like you said, Joy. It will blow your cover but, hey, Fiona won't breathe a word to your parents about us not really being together.' Fiona's mouth drops open and her eyes grow round. 'Will you, Fiona?' Liam says in a stern voice.

She ignores this question and asks, 'You're not together? So, what … are you saying you made it all up?' Fiona looks at me, bewildered.

Great. Fiona is not the best at keeping a secret, so Mum will have her matchmaking hat on again pronto. Mind you, Maggie will no doubt tell her all about the fight anyway. I sigh. 'No. We made it up to keep people like you from trying to set me up with an irresistible new love. You know, like the up-himself bird-brain, Brad. That went well, didn't it?' Mark bristles at the mention of Brad's name, but says nothing.

Fiona leans forward, rests her chin on her knuckles. 'I'm intrigued. So, tell me all, Liam.'

Liam shrugs. 'I had a fight with my dad. I came out to him, he's a homophobe, he threw a few punches and I replied in kind. Okay?'

Fiona's chin falls off her hand. 'You're gay? No way!'

'Way,' Liam says.

'Bloody hell. I would never have guessed…' Fiona pulls a sad little face. 'What a blow for womankind, eh, Joy?'

'Oh, for goodness sake, Fi,' I huff and give her a hard stare.

'Just joking, keep your pants on!' she laughs, and I can't help but smile back.

'Will your dad come round?' Mark asks.

'Doubt it. And I can't say as I'm bothered. We've never seen eye-to-eye.'

Fiona sits back in her chair and folds her arms. 'Well, well, well.' Then she looks at me, wiggles her eyebrows up and down. 'And I know you said I have to stop trying to find you a man, but that gorgeous Jowan at your party couldn't keep his eyes off you, Joy. Is he single?'

He couldn't keep his eyes off me? I must have missed something there. 'I'm not having this conversation.'

'You like him, don't you? I can tell.' Fiona's eyes lock onto mine like two truth-seeking missiles.

'Of course I like him, he's our deputy head – a good guy.' I throw my hands up, exasperated. 'Everyone likes him.'

Fiona points a finger. 'You *know* what I mean. And you *do* like him, you've gone scarlet!'

My colour deepens as three pairs of eyes scrutinise my face. 'That's because you're pointing fingers and talking a load of bollocks!' I jump up, grab the cups, some of which are still half full, and stomp over to the sink, run water into it. My heart's hammering, and anger is bubbling up from my depths, threatening to pop out in another torrent of expletives. Fucking Fiona! Why did she have to come round and poke me in front of a bloody audience?

Into the stunned silence, Mark says, 'I think you need to apologise, Fi. You let yourself go too far sometimes.'

Sometimes? All the sodding time.

Fiona comes up behind me and puts a hand on my shoulder. 'Hey, Joy. I was only having a bit of fun. You know what I'm like.'

Her tone is apologetic. Sad. Swallowing down a ball of emotion, and bewildered at my out-of-character response to Fiona being … well, Fiona, I take a breath, turn to face her. 'It's okay, I overreacted. I've not been sleeping well lately.' A lie, but who cares?

'Right. Well, I'm sorry, hon.' She gives a little smile. Then she goes back to the table and picks up her bag. 'Anyway, we must be off,' she says brightly. Too brightly. The kind of brightly that's trying too hard. 'We are going to pop into a few hotels to ask about their wedding packages, aren't we, Mark?'

'Yep.' He smiles, but I can tell it isn't his ideal Saturday afternoon activity.

Liam says, 'Lucky you, Mark,' and gives him a wink. Then we say our goodbyes and Liam shows them out.

'Oh God, I was such a bitch,' I say, flopping down on a sofa in the living room, head in hands.

'She deserved it. She went too far. She could see you were upset,' Liam answers, leaning against the door jamb.

'But even so, that's just Fiona…'

'Hmm. Wanna talk about it?'

About to say there's nothing to talk about, I look up at his battered face and something shifts inside me. If he can be honest, so can I. 'Not really… Suffice to say, I think I've fallen for Jowan, but it's very complicated. There's not just me to consider, and I've not the faintest idea how Jowan feels about me. On top of that, we work together. Not a good idea.'

Liam looks at me for a while then says, 'I'll just take my suitcases to the spare room and then I think we could do with something a bit stronger than hot chocolate. You agree?'

Emotion chucks another lump into my throat, so all I can do is nod.

Chapter Twenty-One

Another week back at school has passed and I'm no further forward with the Jowan dilemma, as I've begun to think about it. Liam has been brilliant. In fact, I don't know what I'd do without him to talk things through with. Fiona always tries to impose her view on mine, until my opinion is squashed flat under her steamroller of 'good ideas'. Liam's approach is gentler, and he listens more than he talks. He's given me some good suggestions and, so far, the overall consensus is that I try and get Jowan to one side at school, ask about how he is in general, and then maybe suggest going out for a drink, or even a meal. At least I'd know how he felt, one way or the other. First, I need to ask Helen if she's asked him out again. Because if she has, and he's accepted, my dilemma is solved for me.

The whole thing feels contrived and unnatural to me. Shouldn't these things just happen organically? This is like a military operation. Cold, calculated. But as Liam says, it's necessary if I want to let Jowan know how I feel. Part of me is wrapped in a blanket, feet up eating comfort food, while muttering stuff about things staying as things are, and leaving well alone. This same part prods me now and then with, 'What happened to never letting another man into your life after Sean? What about that, eh?' At the same time, another part of me is dressed in a sequined evening gown and spike heels, yelling, 'We only have one life. Carpe diem!'

At the moment, the blanket-wrapped me is winning, as I walk down the corridor towards Helen's office. It's a few minutes into lunchtime and I promised myself to go for it today upon waking with the Carpe Diem diva dancing in my head. I raise my hand to knock on the office door, but it's whisked open before I can. Helen's glaring wide-eyed at me. 'Joy … you startled me.'

'Ditto.' I smile and shove my hands into the pockets of my trousers to stop them shaking.

She knits her eyebrows together. 'What can I do for you? I'm on my way to a meeting.'

'In that case, don't worry,' I say, the blanket-wrapped me sighing with relief.

Helen's eyes soften and she glances at her watch. 'No, come in. I have a few moments.' Then the frown is back. 'Unless this is going to take ages?'

I give a quick shake of my head and the diva pushes me through the door. Helen waits at the window, head on one side. *Come on, Joy. Just say it – no umming and ahhing.* 'It's about what we talked about at my birthday party…' Her eyes narrow and her red lips draw themselves into a tight knot. 'Have you managed to ask Jowan if he ... um ... ah, that is to say—'

'Why are you asking me this? I made it quite clear I didn't want to discuss it further.'

My face feels like it's on fire now, and her narrowed eyes have more than a glint of suspicion in them. 'Oh ... I just wanted to see if I could help with it all, if needs be... You opened up to me and—'

'Which was a colossal mistake,' Helen snaps, folding her arms tight across her chest as if she's scared of letting any feelings escape.

'Okay. Sorry, I—'

'No, I'm sorry.' She holds her hands up, heaves a deep sigh and tries a smile. 'Truth is, I was embarrassed about getting drunk and spilling my guts. My whole life story, in fact. I never do that. Ever.'

Hmm, but then you've never met a collector before.

'In the cold light of day, I thought it over and decided to let sleeping dogs lie. I can't change my feelings towards Jowan.' She blinks her eyes rapidly. 'God knows, I've tried. But there's no way I'm letting my heart rule my head. If he rejected me again, it would be the living end. It wouldn't work.' Helen grabs her bag and moves towards me. 'Thanks for thinking of me, Joy. Appreciate it. But let's leave it there, shall we?' she says, awkwardly patting me on the shoulder.

I nod and open the door for her. She nods back and hurries away along the corridor. The blanket-wrapped me tells me I have no morals, lying to the poor woman and pretending I wanted to help her with Jowan. How could I? I reply she's absolutely right, and I have no idea what kind of person I'm turning into. Sparkly Diva turns up and whispers in my ear that love will do that to a person. Love? Really? I shut the pair of them into an empty room and let them fight it out, while I step out into a squally shower to commence playground duty. Great. It was sunny a moment ago. Serves me right.

———————————

After a hasty sandwich ten minutes before afternoon school, I make my way along the corridor to Gilly's classroom. I said I'd help her set up before registration. Playground duty has passed in a blur. My head is still full of conflicting messages and ponderings, so I'm not really aware of my surroundings, until I'm about to step through the open classroom doorway.

'Miss Pentire, can I have a word?' comes Jowan's voice a little way behind me.

My stomach flips over as I turn round and take a deep breath to calm myself. 'Of course,' I manage, in an unnaturally high voice. It's the kind of voice that says I'm guilty of something. Thankfully, only I know what it is.

Jowan closes the gap between us. He's dressed in charcoal grey trousers and a stripy blue and white shirt. His wavy dark hair is damp from the rain and he smells of fresh air and a lemony spiced aftershave. Jowan's sky-blue eyes lock onto mine and I can hear my heart thudding in my ears. What would it be like to just reach up and kiss his lips? Run my fingers through his... 'Pardon?' I say, as his first few words register, exploding any idea of kisses into tiny pieces.

Jowan folds his arms, and a few dark clouds scud across the sky blues. 'I *said*, I wasn't impressed with your lack of authority just now.'

I haven't misheard, then. What the hell? 'When?'

'In the playground. I was looking out of my office window and noticed you didn't intervene in the obvious bullying of Leo Mellor going on right in front of your eyes. Then you just walked off as if you were in a trance. I had to hurry down and sort it myself.'

My stomach flips again but for a different reason and then shrivels into a tiny ball. 'I … I had no idea Leo was being—'

'Clearly. But God knows why not. He was in the corner of the playground and three Year Fives were taunting him about his hair. You were just standing there staring into space, apparently.'

A vague image of Leo in the playground comes to me. Leo's got a pink face, laughing at some other children who are ruffling his red hair. Were they bullying? Perhaps… I'd not being paying much attention as my head was full of Jowan. 'But Leo was laughing, I assumed—'

'Leo never makes a fuss. But I could tell he was upset. You need to pay more attention to detail, Miss Pentire.'

Miss Pentire. There are no children around, yet he's insisting on addressing me formally. His whole demeanour is bordering on the aggressive and I feel like a naughty pupil caught in the act. Demeaned, awkward and hurt. Very hurt. It's as if my visit to his house never happened … the closeness we shared, a figment of my imagination. 'I'm so sorry.' I avoid his eyes and swallow hard. 'I had no idea he was upset. Is he … is he okay now?'

'Yes. I got the others to apologise. Leo shrugged it off, of course, but they know in no uncertain terms that if I catch them again, parents will be involved. Please make sure you are vigilant at all times. Okay?' His brief smile is as warm as a winter's day.

Nodding, I'm about to apologise again, but he's off down the corridor before I can draw breath. Receiving such a telling off would have been unpleasant from anyone, but from him it was like a punch in the gut. Bewildered, I stare at the wall and try to swallow down a choking sensation in my throat. Gilly pops her head round the classroom door and takes in my swimming eyes and wobbly lip. 'Bloody hell, Joy, what the hell is up with Jowan? Harsh or what!'

Great. Not only have I been humiliated, it's been overheard too. This tips me over the edge and tears spill from my eyes and pour down my cheeks. Gilly takes my arm and pulls me inside the room, and gives me a big hug. 'Sorry, I'll be okay in a mo,' I sniffle into her shoulder.

'Don't apologise. Come on, sit down. Have a sip of water.' She hands me her water bottle. 'God knows what's got into him. I've never known him speak to anyone like that. I've a good mind to have a word with Helen about it.'

I nearly choke on the water. 'No! That's the last thing I want.'

'But he was out of order.' She hands me a tissue.

'Maybe, but I can't have her involved.' I wipe my nose,

conscious of the time. The children will be arriving any second. I need to get hold of myself.

Gilly gives me a knowing look. 'There's more to this than meets the eye, isn't there?' I shrug, blot under my lashes with a tissue. 'Hmm. We're going to have a chat after school. My place?'

'It's fine, honest,' I say, with a forced smile.

'And I'm the Queen of Sheba.'

'Yes, Your Majesty.'

'So you'll come?'

'Okay.'

Gill's Truro apartment is in a converted warehouse overlooking the river. It's quite small, but it's open plan, and its huge patio windows let in lots of light. Perfect for Gilly's bright and breezy personality. I sit in a red comfy chair by the window and watch a little boat gliding by, the early evening sunshine glinting off its windows. 'Right, now get ready to tell me all about it,' she says, handing me a glass of wine. I take it, but wonder if I should on an empty stomach. I do have to drive home. As if she read my mind, she comes back from the kitchen with a bowl of peanuts and Mini Cheddars. Making herself comfy on the opposite chair, she says, 'Okay. Spill it.'

Uncomfortable with telling her about Helen, I realise I can't tell the story properly at all. It would come across as disjointed, which would prompt her to ask more questions and I'd have to lie. Best to be honest. 'The thing is, Gilly, there's a confidence wrapped up in all this which I feel loath to break.'

'Because of Helen.' Gilly takes a sip of wine and leans back in her chair.

'How the hell…?'

'An educated guess. I saw you chatting in the summerhouse at your party when I was helping you mum look for you. I came down the path, but then saw Helen crying, so decided not to interrupt.'

'Right.' I sigh and take a handful of peanuts. 'So you see, it's tricky.'

'Yeah. But I'm much more concerned about you than I am about Helen, and I give you my solemn promise that I won't breathe a word of this to anyone.'

Gilly is nothing if not trustworthy, so after a few moments' consideration, I tell her about meeting Jowan on the beach, and Helen's confession, and my subsequent admission to myself about how I feel about him. 'That's why it hurt so much earlier. I should have realised he had no feelings for me, when he ignored me and rushed off at my party. And he's hardly spoken to me since. What was I thinking? I'd *actually* planned to tell him how I felt today.' I take a big glug of wine to wash down a lump of emotion.

She frowns and leans forward in her chair. 'But I thought you and Liam were together?'

'That was a big fib.' I explain why, and all the while Gilly's shaking her head disparagingly.

'What a dumb thing to do.'

'Yes. It was.' As if I wasn't fed up enough, without Gilly stating the obvious.

She gives me an intense stare, the green bits in her hazel eyes glowing as the sunlight catches them. After a moment or two, she sits back, tosses a few peanuts into her mouth and says through them, 'I think Jowan's mad about you.'

Mid-sip, I nearly snort the wine through my nostrils. 'Oh yeah. He's bloody mad alright. He was furious today.'

'With himself.'

'Eh?'

'Because he was nasty to you, ignored you at the party, because he's jealous of you and Liam. Angry that he feels something for you, but can't have you. It's obvious, really.' Gilly twists her mouth to the side. 'Yup. He's protecting himself. Poor guy's been through so much lately. His head's messed up.' She takes a sip of wine and twists her dark ponytail around her hand. 'I can't see him behaving like that if he was thinking properly.'

No chance. She's way off there ... isn't she? My mind re-runs a few scenes for me. The way Jowan looked at me sometimes across the staffroom; the way the chemistry between us could have powered a small town the day I wiped paint off his shirt on the field; the way he was with me at his house that day. The look he had in his eyes when I held him, the warm conversation and banter, and his grateful appreciation when I tucked the red and yellow checked blanket over him and made him sleep. Then I remember him avoiding me at the party, his stand-offishness at school and then today, when he tore into me. Could what Gilly suggested be true? Then another truth rolls its sleeves up and punches any hope I might have to the floor. 'Hang on. Your wild theory might just have worked, but he was cool with me the week he came back to school after the funeral. That was *before* my party. Before he even knew about Liam.'

Gilly strokes a hand down her chin and considers this. Then she sticks a finger in the air in triumph. 'Not if you know what I know!'

'Which is?'

'A few months after the start of the school year, we had a quick meeting, as he's my mentor. Anyway, he asked how you were getting along in your new post and I said you were brilliant and wonderful and everything. Then he casually asked if you were married or had kids, just general stuff.' Gilly stops, takes some wine.

'And?'

'And what?' Her eyes are twinkling with mischief.

'Gill-y…'

'Okay. I said you were a widow, no kids and that you were set to stay single. You couldn't cope with being hurt again.'

'Gilly. For God's sake!'

She flings her arms wide and a splash of wine lands on the stripped-pine floorboards. 'What? That's what you told me.'

'Yeah, but I didn't expect you to blurt it to the deputy head!'

'It was the truth, wasn't it? And you never told me to keep it a secret.'

I heave a sigh of frustration. That's how Jowan knew Sean had died. Gilly. I thought as much at the time, but I hadn't realised she'd told him about me wanting to be single. 'I see.'

Gilly leans forward, her expression troubled. 'So sorry if I did the wrong thing, Joy. It was only a casual conversation. I'd no idea that he liked you.'

'It's okay. He might not, we don't actually know. But if he did, he wouldn't have been pleased that I was with Liam.' Thinking back again over the previous scenes I've just run in my head, I decide there was definitely something between us that day at his – what exactly, I'm not sure. Maybe he thought I'd begin to change my mind about having someone in my life … that there was a chance for us? Then I go and ruin it all with the Liam thing.

Gilly gives me a sympathetic smile. 'It's not too late. Tell him the truth.'

'No chance. If he isn't interested in me, he'll think I've gone nuts. What would it matter to him that I'm not with Liam? Besides, it will take me a long time to forget how horrible he was to me today. Then there's all the Helen thing. If he was interested in me, she would be devastated. We'd be rubbing her nose in it. Imagine what life at work would be like!'

Gilly gives a quick shake of her head. 'You owe Helen nothing, Joy. She only cares about herself. Hard-faced cow.'

'She might be hard-faced, but there's a reason for that. I didn't tell you everything she confessed to me in the summerhouse. Suffice to say, her upbringing wasn't great. Helen's more vulnerable than you might think.'

Gilly snorts, 'Helen, vulnerable?' But she says no more after I give her the raised eyebrow.

I drain my glass and stand up. 'I can't be doing with romance anyway. The blanket-wrapped me was right all along. I'm better off on my own. Much more sensible. Thanks so much for the wine and the chat, Gilly. But I'd best get off now.'

Gilly puts her glass down and asks, 'Who's the blanket-wrapped you?'

'Oh, ignore that. It's just my name for my cautious, sensible side. Wished I'd listened to her instead of being reckless.'

'Hardly reckless,' she says, following me to the door. 'Why don't you let me speak to Jowan? I'm sure I could find out what he thinks without asking him directly and—'

'No way.' I turn from the front door, give her a hard stare. 'Promise me, Gilly. You'll not breathe a word of this to him, or anyone else, come to that. Not even Steve. Okay?'

She puts her hands up in surrender. 'Okay, okay. But I think you're making a mistake. You two are made for each other.'

I open the door and walk through it. 'Yeah. And I'm the Queen of Sheba.'

Chapter Twenty-Two

It's not really the ideal kind of day for a stroll on the beach. The lovely May sunshine we've been spoilt with has abandoned the north Cornwall stage for the past three days and sent a chill wind as its understudy. It feels more like October than almost summer. There's a huddle of dark cloud pinning itself to the low charcoal horizon, and the cold wind is practising spitting a fine mizzle into my face as I stride along the sand. Luckily, I'm wrapped in my big green coat with its snuggly fur-edged hood. Nothing like being prepared. It took me a while to muster the energy to get myself out of the house. But having spent most of the weekend crying over the freshly dug grave in which I've buried the Jowan dilemma, it was crucial that I came down here to allow the elements to blow the cobwebs from my cluttered brain.

I've got used to the faces of the regulars walking this beach. We rarely pass by each other without acknowledgement; mostly we smile, nod, or sometimes say good morning or afternoon. Some walk alone like me, others are in couples or families, but the majority have a dog in tow. And today is no exception. A black and white Collie barks at a caramel Labrador a little way off, and both owners raise a hand to me in acknowledgement. The idea of a dog is very appealing to me. The pure joy they display galloping towards the sea, the wind making waves of their fur, their pink tongues lolling from their mouths as they do their big daft dribbly grins. Dogs love the seaside. Fact. Though the idea of a dog is appealing, the reality isn't. Sebastian, for one, would have something to say about it, and I'd feel bad leaving it in the house all day while I was at work.

Coming towards me in the near distance, slowly but surely, her slight frame battling the wind, head in a purple bobble-hat determinedly thrust forward, as if streamlining might aid her journey, is an elderly lady who always smiles and waves. We've never chatted, but over the last few years we've got as far as exchanging pleasantries about the weather upon passing. But today there's something missing. It's her dog. An elderly dog with stiff back legs and an unsteady gait. A dog that's mostly black but has ginger patches and a grey muzzle. The lady looks incomplete without it … lost.

As we get closer, the lady stops abruptly and looks back to the shoreline. There's a big lolloping dog splashing through the water, barking at its owner as if telling him to hurry up. It's black and brownish, and full of energy. The lady watches it for a while, then her shoulders start to shake and she covers her hands with her face. Then she turns and makes for one of the caves under the cliffs. Now what? Do I follow and see how she is, or walk on? She's obviously upset and might not thank me for sticking my beak in. Watching her retreating back, I make a decision. The poor woman looks so dejected, I can only offer my help, then go on my way if it's not needed.

At the entrance to the cave, I stop and clear my throat so I don't startle her. She's sitting on a boulder just inside, wiping away tears. Raising her head, she sniffs and gives a watery smile in recognition. 'Oh, hello. Don't mind me… I'm having a moment, as people say nowadays.' Blowing her nose on a tissue, she adds, 'You come to get out of the wind?'

'I came to see you, actually. I noticed you were upset on the beach and wondered if I could help.'

The watery smile becomes more substantial and she tucks the tissue into her pocket. 'That's a very nice thing to do. But I'm afraid you can't help me. I have to ride the storm and hope for calmer waters.'

'Are you sure?'

'I am … but I wouldn't mind a chat.' She sticks her hand out. 'I'm Grace, by the way.'

'Joy.' I shake her hand and sit on a boulder nearby.

'Nice name.'

'So's yours.'

Grace opens her mouth then closes it again. She zips her quilted yellow coat down a little at the neck and sighs. 'Not sure where to start…' She tucks a loose strand of long, messy, grey hair under her hat. 'The thing is, it's my dog, Sam … he died last week.'

'Oh, I'm so sorry. I did wonder where he was.'

'He was going on for fifteen, a good age, and he didn't suffer. But I've been devastated. When I heard that young 'un barking just now, I turned to look because he sounded exactly like Sam used to when he was a pup. Resembled him a bit too. Brought everything gushing back, you know?' Fresh tears well in Grace's eyes and I nod. 'When he was a pup, me and my husband Barry used to walk him here. Barry's been gone three years now … we moved down here from up north about twenty years back. It was a dream of ours to retire here. And we bloody did it!' Grace's quick brown eyes are lit with pride and then the light dies. She stares into the mizzle, watching some image only she can see.

'Memories are treasures. They might have sharp edges, like now, and leave deep wounds, but they can be a comfort too. Some might fade a bit, but you'll always have them.'

She nods. 'That's it exactly … you must be no stranger to loss. A shame in one so young.'

'Yes. I lost my husband.' I tell her all about Sean and how much I still miss him.

Grace pats my hand. 'How terrible. I'm eighty, and had my Barry for nearly sixty years. So, I've been very lucky… Sam helped me struggle on after he died, but now … now there's just me and I feel so alone … so alone.' Her lip trembles and she puts her hand over her mouth. 'You must think I'm an ungrateful so-and-so, after losing your love so young.'

As she's been talking, a charcoal aura has draped across her shoulders like a shawl. Sadness again. So many people wearing it in the world and in so many different hues. I want to hug her, but I'm worried that will set her off again, so I say, 'No, of course I don't. You must be devastated, and rightly so. Walking on the beach and seeing that dog has reminded you of everything you've lost.'

'It has. And I know it was a struggle to walk Sam with my arthritis these days … and his.' She gives a little chuckle. 'But at least we were together and enjoying what time we have left.' Grace blinks back more tears. 'Had, in poor Sam's case.'

We sit for a few moments and watch the beach walkers, listening to our thoughts and to the shush of the waves breaking on the shore. Grace is sad, but I think the worst of it is her loneliness. Loneliness is a terrible thing, especially for older people. Some residents at St Margaret's used to tell me that they used to go for weeks sometimes without speaking to a soul, until they moved there. Maybe Grace lives nearby. If she does, I could pop round and slip her the happiness pebble I got from Fiona. It might help a little, a temporary salve to the wound, while I think of a solution to her longer-term problems. 'Do you live near the beach, Grace?'

'Yes, just up the road. I drive up and down now though. Tackling that hill on my own two legs would send me to meet Barry and Sam pretty damn fast!' She laughs and I'm drawn to her. There's a strength and warmth to her character. I can see her becoming a friend.

I explain where I live and we're amazed to find we live

three streets away from each other. 'Wonderful! Can I make dinner for you one evening, Grace? You can meet my crazy cat Sebastian. I'd come and get you, so no need to worry about walking.'

Grace's thoughtful expression threatens to crumble and she loses the shawl. 'Joy, you're so kind. But please don't feel obliged. I'll be okay, honestly. You caught me at a low point, that's all.'

'No obligation at all. I'd love to get to know you better, truly.'

We arrange a date for next Wednesday and walk arm in arm together along the beach. At the end, we both smile as we watch a dancing child, with an aura as bright as the sun, circle her parents, and bow to an imaginary audience. Grace remarks how joyful she is, which is actually pretty accurate, and as we pass the girl, I smell chocolate. Now that's a *great* aura to have. I remember I have some with my name on them at home, I'll open them when I get back! We cross the road and make our way to the carpark at the back of The Merrymoor, and as I wave Grace's little red car off, there's a lift in my mood. Something tells me I've just made a friend for life.

Later that same afternoon I'm in a bubble bath, indulging myself with a glass of red wine, and some chocolates that Liam bought me the other day. He said they were apropos of nothing, apart from the fact that I am one of the most wonderful people he's ever met. That made me smile. It's such a delight having him stay that when he leaves, it will likely feel a bit empty, I think. I'm contemplating washing my hair, when I think I hear a knock on the front door. Straining my ears, I hear a rumble of voices and then footsteps moving inside, towards the living room, as far as I can tell from here in the bathroom.

Who on earth can it be? Must be someone who Liam knows because he's not shouted upstairs to me. God, I hope it's not his dad, because Liam's been coping well so far. A visit from his father might set him back again. Maybe his mum? They talk on the phone often, but he hasn't seen Maggie, as she said it would be 'awkward' if his dad knew. Maybe she's had enough of being told what to do and come over to see her son properly? Could it be my parents? Unlikely, as I spoke to Mum yesterday and we arranged to meet for lunch next weekend. She's still smarting about me not telling the truth about Liam. Maggie told her everything, predictably. So it's not Mum and Dad. Besides, Liam would tell me they were here. I pop another chocolate into my mouth and finish the wine. My hair can wait. I'm too curious to stay here for another second.

A quick rub with a fluffy towel leaves me almost dry, and I slip into my light-blue bathrobe that's seen better days and re-twist my hair up into a messy bun. Some bits are damp, but never mind. Should I get dressed? Nah. I'm putting my PJs on in a bit anyway, so no point. I might not look my best, but I have nobody to impress, whoever it turns out to be. Tiptoeing along the landing, I stop and listen at the top of the stairs. I can hear voices. Liam's I know but I can't make out the other. I'm sure it's male. Must be his dad because he knows nobody else. Liam laughs and then I hear the living room door open.

'Joy!' He calls from the foot of the stairs. 'You have a visitor!'

I have a visitor? Who the hell can it be? I gather the robe tightly to me and descend the first few steps. Liam's at the bottom, eyes full of excitement. 'Who is it?' I whisper.

'Come and find out.' Then before I can ask anything more, he shouts over his shoulder in the direction of the living room. 'She's out of the bath. Won't be a mo!'

I hurry down to him. 'But who is it? I'm in my robe here,' I hiss, sweeping my hand across my body, unnecessarily.

'You'll do. Come on.' He grabs my hand and pulls me along the hallway. He ignores my insistence that he tells me who it is, and intuition is suggesting this might not be a good idea. Liam's excitement is freaking me out, so at the door I hang back, until he gives me a little push into the room. Sitting on the sofa with a huge bunch of yellow roses on his lap is Jowan. He stands up and holds them out to me. He's wearing jeans, a red shirt and a huge smile on his face. His blue eyes are radiating warmth and the Jowan that I remember from the afternoon we spent together is back with a bang. The air between us feels charged with emotion and I've never been so embarrassed about my appearance. Twice he's been to my house and both times I've looked like a dog's dinner. At least I'm not sweaty today.

'Jowan…' I take the flowers. 'Thanks. But why?'

He swaps the smile for a sincere expression. 'Because of my appalling behaviour towards you the other day at school. It's been on my conscience ever since, so I thought some flowers and an apology might help.'

'Oh. Well, I must say I was a bit shocked. But then bullying is a serious issue, and if I wasn't on top of my game...'

Hang on, why am I letting him off the hook?

'Yes, but the incident wasn't as serious as I was making out. It was inexcusable to talk to you in that way. I'm so sorry, Joy.' Jowan gives me an intense stare. So I look away, uncertain what to do or say next.

'Apology accepted.' I smile and nod at the flowers. 'I'll put these in water, and then put the kettle on ... if you want to stay, that is?'

'Already done it,' Liam says, bounding into the room like an overgrown puppy. He snatches the flowers from my hands. 'I can put these in water. You two need to talk.' He gives Jowan a pointed look – causing him to flush pink – and then Liam leaves the room. This is fishy. Very fishy indeed. Jowan sits back down and avoids my eyes.

'Okay. What's going on?' I say, sitting in an armchair opposite. 'What does Liam know that I don't?'

Raising his head, Jowan smiles. 'When I arrived today, I wasn't sure how Liam would take it. You know, me rocking up with flowers for his girlfriend? I explained I was here to apologise, and he more or less dragged me into the house and told me a very odd story. A *very* odd story all about how you and he were not really together. And about how you had feelings for me.' Jowan stops and takes a deep breath. 'Joy, I was over the bloody moon, I can tell you, because I have feelings for you too.'

While he's been speaking, my heartrate has rocketed and now it almost stops in shock. *He has feelings for me?* Oh my God! He has feelings for me! A wave of emotion surges through my body, rendering me speechless. Almost. 'But … but why were you so awful to me the other day, then?'

Jowan shrugs, looks sheepish. 'Because I wanted to hurt you. I was lashing out because Liam had you and I didn't. I was drawn to you from the first time I saw you. When I popped round to drop off the file, remember? Even though you were a bit sweaty from running.' He laughs and I manage a smile.

'Thanks for reminding me, Jowan.'

'You're welcome. Then, the day you wiped paint from my chest – the tipi day, remember?' I did. 'I could feel the attraction between us. It was all I could do to stop myself kissing you there and then in front of your whole damn class.' He laughs again and his cheeks turn pink. 'But it was on the day you came to my house, I thought we might have had something real growing between us, not just lust. I could feel it, or so I thought. But then I remembered that Gilly had told me you wanted to keep single because your husband's death had broken you … and then at your party Liam told me you were with him and … I just saw red. It's been a tricky time, with my mum and whatnot. But that's no excuse.'

He falls silent and my thoughts are in freefall. One is caught and spat out: 'Hang on. Have you been taking to Gilly about this?'

'No. Why?'

'Because what you just said is more or less what she thought about it all.'

'Clever Gilly. Wish she'd told me, 'cos the way I've been feeling and my behaviour has been a proper mystery to me. Until today.'

'Today?'

'Yeah. I woke up and realised that I needed to say sorry to you. I realised I'd been a bloody fool and none of it was your fault. So even though I couldn't have you, I needed to get a grip.' Jowan's face lights up. 'I couldn't believe my ears when Liam told me everything.'

We do stretchy grins across the room at each other for a few seconds and my stomach turns over. Is this really happening? 'Good old Liam.'

'So it's true then … not another daft prank?' Jowan puts his head on one side.

'It's true,' I say, in a wobbly voice. He stands up and so do I, pulling my tatty dressing gown belt tighter, not sure he'd want a full-frontal … or yes, actually, he probably would. 'I wish I was dressed in something a bit nicer,' I laugh and tuck my damp hair behind my ears.

Jowan comes over, takes me in his arms and gazes into my eyes. 'You couldn't look more beautiful now if you were hung in diamonds.'

'I'm not sure I believe—' I begin, but he stops my words with his lips, and I sink into him, breathe in his scent, feel the prickle of his stubble against my cheek. My imagination about such a moment over the past few weeks doesn't come close. We fit together like puzzle pieces, hands roaming, exploring. He's strong, solid, every muscle defined and firm under my fingertips.

'Oops! Sorry. I'll make myself scarce,' comes Liam's voice from the door. We break apart to see him standing there in the doorway, beaming at us with a trayful of mugs.

He backs out, but I say, 'Not so fast, loose lips. I want a word with you.'

Chapter Twenty-Three

The prosecco has gone to my head, but not as much as the emotional high put there by Jowan a few hours ago. Liam was thrilled when, instead of telling him off for having loose lips, I put a smacker on his own and gave him a huge hug. If it hadn't been for him, I doubt Jowan and me would have ever got together. At least not so quickly, at any rate. Liam, ever resourceful, had presented us with some prosecco he'd been saving for an occasion such as this. He'd shared a small glass, and then suddenly remembered he had to pop off to town to get a few essentials.

Jowan's having a chat with Sebastian at the kitchen table, while I make us a bite to eat. Something to soak up the prosecco, but mainly a master plot of mine to keep him here longer. Not that he looks ready to rush off anywhere. Thankfully I'm looking a bit more presentable now, dressed in a floral summer cotton top and jeans. I also managed to apply a bit of mascara and a slick of pink lip gloss. My hair leaves something to be desired, but it could be argued it often does. It's about time I accepted my tawny mane and stopped trying to tame it. I'm washing lettuce in the colander when I feel Jowan come up behind me, lift the weight of my hair and plant some hot lingering kisses along my neck. This does unspeakable things to my libido and I step to one side. 'Hey, that's going to put me off making the dinner,' I say with a chuckle.

He gives me a quizzical glance. 'Too much too soon?'

Is it? Perhaps. There's still the Helen avalanche ready to slide down the mountain. I'm loath to watch it happen, but I have to share her information with Jowan. There's no other way, is there? 'Too soon?' I shake a lettuce leaf at his nose and he brushes away the water droplets with a wry smile. 'I'm not sure. My instinct is telling me to take things slowly.'

Jowan's eyes shine with passion and he traces a fingertip across my lips. 'Hm. My instincts are telling me something else entirely.' Then he goes back to Sebastian. 'But, yes, I think you're right. We need to get to know each other properly. I haven't the first idea about your life, your family, your friends, what you like to do – hobbies and so forth, for example.'

I bring the chopping board over to the table, sit opposite and slice some tomatoes. 'You met my family and many of my friends at the party.'

He tickles Seb under the chin. 'Yeah, but I wasn't there long enough to have a proper chat though.'

'I noticed. How come you rushed off?'

'After Liam told me you and he were together, I had to

get out of there.' Jowan shrugs. 'Wish I'd known the truth then.'

Raising my head, I hold his gaze. 'I'm really sorry about that. But...' I put the knife down and clear my throat. 'There's some other stuff you need to know before we can really start this relationship properly. It affects work and—'

Jowan holds up a silencing finger as if I'm one of the children at school. 'I've thought of that. We should carry on as if nothing's happened for a while. We can't let everyone know about us until...' He rubs his chin, looks thoughtful. 'Well. Until we're sure we're serious.' I open my mouth, but he carries on in earnest, his words tumbling out in a rush: 'Hey. I hope that doesn't sound presumptuous, or that I'm giving the impression that I don't think we *will* be serious. Because that's not it, I just mean that...'

My own silencing finger shuts him up. 'I know exactly what you mean, and I agree. We don't want the added pressure of people gossiping about us.' I take his hand and give it a squeeze. Relief flows through me, because now I don't have to tell Jowan about Helen's secret love for him. 'Gilly will have to know, because she'll guess anyway, and she's been a good friend to me. She's the soul of discretion though.'

'Okay. Not sure I'll mention it to Helen ... she's been very supportive lately over my mum and so forth. But not sure she needs to know ab—'

'No!' I say, louder than I'd intended.

Jowan's eyebrows shoot up and he sits back, his cool blue eyes searching my face. 'O-kay. Is there a problem?'

'No.' A high-pitched laugh escapes me which hangs in

the air between us like an admission of guilt. I can almost see the suspicion gathering in his head. Never any good at telling bare-faced fibs to someone's face, I grab the chopping board and take it over to the worktop. 'No problem at all,' I say over my shoulder, opening the fridge and rummaging inside for nothing at all. At least the cold is cooling my cheeks. 'It's only that I want things to remain between us. Helen's a bit bossy with me sometimes, and I don't want her sticking her oar in. Please don't tell her anything.'

'Of course I won't, if you don't want me to. Promise.'

If I look at him, he'll see the truth trying to wriggle out from behind the lie in my eyes, so I take some chicken breasts out of the fridge and still with my back to him ask, 'Spicy chicken kebabs, rice and salad, do you think?'

'Wow. Sounds delicious. Beautiful and a good cook – how lucky am I?'

'You haven't tasted it yet,' I reply with a chuckle. Phew. Think I've managed to get out of that one.

———

Just before breaktime on Monday morning, I'm in the store cupboard at the back of the classroom stacking some books when Gilly startles me by shooting in and grabbing my arm. 'Spill it, Pentire,' she hisses, checking behind to ensure none of the children are around. 'And don't tell me there's nothing to spill.'

'Eh? I've no idea what you're on about.'

'Don't give me that.' Gilly's hazel eyes narrow, and she

prods me in the shoulder. 'I saw the way you and Jowan looked at each other in assembly. Mooning across the hall at each other like lovesick teenagers.'

Heat sends a flare to my cheeks. Had we been mooning? Maybe we had… This is bad news. If Gilly noticed, then Helen might have. 'Um … let's say things have moved on a bit since we spoke on Friday. I was going to tell you at breaktime.'

'I knew it!' Gilly punches the air and jumps up and down.

'Shh!' I point behind her towards the classroom. 'We don't want anyone to know yet, especially Helen.'

'Jowan knows about her?'

'No. I managed to swerve it so far, but he agrees we need to carry on as normal until we're totally sure it's going to work between us.'

She chuckles. 'The carrying on as normal has gone well so far then. Especially in assembly.' Gilly flutters her eyelashes, pulls a lovesick face and makes a heart shape of her thumbs and forefingers.

Despite the worry of Helen finding out, I have to laugh. 'Hm, we'll have to be more careful, obviously.'

'Okay. Tell me all about it. How you miraculously got together this weekend. What he said. What you said. All. Of. It.'

'Gilly. We're in a stock cupboard with a classroom full of kids outside. I'll tell you at break.'

'You have a point. But just tell me this. Did you do the deed?' Gilly does lewd movements with her pelvis just as Callum Pengelley appears at the door picking his nose.

'No we didn't! And I think Callum needs help with his spellings.' I flash my eyes at her and point to the door.

Gilly stops thrusting her pelvis and spins round. 'You okay, there, Callum?' Her voice sounds like she borrowed it from Mickey Mouse.

'Yes, Miss. Why were you doing that wiggly dance? And is doing the deed like the good deeds people do when they're helping others?'

'Um, yes. Yes, it is.' She shoots a guilty glance at me and walks towards him. 'Come on, let's see your spellings.'

'Why didn't you do the deed, Miss Pentire? I thought you liked to help people.'

Any sensible reply escapes me as I stare at him, mute. Then I'm literally saved by the bell ringing for break and Gilly dismisses the class. Afterwards, she collapses at her desk in fits of giggles. I stand in front of her, arms folded. 'Bloody hell, Gilly. It's not funny. What if he tells his parents?'

'Don't be daft, he won't. He'll have forgotten all about it by now. And it *is* funny. It's hilarious!' She howls again and it's infectious. We both crack up together for a good few minutes. Once we've recovered, we go to the staffroom for coffee. On the way, I text Jowan and tell him not to even look at me and the reason why. Then I add a heart and three kisses.

In a quiet corner of the staffroom, Gilly is suitably satisfied after I quickly tell her all about Jowan coming to the house to apologise and Liam's part in it all. She still can't understand why I haven't slept with him yet. Straight away I tell her it's because we both decided to take things slowly, and when the time is right, we'll know. But her words have planted a seed or two of doubt. Jowan clearly wanted to take things further yesterday when he was kissing the back of my neck. It was me that stopped it, mentioned taking things slow. After a few moments' deliberation I decide that maybe it's because of Sean. Maybe in some distant corner of my psyche, there's the idea that I'd be betraying him. He's gone. I know that, but I still feel married to him. I'm still wearing my rings.

Gilly's talking to me about something, but I'm not really paying much attention. I turn my wedding and engagement rings around and around my finger, remembering my wedding day and the look in Sean's eyes as I said 'I do.' Guilt floods through me like a tsunami. I've barely thought of him lately. My mind has been too full of Jowan. A familiar tightening in my throat threatens to push a few tears into my eyes, so I take a gulp of coffee to wash it away.

'So, I think it might be really worthwhile. Would you be interested in helping now and then?'

Raising my head from my rings, I look at Gilly's expectant face. 'Sorry? Helping with what?'

She rolls her eyes. 'I knew I was talking to myself. Me and my neighbour Sally are going to set up a story-telling group in our local church hall. She's an ex-teacher who does counselling with women and children who've left violent relationships and live in the refuge in town.' Gilly smiles. 'It was my idea. Just came to me out the blue when I was chatting to Sally about her work. The children could write and tell stories and do other creative stuff too. It will be a safe outlet for their emotions. Their mums could join in too, if they liked.'

My spirits lift. So that's Gilly's random act of kindness, I'd been wondering what she'd do. 'It's a wonderful idea, and yes I'd be pleased to come along and help sometimes.'

As we're getting up to go back to class, Helen comes in and looks like she's searching the staffroom for someone. Her gaze lands on Jowan and she studies him for some time. He's oblivious, sipping his coffee and chatting to Holly, one of the student teachers we have this term on placement. I watch him too. It's hard not to, his bright-blue eyes crinkling at the corners in a smile, the way he raises his hand and runs it through his dark curls. Holly tosses her long blonde hair and puts her hand on his arm as she laughs coquettishly at something he said. Unbidden, a tickle of pride swells my chest. *You can't have him, Holly. He's mine.* Jowan looks over at me then and shoots me a look that's both intense and steamy. Unable to stop myself, I smoulder back and do a pouty smile. When I look back to Helen, I see she's no longer watching Jowan. She's watching me.

Chapter Twenty-Four

I t's Wednesday already and I've not seen Jowan. Well, I've seen him at school, obviously, but he had prior engagements he couldn't get out of last night and Monday. He suggested I went round to his tonight, but I have Grace coming over for dinner. If I'd wanted to, I could have rearranged. Grace wouldn't have minded, I'm sure. But something stopped me. If I'm honest, Sean did. Or his memory. The guilt of betraying him. Every time I think about Jowan or have a long, lovely chat on the phone, as we have been doing daily since Sunday, there's a voice whispering in my ear that it will never work. It will never work because I'm still in love with Sean. And Helen. Let's not forget her. Helen's always there, hovering in the background. Scowling in my mind's eye when my heart skips a beat upon hearing his sexy voice down the line, or if I see him across the staffroom.

As I prepare a lasagne and a mixed salad, the idea that Helen's on to us won't go away. I saw it in her eyes on

Monday when she clocked me watching Jowan and Holly. She hasn't said anything, but maybe she's biding her time. Since then, I've been extra careful not to look at Jowan for longer than a nanosecond. He's not so careful though. A case in point is when he popped into the classroom this morning and gave me a cheeky wink. It's a wonder Callum, David or Ellie didn't pounce on that. They didn't, thankfully. But they will eventually. Maybe I have to nip this thing in the bud before it's actually got off the ground. There's the guilt eating me up on the one hand, and the untenable work situation on the other. It's doomed to fail.

After I pop the lasagne in the oven, I'm about to grab my car keys and get Grace, when a text comes through from her. She's on her way and will be five minutes. It's a fine late-spring evening, but there's a nip in the air and she does have trouble with her arthritis. So maybe I should drive down and pick her up anyway? I decide to call her, when there's a knock on the door. A grinning Grace is standing there dressed in a tan jacket, sparkly red top, black jeans and holding a bottle of brandy. Her silver-grey hair, which on the beach the other day was long and messy, has been expertly cut into a choppy chin-length bob and she's wearing subtle make-up too. 'It's not often I get asked out for dinner, so I brought this! Hence me leaving Tommy at home.'

'Tommy?' I ask, showing her in.

'My car,' she says, with a chuckle. 'It's tomato-red. So, Tommy. I always name my cars.'

'You look lovely, Grace. New hair-do?'

She smiles and pats her hair. 'Yes. I fancied a change.'

'It really suits you. And it would have been no bother to pick you up, you know.' I hang her jacket on the peg and take the brandy.

'I know, but it is literally a cut through the field. I bet I could beat you on foot, if you go the long way round in the car. Ooh, and what's that delicious smell coming from the kitchen?'

Grace's bubbly personality is infectious. She's lost her sadness from the other day and is wandering around my cottage complimenting me on my taste and style of decor and the general ambience of my home. 'Glad you like it, Grace.'

'Like it? I love it. My place is nice, but it needs brightening up a bit. I might get some colourful throws like you have on that sofa.' She points at the throw and then notices Sebastian's big green eyes watching her from Sean's chair. 'Oh, my! What a gorgeous cat. What's his name?' She goes over and gives him a tentative stroke.

'Sebastian. He's my baby and I adore him.' I kneel in front of him and take his big fury face between my hands, plant a kiss on his nose, which he's not too sure about and twists out of my grasp.

Grace goes over to the kitchen table and pulls out a chair, leans an elbow on the back of it. 'Yes. I can see how much you adore him,' she says, matter of fact. 'Your aura is pure love. Pink and lemon, smells like Battenburg.'

The bottom drops out of my stomach and I'm glad I'm kneeling, because I'm sure my legs wouldn't hold me right now. We stare at each other and then I manage, 'What… what did you just say?'

'I think you heard me, judging by your face.' Grace chuckles and sits down at the table. 'Hope you don't mind me making myself comfy, I can't stand for long.'

'You can see auras? Smell them?'

'Yes. And so can you.'

My hand flies to my mouth and I can't speak, but my thoughts are many and shouty and crash into each other, until a rising panic in my belly makes me nauseous. How the *hell* does she know? Hope told me I should never talk to anyone else about collecting, so if Grace is a collector, why is she? But she might not be a collector. She might only see auras … but that still doesn't answer the question of how she knows that I can see them too.

'Take a few deep breaths, lovely,' Grace says, hurrying over to the sink and running the tap. 'You've gone a bit pale.' She hands me the glass. 'Drink it and then take more deep breaths. I shouldn't have sprung it on you, like that. Silly old fool, I am.'

Grasping the glass, it's a few seconds before I can steady my hand enough to bring the water to my lips without spilling it. While I drink, she looks at me, worry clouding her sparkly brown eyes. When I feel I can, I say, 'How did you know that I can see auras?'

She puts her head on one side, bird-like, and ponders. 'I wasn't absolutely sure until today. But on the beach when we met that day, I noticed that you were glancing at all the people we passed who had auras. I thought it could just be coincidence, but I was almost certain when we reached the end of the beach, and saw the little girl who was dancing with the bright-yellow one. It was pure joy and the smell of chocolate was really strong. You muttered "chocolate" under your breath.'

My mouth drops open. 'I did?'

'Yes.'

I shake my head in bewilderment. Am I dreaming? 'What did you mean about you weren't absolutely sure until today?'

'Well. It was possible that you muttered the word "chocolate" because you wanted some, but a gut instinct told me you were like me.'

'Yes, but you still haven't said what happened today to make you sure.'

Grace points at my big jar of pebbles on the side next to the kettle. 'I saw those. You're a collector, aren't you, Joy?' She smiles and sits down at the table again.

Oh. My. God. 'I … I … I need a glass of that bloody brandy.'

A few minutes later I'm looking at the bottom of an empty glass and considering another. Grace is sipping hers slowly. She raises her glass. 'This is the main reason I brought a bottle. Something told me you might need it.'

'Let me check to see the lasagne isn't burning, and then I have a few questions or fifty to ask you.' Deciding it needs another ten minutes, I bring the salad and garlic bread to the table. Then I go back for the brandy. My gran used to say it was for medicinal purposes and that's good enough for me.

'Can I pinch a bit of garlic bread, Joy? I'm a little peckish.'

'Go for it. I will too.' We crunch into the bread and chew

thoughtfully for a few moments. Then I say, 'Right. First of all, Hope, the lady who bequeathed me the death-bed gift of collecting, told me never to speak of it, or I'd lose it. Is that your understanding?'

'Yep. Old Constance said the same to me. She was my mum's neighbour and was most insistent that I didn't tell.'

I'm incredulous. 'Then why the hell did you?'

'Because it's permitted to tell another collector.' Grace dabs garlic butter from the side of her mouth with a bit of kitchen roll. 'This is something I discovered a good twenty years into my collecting. Constance passed it on when I was seventeen, and I'd kept it secret. When I got married, I was desperate to tell Barry a few times, but knew it would mean the end of it. If I couldn't help people anymore, my life would only be half a life. I love it so. Do you?'

'I do. It's so rewarding.'

'Yes.' Grace's eyes twinkle and she says through a mouthful of bread, 'I don't get the opportunity as much nowadays, it's difficult to go places to meet people at my age, and with my arthritic knees. But I still try to help as many as I can.'

I'm beginning to realise that Grace goes around the houses and meanders off in different directions instead of explaining her main points. 'You said it was a good twenty years later that you discovered it was permitted. How?'

'Ah yes. It happened a bit like it did with me and you. I'd taken our dog for a walk round the park. Not Sam. No, this was years ago. Herbert was his name. He was an Alsatian and such a soppy lad. He was always stopping and talking to people. Well, when I say talking, I mean he'd lope up to them and lick their hand or drop a ball at their feet for them to throw.'

A faraway expression finds a home on Grace's face and she takes another bite of bread. 'And what happened at the park?' I prompt.

'Sorry, Joy. I tend to drift off these days. I live in the past more than is good for me.' She sighs. 'Anyway, our Herbert goes running up to this old lady sitting on a bench in the park and licks her hand. She laughs and pats him. When I catch up to him, I apologise, as some people don't like dogs just bounding up. But she says she thinks he's lovely. I give Herbert a cuddle and say I think he is too. She nods and says that she could see that. She was watching us apparently, playing ball in the park, and she said my aura was delightful.'

'Wow. I bet that was a shock,' I say and get up to take the lasagne out. While I'm getting plates and drinks, Grace tells me that the old lady asked if she was a collector and explained that she'd been told by her bequeather, that if she ever met another collector, it was fine to share her experiences. The lady, Faith, also said that she'd know instinctively when she met one.

'But I didn't know about you,' I say, bringing the lasagne to the table.

'And I didn't know about Faith. But I knew about you. I think it's something that must come with age.'

'Maybe.' I put a helping of lasagne onto Grace's plate and pass the salad. 'I did feel like we would be good friends, though.'

Grace beams. 'Oh, me too. Faith died shortly after we

met, so we didn't have long to chat about our experiences. But meeting you at the weekend really perked me up. I went and had my hair done, bought a new top. Put myself back in the land of the living. I'd been so miserable, and you were like a ray of sunshine.'

'That's wonderful,' I say with a smile. We dig in. 'There's more questions than answers with this aura seeing, and collecting in general, I've found. For example, why do I only smell some auras and not others?'

'No idea. I've given up trying to understand it, and I've been doing it for over sixty years.'

'And why do we see others' auras, but not our own?'

'Again. No idea.' Grace takes a big forkful of food and closes her eyes to savour it. 'This lasagne is really fantastic, Joy. I could eat another helping!'

'You're welcome to, there's loads.'

'Don't tempt me.'

'I am a bit worried that so far all I've had are successes, and I'm a bit scared that something's bound to go wrong soon.'

'It does go wrong. But not very often. Because what's the point of having the power to help people if it keeps going wrong, and you leave the poor buggers more in a pickle than they were before you gave them a pebble?'

I chew this over with my food for a moment or two, hoping she's right. 'How many missions have you had go wrong in sixty years, Grace?'

She shuts her eyes and furrows her brow as she considers my question. 'Er, I suppose about seven or so … possibly ten? And nothing that was life or death.'

This is comforting. I'm not sure if I could cope with too many disasters. 'Right. And did you ever meet another collector apart from Faith?'

'One. About ten years ago. Charity. She was lovely, emigrated to Australia though, and I do miss chatting about our collecting.'

'Well you have me now, so all's good.' I chuckle when I remember one of the reasons why I asked Grace to dinner. 'And to think I planned to slip you a happiness pebble later. Not sure you need it now anyway.'

She dabs her mouth and pushes her plate away. 'Do you know, I really don't think I do. Don't get me wrong, I'm still sad about losing Sam, but I've got a new perspective on things now, thanks to you.' She drains her glass and smiles. 'Now, tell me all about you. About your life, your job, everything.'

While I cut Grace a slice of lemon meringue pie and make coffee, I tell her all about Sean, my parents, friends, and my job. I keep Jowan out of it, apart from mentioning his name when explaining who works with me. I skim over Helen too. No point in bringing all that misery into our cheerful dinner. In turn, Grace tells me more about her life and I find she used to be a nurse many years ago. I can see how she'd be suited to a job like that. She has a calming way about her. I'm about to ask if she'd like more pie or coffee when she startles me by saying:

'My guess is, you need the happiness pebble more than I do. Is there someone special in your life, Joy? I feel there might be, but you're holding back. Keeping him secret.'

How on earth does she know that? This energy collecting hasn't morphed into clairvoyance, has it?

'I… Yes, but how do you know?'

'When you mentioned the deputy head, Jowan, a flash of scarlet edged with magenta surrounded you. One of the most dramatic declarations of love I've ever seen.' Grace's eyes crinkle at the corners as mine grow moist. 'But as you buried him under the names of others, the aura faded to grey and disappeared.'

I heave a deep sigh and tell her everything. How could I not?

'So the idea of hurting Helen is stopping you two from being together?'

'She's just one thing. There's feeling guilty about Sean, as I said, and the fact we work together. If it didn't work out, the situation would be very awkward.'

'Yes, but if you don't try, you'll never know, will you?' Grace gets up and pours us a couple of brandies. 'And Helen will have to cope with it, I'm afraid. You're always putting others first, Joy. Even I can tell that and I've not known you five minutes. You deserve to be happy. Sean would want you to be happy. I understand the guilt thing, but it will fade as love takes over. You just have to let it. Stop fighting it off as if it's a deadly virus. Live up to your name, embrace the joy and shake off that dark cloak of misery you're wearing.' She gives both my shoulders a quick brush down with her hands and raises her glass.

'I'm wearing a dark cloak?' I take a sip of brandy, relish the fire-path it cuts down my throat, and cup my hands around the wide bowl.

'You were. It's receding now.'

'Must be the brandy.'

'Must be.'

We sit and sip. Sip and sit for another few minutes. The silence between us is comfortable, contemplative. Grace's calm is transferring through it, settling in my head, my chest, my heart. Jowan deserves a chance. I deserve a chance. We deserve a chance *together*. Grace swirls the last of her amber liquid around her glass and tips it to her mouth. 'Okay. I'll pop off. I've had a lovely time, but I don't want to outstay my welcome.'

The clock on the microwave says just past eight thirty. 'It's not late. Surely you can stay a bit longer?'

'I'm an old woman, Joy. I'm in bed by half-nine most nights. And this is a school night – literally, for you! I'll stay a bit longer next time. Or you come to me.'

'You're welcome any time.'

'Thank you, dear.' Grace shrugs her coat on and Sebastian looks up from Sean's chair by the fireplace. 'It's been lovely to meet you too,' she says, going through the alcove into the living room to stroke him. 'You must be such a comfort to your mummy.' Sebastian purrs and bumps his head into her hand.

'Will you get another dog, Grace?'

'No. There's no way I could walk a puppy. Too lively, And I wouldn't want an older dog. They're too set in their ways, like us. Besides, I couldn't walk an older dog properly either, if I'm honest.'

'How about a cat? They are very independent; all you need is a cat door. And they are very loving, as you've seen with this one here.' I tickle Seb under the chin and he rolls upside down, looks at us both with his big green saucer eyes.

'Hmm. I've always been a dog person ... but we did have a cat when I was little. Lovely old moggy, she was.' Grace shakes Sebastian's paw and laughs.

I think it would be a great idea. And I know just the person who has some gorgeous kittens she needs homes for.

———

An hour later, I'm sitting with my feet up on the sofa, wondering if I should have another brandy. It would probably be a bad idea, but the others were only tiny ones. I'm feeling very pleased with myself, so I deserve a reward. Fiona was really thrilled when I phoned to say that Grace might want a kitten. I said I'd take Grace round there at the weekend to look at them. And I'm feeling much better about making a go of it with Jowan. I'll phone him in a moment and have a quick chat about it. Or shall I? Maybe it can wait. An image of his lovely face comes to mind and I close my eyes, savour it. Remember the smell of his skin, the feel of his lips on mine, the sound of his laughter.

Opening my eyes, I look at my wedding and engagement rings, turn them round on my finger and something shifts inside me. I take a big breath, let it out slowly and admit to myself that it's time. It's time and I need to take them off. Take them off and keep them safe, exactly the way I do with Sean's memory. Grace put the seal of approval on the decision I've been putting off for a few months now. As she said earlier, it's time I allowed myself some happiness. I deserve it. Sean will always be with me. He has a piece of my heart that will never be anyone else's. His memory, his love is sacred. Always was, always will be. I twist the rings off and fold them into my palm. My finger's base has a white band of skin and it looks naked, like it doesn't belong to me. Then, before I can change my mind, I go upstairs and put the rings in my bedside cabinet.

Back downstairs, I pour that brandy and grab my phone. There's a gardenful of butterflies in my belly churning my nerves to mush, but I quickly scroll to Jowan's number. Is this wise? No. No, but like the waves rushing to the shore nearby, my decision is unstoppable.

'Joy. Great to hear from you. Did your dinner go well?'

'It was lovely, thanks. I was wondering if you wanted to come over for a nightcap.' Did I really say that? I hold my breath, listen to my heart thump in my ears.

After a few beats he asks in a low voice, 'What, now?'

'Yes.'

'I'll be there in five.'

Chapter Twenty-Five

From a crack in the curtain, a golden finger of sunlight caresses the finely muscled arm of the man lying beside me. At this early hour, the rest of my room belongs to sleepy grey shadows and the gentle in and out of Jowan's breathing. I've been awake for twenty minutes now, gazing at his sleeping form, listening to the dawn chorus and the sound of him breathing, relishing this quiet time before my alarm clock squeals into action. I flick the button to off and close my eyes. But it won't help to hide. It's almost six-thirty and I know that once the curtains are opened, the bright early sunshine will flood the room, heralding the day, signalling our time together hidden from the world is over. Just a few more minutes, then I'll wake him.

What a wonderful night it was, though. I snuggle down under the quilt. Our first night, and hopefully many more to come. My worries of feeling guilt and betrayal were unfounded as he led me to bed. It was passionate, exhilarating, beautiful. Afterwards, he held me as if he never meant to let go, said how much he needed me, wanted me. How had I ever believed I could push him away? Making love with him was as natural as breathing to me. Grace said that Sean would want me to be happy and she's right. I can sense it … maybe that's why I don't feel guilty anymore. Being with Jowan feels so right. I remember Hope's words too. She said happiness was within my grasp. She was right too.

'Morning, my beautiful sleepyhead,' Jowan says, ending my ponderings and brushing my cheek with his lips. 'Time to get up. It's almost six-forty.'

'Sleepyhead? I've been awake ages,' I say with a smile, and stretch my arms above my head. In doing so, the quilt falls away from my naked breasts.

Jowan stares at my chest and moans, 'Oh God. Don't do that or we'll both be very late for school, and how would that look to Helen? Both of us rocking up with big satisfied grins on our faces.'

'I don't care.' Our eyes lock and I reach my hand up around his neck, stroke my fingers through his curls and tighten my grip. My need for him is both physical and cerebral. I want to consume him totally, feel him inside me, his whole being coursing through my blood until we are one. Increasing pressure on his neck, I bring his face to mine, open his mouth with my tongue and stroke my fingers slowly down his chest. The contact from every muscle and contour sends little electric shocks.

A moan escapes him and he pulls back slightly. 'God, Joy. I want you so much, but we are going to be seriously late.'

I know he's right, but there's a devil driving me. Relaxing back against the pillows, I give him an intense stare, part my legs, trace a finger over my breasts and say, 'Okay. We'd better not, then.'

Eyes lit with raw passion, he covers my body with his. 'You are so bad for me, Miss Pentire, but so very, very good.' Then his kisses ignite every part of me until we're both lost in the fire.

A little while later, I say, 'Come on. Why are you still lazing here in bed? We'll be late!' I laugh, ruffle his hair and swing my legs out of bed. Slipping into my dressing gown, I wonder if Helen will make a thing out of us arriving late. It will only be about ten minutes, but we don't want to draw attention. Then a pang of regret that I had to tell Jowan about Helen surfaces. There was no choice though. If we are to have any chance of a successful relationship, we must keep it from her at all costs. Now Jowan knows the seriousness of it, he will be able to do a much better job of keeping his feelings for me hidden. He'll have to. As will I. Jowan wasn't really surprised about her, actually. He said he knew she was carrying a bit of a torch, even though she'd not mentioned anything since the first time she'd asked him out. But there had been glances and touches which he could tell were more than friendly. He wasn't interested, never had been. I impressed upon him the importance of keeping his feelings about her interest in him secret too. We agreed it isn't going to be an easy ride, but we'd get there.

Breakfast over, Jowan gives Sebastian a cuddle and sits in Sean's chair to do it. This is where the guilt kicks in then. Or is it just sadness? Emotion swells in my throat and I busy myself at the sink. If this happens every time a memory is triggered, I'll be a blubbering mess each day. Then I tell myself again that Sean would want me to be happy. Maybe I need to allow these feelings to be acknowledged and accepted. It was Sean's chair, but now it's not. Because Sean is gone. Gone physically, but he will always be with me. Jowan's hand on my shoulder makes me jump. 'Oh, I didn't hear you come over. Would you like more tea?'

'No thanks, we haven't time. I need to pop back to mine to have a very fast shower and change my clothes.' He drops a kiss on my lips. 'I'll see you at work.' Then he lifts a finger. 'Actually, make that – I'll ignore you at work, Miss Pentire.'

'Ditto, Mr Williams.' We kiss and I follow him to the front door.

As he's about to go through it he turns and says, 'Thanks for a wonderful evening, Joy. Can't wait to do it again very soon. I'll call you later.'

'I'll look forward to it, Jowan.' As I watch him walk away down the sunlit path, my heart soars higher than the seagull gliding through the blue above his head.

Thankfully we are both better actors now there's so much at stake. Jowan has barely glanced in my direction all week, and when I had to ask his advice on one of the children, he was very professional and just gave me a brief smile at the end of our conversation. Gilly thinks the whole situation is hilarious and whispers innuendo in my ear whenever he's near. It's funny. But it does unnerve me a little. Helen might get suspicious if she keeps it up. Unlikely though; why would she? Every evening except one this week has been spent either at mine or Jowan's, where we've been far from professional. And now on Saturday morning, I'm on my way to pop Grace over to see Fiona's kittens. Jowan's cooking for me tonight, and then we're going to drive down to Sennen early Sunday morning, before anyone is out and about, for a nice walk on the beach. It's far enough away from where we live. A shame we can't be seen together, but there we are.

Grace is suitably impressed on the drive over when she discovers Jowan and I have moved our relationship on. She gives me a knowing smile when I open the car door for her outside Fiona's. 'I thought you had a certain glow about you that wasn't there last time I saw you, Joy. It's the kind of glow only one thing can give you.'

'What's that?' I ask, expecting her to say 'love'. Although I'm not sure I'm quite at that stage.

'Sex,' she says, and laughs at my shocked expression.

'Grace Orwin, I'm astonished that you should suggest such a thing!'

She gets out of the car and looks me in the eye. 'Don't

give me that. You've been at it like rabbits!' Then her face creases with laughter and she sets me off.

'What's so hilarious?' comes Fiona's voice from the doorway.

'Nothing,' I say, wiping the corners of my eyes. 'Just something Grace said.'

'Hm. Well, I bet it was something inappropriate or you'd tell me.' Fiona holds her hand out to Grace. 'Hi, I'm Fiona, or Catwoman, if you prefer. I'm one of Joy's oldest friends and she'd be lost without me, don't you know?' Fiona does the plait tossing and I can tell Grace doesn't quite know how to take her theatrics.

'She's always like this, don't worry,' I say, taking Grace's arm and guiding her down Fiona's hallway to the kitchen. 'Such a drama queen.'

'*She* is in the room, you know, and she *can* hear.'

Grace smiles. 'I can tell you're full of fun, Fiona, and I'm sure you are a great Catwoman too.'

'See!' Fiona jabs a finger through the air at me. 'Someone who appreciates me.'

I give her a wink, thankful that we're back to normal after my outburst a few weeks back when she pressed me over Jowan. I've phoned her since, apologised, and told her she was right and Jowan and I are together. Fiona doesn't bear grudges, thank goodness.

We go through into the large sunny living room and at one end, near the patio doors, is a big basket full of wriggling fluff and big saucer eyes. Five kittens varying in colour from ginger to black are at play, some feeding, while their mother, a grey tabby, looks less than enthusiastic. She has the expression of many new mothers – exhausted, bewildered and ready for some time alone. 'Oh my goodness,' Grace says, crouching down next to the basket. 'Aren't they totally adorable?'

'They are,' Fiona says, picking three wriggling bodies up in her arms. 'These three are spoken for, the other two are going spare.'

Kneeling down, I peer at them both. One is black and white; one is ginger and white. They both have huge green eyes and send us cute little meows from sugar-pink mouths. 'So gorgeous. I'd not be able to choose.' I glance up at Fiona. 'Girls or boys?'

'Two boys.'

'Easier when it comes to neutering,' Grace says, thoughtfully.

'Which do you like best?' I ask, picking up the ginger-and-white one and handing him to Grace.

She kisses the top of his head and inhales his fresh kitteny smell. Then she picks the other one up and does the same. 'I can't decide, they are such sweethearts.'

'They have another week before they can leave Mum. I can let you know if anyone else is interested, if you want time to think?' Fiona says. Then she points through the doors into the garden at a large ginger cat. 'There's Dad. He does bugger all to help. Typical male.'

Grace fixes me with her sparkly brown eyes and cocks her head to the side. 'I might take both, Joy. What do you think?'

'Two cats. Are you sure they won't be too much for you?'

Fiona raises an eyebrow and smiles. 'From what I've seen of Grace, I think she knows what she's doing.'

Grace smirks. 'Not sure about that, but I think it would be nice to have two little monkeys around the place. They can keep each other company when I go shopping.' Rubbing her cheek on the heads of the two little monkeys, she asks in a baby voice, 'Can't you, eh? You can, yes. Yes. You can.' They both meow back at her and she laughs. 'I reckon it's a done deal.'

We stay for coffee and then I take Grace back to her house. She has a cosy home, Cornish stone and set back from the road along a beautiful front garden burgeoning with early summer flowers. As we walk along her path, I see a huge clump of agapanthus in a barrel tub to the side of her front door. I adore them and have some blue ones by my back door. They aren't yet in bloom, and neither are Grace's, but the green buds are lined with white edges, a kiss of the promise to come. 'White aggies,' I say and gently stroke the edges of one of the spears.

'You call them aggies too?' Grace shields her eyes against the sun and smiles at me. 'I call mine Madam Agatha Panthers to her face, but behind her back, it's plain Aggie.'

'Shh, she'll hear you.'

I receive a withering look. And in a heavy Yorkshire accent she says, 'I'm not sure who's daftest. Me or thee.'

The inside of the cottage is quite small; the decor needs a lick of paint and the furnishings are worn, but the ambience is welcoming. Grace lives here, so it would be. 'It's lovely,

Grace,' I say, and sit on her two-seater flowery patterned sofa.

Slipping her coat onto the back of a dining chair, she shakes her head at me. 'It's not lovely, by any stretch of the imagination. It's seen better days, like me.' She gives a wheezy chuckle. 'But it's comfortable. Like I said when I came to yours, it needs a brighten-up. Will you help think of some ideas?'

'Of course I will. You'd better not have anything too posh, though, until the kittens grow up a bit. They have very sharp little claws and get into everything. I once found Sebastian hanging upside down behind the curtains. He'd got a claw stuck and yelled his head off.'

Grace laughs. 'Now, can I get you a gin and tonic?'

'Eh? No thanks. It's only half-three in the afternoon. I'd planned to have a nice bath too before going to Jowan's.'

Her face falls. 'Oh. I won't keep you long but I did want a chat about collecting. Gin will help me concentrate.'

'Gin helps you concentrate. Really? If I didn't know better I'd think you were using that as an excuse.'

'Moi?' she feigns offence. 'I hardly touch a drop of alcohol these days.' Then she gives me a cheeky wink and hurries into the kitchen.

Gin in hand, we toast the imminent arrival of Tom and Jerry, the names Grace has given to the kittens. Then she takes a sip of her drink and stares into space. After a few moments I prompt. 'You said you wanted to talk about collecting.'

'Hmm. I was wondering where you got your energies from. Do you get them by chance, or go actively looking?'

'Both. I sourced some courage from a lovely old gentleman whom I used to know when I worked at St Margaret's. He'd been at the D-Day landings. Often it's by chance, though. Fiona came to tell me she's getting married and I grabbed a pebbleful of happiness while I could. Still got it, unused. It had your name on it, as you know.' I smile and take another sip of my drink.

'But you don't have a stock of fully charged pebbles, just waiting?'

'No. I have just the one right now.'

'So that jar of pebbles at your house is just a jar of pebbles?' Grace frowns.

'Well, yes.' I'm beginning to feel like I'm doing something wrong.

She nods. 'Yes, I thought as much. I used to do the same, particularly when I was working full time. I was always too busy to build a stock. But that's what you should be doing. If you collect and then redistribute randomly, then it's easier to help more people. You don't always have to meet the person you're going to help, though of course, you can and do. But it's often strangers that will benefit. Besides, doing one at a time and getting involved in their lives can be very draining, I've found. And, the more people you help, the stronger you'll become in terms of collecting.' She puts her head on one side and swills some gin around her mouth. 'No. Stronger's the wrong word. More experienced, is what I mean. It will all become second nature to you. At the moment it's still new, awkward, isn't it?'

'Um … yes, I suppose it is at times.' I can see her logic. And it will be fairly easy to collect energy from random strangers, like when I took some joy from the little child's mum, the first time I collected when I was helping Jack. But how on earth will I pass it on again, randomly? How will I decide who needs it more than others? And how does she know it will make me more experienced?

As if Grace can read my thoughts she says, 'Faith told me about it. And I thought it would be so hard to decide who to help, as there's so many people walking the earth who are in desperate need, their auras signalling desperation, sadness, misery … but it's not hard. Instinctively you know who to help, so you slip the pebble in their pocket, or bag. I pick a day to do a happiness drop – say, five or so people. Then another day I'll do confidence or something. Keep a diary. I do.' She heaves herself up from her chair. 'That reminds me, I think I need to do a joy drop tomorrow.' From a drawer in an old wooden sideboard, she pulls out a red book and runs her finger down the page. 'Yup. Joy in Newquay. Perhaps start in Asda and walk through town, dropping as I go.' She looks at me. 'I only do one or two drops a month nowadays, as it's tiring. Not bad for a woman of my age though, eh?'

My God. She puts me to shame. 'That's fantastic, Grace. I had no idea, or I would have been doing more.'

Grace flaps a hand at me and sits back down. 'Of course you would! And don't feel bad. I can tell you do, and I felt the same when old Faith explained it all to me. Now you know, you can get cracking!'

'I will. It's all very exciting, to think I can help so many people at once.'

'It is. Makes you feel like a superhero, but I draw the line at wearing my pants outside my tights!'

We laugh and then a thought occurs. 'How do you know if the pebble's power works if there is no interaction between you and the person? I've told the people I've helped so far that it's a lucky pebble and because they know me, I think they accept it. A random stranger might just find the pebble and toss it on the floor.'

'That's what I thought.' Grace points a finger at me. 'But it's the darnedest thing. Immediately after you drop the pebble, they pick it up and you can see it taking effect. Whatever negative aura they are wearing changes into a positive one almost within seconds.'

'But why? How does it work?'

'Ours is not to reason why, young Joy. Now, go home and have that bath. Then go over to Jowan's and have a lovely evening.' I get another cheeky wink. 'We'll catch up soon.'

I do a mock salute. 'Yes, ma'am.'

———————

As I drive round the corner, my heart floats as light as a party balloon. How lucky am I to be able to give joy to so many? And how wonderful that I have a lovely friend whom I can discuss it all with. Grace looked a little lonely, though, as she waved to me from her door just now. I remember that all of her close friends have either died or moved away. It's hard to make new friends at any age, let alone when you're eighty. Trouble is, I don't know any other elderly people, apart from a few in St Margaret's, but mostly they are too poorly to do an awful lot.

In the bath I eat the very last chocolate that Liam bought me and ponder on Grace some more. Mum phoned last night and was chatting about a new song she was learning at choir. I wonder if Grace would be up for that? It's only in Porth, a short drive from here, and she'd certainly meet more people that way. Relaxing back into the bubbles, I think about my new random collecting and distributing mission, and also about the remaining happiness pebble. Who will I give it to? A few moments later, I think I have the answer.

Chapter Twenty-Six

Helen dismisses assembly with a face as sour as curdled clotted cream. She's been more miserable than usual lately and it's time she smiled again. Even if it's the big, false, red-rimmed shark grin she used to favour us with, it's better than nothing. In my trouser pocket the weight of the pebble shifts against my thigh as I walk along the corridor to her office. It's only a small pebble, but it feels as big as an ostrich egg. There are so many 'what ifs'. What if she sneers at my usual explanation – it's a lucky pebble? Mind you, that would mean me handing it to her, and wouldn't that seem a bit out of the blue? I could slip it into her handbag instead, but what if she has no reaction to it whatsoever, because she really *is* a robot, like I first suspected on the day of my interview? What if my excuse for showing up at her office to see if she'd come and judge a poetry competition in our class comes out jumbled and unintelligible because I'm nervous? What if Gilly's cross

295

when I tell her that I've asked Helen to judge it, without discussing it with her first?

More 'what ifs' circle in my mind like vultures waiting to swoop on carrion as I stand in front of her office door, but before I can knock, it opens and Jowan comes out. His eyes pop when he sees me, but, to give him his due, he recovers quickly, and after a brief 'Good morning, Miss Pentire,' he goes on his way. My words, on the other hand, have been eaten by the vultures, and I can barely breathe when Helen beckons me inside.

'Joy, how can I help you?' Helen allows the right side of her mouth a half-hearted curl.

'It's the competition,' I blurt like a nervous child might in our class. Actually, more like reception class.

Helen sits, steeples her forefingers, stares at me, a slight frown furrowing her dark eyebrows. 'What competition?'

'A poetry one. In our class.'

'Uh-huh.' The keen green eyes sweep the length of me as she waits.

She waits? 'Oh, yeah, sorry. We'd like you to judging it. I mean, judge it. If it's not a problem.' No response. 'I could see if Jowan …' my face catches fire, '… I mean, Mr Williams could do it, if you're busy and that.' *And that?* I never say 'and that'.

The slight furrow becomes a ploughed field as she watches my embarrassment deepen. Then she coolly replies, 'No. I can do it, no problem at all.'

'Oh good. Good. That's good, then. Great.'

'When do you want me to come?'

'Tomorrow, not sure when time. I mean, what time…' God, I need to get a grip.

'Joy, are you okay? You seem a bit …' she twists her red mouth to the side, '… odd.'

Releasing my breath, I decide to come clean. 'I'm okay. I was just plucking up courage to ask how you were. You see, I don't think you've been yourself lately. You seem very sad, and I was wondering if it had anything to do with Jowan and what we talked about before?' *And because I feel as guilty as hell, as I'm in a relationship with him and haven't told you.* 'I know you said it was a mistake and you didn't want to talk about it, last time I came to see you, and—'

Helen holds up her hand to silence me. 'Look, why don't you sit down? You're getting all flustered.' I sit and take another deep breath, try to calm my heartrate. She continues, 'Yes, it was a mistake, but I still can't get him out of my head. And yes, it's making me thoroughly miserable.'

Now, Joy. Now is the time to hand her the pebble. Do it now before you change your mind. 'Here you are, Helen. It's a lucky pebble that might make you feel better. I picked it from the beach especially.'

Helen looks at me as if I've just said, 'Here you are, Helen, here's a goblin that I captured at breaktime in the staffroom.' Nevertheless, I sit with my hand out, the light-grey pebble on my open palm for a few seconds like an offering to the Gods. She heaves a sigh through a patronising look, but she takes it, closes her fingers around it and goes to stand up … then instead, she sits back down and a wobbly smile shapes her lips. 'You're so kind, Joy.

Bringing me a pebble, caring about me... It's definitely cheering me up.'

This kills me inside. 'Oh good. Pebbles from the beach have a certain positive energy, I find...' *What a fraud I am. I'm not as nice as you think. I've gone behind your back and...*

Then she starts to cry. I can't bear it. All the deception and sneaking around. It's not who I want to be. I decide to resign there and then, until she startles me with, 'Don't worry, Joy. These are happy tears. I'm leaving soon. I realised – actually, *you* made me realise it's not too late to do something I love. Remember, at your party you said life's too short?' She dabs the corners of her eyes with a tissue. 'As you know, teaching never made me happy, being headteacher doesn't make me happy, mooning after a man who doesn't have the slightest interest in me, doesn't make me happy.' Helen uncurls her fingers and looks at the pebble with reverence. 'Being happy is what we're supposed to be, or what's the point of life?' She sniffs and gives a dazzling smile. 'I'm going to buy that little shop by the sea. Fill it with my art and be happy, Joy. What do you think of that?'

What do I think? I think it's fantastic and it means Jowan and I are off the hook too. No more sneaking around and pretending. The pebble has allowed her to come clean, added to her self-belief, and for that I'm grateful. 'Wow! I think it's wonderful. Have you told your parents?'

'Yes. They were predictably disappointed, but they'll get over it. And if they don't, so what? It's my life and it's about time I lived it!' She tips her head back and laughs. Not a false hyena bray, but a genuine, rich belly laugh. 'Once I get out of this place, shuck off the responsibility of the job, and unrequited love, and start living "my best life", as they say nowadays, I'm sure I'll be happier!' Helen looks at the pebble again and slips it into her trouser pocket. 'Thanks so much for the pebble, Joy. And for everything.'

She's being so open and honest; she's showing me her true self. What a change from the other Helen. This is someone whom I could see being a friend. Then guilt kicks me in the shin and before I can stop myself, I say, 'I'm so happy for you, Helen. But I've not been totally honest with you about my relationship with … with—'

'Jowan?'

This is like a punch to my stomach and I take a moment to recover. 'I … how…?'

'I wasn't a hundred per cent sure, but as good as. And your reaction just now confirmed it. I'm not blind.' She folds her arms and holds my gaze, a sad little smile playing at the corners of her lips. 'I noticed the way you two looked at each other in the staffroom a few weeks back when you thought nobody was watching. Then, just recently, you've been studiously ignoring each other every time you're in the same room. It was this realisation that gave me the extra push I needed to get out of here, so I should be grateful.'

My eyes well, and my hand flies to my mouth. This is unbearably sad. She's known for ages and never said. No wonder she was rude last time I came to see her. 'Oh, Helen. I'm really sorry. We—'

She holds her hand up. 'Please don't apologise. Love has no conscience. It happens and there's not a bloody thing we can do about it.'

'That's true, but I—'

'Joy. Stop.' She stands and brushes a crease from her pink jacket. 'I'll be gone at the end of this school year, and I'm genuinely excited about it. It's not your fault that you fell for Jowan. You couldn't help it, just like I couldn't.' Helen picks up her bag and hooks it over her shoulder. Then she smiles again and it's warm, genuine. 'And who knows? If I'm lucky, who's to say I won't meet someone just as nice in the future? Come on, time for class.' She slips her arm through mine and walks me down the corridor to Gilly's classroom. I don't say anything. I can't, because my throat's restricted by a swelling knot of emotion.

Helen flings open the door and says to Gilly, 'Miss Pentire reporting for duty.' Then she grins at the children. 'And I'll be along tomorrow to judge all that wonderful poetry you little monkeys are working on.' They giggle, obviously delighted at being called little monkeys. Gilly smiles and sends me a questioning look across the classroom as I turn to thank Helen, but I find she's already gone.

The last few weeks have been manic. I've been helping out at the refuge with Gilly and thoroughly enjoying it. The children are so eager to learn and have had some brilliant writing ideas. I've also done two random collections of joy, peace and happiness around Truro and Newquay. I need to distribute them at the weekend, before more stuff takes over. I also need to take Grace some apple-green throws that

I picked up at the market too. They will look wonderful on her old sofa, providing Tom and Jerry don't pull threads in them. They really are the most adorable kittens, and seeing Grace's aura of joy when she's playing with them is a joy in itself.

Jowan and I have been together every evening; it's so wonderful not to have to hide anymore and to go wherever we like. I tend to be spending more time at his than mine. It makes sense, as his place is bigger, and has that to-die-for view. We've spent many early summer evenings after dinner on his balcony, with a glass of wine, chatting and watching the ocean roll in. Absolute heaven. Sebastian's come over a few times, as I don't like leaving him alone too much, and seems to be making himself at home there too. He adores Jowan almost as much as I do.

Liam's hardly been home; he's working all hours at the restaurant and I have a feeling he'll be gone before long. He was saying the other day that there might be a chance of a small flat in Padstow. He'd be nearer to his work, which would mean he could leave later in the mornings, and anyway, it's time he had a place of his own. I guess it is, but I'll still miss him.

After an exhausting week of racing here, there and everywhere, I'm glad that the peaceful weekend's just a day away. I might phone Dad and insist he comes for that swim with me on Saturday. It's time I told him and Mum about Jowan too. I've just been waiting for the right moment.

I put Seb's food in his dish and tell him I'll see him in the morning. I'll take him over to stay for the weekend tomorrow night. Liam will be back later, so he won't be alone. I grab my overnight bag as I'm about to drive over to Jowan's, thinking about how different my life has become lately. What a whirlwind of activity it is. I yawn loud and long and wonder if I'll be able to keep my eyes open after dinner. Being busy is something to be thankful for, though, because I've had little time to worry about Helen. She's seemed more like her old self. Because of this, Jowan and I have been more relaxed at work. We've still been discreet but not to the point of blanking each other anymore. Jowan's toying with the idea of applying for her position, but can't make his mind up. He thinks it will be a bit like jumping in her grave, even though she isn't dead. I tell him she'd probably like him being headteacher, rather than some newcomer. Besides, let's not forget she hated the job anyway. The thought of working under a complete stranger, who Jowan might not get on with, in a job he already knows inside out, in my view will push him to apply.

Just as I'm about to leave, my phone rings. Probably Jowan reminding me to bring the bread I made earlier. A quick glance tells me it's Helen. Odd?

'Hi, Helen.'

'Good, you're in. I'm about five minutes away … need to speak to you. Won't keep yer long.'

God. Has she been drinking? 'Oh … I was about to go out—'

'As I said, won't take a minute.' The line goes dead and I stare at my phone, my gut rolling in anticipation. Last time she was drunk she had a lot to say. And why is she driving? The answer to that is revealed as a taxi pulls up outside.

Helen instructs the taxi driver to wait in an imperious

tone that loses its gravity because of her inebriated state. Then, weaving her way along my path, she jabs a finger at me as I stand at the door. 'I had a think after school today. I had a think and it's about time you learned a few home truths, madam.'

The taxi driver's looking on, a bemused smile on his face, obviously waiting to be entertained, so I take her arm. 'Let's go inside. I'll make you a coffee.'

The force she uses to shake off my hand flings my arm into the door jamb, and her red-rimmed, mascara-smudged eyes narrow, blue steel pinning me to the spot. 'I won't set foot in your house, you vile snake in the grass!' Helen hitches her arms under her bosom. The white blouse has lost a button, and the fuchsia suit she wears for school is creased and wine-stained.

At a loss as to what's brought her here in this state, I ask calmly, 'Helen. What's wrong? What is it that you think I've done?'

'Ha! That's typical of you. Always little miss perfect. Bet Snow White is your flavourite fairy tale.' Helen winces at the mispronunciation. 'No. Not flavourite. Favour-ite.'

We look at each other in silence. She sways to the right, sticks out an arm, slaps a hand against the jamb to balance herself. Alarmed, I step back. 'Please come inside, Helen. You can have a sit down.'

'No… No!' She gives her head a quick shake as if she's trying to rid her mind of any compliance with my suggestion. 'I'll say what I came here for and go.' She draws in a deep breath. 'Two weeks ago you came into my office and gave me a pebble. A lucky pebble.' Helen's eyes flash. If they were blue steel before, they're molten lead now. 'How fucking condescending was that? Since your party, you had pretended to care about me, asked after me, wondered if I'd mentioned my feelings to Jowan, stuff like that. When all the time…' She jabs a finger at me, just stopping short of my chin. 'All the time you had been after him yourself.'

Her voice trembles on the last few words and her eyes swim with unshed tears. Adrenaline gallops through my veins and shame turns my face into a furnace. I have no argument. Because some of this is true, isn't it? 'Helen, I—'

'No, you don't get to speak. You listen!' The back of her hand wipes some spittle from the red-lipstick slash of her mouth, smearing it across her chin, giving her a lopsided sneer. 'You took advantage of me. Of my life story, when I was weak that night. You pounced, dug in your talons and dragged out my soft middle like a carrion crow on a lamb. Then you used it. You lied to me. Pretended to care. I knew what was going on between you and him, with all those lovestruck googly eyes across the staffroom and assembly too, I saw it all. Bet you had a right laugh at my expense behind my back. But what did I do when you gave me the stupid pebble? I said it was all okay. That pebble must have done something to my brain, gullible fool that I was. I said I gave you both my blessing. Well, I don't.' She holds her hand up. 'Oh, don't get me wrong. I don't want him now, I knew that was a non-starter a long time back. But I needed to tell you that you're not a very nice person, despite what everyone thinks.'

This is all too much. The poor woman thinks we've been

mocking her and my heart fills with compassion and pity. 'Please, Helen. It wasn't like that!'

'Really? Oh, I think it was. I think it always has been. I didn't do this two weeks ago in my office, more fool me, but I'm doing it now. You need to take a long, hard look at yourself, Joy. Admit to yourself what you really are. Who you really are. A conniving, false, self-serving little bitch.'

The quietness of her voice does nothing to detract from the menace, and before she turns for the taxi, she spits on the ground between my feet. A sob breaks free from my lips and I call after her, 'Helen. Helen, come back. Let's talk about this!' But all I get is a V sign as she stumbles into the back of the taxi. As I watch it drive away, like Helen before me, I have to grab the door jamb to steady myself. I'm not drunk, but in shock. In shock and, oh, so sad.

Chapter Twenty-Seven

The last of the early evening light has almost gone without me noticing. I've just been staring at the kitchen table, my head in my hands, tears splashing onto the pine surface. Jowan will be calling soon if I don't get round to his. I said I'd be there half an hour ago. But how can I go, after Helen's visit? There's a dark cloak of wretchedness wrapped around me, and I don't need to be able to see auras to know it. Poor Helen is in so much pain, so how can I go to see my lovely man and behave like nothing's happened? Do I even deserve happiness? Am I the kind of person she said I was? Remembering the look of contempt on her face is enough to bring fresh tears, but a knock on the door stops me giving them free rein. Scrubbing my fists into my eyes, I stand up and walk to the door. Probably Jowan coming to get me. If it's Helen again, I don't think I'll be able to hold it together.

The kindly figure of Grace on my path with a cake tin has a similar effect, and, before I know it, I'm sobbing my heart out on her shoulder in my kitchen. 'Hey, hey. What's happened, my lovely?'

'Oh, G-Grace.' Hiccupping sobs force me to sit down and take some breaths. Grace hands me a glass of water and she sits opposite at the table. When I'm calmer, I recount Helen's visit. 'And the worst of it is, I'm wondering if she's right. I mean, I did keep my feelings for him secret, didn't I? Secret when I knew how she felt about him. Thought a bloody joy pebble would make it all right. How lame is that?'

Grace shakes her head and grabs my hand. 'Now you listen here, lass. There's not a conniving, self-serving, false or bitchy bone in your body. You're a loving and caring, wonderful girl who goes out of her way to make others happy. You don't have to, it's not the law. There would be many who would have laughed off Hope's gift and chucked the pebbles in the bin. But not you. You're a good egg. The best.'

I take a gulp of water. 'But I was out for myself in the beginning. I was hoping that Helen hadn't asked Jowan out again. Hoping that he wouldn't say yes.'

Grace frowns, her quick brown eyes intense in the low lights. 'That's as may be. You wouldn't be human if you thought otherwise. But all the time you cared about her – were mindful of her feelings. She said you pretended to care. That's not true, is it? You actually did care.'

'Yes. Of course I did, but—'

'No buts. Helen is a damaged soul, she's been living a miserable life in a job that's not right for her. Thankfully, she's leaving and following her dream in a matter of weeks.

That's down to you in part, she said as much the day you gave her the pebble, remember? And why, exactly, did you give her the joy pebble?'

I blow my nose on a tissue. 'Why?' I ask, thinking the answer is obvious. 'Because I could see she was miserable, wanted her to be happy.'

'Exactly!' Grace does a twinkly smile. 'How many self-serving, conniving bitches would give a flying one?'

Such a phrase coming from Grace makes me crack out laughing, and she joins in. I drink more water and start to feel better. What Grace said about Helen being damaged is true, and I did care about her. If I didn't, I wouldn't have hidden my feelings for Jowan. We wouldn't have snuck around. Yes, she could have made our lives difficult, but so what? No, we kept our relationship from her because we wanted to spare her feelings. So I can't be all those things she said about me, can I?

'Penny for 'em?' Grace asks, patting my hand.

'I'm thinking you're right overall, Grace.'

'Of course.' She winks. 'I'm always right.'

Another thought that's been bubbling up surfaces on my tongue. 'Thing is, I am off to Jowan's tonight. What on earth am I going to say about all this?'

Grace pulls her neck back. 'Nothing. It won't help anyone. Jowan might fly off the handle at her, and it will make it awkward for him and Helen during their last few weeks of working together. Also, Helen will sober up and apologise to you. Or at least, she'll say she was out of order, or summat.'

'You a clairvoyant now?'

'No. Just an experienced old lady who's very wise and been round the block once or twice.'

I laugh and squeeze her hand. 'Thank God you popped round right when I needed you. Not like you to come after sundown. Was it anything in particular you wanted me for?'

Grace frowns, then slaps her forehead. 'Cake! That's why I came. I made it this morning and forgot until now. I drove Tommy round here to drop it.' She reaches under the table and retrieves the cake tin. 'Take it to Jowan's and give him my love.'

'Thanks, Grace. Your cakes are legendary.' I sigh as I think of Helen and the day of the interview when I was eating cake in her office. 'I wish things were different between me and Helen.'

'You have nothing to reprimand yourself for. You did your best for her … she'll come round, or she won't. Either way, she's going to have a better life once she gets that shop, and hopefully one day she'll be happy.'

I nod. 'Why didn't the pebble work, do you think?'

'It did, she was happy the day you gave it. But not long term. My guess is she resented you too much to accept the gift totally, I suppose. Anyway, no more worrying about Helen. Go and see your man.' Grace kisses me on the cheek and then I see her to the door. As she drives round the corner in her little red car, I thank my lucky stars I bumped into her on the beach that day. She's a wonderful friend, and sharing my collecting journey is such a blessing.

Jowan opens the door and dual aromas of curry spice mixed with bergamot cologne rush past him into the cooling twilight air. 'Yum, something smells good,' I say, as he takes my bag and draws me into his arms.

'Is it me?' he smiles and kisses me on the mouth.

'Well, it might be…' I murmur between kisses. 'But I think it's probably the curry.'

'You know how to wound a man, Joy. I have on my very best cologne, specially for you.' Jowan does a pretend pouty lip.

'It is gorgeous. But then so are you.' I wind my fingers into the hair at the back of his neck and pull his face back down to mine. 'Everything about you is gorgeous.'

Jowan kisses me again, strokes his hands along my back and cups my bottom. Every nerve ending in my body is sparking, reaching for him. 'Want to put the curry on hold?'

I do, but Helen's face, voice, and pain are still fresh in my mind, cooling my ardour. I give him a playful push and go inside. 'No, I'm starving. Plenty of time for that later.'

In the kitchen, I kick off my shoes and grab a poppadom from a plate on the side. 'Beer, lager, wine, or gin and tonic?' he asks, with his head in the fridge.

'Lager, I think. Normally works well with curry.'

'There you go.' He cracks the cap off and hands the bottle over. 'It will be ready in five. Wanna sit here or out on the balcony? Though it's a bit nippy tonight with the clear sky.'

'I don't care. I've got my jeans and a long-sleeved top on, and I'll put my coat on if necessary, it's my favourite spot.' Gathering cutlery, my lager and the poppadoms, I go outside and place everything on the white wrought-iron table. Then I stretch my arms above my head, gaze at the navy ocean underlining a petrol-blue sky and take a big breath of salt air. One or two figures dot the darkening sand and a few canine companions run ahead, barking at seagulls, while high above me, a single star winks from a cloudless heaven. This is exactly what I needed after that awful run-in with Helen. I sigh and take a swig of lager. Jowan's right, it is a bit chilly, but then it's only early June and the drink and the curry should warm us up. Wrapping my arms around myself, I allow a spot of daydreaming. What if we could eat here every night, watching the waves below and the stars above switch on one by one, as if scattered by an unseen hand? What if I could watch this scene every morning? What if I could just walk along the lane outside and down the steps to the beach in five minutes? *What if lived here?*

'Dinner is served, young lady,' Jowan says, holding a tray aloft and then setting two plates down with a flourish. 'Onion bhajis to start, with mint sauce and mango chutney.'

I'm glad we only have the outside light on, as my face is a bit hot after my daydreams. Thoughts have a funny way of surprising you. Living here? Might be a tad too soon. I smile up at him. 'Starters too? You're spoiling me.'

'Of course. You deserve spoiling.' He mirrors my smile and sits down. I join him and we do a cheers, clinking our lager bottles together.

We chat about nothing in particular all through dinner. That's one of the things I love about our relationship, we never get stuck for something to say. It's so tempting to share about Helen, but it wouldn't be right. Grace made a good call. The last thing we need is Jowan going off at the deep end on Monday at her. Right then I decide to push Helen out of my mind, for tonight at least, and enjoy the evening.

The curry is delicious, and apart from a few bits of naan bread, my plate is very soon empty. 'That was wonderful, thanks, Jowan. You're almost as good a cook as me.' I raise my lager bottle in a toast to him and take a swig.

'Praise indeed from the lasagne queen of Cornwall.' He raises his bottle too and nods at my plate. 'And you like your food almost as much as me.'

'Waste not, want not.' I pat my stomach. 'As long as I keep up my exercise, I can eat more or less anything.' Swimming pops into my head. 'Oh, that reminds me. I'm going to ask Dad if he wants to go swimming with me on Saturday morning. He keeps putting me off, but I know he'll love it once he gets in there.' I nod at the darkening ocean and notice more stars have come out to play, while the new moon curves the suggestion of a smile.

'That will be nice. And it's about time I got to meet your folks, isn't it?' Jowan says in a matter-of-fact tone, but I can detect a wobble running through.

Trying to hide my surprise and my own wobble, I say, 'Oh … yeah. I mean, one of the reasons for meeting up with Dad is so that I can tell him about you. Mum too, obviously.'

Jowan furrows his thick dark brows. 'You haven't told them about me, yet?'

Now what? He looks a bit put out, as if I've made him

feel unimportant. But the reason I've not told them is the total opposite. 'No. The thing is, I've wanted to tell them for ages, but I haven't, because I wanted to be sure that our little ship is heading for serious waters.' What the hell? Little ship? I've only had one drink. 'I told them I'd stay single after Sean, so it's a big deal for me. So anyway, I am now.' Shit, this isn't making sense.

'You are now what?' Jowan says. His frown's gone, but he looks unsure.

'I'm sure that it's serious between us … or I'm serious about you, at least. I'm not assuming…' This is painful. I go to take a swig of lager but the bottle's empty.

My words hang in the air between us and he looks at the beach. The silence draws out, elongates, stretches from awkward to embarrassing, to excruciating, until I can hardly stand it. So much for me thinking we are never stuck for something to say. Then he looks deep into my eyes and says, 'I… I… Yes, of course it's serious.' He looks away, gives an embarrassed chuckle. 'Look, I've had an idea. Let's throw a barbeque here on Saturday. Invite your parents, our friends. Make a big party out of us being serious?'

Unsure of what to make of his response, but glad the awkwardness is slipping into the shadows, I say, 'Sounds like a plan. But it's Thursday evening now. Even if we message everyone in the morning, isn't it a bit short notice?'

'A bit, but it's impromptu and informal. Tell people they can just pop in and go, if they have other plans.' He's enthusiastic now, waving his arms about. 'We'll have it early enough to incorporate that. Start about four. Some who want to stay late can, others can leave. What do you think?'

'I think it's a great idea. I'll pop into town on Saturday before swimming with Dad and get some food for it.' *And then distribute joy, peace and happiness to the good people of Newquay.* 'It will be a fab party. I can tell.'

'Excellent! I'll get the barbeque bricks and anything else we need. Booze. That is a must.' He laughs then rubs his arms. 'Talking of which, let's go inside and have another. It's bloody freezing out here.'

I help him stack the plates and leftovers on the tray, while thinking how wonderful the Saturday barbeque will be. Family, friends, all here in this wonderful house to celebrate our relationship. But as I follow him inside, another, more unwelcome thought pops into my mind. If he's serious about me, what was all that awkwardness about earlier? What had he been about to say before he changed the subject with barbeque plans? Telling myself off for overthinking as usual, I slip into his arms, and soon any worries have melted away under the heat of his kiss.

Chapter Twenty-Eight

We've had only one person decline our invitation, so it's going to be a busy party. As I make the list of things we need, I do a rough count in my head: Gilly and Steve, Daisy, Mum and Dad, Liam, Fiona and Mark, Grace, two of my friends from St Margaret's, two of Jowan's friends and their partners. I pause, pen poised over the paper. Bloody hell, maybe we were a bit too free with the invites. I'm going to need fifty tonnes of burgers and sausages. Jowan wondered whether to ask Helen, but I said I didn't think she'd appreciate it, despite her originally saying she wished us well. He accepted it and I changed the subject. Grace's prediction that she'd apologise didn't happen on Friday. Helen arrived in school late, then apparently went home with a migraine. I knew this was obviously a hangover, but I only saw her from a distance as she got into her car. Time will tell if she'll try to make things right between us. But though I still care, it has to be down to her.

My mind goes back to the food. Okay, Jowan's getting the bread rolls, booze and condiments from the local deli, and he said people will likely each bring a bottle too. He also said in the invite message that people can muck in and cook their own stuff. We'll do some, of course, but if others don't chip in, they'll be waiting ages for their grub. Jowan's begged and borrowed two extra barbeques, so we'll be fine. I hope…

My next list is 'things to do': *Sainsbury's BBQ food, distribute pebbles, take Grace's throws, Dad – swim, prepare BBQ food.* That should be enough to keep me out of mischief. After checking that Sebastian is happy in Jowan's bedroom, I pop out to see Jowan in the garden and tell him I'm off shopping. He's about to mow the lawn and then clean the garden chairs. 'Do you think people will be okay sitting on the patio wall? I've only found six chairs.' He ruffles his dark curls and sighs.

'Yes, with a view over the ocean like that, they'll be happy to.' I look down the long sweep of lawn, edged by honeysuckle and a riot of summer colour, to the Cornish stone wall around the patio and the blue horizon beyond. 'I'll ask Dad to bring some chairs just in case, and why don't you ask your friends to bring some too? Then we'll be absolutely sure. Also, there's the beach blankets in your shed if need be. I found them yesterday when I was looking at the barbeque. People can sit on the lawn.'

Jowan's eyes reflect the sky and crinkle at the corners. 'You are full of ideas and very well organised, Miss Pentire. What on earth would I do without you?'

'I have no idea, Mr Williams. You'd probably sit in a corner sobbing quietly and rocking to-and-fro.'

He kisses my cheek and gives me an intense stare. 'I would. And that's no joke.'

My heart swells and I give him a quick hug. 'All I have to say to that is, paper plates.' I pat him on the shoulder and hurry back towards the house.

'Eh?'

'Don't forget to buy some when you get the booze.' As I get in my car, I make a mental note to get some anyway, just in case he does forget. The familiarity of such a small thought sends a warmth through me. Since Sean, I've missed this. This doing things together, working as a team. Second guessing what the other will do and say. An image of Sean smiling comes to mind; he seems to approve. I blow him a kiss and turn on the ignition.

———

With the shopping safely stowed in cool-bags in the boot, I make my way down the steps out of the supermarket carpark and into the narrow streets of Newquay centre. Three pockets of my green dungarees are loaded with pebbles. Right pocket is joy, left is peace and bib is happiness. Aware that sometimes it's hard to decide who is wearing what aura, I hope that random dispersal of these powerful emotions will help with whatever negative emotion is weighing these people down. Maybe if I see an aura of what I think is despair, I could give pebbles of peace, happiness or joy. Any of them will make a difference. I'm so thrilled Grace told me about this part of the job. I love the one-to-ones I've had so far, getting to know the stories behind the auras, but it's not always possible, and this is a great way of spreading positivity.

With a spring in my step, the first person I see is wearing misery. It's brown and black and the young woman burdened with it is hunched over as she trudges along the pavement towards me, glancing in shop windows, but not stopping to have a proper look in any of them. Maybe she's got no money and it's getting to her. She has a large green canvas bag over her shoulder, which being empty flaps against her side like a leaf in the wind. As she passes, I drop a happiness pebble into it and, just like Grace said, she immediately stuffs her hand in and pulls it out. She stops and looks at it, and actually laughs out loud. Her aura turns yellow and she holds the pebble up to the sun, then folds it tight into her palm and glances around, maybe to see who put it in her bag. I'm opposite in a doorway, and pretend to look at my phone when I feel her gaze on me. When I raise my eyes she's walked on, no longer hunched, but tall, and there's a length and bounce to her stride that wasn't there before. Wow. What a brilliant job this collecting is.

A few minutes later I'm pretending to look in Specsavers while glancing up and down the street for troubled souls. This is such fun; I feel like a modern-day fairy godmother. As I'm about to move on, out of Specsavers steps a plump, red-haired, middle-aged lady, wearing a floral dress and a dark cloak of grief. Deep furrows knit her brow and run deeper lines down her face to tug at the corners of her mouth. She barely notices me and brushes past, a vacant stare in her eyes. Now what? Do I follow her, try and slip some joy into her pocket? I set off at a little distance, still pondering. Her bag is tight to her body, so I don't think I'd be able to… She stops abruptly to look in a shop window and I almost bump into her. Aware of me, she spins round.

'Sorry,' I say. 'I was miles away.' She sighs and looks back at the window, but I can tell she's not really looking at the greeting cards and ornaments. The poor woman is bewildered, going through the motions. Maybe being out of the house is keeping her sane.

'What are you staring at?' she asks without moving her head. She must be able to see me from the reflection in the glass.

I clear my throat, decide to tackle it head on. Even though Grace said just do the drop, I can't see as I have a choice. 'I noticed you look very sad and was wondering how I could help.'

The woman glares at me, the vacancy in her eyes now occupied by contempt. 'Nobody can help. I've just lost my daughter to cancer. Thirty-two is all she was.' She turns back to the shop window and, as if to herself, whispers, 'Thirty-two.'

'I'm so, so sorry.' I look at the bag again and see a flap in the side, but her arm is over it and there's no way I could put a pebble in there without her knowing. So there's only one thing for it. 'You might think this a little odd, but I have a lucky pebble here that I'd like to give you. Lucky pebbles can bring comfort and—'

'Are you nuts? How the fuck can a lucky pebble help

me?' She brings her face close to mine, the contempt I saw earlier now blazing fury. 'I. Lost. My. Daughter.'

My heart's racing and I'm torn between walking away and pressing on. My gut says walk away, leave the woman be. I take a step back and then I stop, reassess. Never mind me being torn, this poor lady is being ripped apart by her grief, and if I can help soothe her soul a little, I have to try. I grasp her hand and slip joy into it. 'Just hold this a moment, I'm sure it will help.'

The woman looks at the flat grey pebble on her palm in bewilderment. A smile transforms her features, while tears fall silently down her cheeks. She opens and closes her mouth, but words fail her. Then as if some inner force has taken hold of her, she glares at me and hurls the pebble with all of her might along the high street. 'What the hell was that?!'

Shock spikes through me. Never have I seen such a reaction to a gift of joy. 'It … it was supposed to make you feel better,' I say in a small voice.

A humourless bark of laughter assaults my ears. 'It did to begin with, but I don't want to. If I feel better, I'll be forgetting my daughter, betraying her, leaving her all alone.' Her eyes have become wild, manic. 'My grief binds me to her. In a strange way it comforts me. It's all I have left. Now piss off and leave me alone!' Like lightning, her hand flies out and my head flicks to the side as her palm finds my cheek.

A couple of shoppers hurry over to me as I rub my stinging face, watching the woman's retreating figure hurry down the street and round the corner. They ask if

I'm okay and I nod and hurry away too, but I can hardly see where I'm going through my tears. I find a bench and flop down, dab at my eyes and take some deep breaths. How stupid. How very stupid of me to think collecting was fun earlier. The realisation that this isn't a game, and I am NOT a fairy godmother, slaps me across my other cheek. I've become complacent, because so far everything has gone well, been successful. But this woman was like a wounded animal. I know from bitter experience that grief has to be lived through sometimes, not just magicked away. Grace said she'd had missions go wrong ten times, but I didn't really think it could happen to me this early in my career.

A seagull alights on the arm of the bench and cocks a beady eye, regarding me down a yellow beak, ruffles its feathers. Mine are ruffled too. I say hello to it and it cocks its head as if it's listening. Letting out a long sigh, I calm myself and realise the need to take note, listen to my instincts. I was going to step away from the woman, wasn't I? Go with my gut – but no, no, I knew best. Ignored it. Ridiculous. Maybe I was trying to overcompensate because of the upset with Helen? God only knows. The seagull squawks as if agreeing with my thoughts and flies off. Maybe I should too. Abandon further missions for today. Shifting my position, in my pocket the weight of pebbles pushes against my leg and I wish I had Grace to talk to. Perhaps I'll call her.

'Hello, Joy. How are you?'

Grace's familiar voice down the line feels like a warm hug and I tell her everything that's just happened. 'How could I have been so stupid? It's not as if I don't know what grief's about.'

'Look, you just got carried away, that's all. You're young, enthusiastic, and have the biggest heart. You wanted to help a broken spirit, and up until now you have done so much good. Helped lots of people in need. Time to get back on the horse, Joy.'

'What, today? No. I don't think I could. In fact, at this moment I don't want to do any more missions. Ever.' I catch sight of my pouty face in the glass door of Peacock's and look away, ashamed.

'Yes, today. You have a pocketful of pebbles that need a home. And I don't want to hear any more of that defeatist talk. What would the old boy who was at D-Day make of you, eh? Imagine if he just gave up when things got a bit rocky?'

My pouty face becomes a scowl and I thump the bench with the heel of my hand. 'Thanks, Grace, for making me feel a total failure.' As soon as the words are out, I wish them in again. Into the hurt silence on the line I say, 'No, I didn't mean that, Grace. I'm so sorry—'

'I know you are. Now stop wallowing and go forth and spread happiness and joy, Joy.' She laughs at her play on words. 'You have the rest of your life to learn from your mistakes. And don't come home until your pockets are empty, okay?'

Heaving a sigh, I turn my scowl into a smile, albeit it a watery one. 'Okay. See you later, and thank you.'

Half an hour later I've just one pebble left in my right pocket – joy. Apart from the one horrendous misjudgement, it's been a successful trip, thanks to Grace's sage advice. First with Helen, now with this. I'm so lucky to have her. After a shaky start, my confidence came back enough for me to plough on, but I need to finish here and get on with the rest of my to-do list for the day. There's nobody obvious in the immediate vicinity, so I stand next to Boots and wait for the last recipient to come into view. Luckily, I don't have to wait too long, as out of Poundland comes an elderly man leaning heavily on a walking stick. His steps are short and unsteady and a battered carrier-bag dangles from his left hand. Across his shoulders is a deep-purple cloak of what I think is sadness. So my last pebble will do nicely. Crossing the street, I nip in behind him and wait for my opportunity. He stops for a breather by Clarks shoe shop and gazes in the window. I hurry past and deliver my pebble into his carrier with a rustle and thump.

From the Specsavers shop doorway, I watch him frown and look behind and to the pavement. He must have heard the rustle and thinks something's fallen out of his bag, maybe through a hole. Then he peers into the bag and lifts the pebble out, marvels at it, closes his hand around it and leans against the shop window as if he's lost the strength in his legs. Slowly his frown recedes and his thin lips stretch into a smile, his eyes crinkle with mirth and tears flow silently down his cheeks. The purple thins, until all around the edges of the man's body is a bright-silver light, as if he's a storm cloud with the sun breaking through.

Emotion rushes me and I swallow hard. So glad I didn't

throw in the towel. Wow. The power of joy at work is so wonderful to watch. And I'm so privileged to be able to share it. After a few moments, the man wipes his eyes with a big hanky and puts the pebble in his pocket. As he goes on his way, he still uses his stick, but his step is longer, more sure of itself, and this lifts my heart.

About to hurry back to the carpark, I notice a familiar figure: tall, long dark hair lifting on the breeze, he's chatting to a *Big Issue* seller. It's a while since I last saw him and he's certainly much smarter now. But I'd know that face anywhere. I'm running late, but I can't just go past without saying hello. I've been wondering how he's getting on but have been too busy to call him. 'Jack!' I tap him on the shoulder. 'How the devil are you?'

Surprised, Jack spins round. 'Joy! Great to see you.' He flings his arms round me. 'I've been meaning to call you but I never get round to it.'

'Ditto!' I hold him at arm's length and study his face. His amber eyes are alight with happiness, his skin is clear and the matted bird's nest is soft and silky. 'You're looking fantastic!'

'A bit better than last time we met, eh?' He laughs.

'Just a bit.'

'Do you want to go for a coffee or something and catch up?'

'There's nothing I'd like better, but I'm rushing around like a headless chicken today. Me and my boyfriend are having a barbeque tonight, so there's all sorts to do for that.'

'Boyfriend, eh? Nice.'

'Yeah. I think we're going to make a real go of it.' I told

Jack when we spoke on the phone a few months back about Sean, but not the details.

Jack smiles and hugs me again. 'I'm thrilled for you, Joy! Though I am a bit jel too. Wish I had a boyfriend to have a cosy barbeque with.' He rolls his eyes and does a big sigh.

'You're gay? I didn't realise.'

'Why would you? I never mentioned it. And to be honest, it wasn't the first thing on my mind to tell you when last we met.'

'True.' I chuckle and then a thought occurs. 'How about coming to the barbeque tonight? We could have a catch-up and you could meet my friends.'

At first, he looks like he's going to accept, then he knits his brows together. 'A great idea, but how would I explain how I met you? I'm not ready to talk about my darkest time to strangers, to be honest.'

'Hmm. I hadn't thought of that.' Then I look across at the guy selling *The Big Issue* and an idea surfaces. 'How about we say we met a while back when I was buying *The Big Issue* and you were helping out with the homeless charity? I could say we talked about you possibly doing a talk at school about homeless people? Then I met you again today and we went for a coffee. I asked you to the barbeque.'

'Wow, you think on your feet, don't you?' He laughs. 'I think that would work, and maybe I could come and do the talk for real, sometime?'

'You could. I'll ask Jowan, he's my boyfriend and the deputy head.'

'Nice. Okay, thank you. What time shall I come?'

'It starts at four and ends whenever you want to leave.'
'That's flexible then! Looking forward to it.'

———————————

Grace loved her throws and she's so looking forward to the barbeque too. She said how proud of me she was for continuing today after the upset. I unpack the shopping, make Jowan and I a quick sandwich and then run down the steps to the beach to meet Dad. As I make my way across the sand, I think about Mum. When I phoned Dad, it was a bugger to get him to agree to come at first, until I told him I had something important to share with him. Mum overheard our conversation and I could hear her in the background asking him, 'What's important?' And 'Why hasn't she mentioned it to me?' And 'Is she okay? God. Do you think she's poorly?' This is exactly why I've decided to pass my news on to Dad instead of her. She would get in a flap and ask twenty million questions about Jowan. She'd doubt everything and say stuff like: 'Are you sure he's serious, and how do you know you won't get hurt?' All the questions I try not to ask myself too often. Mum's matchmaking with Liam was fine because she was in on it. But she's never been good at me doing important things without telling her. My good news would end up buried under a pile of worry for no reason. Dad can be in the know first for once, and he can tell her.

'Bloody hell! This water is freezing!' Dad's up to his waist and turns back to the shore.

'Not so fast!' I grab his goosepimply arm. 'It's only

because the sun is so warm. Once you submerge your body, it will be fine.'

'Er … you go ahead and submerge, love. I'll watch you from the beach.' His eyes reflect the water and sparkle with mischief.

'Nope. We are doing this, with an emphasis on *we*.' Dad ignores this and takes a step towards the beach. So I leap on his back and we both go under with an almighty splash!

Dad torpedoes up, gasping for breath as he breaks the surface and pushing his hair out of his eyes. 'You maniac! You could have bloody drowned me!' he yells.

I can't reply for a moment as I'm laughing too much. He looks like an indignant sea-lion with his grey hair and stubble, brown sun-tanned skin stretched across the beginnings of a beer belly. Too much sitting on his bum being the manager, I expect. 'Oh, Dad. We're up to our waists. Can't see us drowning.'

'Really?' He narrows his eyes at me and I see a gleam of devilment as they catch the sun. 'Let's see how you like it then!'

Before I can run, he launches himself at me, picks me up and dumps me into the waves from a great height. I pop up again laughing, and coughing because seawater has gone up my nose and down my throat. It's years since we've done anything like this. Larked around together. In fact, I can't remember when we did. Must have been a teenager. 'You got me!' I hold my hands up. 'Now, let's do what we came for.' I turn to the horizon and secure my ponytail. 'On your marks, get set…'

Dad shouts, 'Go!' and sets off at a fast front-crawl before I can draw breath.

'Cheater!' I yell after him and power forward, exhilarated as the cold seeps through my skin and into my bones. After a few minutes the cold's replaced by comfortable salt-hug as my temperature adjusts with every stroke of my arms and kicking legs. Pausing to see where Dad is, I see he's only just ahead, but determined to win. I'll allow him this victory. I smile and, on my back, I float, weightless. Above me the sky paints a few herringbones and vapour trails across itself for variety, and a tiny puff of cloud competes against freewheeling seagulls for centre stage. Bliss.

'Oi!' Dad's voice breaks through my tranquillity as he swims up to me.

'You bellowed?'

'Thought we were racing?'

'We were. You won.'

'You stopped.'

'Only because I couldn't beat you, Dad.'

'Hmm. A likely story.'

'Lie on your back and look at the sky. It's lovely.'

'No. The water goes in my ears.'

'Yeah. So what?'

'It makes me deaf.'

'Pardon?'

'Oh, very funny.'

I roll onto my front. 'Okay, I'll race you back to shore. On your marks,' I begin, and Dad's off again like a mad herring trying to avoid a fishing trawler.

On the beach, wrapped in towels, perched on sun-warmed boulders, we sit sipping hot chocolate from a flask Dad brought. 'This is nice,' I say. 'Even in sunny weather, it's just what you need after a swim.'

'Yep. I always used to bring hot chocolate when we went swimming years ago, remember?'

'Yeah. It was the law.'

We sit and watch the beach activity. Surfers, picnickers, walkers, children building sand castles. Then Dad nudges me, 'Come on then. What's the important news? Your mum's been driving me nuts since you called. She's worried it's something bad. But then she worries for no reason. I told her it wouldn't be something bad.' He gives me a wink, but I can tell he's not entirely convinced. 'She also wondered why you couldn't tell us both tonight at this barbeque at yours.'

A tickle of excitement grows in my belly at the thought of springing Jowan on him. It's the best news I've had for a very long time and I need to share it. 'Well, for one thing it's not a barbeque at mine. I said come to a barbeque on Saturday. I didn't say where.'

Dad screws the cap onto the flask and frowns. 'Where is it then?'

'See that lovely house on the cliff up there? The one with the balcony and window in the roof?'

Dad's eye-line follows my finger. 'Yeah?'

'That's where it is. The house belongs to Jowan. He's the deputy head at my school. You met him at my party.'

Dad's frown is still furrowing his brow and he looks at me. 'Yes, I remember. Nice guy. He left quite soon, though, as far as I remember … but why are we going there?' My face must have given the game away because he says, 'Are you seeing him?'

'Yes.' I beam. 'Yes I am, and we're serious. That's why we're having the barbeque – so our friends and family can meet and see we're together too.'

'You're getting married?'

I laugh. 'No. No, we've only been together a short time, but decided to keep it under wraps. Now we'd like to go public.'

Dad hugs me. 'That's great, love. But why have you kept it secret?'

I tell him all about Helen. Also, the fact that I wanted to be absolutely sure before I made Jowan common knowledge. 'You know what Mum's like. If I told her right from the beginning, she would have worried about everything and chewed my ear off twenty-four-seven. So tonight, she can meet him and hopefully see how good we are together. Set her mind at rest.'

Dad nods and gives me a beaming smile. 'You've done the right thing. And I, for one, am over the moon for you. I knew you'd meet a nice man eventually. Even though you said you'd always stay single.'

'Really?'

'Really. And I can literally see how happy you are. It's shining out of your eyes – well, all over you – like a ray of sunshine.'

That stops me in my tracks. My smile feels fixed in

cement. *Dad can see auras too?* Making my tone light, I ask, 'You can literally see my happiness?'

'Eh? Figuratively I mean, dafty.'

Phew. What a relief. 'That's a big word for you, Dad.' I give him a playful push.

'Dafty?'

'No. Fig—' When I see his mischievous smirk, I snap my mouth shut and push him again. Then I stand up and grab my stuff. 'Okay. Time we went. I have a barbeque to prepare. See you later.' I drop him a wink. 'And good luck telling Mum about Jowan. Hope she doesn't drive you mad with questions!' Then I turn and scarper off up the beach.

Dad yells after me, 'Hey! That's not fair!' but I laugh and just keep running.

Chapter Twenty-Nine

L iam's the first to arrive. He's over the moon that he's got Saturday night off, the first in about six weeks. He's looking so much happier now, and though he's still careful about his appearance, the days of having to dress in the most expensive designer gear because of his controlling ex are long behind him. He's wearing a black T-shirt and denim shorts and his chestnut-brown hair is more natural and no longer hairsprayed to within an inch of its life. He's helping me prepare the salads and adding a few cheffy touches to dressings and marinades.

'You're welcome to do it all if you like, Liam. I'll just put my feet up and have a glass of wine.'

I get an eyebrow raise and a pointy fork. 'Er, I don't think so. This is my night off, young lady.'

'A girl has to try.' I smile and slice a red onion.

'Oh and guess what? You know I was telling you about all that left-over food we have at the restaurant? The stuff that's a nanosecond or two past its sell-by, and some veg that isn't completely perfect enough to grace our clients' plates?'

'I do.'

'Well, to save it just being dumped as normal, I organised it to go to a local food-bank. It seems such a waste when people can make good use of it. The boss was reluctant at first, but I said I'd organise it all, so he was cool.'

'Brilliant!' So this is Liam's random act of kindness. How useful!

'Yeah. It gives your heart a lift to do something good, doesn't it?'

'Totally.' We do stretchy smiles at each other and it's times like this that I wish I could share my collecting activities. Never mind, at least I'll have Grace to chat to later.

Jowan pops his head round to say Fiona, Mark, Gilly and Steve are here, so Liam and I take a tray of nibbles and drinks out into the sun-drenched late afternoon. Everyone is saying what a fantastic house and garden Jowan has, and I'm pleased that a gathering of very different personalities seem to be getting on so easily. Fiona is dressed in what can only be described as an outrageously flamboyant ensemble. A pink and yellow tutu paired with a green and blue sequinned shoe-string top. On her feet are some 1970s-style platform sandals, and her white-blonde hair has been divided into four plaits and woven into what looks like a giant pretzel atop her head. But strangely, it works. All of it.

'Fiona,' I hand her a drink and take a step back. 'You look absolutely…'

A Secret Gift

'Bloody amazing. Yeah, I know!' she says, modestly. Mark rolls his eyes and says nothing.

'Will you be wearing something like that for the wedding?' Gilly asks, giving me side-eyes.

'Not quite. But it's kind of special.' Fiona winks at her and raises her glass. 'Can't say too much with my husband-to-be listening.' Again, Mark says nothing. I think he's going to be long-suffering, but I can tell he loves her.

Steve is chattier and talks about his teacher training, and how much he's looking forward to becoming a teacher, which draws Jowan in. Before long, the three men have wandered off together to drink beer and sort out the cooking of meat. Liam comes back outside with more nibbles and nods over at them. 'I see the boys are being the traditional hunter-gatherer types. Wrestling the beef burgers to the floor and providing food for the tribe?'

'Yep.' Gilly laughs. 'What is it about barbeques that means men tend to do it? The rest of the time Steve barely sets foot in the kitchen.'

As we're discussing how far the traditional division of labour has changed in the twenty-first century, Mum and Dad come round the side of the house. Dad's wearing a big grin, Mum's doing her tight polite smile, which actually means underneath is a seething mass of disgruntlement. Dad spreads his arms wide and turns in a circle in the middle of the lawn. 'Bloody hell, this is a place and a half, isn't it? Look at that view!'

I hurry over and give him a hug. 'It is very lovely, isn't it.'

Mum gives me the smallest of kisses and steps back as if

I've given her an electric shock. 'Yes, you've done very well for yourself,' she says, stiffly.

Oh, for God's sake. Does she think I'm with Jowan for the house? There are so many things I could say to her, but I keep them all locked down in a shouty swear-box. Taking a deep breath, I say to them, 'Come and meet Jowan properly.'

The force of Jowan's charm has Mum coming out of her shell in no time and she's laughing and joking with him about the sausages. 'Well if I were you, I'd say at least five more minutes for that one. It looks like Donald Trump without the fake tan.'

'It really does!' Jowan laughs. 'Right down to the weaselly little smile where the skin's cracking.'

Dad's chatting to Mark, so I leave them to it and check on the bread rolls in the oven. As I'm taking them out, Liam pops up behind me. 'Who is that gorgeous man who's just arrived?'

'Given that I'm in here and not outside, I can't help you with that.' I waft a tea-towel over the rolls. One looks a bit burnt. 'Can you dress the salads and take them out for me, please, Liam?'

'Not until you come and introduce me to the Viking.' Liam does a warrior stance and pretends to flick back a mane of hair.

'Viking?' I fold my arms and run through who's been invited. Might be a friend of Jowan's. 'Has he got long hair, then?'

'Yeah. Tall, young, gorgeous light-hazel eyes. No not hazel, they're more, er … what do you call it…?' Liam looks up to the left, as if a better description is written on the ceiling.

The penny drops. 'Amber. And I think you mean Jack. He's a friend of mine but a little too young for you.' I tip the rolls onto a big oval plate and wonder if seven years *is* actually too young. Jack and Liam would actually make a great couple...

'Too young? I think the main obstacle would be him being straight. I suppose he is? Straight, I mean.' Liam puts his head on one side, his chocolate-brown eyes staring out of the kitchen window at the gathered throng. 'All the gorgeous ones are, or in a relationship,' he adds with a sigh.

'You're gorgeous, and single, aren't you?' I prod him and put the plate of rolls in his hands. Then I whack him on the bum with the flat of my hand. 'Now, go and hand out these rolls, and ask if you can get our Jack a drink.'

Liam rolls his eyes. 'You're working me hard today, woman.'

'I am.' I wait until he's almost at the door and say, 'And by the way, Jack isn't straight.'

Liam stops so fast, the rolls nearly fly off the plate. 'He's not?'

'Nope.' I grin and watch his face flush with excitement. '*And* he's single ... said the other day that he wished he had a boyfriend to have a barbeque with.'

His mouth drops open. 'Then why the hell didn't you tell me about him?'

'Honestly, I've been so busy ... it never crossed my mind. And he's only just twenty ... but he's mature and I'm sure you'll get on. Go and meet him, make the most of it.'

'Oh. My. God. I'm all hot and nervous now. What if I mess it up? What if he doesn't fancy me?' He puts the plate down on the side. 'I think I'll have another drink first.'

'Liam?'

'What?'

'Go and say hello. It will all be fine, promise.'

'But...'

'Go. Now.'

'Okay.'

Back outside, after a quick head-count, I see that everyone is here apart from Daisy. She said she was coming later. I'm introduced to Jowan's friends who he's known from college and their wives, and they all seem such a nice bunch. Grace is chatting on the balcony with Mum about the choir. At first, Grace was reluctant to give it a go, saying she has a voice like a bullfrog. But Mum convinced her and they seem to be getting on really well. Mum still hasn't said more than two words to me all evening, however. Jack and Liam have been sitting on the far patio wall together, overlooking the ocean, while chatting nineteen to the dozen. I've lost my kitchen helper, but that's okay. It's great that they seem to be getting on so well, and Fiona and Gilly are helping out now, so all is good ... apart from the incident when we lost a plate of burgers, because Fiona fell off her platforms, tottering squiffily across the lawn.

Daisy arrives about eight, and brings a male friend she's met at the library. Claude is half French and such a gentle soul. Just what Daisy needs after the awful life she led with her ex-husband. When Claude goes to get a burger, Daisy insists they are just friends when I suggest otherwise, but I can tell they are on the way to becoming something more. I'm so happy for her. It seems like everyone is having a fun time, and all my worry about getting it right and the face-slapping incident today drains away. Taking a bite of a much-needed hot dog, I gaze out over the navy ocean and watch the sunset's palette spill colours of magenta and tangerine across a lemon and turquoise sky.

Jowan's chatting to Gilly and Steve and I catch his eye. He blows a kiss and raises his beer bottle. We've not had more than five minutes together tonight. I'm just about to rectify that, when from behind me, Mum's voice says, 'Can I have a quiet word, Joy?'

My heart sinks. I know all about Mum's quiet words. I turn round. 'Yes, of course. Do you want to go inside?'

'No. Let's go and sit on your lovely balcony. Grace is chatting to your friend Daisy on the lawn, so it's free.'

We sit at the table and sip our drinks while watching the sunset change colour over the ocean. 'My God, this view is stunning. You are so lucky,' Mum says, but she's not being snarky this time.

'Yes. Though I don't live here, you know.'

'You will, before long.'

'I'm not sure about that—'

'Why didn't you tell me about Jowan before? You've always confided in me since you were little … and, truth be told, I was hurt when your dad told me your news.' Mum's jade eyes are soft, but there's sorrow in them. She puts her drink down and twists her auburn curls around her fingers. Something she always does when she's unsure.

I look away and consider saying I was busy or something ridiculous, but then realise I have to tell the truth. 'Because I wasn't sure what the hell I was feeling, Mum. I was a mess. There was all the guilt piling in because of Sean, there was denial, and there was Helen's dilemma to deal with. Dad told you about that?' She nods. *Plus the fact that I was coming to terms with collecting, and thought I was going crazy, to start with, for believing all of that.* Once again, I wish I could share, but I can't. I take a breath, calm myself. 'I knew if I told you, you'd want to give advice, maybe say things were moving too fast. God, I don't know...' I look at Mum and see her eyes are shimmering, so I look back at the sunset, where fingers of yellow and scarlet are threading through a violet canvas.

Mum sighs and sips her drink for a few moments, then at exactly the same time, we both say, 'Sorry.'

We smile and Mum stretches her hand across the table, takes mine in hers, and the warmth of her grasp anchors me. 'No. I'm sorry. I admit I can be a bit full-on, and yes, I probably would have put my oar in. But I only do what I think is best for you. Me and your dad have only ever wanted you to be happy, and I go overboard because of it, often without thinking. Maybe I need to learn from this, and be there for you when *you* need me, not when *I* think you do.'

'Oh, Mum. I know you love me, and I love you too.' I give her hand a squeeze and wipe away a tear with my other. 'Truth is, I suppose I didn't want to hear any doubts you might have had, because I was thinking them already. But now I'm sure about Jowan. One hundred per cent. And after Sean…' I swallow and clear my throat. 'After losing him, I wasn't sure if I'd even survive living my life, let alone be with anyone else. The thought of getting hurt again, being in such a dark place, terrifies me.' Mum nods her understanding, an encouraging smile curling one edge of her mouth. 'But if it doesn't work out and I get hurt, then so be it. At least I allowed us a chance.'

'It will work out, my darling. I can feel it in my bones.' Mum grins. 'Jowan is such a lovely man. And you've made so many new friends who all speak so highly of you. I'm so proud of you, Joy.'

'Me too,' comes Dad's voice from behind us. He steps through the door with Sebastian in his arms and kisses me on the top of my head. 'This one says he's hungry.'

I laugh and take him from Dad. 'He's always hungry. Mind you, he's only been fed about four times today, poor thing. And I saw him begging some sausage and bits of burger from the guests earlier.'

Sebastian yawns and jumps from my lap, makes his way down the steps from the balcony to the garden where a few sausages are still cooking. We three stand at the top of the steps arm in arm and watch the solar lights come on that Jowan has rigged up around the lawn. People are chatting, laughing and having a wonderful time. My heart is as full as a hot-air balloon as I count my blessings. They are a multitude, and brighter than the stars switching themselves on in the heavens above.

At almost ten o'clock, the last of the guests make their way home, leaving us with hugs, kisses and thanks for a fabulous barbeque. We're also left with good wishes and kind words from all about how right we are together. Grace tells us we are cut from the same cloth, and expects us to make a good wardrobe of clothes together over the years. I whisper that she might be jumping the gun a bit, and she whispers back that Jowan and I are wearing the same vibrant auras. 'That's love if ever I saw it,' she says out of Jowan's earshot and chuckles to herself as she leaves arm in arm with Mum.

Liam and Jack leave arm in arm too, after Liam confided in me that he's not felt so positive about a guy since forever. 'He really gets me, Joy. You know?' I said I did, funnily enough. Liam also said that Jack's going to go and look at the new flat with him next week, to give his advice. I'm so chuffed for them both. It's about time they had some real happiness.

'Nightcap, Miss Pentire?' Jowan asks, kissing my cheek and leading me back up onto the balcony.

'Don't mind if I do, Mr Williams.'

'It went really well tonight, didn't it?' Jowan pours me a brandy and clinks his glass against mine.

'It did. Just perfect.' I light a candle in the middle of the table between us, take a deep breath of salt air and exhale, feeling peace and calm flowing through my entire body.

'You know you said I should go for Helen's job?' I nod.

'I've decided I will. You were right, I'd regret it if I didn't, and ended up working for someone who's not very good.'

'Yay! That's great news. You'll be a wonderful headteacher, Jo.'

'You called me Jo! My mum used to…' Jowan's eyes glisten in the candlelight and he clears his throat.

'I'm sorry. I didn't realise—'

'No. Don't be sorry, I like it. She would have loved you.' He clears his throat again and says, 'Just like I do.'

I nearly choke on my brandy but manage to swallow it without spitting it all over the table. Thankfully. 'Really?' Though I don't have to ask, because a golden aura is brightening around his shoulders and across his chest.

'Yes, *really*. I was going to say it on Thursday when we were out here after the curry, but I bottled it.'

A bark of joy burst from me. 'So *that's* what you were going to say. I was worried you didn't feel the same way, and then there was that awful awkward silence.'

'Because I didn't want to pressure you to say you loved me back, if you didn't.' He smiles and kisses the back of my hand. 'I didn't want to just spring it on you, but I couldn't help myself just now. Hope that's okay?' The doubt is back, the vulnerability he always tries to hide, clear in his eyes.

'It's more than okay. It's bloody brilliant. Because I love you too!' Until I said it out loud, I hadn't believed it was really possible. I was almost there, but now I'm sure. I love this man. I do. With all my heart, body and soul, and there's nobody else I want to spend the rest of my life with.

Okay, let's not get too crazy … glad I didn't say that out loud.

Jowan comes round the table and picks me up, spins me

round. 'Thank goodness for that!' He gives me a long lingering kiss and puts me back in my chair.

'What a brilliant night it's been. One of the happiest of my life. The food was great, the company worked, everyone got on. Even Mum was lovely to me.' I gesture to the lights in the garden and the moonlit sky. 'And this place. God, I love it here!'

'Then move in with me,' he says quietly and drains his glass. 'Makes sense. You're here more than you're home, anyway.'

Open-mouthed, I gape like some landed fish. 'What. Already? We've only been together a short while and...'

'Unless you don't want to.' He folds his arms, gives a little smile. 'If you don't, that's absolutely fine. I don't want to rush you into anyth—'

'Yes please.'

His eyebrows shoot up. 'Really?'

'Really.'

He shakes his head. 'Wow.'

'I know.' We lock smiles and stay like that for some time. Then I say, 'Anyway, I knew you loved me just before you said so.'

Jowan twists his mouth to the side. 'Oh, you did, did you?'

'Yeah. Because I could see it literally shining from you.'

'Hmm. I think you mean figuratively.'

'Do you? No. I know exactly what I mean.'

Before he can say anything more, I pick up an empty crisp bowl from the chair next to me and jump up. 'Come on, Jo. Let's go and collect some pebbles from the beach in the moonlight.'

'Pebbles?' He frowns as I pull him to his feet.

'Pebbles. Yeah, they are charged with the energy of the elements, and on nights like this they're magical, you know.'

Jowan shakes his head and follows me down the steps. 'It's you that's magical, Joy,' he whispers in my ear.

My heart's too full to answer, so I smile at him, and together we walk hand in hand down the path to the moonlit shore.

Acknowledgments

There are so many people to thank for their support and encouragement of me and my writing. The first huge mention has to go to my wonderful editor and Publishing Director, Charlotte Ledger, or legend, as I think of her. She approaches each project with phenomenal energy, passion and commitment – a complete tour de force. I will be forever grateful to her for taking me on and believing in me and my stories. It means more to me than she will ever know. Thank you, Charlotte, so, so much!

A massive thanks also to my writer friends who read an early copy of *A Secret Gift* and were kind enough to say wonderful things about it and provide quotes. Celia Anderson, Linda Huber, Kelly Florentia, Lynda Stacey and Debbie Viggiano. They have been a huge support on days when writing didn't seem such a good idea, and to share in celebrations on days when it did! Longing for the days when we can all meet up again in person.

Huge thanks must go to the wonderful and inimitable

Katie Fforde, President of the Romantic Novelist Association, for taking time out of her busy schedule to read and provide a cover quote for this book too. Very much appreciated!

And last but not least, to my husband Brian who has to live with me and put up with my angst and woes! Love you lots. Love to my daughter and wider family too, for always being there. Tanya bought me a little velvet bag of crystals at Christmas two years ago, which helped me pull together the idea for this book. Joy would love to see them, I'm sure.

The Garden by the Sea: Preview

Read on for an exclusive preview of *The Garden by the Sea*, the next charming and heartwarming novel by Amanda James...

1980

Tamsin Rowe had been up in the loft, sitting on the packing crate, for far too long. What had started as a mission to find her mother's sewing kit had turned into a two-hour stroll down memory lane. Big bundles of her past were up here, and quite a few were undone and scattered around her feet, like presents on Christmas morning. Right now, she was back in her wedding day, twenty years ago. With the wedding album across her knees, she ran a finger along the edge of the bride's veil and wondered where that slip of a girl had gone. In the elegant high-necked gown, confetti in her hair with her new husband smiling down at her, love shining from his eyes, she'd thought she was the luckiest woman alive. And she had been. But Tamsin would be forty-four next birthday, and although she couldn't wish for a better man to share her life with, there was something missing for both of them. No, not something. Someone.

Still, no use yearning for things that weren't mean to be. Tamsin placed the wedding album back in its white box and tied the pink ribbon around it. She was just about to take the sewing kit and go, when she noticed the corner of an old carved wooden box sticking out from under some old curtains she'd been meaning to throw away. Pulling it free, she smiled. This was the old 'magical' Tintagel seed-box that had been passed down from her great-grandmother and her mother before that, and on down the line. Tamsin's own mother had told her some nonsense about it being magical and having soil inside from the garden of the legendary King Arthur. Tamsin should have chucked it years ago, but her mum believed the old tales. It had a lovely carving of a tree on it too.

Ten minutes later, she was still there with the box on her lap thinking about her parents, the hopes and dreams of her youth, and wondering what the future had in store. *No use getting maudlin, Tamsin. You have to make the most of what you have, and what you have is so much more than many people.* To cheer herself up, she decided that she'd make a lovely dinner for Derek when he got home and wear that dress he loved so much. The yellow one with the big red poppies. It wasn't new, but he said it made her look like a summer's day. Tamsin had much to be happy about and the thought of being in Derek's arms lifted her spirits.

About to shove the box back where she'd found it, she

hesitated and remembered her mum's words. Tamsin held it to her chest and said to the wooden rafters above, 'Dear Magic Box, please grant me my heart's desire. Bless me and Derek with the child we've always wanted.' In the loft space, her voice sounded small, feeble and more than a bit desperate. Feeling slightly daft, she sighed and put the box back. Wishes were for kids on starry nights, not silly middle-aged women who should know better. Still, she thought, as she extinguished the light and climbed down the loft ladder. Sometimes miracles do happen.

The Garden by the Sea: Chapter One

Present Day

If you have a garden and a library, you have everything you need
– Cicero

Benches are often taken for granted, or worse, ignored, their importance not even crossing the minds of those sitting upon them. Lowena shifts position on hers, feeling the old wood creak under her, and decides they are invaluable. She also considers the hundreds of people over the years who have sat where she's sitting, gazing out across the Atlantic in all its moods, watching the gulls wheel above, broadcasting their plaintive cries across an ever changing sky. A bench with a view like this is conducive to contemplation. The hopes, dreams and fears of those bench-sitters, emotions both happy and sad, will have found a temporary home here, as their owners sought a place to rest.

Maybe this bench is a keeper of secrets whispered to the wind, or mumbled into damp tissues. A silent confidant of deep desires, heart-felt wishes, and regrets. Lowena has a few of those, though thankfully not that many for a woman who's almost forty. At this time of day and this time of year, sitting on a coastal bench in north Cornwall, Lowena thinks she is one of the luckiest people in the world. A fresh salt breeze tousling her shoulder-length curls, gentle waves rolling to a damp beach, tinged pink by the fingers of a languid sunset, and a hearty casserole waiting at home in the slow cooker. Simple pleasures.

A glance at her watch and a chill seeping through her warm parka tell Lowena its's time to go. She's not done bad though, sitting here for nearly an hour on an early spring evening. It was just what she needed after working in the library all day. She loves her job, but it's a bit short on fresh air. On the walk back to the car park, she realises it's April tomorrow, and Mum's favourite month. She remembers every year Tamsin Rowe always saying the same thing – *March is too much like winter, and May is too much like summer, but April. April is the epitome of spring.* It won't be long before Mum will be out in her little patch of garden, weeding and organising new planting for her borders and pots, buying tomato plants and seed potatoes to layer under rich compost in the trusty old barrel she's had since she was a new bride.

At eighty-five, Lowena wonders where her mum gets the energy. Since her dad passed away three years ago, her mum has thrown herself into her garden, her various clubs and recently has even started beach cleaning. Lowena's reached the conclusion that Mum's keeping every minute occupied is probably a barrier against loneliness, and preventing memories of almost sixty happy years with her husband swamping her days. After dinner, Lowena will ring and see how she is. They haven't spoken for a couple of days and last time they did, her mum said she felt like doing a spot of painting in the kitchen. Skirting boards and possibly the window sills. Lowena wondered if she was taking on too much, but didn't say so. It would have made Mum more likely to do it. She sighs. Although her mum is fit as a fiddle, there's a fine line at eighty-five between being fiercely independent, and plain reckless.

As twilight is consumed by night, Lowena puts her key in the door of her Truro home and is greeted by two things. The wonderful aroma of casserole, and the pitiful meow of her black and white cat, Conrad. 'Oh, come on, Conrad. Stop putting it on, I'm only an hour or so later than usual.' Conrad, unimpressed, circles her legs and then sits looking pointedly at the food cupboard. Lowena crouches down and gives him a tickle behind his ears. 'I just fancied a run out to Treyarnon Bay after work as it was such a sunny afternoon. You have biscuits in your dish, anyway.' Conrad walks to the food cupboard and glares up at her. 'Yes, okay. Don't get your whiskers in a twist.' As she spoons food into his dish, Lowena imagines that all over the UK, other cat owners are having a one-sided conversation like this. Conrad threads himself around her legs some more, and then as soon as the dish hits the floor, attacks the food as if he's not eaten for days. 'You're a pain in the bum, aren't you?' She strokes his head. 'But I adore you.'

As Lowena pushes her own plate away half-an-hour later, the phone rings. Must be Mum, she's the only one who uses the landline nowadays. She says mobile phones sound too distant, as if the person talking is down a well, or up a mountain, and what's the point of them anyway? Why does everyone need to be in constant contact? When she was a girl nobody had a phone. And we were no worse off for it. Smiling at this, Lowena picks up the phone and makes herself comfy on the sofa. 'Hi, Mum.'

Silence.

'Mum?'

A rasping breath and a cough.

Lowena leaps up. 'Mum! What's happened? Mum!'

'I ... I've had a f—fall...'

'Oh my God! Where? Are you hurt?'

'...yes, I've been on the floor ... a good while ... enna?'

The line goes dead and Lowena's stomach rolls as she imagines her poor mum lying on the cold kitchen floor. Has she fallen while painting? Broken something? Why the hell didn't Lowena warn her against tackling such a job? She'll never forgive herself if ... stifling a sob, she calls an ambulance and flies out of the house.

———

Lowena watches her mother sleeping. She's been watching her sleep for the last two hours, her nose and mouth covered with an oxygen mask, a drip by the bed, various tubes creeping around her body like synthetic vines. Her mum's face is as white as the starched white pillows propping her up, her slender frame tucked in under crisp sheets secured by hospital corners. A white cast on her left arm. Only the remnants of her once dark-brown curls mixed with waves of silver-grey save her from totally disappearing. A nurse said the doctor would be popping in to speak to her around midnight. Just a few more minutes to wait. Nobody is very sure what happened to Mum, just that she fell, has a broken wrist, fractured hip and is very poorly. She's on an antibiotic drip and the doctor will be able to tell her more.

The feel of her mum's hand in hers is a comfort. Even though it's as light and dry as an autumn leaf, it's warm, and the blue raised vein under Lowena's fingers, throbs with a steady pulse. She raises the back of her mum's hand to her mouth and brushes her lips across it.

'Don't worry. You'll soon be home and back to normal, Mum,' she says. Then she sighs. Ignoring how frail mum has become is something well-practiced for Lowena over the past few months. It's her defence against reality. But her mind only allows ignorance for a while. Sometimes upon waking, in the small hours, worry burrows a path into Lowena's consciousness and asks difficult questions about the future. She's mostly successful in giving partial answers and dismissing unwelcome thoughts, but right now under the harsh strip light, curtained off from the rest of the ward and the world, these questions won't be silenced.

'Lowena Rowe?'

Lowena looks up at a young male doctor who's just stepped through the curtain. 'Yes?'

'My name's Doctor Lawson,' he says with a smile, and they shake hands. Despite his youth, his gentle brown eyes are underscored by dark circles and his smile struggles to sustain its shape, as if it has run out of energy. Lowena wonders how long he's been on shift. 'I expect you have a few questions, so I'll quickly give you the upshot of your mum's condition.'

'Thank you,' Lowena says, unsurprised to hear a tremble in her voice.

He pulls up a plastic chair and sits opposite. 'Okay. We think your mum fell from a step ladder that was propped against the sink. I understand she'd been painting the kitchen windowsill above it?'

'I think so, yes. There was a paint pot and brushes on the sink. When I arrived at her house earlier, the paramedics said she'd obviously climbed back onto the ladder to get down, and her foot slipped, or the ladder toppled.'

Dr Lawson pulls a sympathetic face. 'Yes. Older people can sometimes forget they're not as nimble as they once were, I'm afraid. We think your mum, as well as breaking her wrist, and fracturing her hip, might have bumped her head and become unconscious, disoriented. She may have been on the floor as long as two days, because she's very dehydrated and weak.'

Lowena's hand flies to her mouth. Dear God. Poor Mum! On her own, in pain, frightened, but unable to move. Blinking tears away she says, 'Two days … oh no. I had no idea. We keep in touch regularly and Dot, her friend and neighbour, goes round every day.' Lowena shakes her head. 'But I'd forgotten she's gone to stay with her daughter in Devon for a week.'

'Hey, it's not your fault, Lowena.' He passes her a box of tissues. 'You can't be held responsible for your mum's actions 24/7.'

Blowing her nose, she says, 'Mum must have been in so much pain dragging herself from the kitchen to the phone in the living room.'

Dr Lawson nods. 'Hmm. But the main thing is that she did it eventually, and now she's with us and receiving the best care. She's being rehydrated and is on painkillers and antibiotics as she has a chest infection.' He looks at Lowena's mum. 'She is very poorly. But she's not ready for intensive care just yet. Hopefully it won't develop into pneumonia. The next twenty-four hours will be crucial.'

His words send a chill through the length of her. Crucial? What exactly does he mean? 'Are you saying her condition could worsen and...' The rest of the sentence is left unsaid, though loud in the silence.

'Let's not get ahead of ourselves.' Dr Lawson stands and puts a hand on her shoulder. 'Mrs Rowe is a determined woman, as many of her generation are, and as we've seen from her painting exploits.' A corner of his mouth lifts. 'But as I said, she is very poorly. We'll just have to see how things go, okay?'

Lowena nods as numbness wraps itself around her chest.

'Do you have any more questions?'

'No ... I don't think so. Thank you, doctor.'

'I'll be off then. And so should you be. Get some rest and come back tomorrow. You need your sleep. We'll phone if there's a change.'

Once more alone with her mum, Lowena fights back tears. She knows her mum can't see her crying, but she needs to keep strong for her. Losing her now, so quickly, so unexpectedly, cannot happen. Taking her mum's hand between both of hers, she tells her how much she loves her and sends a silent plea to whoever might be listening. 'Not yet. Please. Not yet.'

Lowena's been home ten minutes when she realises she left her mobile on the bedside cabinet in the hospital. *Shit!* There's no way it can wait until tomorrow in case the hospital tries to phone during the night. They don't have her home number. Lowena's bedside clock says one-thirty a.m. Wearily, she pulls her coat back on and heads out.

When she arrives back at The Royal Cornwall hospital, the ward station is unmanned, but Lowena can hear low voices coming from behind a curtain just inside the door. Now what? Should she wait for the nurse to come back out? No telling how long she'll be though. Lowena's sure it will be okay to pop through without asking permission first. She just wants to grab her phone and go. Hurrying along to her mum's bedside, she stops and looks around. The curtains of her mum's bay are pulled back and the bed's made. Lowena is sure this was the bed? Could it have been … but the next bed has the sleeping form of a much younger woman. This woman was in the bed next to mum's earlier. She spins round when she feels a hand on her shoulder.

'Miss Rowe?'

It's the nurse who she spoke to earlier in the evening. 'Yeah. I forgot my phone ... I'm just looking for my mum. Have you moved her to intensive care?'

'No. Can I have a word privately?' The compassion in her voice and eyes full of sorrow strike Lowena dumb, and she allows the nurse to take her arm and lead her out of the ward. Doom ladened thoughts crowd to the front of her mind and she tries to erect a barrier against them, but her gut instinct allows them through. Lowena's offered a seat on a plastic chair in the office and the nurse says, 'I'm afraid your mum passed away not long after you left. We tried to phone, but obviously your phone rang here in the ward.'

Lowena shakes her head as the bottom drops out of her world. This can't be happening. Can. Not. 'No. Doctor Lawson said she didn't have pneumonia ... she wasn't ready for intensive care ... and...' A lump swells in her throat, strangling further speech.

'I'm afraid she went into cardiac arrest. Your mother had suffered trauma and shock. She was very weak. Her system couldn't cope ... plus the chest infection and her injuries...' The nurse gives a sad smile. 'I'm so sorry.'

Lowena crumbles mentally and physically. Wraps her arms around her middle, slumps forward in her chair and lets the tears come. The nurse rubs her back, makes soothing noises, while all the time running through Lowena's mind is, *Mum ... oh, my lovely mum. I never got to say goodbye.*

The Garden by the Sea: Chapter Two

It's like looking in a mirror. Well, except Lowena's mum looks a good bit younger than her in this wedding photo. But then she would, at only twenty-four. She has the same soft green eyes, straight nose and full mouth, quick to smile. The hair, though curly, is much darker than Lowena's chestnut mane, but other than that, they could be twins. Lowena sits on her parent's bed, places the wedding album on her lap and traces the shape of her mum's face with the tip of her finger. Sunlight slants in through the bedroom window, falling across the photo of the bride and groom, bringing it to life. Mum, in a high-necked beaded wedding gown, confetti in her hair, looking adoringly up at Dad. He's smiling down at her, looking like a film star with his Brylcreemed blonde quiff, shiny shoes and charcoal suit.

Lowena swallows a lump of emotion as she remembers her parents showing her this album when she was little. 'Your dad could charm all the ducks from the pond in his youth,' her mum said.

'But I didn't want them. I went for the most beautiful swan instead,' Dad had replied. They were so in love then, and all the way through their fifty-eight-year marriage. Lowena could never remember a cross word between them. Or between her and them. Lowena's childhood was filled with laughter and happiness, her teens too, even though her mum and dad were in their forties when they had Lowena, they got along more like friends than parents and child. She hopes that they are together now, wherever they may be.

Six weeks have passed, but Lowena thinks she'll never get used to the empty feeling that slips into her chest a few seconds after waking each morning. Her parents' faces blur as her eyes well, and she dabs at the corners with a tissue. Tissues are never far from her hands these days. Taking a deep breath, she has a word with herself. *Come on, Lo*, as her Dad sometimes called her, *time to get on with the job.*

The job, right now, is spending the weekend sorting everything out in her parents' house before it goes on the market next week. It's proving to be a huge task, more so as she keeps stopping to reminisce over photos, ornaments and even Mum's old earthenware mixing bowl Lowena remembers from her childhood. Mum used to let her run a spoon around the left-over cake-mix for a sneaky taste. She stares into space, remembering the baking days they shared together and then notices the time. Not much done so far. Thank goodness Anna, her lovely and very efficient friend from work, is coming over to help organise things. She won't allow all this endless wallowing. She can be a bit bossy and domineering though, but Lowena knows she has the best intentions.

As if Lowena's thoughts have summoned her, there's a knock on the door.

'You finished, then?' is Anna's opener. She has a roll of black bags in her hand and a grin on her face.

'Ha! Chance would be a fine thing. This is my second day and I don't seem to have got very far.'

'I bet you've been agonising over every nick-nack, photo and item of clothing, haven't you?' Anna asks, as she bustles inside.

Lowena follows. 'As if.'

'Hmm.' Anna puts the black bags on the kitchen table next to a pile of crockery and glassware and runs her fingers through her short auburn hair as she eyes the crockery. Then she pulls open a few drawers and cupboards before coming back to the table and folding her arms. Anna sighs and narrows her sharp blue eyes at Lowena. 'How much have you *actually* put aside for charity or the dump?'

'That pile over there is for charity,' she points to the countertop. 'The one near the back door is for the dump.'

Anna laughs. 'Pile? You mean the measly five or six items in each?'

Lowena holds her hands up. 'Okay. You got me.' She tries a smile but it wobbles.

Anna loses the humour. 'Hey, it's going to be fine. Totally understandable that you're taking your time. I remember my mum being the same when my gran died. Me too. We spent more time blubbing than packing things away. But this is why I'm here. I told you the other day that I'd be ruthless, but fair.' She does a cheeky wink and puts a hand on Lowena's arm. 'Come on. Let's make a start.'

Three hours later they stop for tea and cake. The kitchen and dining room are tidy and organised, and the living room is well on its way. 'I couldn't have done this without you, Anna. Thank you.' Lowena puffs a damp curl from her forehead and chases a few crumbs around her plate with a fingertip.

'That's what friends are for. And we'll have finished the upstairs by the end of the day.'

'Hope so. A man with a van's coming for the sideboard, sofa and chairs in the living room. A clearance company for the bed and wardrobes. There's not that much to sort out upstairs after. Mum's clothes will be the h—hardest.'

Anna takes a sip of tea. 'Bound to be.'

Lowena swallows a mouthful of cake and a lump of emotion. 'Clothes are so personal, aren't they? I can see Mum in most of them … can even smell her perfume on some, the scent of the washing powder she's used since forever.' Memories of her mum at various points in her past roll in Lowena's mind like a film reel. Mum on the beach helping her build a sandcastle. Mum in the garden teaching her the names of flowers. Mum in recent times, laughing at something Lowena had said as they had afternoon tea. All those precious moments she'll keep safe in her heart. But oh, how her heart aches for one last afternoon tea, or a walk on the beach.

Anna's voice brings her back to the task at hand. 'There's no reason you can't keep a few. Maybe she has a few nice retro pieces you could make use of?'

Lowena brightens. 'That's a good idea. I think I saw an old sixties summer dress in the wardrobe the other day when I was looking through. Yellow with big red poppies on it. I'd never even seen her in it.'

Anna points a bit of cake at her then pops it in her mouth. 'There you go, then.'

'Mum was a bit of a clothes horse in the sixties, I think, judging by the photos. Matching dresses, handbags, shoes, the lot.' Lowena grabs a pack of photos from the table drawer and pushes them across to Anna.

'Wow, yeah!' Anna shuffles through them. 'She had a real Jackie Onassis thing going on with those shades. Gorgeous woman. Looks just like you.'

Lowena flushes. 'Hardly gorgeous. I'm not bad, I suppose, in a good light. Past my prime now though, as they say.'

'You are not! You're only a few months older than me, aren't you?'

'Forty in December.'

'Well, there you are. I'm thirty-nine next week, and deffo not past my prime, darling!' Anna does a sexy pout and fluffs her elfin haircut.

Lowena bursts out laughing and it feels good. It's been a long time since she's had the inclination. 'You're a great tonic, Anna. Mum would have loved you.'

Carrying on the dramatics, Anna tilts her head to the side, lifts one eyebrow and replies, 'Everyone does, sweet cheeks.' They sip their tea in comfortable silence for a few moments and then Anna asks, 'So how old was your mum when she had you? Can't have been too young.' She frowns. 'Just struck me, if she was in her thirties or so in this nineteen-sixties picture.' She flicks a red nail at the photo in her hand.

'No, she wasn't young. She was almost forty-four. Mum and Dad had been married for twenty-odd years when she fell pregnant with me. Mum always said I was her miracle baby, just as they'd given up hoping. They thought a child of their own was never going to be.'

'That's wonderful. You must have brought them so much joy.'

'I think so.' Lowena looks around the kitchen and then through the garden full of the beautiful array of flowers mum planted last year. Lowena's heart squeezes. She never did get the chance to plant the potatoes in the old barrel … or the tomatoes this year. 'We all got on so well, despite the big age gap.' She swallows. 'This old house was always full of laughter.'

Anna nods and pats Lowena's hand. 'And it will be again, when another family comes to look after it.' She gives Lowena an intense look. 'You know, this house is just bricks and mortar. You'll be taking the memories of your parents with you. Always. And you'll have lots to remember your mum by. She's the one who gave you your love of books, wasn't she?'

'Yes. She worked in a library part-time too. Dad was a plumber and more practically minded. But me and Mum would sit for hours discussing books and wonderful new worlds and the lives and loves we discovered between their pages.'

'Perfect,' Anna says, standing and picking up their mugs and plates. 'And now back to work.'

About to tear off a black bag from the roll, Lowena's hands tremble and out of nowhere comes, 'I feel so guilty, Anna. If I had warned Mum not to do the sodding painting, she might still be here with us. Why didn't I? Too busy? Too full of my own life? Why didn't I offer to do it for her? *Why?*' Fresh tears pour hot and furious down Lowena's cheeks.

'Hey, hey. Where's this come from?' Anna takes the black bags from Lowena's hands and holds them between her own. 'It wasn't your fault. You always said she was stubborn, wouldn't listen to advice. She was a strong, independent woman and not about to admit she couldn't do the stuff she used to.'

Lowena has told herself exactly this for weeks, but it helps to hear it from someone else. But in her mind the guilt's still muttering under its breath. 'Yeah, she was ... but I could have at least tried to do something—'

'It wasn't your fault. Are you listening? Was. Not.' Anna's eyes hold Lowena's in a steady gaze.

Guilt stops muttering as Lowena takes a big breath. 'Okay. Thanks, my friend.' She picks up the black bags. 'Now let's get on with it. All your chattering is holding me up...' Lowena dodges a play punch in the arm and hurries upstairs laughing.

———

Two hours later it's almost done. Just a few little things left in the understairs cupboard and that's it. 'Right,' Anna sighs, shrugging her denim jacket on. 'I'll get going before my husband sends out a search party.'

'Thanks, Anna. I don't know what I'd have done without you today.' Lowena gives her friend a quick hug. 'Apologise to John for me, for stealing you on a Sunday.'

Anna wrinkles her nose. 'I'll do no such thing – besides it got me out of cooking Sunday dinner. He's doing it for once.'

'Lovely. How's Sophie getting on at uni?'

'Loving it, and working hard. Not sure her lazy good-for-nothing brother will be as keen when it's his turn next year.'

'Harry's always been the laid back one, hasn't he?'

'Yeah, like his dad.' Anna laughs and walks down the hallway to the front door, tossing over her shoulder, 'Wouldn't have any of them any other way though. Love the bones of 'em.'

Lowena stands at the door to wave her friend off. 'See you tomorrow at work. Thanks again.'

From the path, Anna nods and then looks up at the roof. 'Just had a thought. Have you cleared the loft?'

Lowena's mouth drops open. 'Bloody hell! I forgot all about it.' Then a quick succession of hazy memories floats through her mind offering tentative relief. 'Hang on. I'm almost sure that we cleared most of it after Dad died.' Having said that, Lowena's not certain, as that was another emotional time. 'He used to stick all his junk up there. Awful hoarder. There are only a few things now ... I think.'

Anna rolls her eyes. 'Come on. Let's go and see.'

The contents of the musty darkness blinks into existence

under the ancient loft light dangling from a rafter. With her head through the hatch, after scanning the area for a few moments, Lowena's heart lifts and she shouts down the steps to Anna waiting on the landing below. 'I was right, thank goodness! There's just Dad's old fishing basket that Mum couldn't bear to part with because of the happy times he had out on the river, some tatty garden furniture that Mum said would come in handy but never did and some old toys of mine.'

'Yay, that's a relief! Do you need me to help?'

Lowena scrambles from the ladder all the way into the loft and tests the weight of the old wicker basket. 'Just with the fishing basket, please. The other stuff is small enough for me to manage on my own.'

'Okay, chuck it down!'

'Er, it's a bit heavy for that!' With a giggle in her throat at the mental image of Anna flat out on the landing with a basket on top of her, Lowena drags the basket to the loft-hatch and manoeuvres it through to Anna, who's halfway up the ladder.

'Okay, got it.' She groans. 'Blimey, it weighs a ton.' She sets the basket down in the spare room and then shouts back up. 'I'll get off now, okay?'

'Yes, see you tomorrow, and thank you!'

Lowena picks up an old folding garden chair by the damp, cold metal arm and shakes her head as she unfolds it. The stripy blue and white plastic material is ripped and frayed and rust grows along the frame like a fast-growing cancer. The material on the whole set is probably rotten through, so it's the tip pile for them, unfortunately. Next are two cardboard boxes full of old dolls, cuddly toys and Lego. Why Mum insisted on keeping these, Lowena doesn't know. Unless she hoped for a grandchild one day? An unexpected wave of sadness rushes over her. One of her few regrets was missing out on the chance to be a mother. Lowena thinks she'd have been good at it. There was a time when she thought she would be, a good few years ago, but it wasn't to be. And getting maudlin isn't going to help her complete this last task. With that in mind, Lowena lugs everything down to the landing and goes back up to the loft for the last check around.

About to leave, her eye is taken by a small grey shape right at the back of the loft. In the dim light, Lowena's unsure if it's actually an object or a shadow of the loft, so she picks her way carefully around the joists to have a closer look. Yes, it's definitely a bundle of something wedged against the bottom of a rafter. Under what turns out to be an old curtain, covered in dust and cobwebs, is an old but rather lovely ornately carved wooden box with a tree at its centre. The twigs of its branches reach out to the far corners like delicate fingers. Something at the back of her consciousness wakes up and paints a picture of small hands holding this box. Her hands. Lowena frowns and searches for more, and then she remembers.

When she was about ten, Mum and her had been up in the loft. She has no idea why. Probably looking for a toy or something. Lowena had found this box and asked her mum what it was. Mum had smiled and told her a very strange tale. Apparently, the box has been passed down through the family for generations. It was originally a 'magical' seed-box, which was thought to contain seeds and soil from Tintagel, the mysterious seat of the legendary King Arthur. It was said that whoever had the box would be blessed with a beautiful garden, bountiful crops and love of their fellow man. Lowena's mother had said it was probably all nonsense of course, but she hadn't the heart to get rid of it. And then her mum had winked and added, 'Besides, I made a wish on it once. I wished for a lovely little child, and not long after, I found I was carrying you. The best little seed in the whole garden!'

This memory sends a flood of warmth to Lowena's heart, and she smiles as she caresses the outline of the carved tree. The old legend was correct in Mum's case. She'd been blessed with a beautiful garden, bountiful crops and she'd always done her best for her fellow man. If Mum could help someone, she did. Lowena disengages the 'S' clasp and opens the lid. Inside is some uninspiring dust-dry soil, just as she remembered, so she shuts the lid again, in case she coughs or sneezes and disperses it all over the loft. What to do with it? Maybe she could use it as a jewellery box and tip the earth out? Mum couldn't bear to part with it and neither can she. It's too beautiful for one thing. Maybe she'll just keep it safe like Mum did. Or better still, take it home and sprinkle the soil on the few patio pots she possesses.

On the drive home she glances at the passengers on the seat next to her. A box of toys, a box of soil and in the back, a fishing basket, a few items of clothing, the earthenware mixing bowl and some ornaments, each of them a symbol of a happy memory from Lowena's youth. A silent promise to her mum is made that she'll use all of them in some way. Perhaps she'll even wear the yellow cotton dress with the red poppies to her friend's engagement party next week. That's settled then.

Far from settled is the answer to a question that Anna asked earlier today, however. What will Lowena do with the proceeds of the house once it's sold? Will she invest it somehow, or just stick it in the bank? This is something Lowena has asked herself over the last few weeks too, but without resolution. As she pulls up outside her house, there's a seed of an idea brewing in the fertile soil of her imagination. The root and branch of this idea is a big step for someone who could be considered set in their ways. And don't 'they' say not to make any big decisions for at least a year after a bereavement? Lowena gets out of the car and collects her passengers.

She thinks that a year might be a bit long … but six months should do it.

Don't forget to order your copy of *The Garden by the Sea* to find out what happens next…